STORMCROW

Creative Texts Publishers products are available at special discounts for bulk purchase for sale promotions, premiums, fund-raising, and educational needs. For details, write Creative Texts Publishers, PO Box 50, Barto, PA 19504, or visit www.creativetexts.com

STORMCROW
by N.C. REED

ISBN: 9780692638439

STORMCROW

By
N.C. REED

For the Ranger, The Clerk, and the Chef.
How I miss you all.

Table of Contents

FROM THE AUTHOR

Stormcrow was an idea given form through other means years ago, at a time when I did not see a future where I was a published author. I bent the character to fit somewhere else and just had fun with it because that was all it would ever be; fun.

But a funny thing happened. Years after the Shade fell, I was suddenly a 'real' writer, with books for sale. Before I could blink it seemed like, I had a publisher, who took the raw material I had self-published and made it better. More.

It was at that point that I realized I could finally take Stormcrow and let him fly on his own. So here is the first installment of that flight in the life of the Stormcrow.

He's not in the Shade anymore.

NCR

CHAPTER ONE

"Husband, the world is growing very large in the window."

Meredith Trenton-Simmons was trying to maintain her calm, but it was becoming difficult.

"Relax," Lincoln Simmons told her from the pilot's seat. "Piece o' cake!"

"Dear, I don't want it to seem as if I question your abilities," Meredith said carefully, "but I am seeing the planet rush up at us very quickly. Much quicker than does seem normal."

"I can see it," Linc replied. "I'm sitting right here."

"And yet we do not seem to be slowing," Meredith noted, her calm tone of voice belying her increasing unease.

"I got it under control, Mere," Linc replied. He made some adjustments to the trim and the *Celia* began to level out a bit.

Meredith and Lincoln Simmons had been married for just under three years, having dated for a year-and-a-half before marriage. Lincoln had given up his career to accompany her into business as an independent freighter Captain right after they were married, having taken piloting classes while Meredith had waded through the bureaucratic labyrinth of paperwork to get the loan to buy her ship. He had passed, barely, and received his license.

His skill behind the controls had not increased much during their time in space together.

As Meredith sat in the co-pilot's chair she was becoming increasingly alarmed.

"Husband!" she added a bit of urgency to her voice as the *Celia* overcorrected and begin to flare, dangerously close to stalling.

"Please don't yell at me when I'm in the middle of a delicate maneuver," Linc asked politely, taking his eyes from the screen and instruments to look at his wife.

"Please don't take your eyes off what you're doing when we're crashing!" Meredith shot back, her alarm now showing plainly.

"We are *not* crashing!" Lincoln's voice raised slightly as he turned his attention back to his job. "We are landing. I have it under control."

Though now completely alarmed, Meredith forced herself to remain silent lest she distract her pilot-husband yet again from his duties.

Then Commander Meredith Trenton had been in command of the Commonwealth Corvette *Celeste* during the Settlement Wars when her ship had come under attack by a Freeborn Destroyer while guarding a convoy of freighters carrying war material and replacement troops. Superior skills had allowed her to fight the larger, stronger ship to a draw, but the battle had left both her and her ship cripples. Neither would fight again in service to the Commonwealth.

After fighting her medical discharge all the way to the CNO of the Commonwealth Navy, Meredith had been at a loss. All she knew, all she'd ever wanted, was to command a ship. And that had been taken from her forever it seemed.

Meredith grasped the seat harness a bit tighter as *Celia* pitched left due to overcorrection. Another overcorrection (from trying to correct the first overcorrection) left the ship yawing dangerously to the right. Just as Meredith was about to yell at her husband again the *Celia* seemed to magically straighten her flight path. Two minutes later the ship settled smoothly into her assigned berth on the planet Halcyon's largest spaceport.

"See, what'd I tell you?" Linc preened, obviously very pleased with himself. "Piece o' cake!" Meredith looked at him in silence for a full minute, composing herself before daring to answer.

"Husband," she said finally, her voice strained as she got to her feet. "There are times when I think that your ineptitude at the controls of this vessel are somewhat feigned, in order that you may amuse yourself at your wife's expense." She straightened to her full height and then tugged her self-appointed uniform of black pants and gray shirt into place.

"If I were to find this is the case," she continued, "that would be regrettable. Firstly, because I would feel as if my trust in you had been betrayed, which would break my heart."

"And secondly, because I would kill you, which would also break my heart." She said this completely straight-faced and was inordinately pleased at the brief look of concern that crossed her husband's face. It was gone in a flicker, but she knew it had been there, which was all the revenge she really needed for what she was almost certain was an exaggerated lack of skill at the controls of their ship and home.

"Mere, honey," Linc looked as if he were wounded. "I would never, ever, do something so crass, so completely disrespectful of my Captain and my -"

"There should be laws against you operating *anything* capable of carrying humans or other live cargo!" a male voice from the passageway off the bridge cut him off. Anthony Giannini, the ship cook and medic, staggered onto the bridge obviously still suffering from the

Celia's approach. Usually dapper and composed, the dark-complected young man's appearance was almost comical. His hair, which was usually styled in the fashions popular on core worlds of the Commonwealth, was askew and looked a bit wild. His silk tie was still draped over his shoulder, loose at the neck where he had obviously been caught by the restraining straps of one of the crash stations throughout the vessel.

"Now, Doc, everything is fine and we're safely on the ground so there's no need to be-"

"How much of that was accident and how much was the grace of God?!" Giannini demanded, almost crossing himself before he realized it. Giannini had come to them as they searched for crew members, having posted job offerings with several listings that catered to spacers.

Polished, prim, obviously well-educated, the Simmons' had often wondered what had led Giannini to space at all, let alone to them. He was all but a doctor, he had told them, having left school just three weeks before receiving his diploma over what he had called a 'misunderstanding'. He was also a fantastic cook, something that had pleased and surprised the Simmons to no end. Since the first meal he'd prepared Giannini had been the ship's permanent cook and many of the duties he would have had as a crewman were instead shared among the remainder of the crew.

"Well I prefer to think of it as skill," Linc shrugged, completing his shut-down sequence and finally standing. Lincoln was a tall man with sandy hair and quite possibly the bluest eyes Meredith had ever seen. His height made him appear skinny but Lincoln was wiry and lean beneath the coverall he normally chose to wear when working. Meredith had asked more than once why he insisted on wearing such clothing even just to sit on the bridge, to which Lincoln had replied that it made him feel like a pilot.

"Skill," Giannini snorted, pausing to compose himself and his clothing, finally realizing how he looked. "A completely disgraceful use of the word," he added as he jerked his tie back into position.

"All right Doc," Meredith interjected, though she agreed in part. "You've had your say. We go through this every time so it shouldn't come as a surprise anymore."

"No, the surprise is that every time we somehow manage to escape *alive*!" Giannini snorted again. Before Linc could defend himself Tony Giannini whirled on his heel and stomped off the bridge.

"Well, another satisfied customer," Linc said at last, grinning. Meredith gawked at her husband for a second before bursting into laughter. His sense of humor was one of the things she loved most about Linc.

"I don't know that satisfied is a good word, Linc," she managed to get out at last.

"Ah, he'll be fine," Linc waved the comment away. "Trust me!"

-

Halcyon was one of those planets that Meredith thought of as 'mid-terior'. Lying too far outside the Sphere to be considered an Interior World, yet not close enough to the outer rings to be called a Frontier World either, Halcyon was a predicable mix of both. Business and industry that one would find on an inner planet sitting right alongside the type of ramshackle, hard-scrabble living that one would expect on any Frontier World.

Planets like Halcyon served as a way station between the Sphere, the collection of first settled planets after mankind had made it to the stars, and the Frontier planets that were often months of travel from the Sphere. As a result, brokerages and shipping firms maintained offices and warehouses on most planets in that ring, using them as transit points for both cargo and passengers. The brokers bartered with independent shippers like Meredith to ship goods on to Frontier worlds as well as carry cargo and passengers Inward. With ships constantly moving, matching freights and passengers with ships going their way was a thriving business.

People who started as brokers often managed to work their way into a position where they had their own warehouses and pads. Meredith routinely took work from one such broker, Mitchell Cauldoon. Cauldoon maintained a series of pads on Halcyon and it was one of those pads that *Celia* had not-so-gracefully settled on.

Meredith made her way down to the cargo hold where her deck hand, Carolyn Faulks, was already lowering the ship's ramp.

A now retired Gunnery Sergeant of the Commonwealth Marines, Faulks was an extremely imposing figure. Six-two, two hundred pounds of pure, ornery meanness was how Linc had often described her and Meredith, at least in private, agreed. Faulks was abrasive, foul-tempered, difficult to work with and prone to bullying those around her.

She was also completely loyal to Meredith, perhaps partly owing to the fact that then Commander Meredith Trenton had defied both logic and protocol to reach into a compartment that was being vented into space to drag a struggling, suffocating Faulks onto the bridge of the badly damaged corvette *Celeste* after a torpedo strike. When Meredith had started looking for people to crew her ship, Faulks had been the first person to sign aboard the *Celia*.

Keeping her hair cut in a style that was only just longer than regulations had allowed when she was a Marine, Faulks dressed in a civilian version of her Marine combat togs and acted as if she were still the senior security officer of a ship. Which, Meredith mused, was technically accurate. While the Interior had little to no trouble with pirates, the same could not be said for the outer fringes of the Commonwealth. Nor was it uncommon for gangs to target ships and crews while on the ground, even in the Interior. Having Faulks around helped to dissuade all but the most determined. Or foolhardy.

Meredith had seen Faulks in action, both with boarding actions and in training. She had never seen Faulks bested physically, and only rarely with firearms. She had routinely beat the men under her command in hand-to-hand training, being certified to teach two different disciplines. All things being even, Faulks was definitely someone you wanted on your side and not opposite you.

"Cap'n," Faulks nodded to Meredith.

"Gunny," Meredith nodded back. "I see the cargo managed to escape damage," she said lightly.

"That man is a threat to everyone he encounters," Faulks all but snarled. "You should space his ass, ma'am, and find someone who can actually fly."

"That is my husband you are speaking of, Gunny," Meredith replied in an amused tone. It was well known that Faulks didn't care for Linc and that the feeling was mutual.

'Mere, that woman has the hots for you', Linc had warned her more than once. Meredith scoffed at that notion, reminding Linc that she had saved Faulks life. '*She merely feels obligated. Something I try not to encourage*.' Linc would shake his head and walk away muttering after each 'discussion'.

"Yes, Cap'n," Faulks schooled her features into the mask she normally wore when off the ship. Meredith had noted that reaction before and assumed it was because she took up for Linc. She also ignored it. Faulks would just have to cope with Linc's flying skills, or lack thereof, along with the rest of them.

"I'm surprised the handlers aren't already out here," Meredith observed, looking down the gangway toward the distant warehouses.

"Probably waiting to see if we crashed and burned before bothering to bring the load out of the warehouse," Faulks muttered, but went silent at a glare from Meredith.

"*Mere, call for you,*" Lincoln's voice cracked across the IC. "*Cauldoon.*" Sighing, Meredith made the trip back to the bridge, her back protesting more than once on the steps. She was missing two discs in her back along with a good bit of extra cartilage and a small chunk of one vertebrae thanks to a razor sharp piece of the *Celeste*'s hull that had been driven deep into her back during the same battle where she had saved Faulks. Meredith had felt the injury but had thought it was just a strain and had ignored it, continuing to fight her ship. Once the battle had ended she had sat down for a brief rest and woke up five days later on a medical ship headed Inward for months of treatment and therapy.

And a pink slip from the Navy.

She arrived on the bridge with carefully schooled features so that Linc wouldn't see her grimace in pain. It was unlikely she could hide it from him but she did try. He worried over her much more than she was sometimes comfortable with. Not that she didn't appreciate it, because it was another of those things that made her cling to him desperately. But she wasn't an invalid despite what the Navy might think. She didn't need coddling.

"What's up?" she asked. Linc pointed to the screen where Mitchell Cauldoon was waiting. She turned to the pickup and smiled.

"Hello Mitchell."

"Meredith," Cauldoon nodded abruptly. Always in a hurry, Cauldoon had no time for pleasantries on most days and this was one of those days. "I wanted to give you a call and let you know the cargo is on its way to you. Should be there by now, almost," he checked his watch.

"Where I was waiting to receive it," Meredith pointed out, cursing mentally at having put the added strain on her already aching back to return to the bridge.

"Yeah, sorry about that, but, thing is. . ." Cauldoon looked away for a minute and then back to the screen. "I've got three people looking for passage outward. I know you don't always do passengers, but . . . one of them is. . .look, she's just a kid, and she's headed for Gateway. She's been away to school or something like that for years and now she's trying to get home. She spent most of her money just getting here, and, well, since you were going that way anyway..." He trailed off, having run out of steam.

"Not like you to do charity cases, Mitch," Meredith said. "What's the real story?"

"That *is* the real story," Cauldoon took no offense at the question. He *wasn't* known for charity work. "It's just. . .aw, hell, Mere she's about five foot nothing at best and looks like she's about eighteen years old. She wouldn't last long on most of the ships that would take her that way and you know it. I got a daughter about her age," he added, looking down at the floor. "I'll pay half her fare," he tacked on a minute later.

"What?" Meredith leaned forward, sure she'd heard that wrong.

"I said I'll pay half of her fare!" Cauldoon repeated, snapping it out this time. "That should at least cover her food and what have you. I know it'll take two, maybe three months for you to get out that way, but that's better than her getting on one of these rattletraps around here and ending up as a slave or a victim."

Meredith considered that. The Commonwealth had strict laws against slavery and enforced them as hard as possible, but space was vast. It was hard to be everywhere at once. And sweet young women were very popular targets. Not all slaves were for manual labor.

"Send her down and I'll take a look at her," Meredith said finally. When Cauldoon's expression turned happy she held up a hand.

"I'm not promising anything," she told him firmly. "But. . .we'll see."

"Thanks, Meredith," he nodded. "Look, I may have a couple jobs that way, too, coming back this way. One's a rush job, but there's two more that are low priority. Be a good way to pay your fuel back this way. Interested?" Meredith knew this was Cauldoon trying to show appreciation. Extra jobs, especially on a return run, were a shippers' milk and honey and most jobs going Frontier in toward the Sphere were shopped around for the best possible rate. By giving her the job he was also cutting his own profit margin down.

"I own a freighter, Mitchell," Meredith snorted. "I'm always interested in good paying jobs."

"I'll send them your way, then," Cauldoon nodded firmly. "And Meredith I really appreciate this."

"I haven't done it, yet," she reminded him.

"You will. Wait and see," he nodded. "Gotta go. Oh, tell Linc that was some show he put on. There's a pool going on whether or not he can get you guys out of atmo when you lift."

"Very funny," Linc muttered behind her, and Meredith hid a smile. Cauldoon was just jerking him around about the pool.

Probably.

"I'll tell him," Meredith promised. "Now I gotta go and meet your crew and this wayward waif of yours. See you, Mitchell." She cut the call off and turned to where Lincoln was glaring at the screen.

"That was uncalled for," he sniffed and Meredith bit down on the inside of her mouth to keep from laughing.

"So it was," she said stoically instead. "Well, I'm going to get a look at this girl and check the load out."

"Keep your girlfriend away from her," Linc called out to her back. She shot him a death glare over her shoulder as she hit the passageway again, Lincoln's laughter chasing her toward the cargo bay.

Meredith didn't often take passengers aboard, having found they were far more trouble than they were worth as a rule. Her ship was meant primarily as a cargo vessel and her amenities were more limited than a regular passenger liner or shuttle service. Room was more limited and creature comforts a bit more thin. That usually led to complaints and ill-tempers which she could do quite well without.

That being said Mitch Cauldoon was not the charitable type. He rarely did anything that didn't have a profit margin attached to it. If he was willing to help this girl get home, then she would at least consider it.

She could hear Faulks bellowing before she ever arrived in the bay. Meredith sighed as she stepped onto the catwalk and started down the steps, wincing at about every other step. She'd have to see if she could wheedle Lincoln into a back rub later tonight.

"Who are you?" she heard Faulks demand and quickened her step. Cauldoon's men were already wheeling the cargo containers aboard, ignoring the bellowing Faulks since this wasn't their first encounter with her. Enraged by their blatant disregard of their authority, Faulks had turned her ire on the first person she could find. A tiny brunette that had to be Cauldoon's charity case.

"Um, I…my name is Jes. . .Jessica Travers? Mister Cauldoon sent me here to-"

"What are you, a mouse?" Faulks demanded. "Speak up, you little runt!"

"I said my n…name is Jessica Travers, and Mister Cauldoon told me to come and see Captain Simmons," the girl repeated perhaps a fraction louder.

"Well, you can go back and tell Mister Cauldoon that the Captain ain't got time for no-"

"Gunny, how about you let the Captain decide what she has time for?" Meredith spoke softly, but the steel in her voice made Faulks stiffen as if shot. She turned on her heel.

"Beg pardon, Cap'n," she said at once. "Didn't know you was here."

"For the future, Gunny," Meredith kept her voice conversational, "when I want you to speak for me, I'll be sure and let you know. Until and unless I do, I'll be doing my own speaking. We clear on that?" The tone was unmistakable, the tone of a commanding officer speaking to her chief NCO. Faulks stiffened to attention out of long habit.

"Aye aye, ma'am!"

"Very well," Meredith nodded, satisfied that she had made her point. "Now that you've terrified this young girl and made yourself feel strong and brave, why don't you make sure that the deck dollies get the load set and tied down correctly. We'll be lifting soon and I'd prefer not to have that load shifting as we do so."

"Ma'am!" Faulks stiffened even further and then stomped toward the dock crew, red-faced from the dressing down. Shaking her head, Meredith turned to regard...

"Miss Travers, was it?" she asked, holding out a hand. "I'm Captain Simmons." The younger woman looked up at her and cautiously held out a hand to clasp Meredith's.

"Yes ma'am," the girl nodded. "I'm Jessica Travers. Mister Cauldoon-"

"He called me," Meredith nodded. "I apologize for Faulks. I'm afraid she's not much good in civilized company. Please feel at ease."

"Yes, ma'am."

"Mitch tells me you're heading for Gateway and looking for a ride?" Meredith got down to it, giving the girl a once over. She was a pretty little thing, Cauldoon had been right about that. Perhaps five two, no more than a hundred and ten pounds with brown hair that trailed over her shoulders and lively green eyes. Eyes that showed more than a little apprehension at the moment, but also hinted at intelligence.

"Yes, ma'am, that's my home," the young woman nodded. "I'm trying to go home for the first time since I left to go to school on Beria. Almost five years ago." Meredith resisted the urge to whistle. Five years away from home to go to school. Poor kid. The girl had one duffel and one shoulder bag along with a small backpack she probably used as a purse. Meredith suspected that everything the girl owned was in those bags.

Her skirt was clean and neat, though Meredith could see at least two places where it had been repaired. Both it and the blouse she wore looked close to threadbare, a hint of the girl's bra showing through the thin fabric of the blouse. Her shoes were clean but clearly had seen long use.

But there was a pride in the girl that Meredith couldn't help but admire. Her stance was not one of cowed submission but simply a healthy fear of strange people and places. Completely understandable and in no way out of place. She began to see why Mitch Cauldoon had wanted to help the girl.

"Well, here's the deal," Meredith looked the girl in the eye. "Yes, we're going that way, but it's going to be a bit roundabout. Probably take right at three months to get there and we'll stop several times along the way to drop off and pick up cargo. Since it's going to take so long the fare won't be very much, basically enough just to cover your keep. And that's been paid already," she added without thinking.

"What?" the girl's eyes widened in shock. "How?"

"Let's just say that you've got at least one friend around who wants to help you make it home," Meredith smiled down at the small young woman. "The accommodations aren't like a liner by any means, but they aren't bad and the food is good. We don't have much in the way of recreational pursuits, I'm afraid," she warned. "We play cards and a few other games around the galley table some nights, and we all read a good bit to pass the time. And like I said, it'll take right at three months give or take to get you there. Are you going to be okay with that?"

"Oh, yes ma'am!" Jessica replied, nodding eagerly. "I've been gone so long, ma'am, a couple more months more or less won't make any difference. I...I spent most of my savings getting this far so I was looking for the best, least expensive way to go on from here."

"Not always a good move this far out of the Sphere," Meredith shook her head. "Things aren't always too nice out here. But if you're from the Frontier I shouldn't have to tell you that."

"No ma'am, you don't," Jessica nodded again, more subdued this time. "I can't possibly thank you enough, ma'am, and I'll work. To help pay my way I mean. I know you said someone-" She stopped as Meredith held up a hand.

"You can help in the kitchen if Doc needs or wants it. Help with the clean-up and such. It'll probably help you pass the time. If you're certain you can spend that much time penned up in here, then. . .welcome aboard, Miss Travers."

"Thank you, Captain!" Meredith watched the girl struggle with her bags for a moment then tried to lend a hand. No sooner had she leaned over though than her back reminded her of why she was no longer in the Navy. A gasp of pain escaped her lips before she could catch it.

"Ma'am, are you okay?" Jessica asked.

"Fine, just a little back trouble," Meredith lied. Damn that had hurt. She carefully straightened up again, testing her ability to stay erect.

"Captain, are you all right?" she heard a familiar voice behind her and grinned. She turned to see her engineer standing close by.

"Sean, this is Jessica Travers," she introduced. "Jessica, this is Sean Galen, our engineer. Sean you are just in time," she added. "Miss Travers will be a guest aboard *Celia* until we hit Gateway. Would you help her with her bags and show her to Dorm Three, please? Make sure she knows where everything is and gets settled in, right?"

"Of course, Captain," Sean nodded and bent to take the duffel bag. He hefted it with ease and then looked at Travers.

"Miss, if you'll follow me I'll get you situated."

"Thank you," Jessica nodded and turned to Meredith. "Ma'am, I sincerely appreciate this. I wish I could help with your back."

"Thank you but I'll be fine in a few minutes," Meredith lied with a smile. "You run on with Sean and he'll get you squared away." She watched the two depart and only when they were gone did she allow herself to show how much she was hurting. She took a halting step or two trying to shake herself down. She needed to get this under control before she got to the bridge and Linc saw her like...

She looked up just then for some reason. The first thing she saw was her husband watching her from the catwalk, a scowl plastered on his normally pleasant features.

Aw, hell.

CHAPTER TWO

Jessica followed Sean Galen up the stairs, passing a tall man in a gray jumpsuit on his way down. The man nodded but never slowed.

"That was the pilot, Lincoln Simmons" Sean told her quietly. "He's the Captain's husband."

"That must be nice, being able to work together," she commented.

"I guess," was the only reply. She followed the taciturn engineer as he led her onto the catwalk and then into the passageway. She noted there were several hatches in the passageway which they passed by, stopping at the last hatch before what looked like an open area.

"Here we are," he said. He opened the hatch and then stepped aside to allow the young woman to enter first. She smiled her thanks and stepped inside. The room was larger than she had expected and looked comfortable.

"There's a head in there," Sean indicated the doorway. "Shares with the other suite, but you're the only passenger so really it's yours alone." He set her bag on the bed. "If you'll come with me I'll give you the rest of the tour." She left her other belongings on the bed and followed him out, closing the hatch behind her.

"This is the galley," he told her as the stepped into the open area outside the passageway. "Off there is the lounge," he pointed to a doorway off the left side of the galley. "Kitchen is through there," he pointed back to the right. "This is the passageway to the bridge and the crew quarters," he indicated the passageway opposite the one they had taken to get there.

"The showers and laundry are off the lounge," he said finally looking down at her. "Unless the Captain gives your permission, the cargo bay, crew quarters and engineering are off limits, as is the bridge. You can go out on the catwalk in the bay, but not down on the floor without permission."

"The lounge has a treadmill and weight machine if you want to exercise. There's a video library and a text library that the Captain keeps fairly up-to-date. There's also several games in the lounge. I guess that's pretty much it." He paused, looking down at her.

"Stay away from Faulks if you can," he told her finally. "That's the large woman who was yelling at you down on the ramp. She's a bully. Try not to be around her alone if you can help it. The Captain won't let her bother you so long as she knows what's happening." He paused again.

"That's pretty much it for the tour," he almost smiled. "If you need anything else. . ." he walked to the com unit on the wall by the passageway entrance, ". . .just hit this green button and call for Sean. I'll hear you call, so just tell me where you are and I'll be there as soon as I can. Might take a minute since I'm usually in engineering."

"Thank you Mister Galen," Jessica smiled at him and he shook his head.

"Just Sean," he told her. "My father was Mister Galen. I'm just Sean."

"All right, Sean," she smiled again. "Thank you."

"Anytime," he nodded. "I'll leave you to settle in, then." With that he disappeared back down the passageway toward the bay. Jessica returned to her cabin and unpacked, thinking about how fortunate she'd been. Thanks to Mister Cauldoon and now Captain Simmons she was going to go home for the first time since leaving to go to school. She had not seen or spoken to her parents since she'd left, the cost of such long distance communication being far too expensive for her family. Letters took a very long time to cross the immense distance between worlds so they had been few and far between. Jessica assumed for every letter she'd received there had been more that she hadn't.

She had written to her parents to tell them she was coming home but there was every possibility that she would get there before her letter did.

Her fare had taken almost all her remaining money, but she had been extraordinarily fortunate to secure passage on a good ship for so small a fee. The fact that she was taking a roundabout route to get home didn't bother her. As she'd told the Captain, two more months, give or take, wasn't that much more time alongside five years away at school.

And when she got home she'd be reunited with her family and have a job as a teacher, helping the children of her under-developed planet get a better education that they could have managed otherwise.

That would make all her sacrifice worth it. Humming happily at the thought, she went about unpacking and settling in.

-

Lincoln had seen Galen leading the girl up the stairs but had no interest in her at the moment. He had seen Meredith from above as she had reeled in pain. A brief flare of anger had been immediately replaced by concern as he had descended the stairs to the bay.

She saw him coming and stood stoically in her place, waiting for the storm she knew was coming. It was kind of unfair, she thought to herself, considering that she hadn't told him because she didn't want him to worry. It wasn't like he could do anything about it that he hadn't already done.

Meredith had spent nearly six months in the Commonwealth Naval Hospital on Wayfair, home of the Navy's Beta Quadrant Fleet Headquarters. In that time she had endured six different surgeries to repair the damage done to her spine during the battle that had cost her both her ship and career. She had been awarded the Navy Cross, the second highest honor available to the military, for her actions in the battle. As a result, the staff had done their best to make her as comfortable as possible while she was being treated. That had included being a bit too free with the pain meds to keep her suffering to a minimum. Despite safeguards that were supposed to prevent such things from happening, Meredith had become addicted to the painkillers.

Upon her release from direct care into rehab she had entered withdrawal. That was the first inkling anyone had that she was addicted to the pain relief medicines that had eased her suffering while confined to her bed. At the same time, she was also dealing with the loss of half her crew in action against the Freeborn Destroyer, the loss of her ship, her career, and a future filled with pain. The Navy had assigned her a counselor to help her deal with all these problems, beginning with her withdrawal from the pain medicines and the survivor's guilt that weighed her down.

That counselor was currently storming across the cargo bay with a mighty frown on his normally pleasant features. He slowed as he reached her, stopping right on top of her. Though Meredith was still a tall woman even after the loss of nearly two inches of height as the result of losing several discs in her spine, Linc towered over her. Normally she enjoyed the feeling of smallness that his build gave her, but in situations like this she was less enamored with his large stature. She looked up at him steadily.

"You're hurting," he said flatly.

"I'm always hurting," she replied evenly. "You know that, Linc," she added softly.

"You're hurting more than normal," he amended, looking down at her as if daring her to challenge the statement. She didn't, merely nodding her agreement.

"You should have told me," he said to her finally.

"Why? So you could stress over something you can't do anything about?" Her voice was kind but firm. "Linc, I love you, but you know there's nothing you can do for this. Well," she corrected, "I was going to ask you for a back rub later," she admitted, allowing a hint of mischief to creep into her eyes.

Lincoln tried to stay upset, but he couldn't. Finally, he grinned slightly and gently put his arms around her, hugging her close to him but careful not to put any pressure on her back. She briefly returned the embrace but then pushed him gently away.

"Let's keep it professional," she joked and he had to laugh in spite of his desire to be angry. It wasn't as if she were wrong. There was nothing he could do. He would hurt for her if he could manage it but he couldn't.

Keep it professional was Meredith's mantra when working. When they were on a job, he was the pilot and she was the Captain. There could only be one boss on a ship, and they had agreed that she was to be it. He knew next to nothing about commanding a ship.

"All right, Captain," Linc replied, taking one step back. "Professional it is. But," he raised a finger, "there will be consequences later," he threatened, eyes twinkling.

"I look forward to it," Meredith replied straight-faced, and she did.

"I'll be on the bridge," Linc told her, turning to go. "Make Faulks do the lifting and tugging, Mere," he added finally, his voice soft. "That's what you pay her for."

"I will," she promised.

-

Faulks had watched the exchange between her Captain and the pilot (she refused to call Lincoln Simmons her Captain's husband) with narrowed eyes, chastising herself for not realizing that her Captain had been in pain. She should have been more aware.

"I think we're finished, ma'am," one of the gang crew said to her, interrupting her thought process. Angry in a flash, Faulks whirled on the man.

"You're finished when *I* say you're finished, maggot!" she stormed and the man flinched in spite of himself. He remembered that she worked for someone who depended on *his* boss for work, however, and steeled himself.

"Actually, we were finished when we got the cargo here," he told her flatly. "Securing the cargo is a courtesy afforded you by Mister Cauldoon. You'd do well to remember that, ma'am, if you want us to continue assisting you in this manner. Otherwise, you'll find yourself handling the loading and tie-down after we leave the cargo and head back to the warehouse."

It amused the man to watch the red creeping up on Faulks face as he spoke. He truly hated this abomination of a woman. Of all the crews he and his men dealt with, she had to be the worst person he'd ever met. And he was tired of her attitude. He turned away from her suddenly, looking toward the *Celia*'s Captain as she approached.

"How dare you speak to me li-"

"Gunny, that will be all," Meredith's voice cut her off, and Faulks whirled to see her Captain standing behind her. Frowning .

"Cap'n," Faulks managed not to stammer. "I was just explainin' to this gentleman-"

"Yes, so I heard," Meredith said dryly. "What say you inspect the load while I sign for it. I assume that all is in order? You've checked the manifest? Since you have the time to explain things to our guests who were lending us a hand?" Faulks face flushed even deeper as she endured the second dressing down from her Captain in less than an hour.

"Yes ma'am!" she braced to attention. "I'll inspect the load now, ma'am." With that she turned on her heel and stalked away, the remainder of the gang crew parting to allow her passage. Meredith shook her head slowly as she turned to the gang crew foreman.

"I'm sorry," she said simply. "I'm afraid Faulks is still in the Marines up here," she pointed to her own temple. "It's a hard mindset to get out of," she admitted from experience.

"It's all right," the foreman sighed. "She's not the first I've met like that, and it's not like the rest of us don't owe veterans for keeping us safe. Just sign here, Captain. We've got you loaded out and ready to fly. Oh, and Mister Cauldoon's compliments, ma'am, there's a food locker we brought aboard from him," he pointed to the insulated carrier. "He said to enjoy," the man added with a smile.

"Tell him I appreciate it," Meredith smiled. "And thanks again for putting up with Faulks."

"No problem Captain," the foreman smiled. "Let's go!" he called louder and his crew assembled outside the ramp.

"Fly safe. . ." the foreman started, then paused as he apparently remembered who he was talking to. And who her pilot was.

"Yes, we'll try," Meredith nodded grimly. "Maybe the pool won't pay out today," she added with a grin and the foreman looked sheepish.

"Good-bye ma'am," he settled for saying and left the ship, his men following in his wake. Meredith turned to find Faulks watching from a distance.

"Load secured?" Meredith asked.

"Yes ma'am," Faulks nodded. "They did a good job," she added, trying to sound friendly.

"Faulks, you need to remember that these men are helping us. If they wanted to, they could just drop the load at the ramp and leave. Is that what you want? To have to load the ship alone and be responsible for securing the load in the bay? Even with all hands on deck, we can only muster two more people to assist you. Doc would try, I'm sure, but he's hardly strong enough to wrestle cargo containers around the bay. That would leave just you, Galen and Linc. How long would this," she indicated the newly acquired cargo, "have taken the three of you?"

"A while, Cap'n," Faulks admitted. "Galen won't be much help," she couldn't stop herself from adding.

"Faulks," Meredith sighed, "I don't know why you can't seem to overcome your urge to bully, but there are two things you need to consider. First, I will not allow you to continue to treat the rest of the crew in such a manner. I'm tired of it and it stops, *now*. I've been patient, knowing from experience how difficult it is to transition from military to civilian life. But after nearly three years you're no better at interaction than you were when you first came on board. Your attitude is starting to affect how my ship runs and how it does business," she pointed to the now distant gangway crew.

"I'll work on it, ma'am," Faulks said stiffly.

"No, you'll *fix* it," Meredith allowed a bit of her anger and frustration to bubble over, fueled by her own pain. "If you don't, then you're out," she added flatly, and Faulks stiffened again.

"Ma'am," she started to protest, but Meredith talked right over her.

"Secondly, your attitude is going to come back to bite you on the ass one day. You're going to try that routine on someone who will beat you into the ground and leave you in a bloody heap. Don't assume even for a minute that it can't happen because you know it can. I've seen *you* do it, more than once," she added. Faulks closed her mouth abruptly at the reminder. Meredith leaned in and despite her size advantage Faulks felt the need to step back. She forced it back and stood her ground, but only just.

"And when that time comes, it had *better* not affect this ship or the rest of this crew, Faulks. Am I clear?"

"Crystal, ma'am!" Faulks snapped out.

"Now," Meredith took a deep breath to clear her mind. "Let's secure the bay and get ready to lift. No one has notified me that we need anything and we are on a tight schedule at the moment. *Do* we need any supplies while we're on the ground?" she asked.

"Not that I'm aware of, Cap'n," Faulks shook her head, still reeling from the Captain's flat declaration.

"Very well," Meredith nodded. "I need you to get it together Faulks," she said more kindly. "I depend on you. I count on you. So I need you to get it together and stop being a bullying ass."

"Yes ma'am!" Faulks stiffened again.

"Right then," Meredith nodded. "Carry on." With that she headed for the bridge, careful to use the handrail when climbing the stairs. Her back was really hurting.

-

Celia was well away from Halcyon by supper time. As the crew gathered in the galley Jessica felt a tiny bit of apprehension at the prospect of facing the large woman, Faulks, again. She watched as Sean Galen took his seat at the far end of the table, and immediately sat down to his right as Faulks filed in and went directly to the seat to the Captain's right. That put her as far from the overbearing woman as possible.

Anthony Giannini had politely refused her offer of assistance in the kitchen, telling her to enjoy her first night on board and relax. She had roamed the ship exploring the areas that she was allowed to visit, always with a wary eye out for Faulks.

Sean Galen had struck her as a very nice and polite young man. For some reason she felt reasonably safe around him and didn't hesitate to trust his advice. It seemed completely natural to her that she would move to his side when he sat down.

The smell from the kitchen had been surprisingly wonderful. Jessica had held no illusions about how good the food quality would be on a freighter but as Giannini set the food on the table she decided she would need to re-evaluate that. Whatever it might taste like, it smelled delicious.

"All right, folks, let's dig in!" Tony called, clapping his hands. Everyone gathered around the table. Jessica watched as the crew sat silently for a moment. Lincoln appeared to be praying and Sean had his eyes closed, his lips moving almost imperceptibly. And then, the moment was over and food was slinging around the table.

"Captain has a moment of silence before meal times," Sean explained softly. "Everyone is free to pray as they deem fit. You don't have to do anything, just respect the rest." Jessica nodded as she accepted a bowl from the cook. She took some of the pasta and passed it along to Sean. Next came a meat sauce which smelled wonderful.

She ladled it onto the pasta and passed the bowl along, accepting bread next.

"This smells wonderful," she smiled at Tony, who beamed.

"Thank you my dear," he bowed slightly. "It's nice to have someone besides the Captain who can appreciate the finer foods available in the world."

"Hey, I enjoy your cooking," Sean offered.

"You do indeed my young mechanical friend, and for that I thank you," Tony allowed. "I was mostly referring to our resident cretin and our designated crasher," he looked down the table.

"Who you callin' cretin, you little pansy?!" Faulks snarled.

"I didn't call anyone cretin directly, but since you responded to it, well..." he trailed off, spreading his hands wide as if to say Faulks had proved her point for him.

"And I must admit I completely object to the title of 'designated crasher'," Linc frowned at the notion that he and Faulks were actually on the same side of any argument.

"I'll try to come up with something else, then," Tony shrugged, taking a bite of his own food.

"Try 'pilot'," Linc suggested.

"Something *accurate,*" Tony amended. Linc frowned at that, muttering under his breath as he returned to his food.

"All right, that's enough," Meredith observed from her place at the head of the table. "We have a guest. Miss Travers will be with us for as long as three months so let's do try to act civilized, can we?"

"Where are we taking you, Miss Travers?" Tony asked politely.

"Gateway," Jessica replied. "And please, just Jessica. Jess even is fine."

"Sounds good, Jess," Tony winked and the girl blushed. Tony Giannini was smooth to say the least. Handsome and sophisticated in a way you rarely saw outside the Sphere. And Beria was not a Sphere world.

"Why in the hell would you want to go to a dump like Gateway?" Faulks demanded around a mouthful of food. Jessica blushed deeper at that.

"It's her home world, Gunny," Meredith's voice was icy and Faulks' face reddened as she realized she had angered her Captain for at least the third time today.

"Sorry," she muttered, casting a withering glance at the girl as if it were Jessica's fault she had been reprimanded.

"I've been away going to school," Jessica explained. "Now, I'm returning home to be a teacher. To help the children of my home world be better educated. Hopefully to improve their lives."

"That sounds like a worthwhile endeavor to me, Jess," Tony told her. "I'm sure your parents are very proud of you."

"I hope so," she admitted. "I haven't seen them since I left home. I get a letter once in a while, but it's not really the same. I can't wait to see them," she admitted.

"Jessica, you've met Sean, and Gunny of course," Meredith cast a quick glare at Faulks. "And I see you've introduced yourself to Tony. This is my husband, Lincoln. He's our pilot."

"Jessica," Linc nodded, smiling. "Nice to meet you."

"Thank you, sir," Jessica smiled. "You as well."

"We don't get passengers aboard very often as you can tell by our conduct," Linc told her. "Try to ignore us if you can," he grinned, and Jessica laughed lightly. She liked this man.

"I'm sure it'll be a blast."

CHAPTER THREE

Over the next week Jessica found a niche in the crew and began to fit in a bit better. Her only difficulty was avoiding Faulks. The overbearing woman had not directly confronted her in the time she'd been aboard, but her hostility was clear to Jessica. She mentioned it to Tony Giannini one evening after supper as she helped with the clean-up.

"She's a bully," he had shrugged. "Captain's got a soft spot for her but I think that's coming to an end. Faulks has gotten on her last nerve lately I'd guess."

"I don't know why I rate her anger," Jessica shrugged helplessly.

"You don't have to do anything to rate it, sweetie," Tony told her. "Poor Galen takes the brunt of her tongue when we're on the move. I don't know how he stands it," he admitted. "I'd have killed her by now."

"She doesn't bother you?" Jess asked.

"She knows better," Tony smirked. "She can mouth at me all she wants but she knows not to push it too far, since I'm not just the cook, I'm also the medic. She just might need me to patch her sorry ass up one day."

"Ah," Jess nodded. "Got it."

-

"We'll be sitting down on Dry Commons later today," Meredith announced at breakfast ten days after Jessica had come aboard. It was the first stop since Jessica had arrived.

"We'll be taking on fuel which means we'll probably stay overnight," the Captain said. "We'll have to stand watch, but we should still be able to get some shore time, considering the fueling delay." Fueling required the engines be shut down completely rather than left on idle. They would need to cool before fueling could begin. Afterwards it would take three to four hours to idle the engines back up and prepare for lift off.

"Anyone who wants to go into Common Place needs to be aware of the dangers," the Captain continued. "It's not exactly lawless but it's not known for its civility, either. Jessica if you want to get off ship, I don't want you going alone. Okay?"

"Yes, Captain," Jessica nodded. "I don't really have a reason to leave the ship anyway," she admitted.

"I'll stand the watch, Captain," Galen volunteered. "I don't have any need to go into town."

"Thank you, Sean," Meredith smiled. "If you'll be aboard, then Linc and I might take advantage of that to have a night on the town, such as it is," she smiled at her husband, who grinned back.

Jessica happened to be looking at Faulks when Meredith spoke and could see the frown pass across the woman's face. It was only there a second, but it was plain to see.

"Tony, do we need any supplies?" Meredith asked.

"No, Captain, we're good," Tony shook his head. "I do believe I'll go into town, however," he added. "Be nice to be out and about, even for a bit."

"Very well," Meredith nodded. "Just make sure you're back by eight hundred hours. Assuming the fueling goes to plan, we'll start prepping for lift-off about nine hundred. Faulks I assume you're going ashore?"

"Yes, Cap'n," Faulks nodded.

"Same for you, then. We'll head out once the cargo is picked up. I'll see to the fueling and any provisioning we'll need. Remember what I said. This planet isn't completely without law, but slavers do frequent here as well as others of a less than savory nature. Be aware of your surroundings at all times, and if you intend to drink to excess you should do so here, aboard ship."

A chorus of 'Aye Captain' and 'Yes Ma'am' replied to her statement.

"Very well."

-

It had been another typical controlled crash landing.

"Damn you, Linc," Meredith didn't quite snarl. "If I ever find out you're doing that on purpose…" she allowed the threat to hang between them.

"I can't believe you would even think such a thing," Linc replied, hurt on his face and in his voice. "And what was so wrong with that landing? I know we had a bit of a rough patch there about mid-way in, but that was due more to atmospheric conditions than anything I might have done."

"*Doc, can you come to the lounge*?" Sean's voice cut through the ship, interrupting the 'discussion' between husband and wife.

"*What's the problem, Sean*?" Tony asked a few seconds later.

"*Girl's a little air sick, I think*," Sean replied. "*We're at the head in the lounge*."

"*On the way,*" Tony replied. Meredith listened to the conversation and then turned a withering glare on her husband.

"See what you've done?" she demanded before heading aft to the lounge.

"It wasn't that bad," she heard Linc complain as she moved out of earshot.

Meredith found Sean standing outside the lounge head bracing the door open with his foot. For once his face wore a look of amused concern rather than the usual blank slate she was used to seeing. Sean Galen was still an enigma after nearly three years of being on the same ship with him.

"She okay?" Meredith asked.

"She will be, I think, once the rest of her lunch is gone," Tony Giannini came out of the head, grinning ruefully. "Poor kid. Hell of a way to be introduced to Lincoln's way of driving a ship." Meredith nodded absently, thinking the same thing. Jessica stumbled out of the head, wiping her mouth with a cloth.

"I'm sorry," she groaned.

"Don't be," Meredith told her, placing an arm around her shoulders. "It's hard to stomach, er, get used to," she corrected.

"I've only been aboard five ships, counting this one," Jessica explained. "I never realized before how rough it can be."

"Better get used to it," Tony warned, gathering up the med kit he'd brought with him. "Par for the course around here."

Jessica nodded weakly, hand still pressed to her stomach.

"I think you might wanna just take a seat for a while, ma'am," Galen said quietly. "You may want to be near the head for a little while til whatever Doc gave you sets in."

"Not a bad idea," Jessica nodded, almost staggering to the nearest seat. "Fortunately I wasn't planning on leaving the ship so I'll have time to recover."

"If you're not feeling better soon call me," Tony warned. "I won't be heading off ship until after the cargo is off-loaded, so I'll be around, somewhere."

"Thank you Doctor," Jessica smiled at him. "I think I'm okay."

"It's just Tony," he waved and returned to the sick bay.

"Sean are we set okay?" Meredith asked as the engineer went to leave.

"Yes ma'am," he nodded. "I made a walk through about two hours ago and checked the inventory. We're in good shape."

"Are you still planning to stand the watch?" she asked, her back aching and threatening to distract her.

"Yes ma'am," he nodded. "Let me know when you head out and I'll close the ship up."

-

"Are you still mad at me?" Linc asked. He and Meredith were walking arm-in-arm down the main causeway into Common Place, less than two miles from the landing pad.

"I wasn't mad, exactly," Meredith told him. "It's just hard for me to believe that you managed to get your license and yet we can't seem to set down anywhere without nearly colliding with the planet in question."

"A series of unfortunate occurrences which I have no control over, whatsoever," Linc told her loftily. "I can't control atmospheric conditions."

"It wasn't 'atmospheric conditions' that caused us to have a near-collision with a star liner shuttle on Midway," Meredith pointed out.

"Smaller vessels have the right of way," Linc sniffed. "I was completely in the right."

"We didn't have the right of way on Danville when we almost plowed into a mountainside trying to get to the port."

"Faulty landing beacon, threw us off course," Linc replied, suddenly taking a great interest in their surroundings.

"And who can forget th-"

"Are we here to have a night out or to talk about ancient history?" Linc cut her off. Meredith shook her head in amusement. Even when almost killing her, Linc made her laugh.

"Fair enough." She saw a familiar figure further down the street.

"There's Tony," Linc pointed, having seen him as well. "Wonder what he's up to?"

"I don't know," Meredith admitted, looking at the building Giannini had entered. "That looks almost like an attorney's office, doesn't it?"

"I can't read the shingle from here," Linc admitted, squinting. "Looks like it, though," he agreed after a minute.

"Well, here we are," Meredith said as they stopped before the nicest hotel in Common Place. "Tony can probably handle whatever he's doing. And I want a nice, hot, soaking bath. I wonder if I'm lucky enough that they have a whirlpool?"

"One way to find out!" Linc smiled. "Shall we?"

-

Unaware that his Captain and her husband were anywhere near him, Tony Giannini stood inside the entrance of the building they had seen him enter, looking around for a minute to get his bearings. He saw a directory, used it to find the name he needed, and then took the elevator up to the top floor.

The lift opened into the lobby of an extremely nice waiting area with a receptionist sitting at an antique desk.

"May I assist you, sir?" she asked, looking up as the door opened.

"I'd like to see Mister Tuttle, please," Tony smiled winningly.

"Do you have an appointment, sir?" the receptionist asked.

"No, but I believe if you give him my name, he'll see me," Tony's smile grew.

"And what name should I give him?"

"Delgado," Tony smiled. "Anthony Delgado."

-

Faulks looked at the building with no small amount of trepidation. She was skating on thin ice with the Captain. Something had to change. Faulks needed an outlet of some kind, and after a good deal of net searching she thought she might have found it.

The tall woman rubbed her short cut hair back and forth as she considered what she was thinking. She couldn't do something like this very often, which meant she'd need to get things done properly. That cost money. Between her pay and her retirement Faulks had a pretty good living but. . .paying for something like this seemed wrong, somehow.

Still, her options were limited and her time was short. She had to be back aboard ship by 08:00. Taking one last deep breath she cast a furtive look down both directions of the street, then stepped off the boardwalk headed for the address she had found on the net.

-

Jessica was feeling much better finally. She had dined on one of the small meals Tony had left prepared for her and Sean for the day and evening and then wandered the ship. She didn't have permission to be on the bridge, but then no one was aboard but her and Sean Galen. Perhaps it wouldn't hurt?

Better to be sure, she decided and walked to the IC.

"Sean, are you on the bridge?" she called. The answer was almost instant.

"*Yes ma'am. What can I do for you*?"

"Honestly I was just wondering; do you think I could join you? Since we're on the ground? I promise not to touch anything."

"*I don't see why not. Come straight up the passageway. It dead ends on the bridge*."

Jessica made her way up the hallway tickled to be getting to see something new. Now she could say she had been on the bridge of a starship and not be lying about it. She passed a half-dozen or so hatches then made a sudden left turn and there she was.

It was larger than she'd imagined. Wide as the ship itself, the bridge was laid out to give everyone on deck plenty of room to work. She could see several systems still working, a bank of gauges and dials that all blinked green or were off completely, and three consoles at different stations. Sean Galen was sitting to her right, looking her way.

"Come on up," he said quietly. "Have a seat," he pointed to what she assumed was either a co-pilot or navigator seat. She sat down carefully at first, but then settled her diminutive frame into the chair.

"This is nice," she said finally. "I expected it to be a lot more cramped."

"Some ships it would be," Galen nodded. "This one is designed pretty well, and built for deep space work. She's meant to haul a larger crew but we don't really need anyone else. If we had another six or eight hands then the room up here would get crowded in a hurry."

"You've been doing this a while I take it?" Jessica asked, looking at the man across from her.

"A little while," he admitted, almost warily. "I had shipped aboard two other boats before the Captain hired me for the *Celia*. Been here since she started."

"She seems very nice," Jessica noted. "I sense a hardness in her, to be sure, but she's been very good to me."

"She is a fine person," Galen nodded. She noticed the knife in his hands and felt a second of trepidation. He saw her gaze and lifted his hands, showing her the knife and the whetstone he was holding in the other hand.

"Helps pass the time," he told her. "And it's a good time to do stuff like this. Sharpen knives, clean guns, things like that."

"I didn't think of that," Jessica admitted. "You stand watches like this when we're under way I suppose?"

"Yeah," Galen nodded, leaning back. "Someone is awake at all times when we're in transit. We don't always stand a watch when we're in port, but this place," he waved to the screen where the lights of the distant town could be seen coming to life, "isn't one of the best spots to be in, to be honest. Standing a watch makes sure nothing happens to the ship."

"Thieves I suppose?" Jessica asked.

"Mostly," Sean nodded. "Sometimes there's a competitor that will try and damage the ship to get a leg up on his competition. Usually nothing major, just enough to force down time for repairs, put you off your schedule. And as you get further out on the Rim, you start to encounter slavers and such. I don't have to tell you that I imagine, being from a Rim world yourself."

"No, I know about that," Jessica nodded. "My parents were always concerned about that. They were especially worried when I left to go to school. And I was too, I admit."

"Worked out okay, seems like," Sean mentioned.

"Yes, it did," Jessica nodded, smiling. "It was hard work, don't get me wrong. I managed to get a scholarship to pay for a large part of my tuition but I had to work the entire time I was there. It took me longer than is standard to get my degree, but yes, it's worth it. Now, I'll be helping children on my home world to get a better education and make their lives better. It might not sound like much, I know," she raised her hands slightly.

"It sounds like an honorable way to serve your people," Sean observed quietly and Jessica was moved by the sincerity in his voice. He meant what he said.

"Thank you," she blushed slightly. "What about you? What led you to be an engineer?"

"Needed a job," Sean shrugged. "I worked as a crewman for a while and then the engineering assistant on a larger ship I was on got hurt and I was promoted. I spent the next six months learning how to keep an old rattletrap ship in space. I eventually moved on and worked as a mechanic until the Captain started hiring. I was lucky to get this job. It's a good ship."

"Except for Faulks," Jessica almost asked.

"Faulks is nothing," Sean said easily. "She's a bully and not overly bright, but she's loyal to the Captain to a fault and she's pretty good at what she does. Just ignore her and you'll be fine." His easy confidence was reassuring to her for some reason.

"I'm pretty sure she hates me just for being here," Jessica shrugged.

"She hates everyone except the Captain," Sean gave a shrug of his own. "It's not personal, really. She's just very insecure for some reason." Jessica looked at him sharply.

"Are we talking about the same woman?" she almost laughed.

"She talks a good fight," Sean admitted. "But honestly, whenever you see someone like that, always looking to bully those around them, they're usually covering up something else. Some deficiency that maybe only they can see. It's kind of sad, really. Like I said, she's pretty capable, so her insecurity lies somewhere rather than her abilities."

"You know," Jessica said suddenly, "I think this is the most I've heard you say in the week I've been aboard. You're a very good conversationalist." She noted a bit of red around his collar as she spoke.

"I don't usually have much to say," he shrugged, this time not as easily. More forced. "I'm not used to being around civilized company for the most part, at least I wasn't until I came aboard *Celia*. It's a hard habit to break after so long. And you're easy to talk to," he added.

"Why is that, you think?" she asked. "I'm hoping I'll be easy to talk to for my students."

"Probably because you're polite and a pretty good conversationalist yourself," he replied after a minute of consideration. "That's not something you get a lot, especially the further out you go from the Middle worlds. You have to remember that we mostly don't move too far from the ports when we put in," he reminded her. "Port towns tend to draw just about the worst people in the galaxy. Thieves, slavers, drug dealers, gun runners, the list is pretty impressive. The further away from the port you get on any world, even a Rim world, the better the people are."

"I...I never thought of that," Jessica admitted. "To me the space port always represented a chance to see other places. To have an adventure, you know?"

"It can definitely be an adventure," Sean nodded grimly. "If you want to survive around places like this," he waved again to view outside the ship, "then you got to learn to be careful. Watchful. Always know what's around you and who's around you."

Jessica considered that even as she considered him. Sean Galen seemed to be a much deeper person than she'd imagined. She'd already known that he was more than he appeared. Now she could see the steel than lay beneath his smooth and quiet exterior. It made a saying of her mother's come to mind; 'Still waters run deep.' She had always thought it as a warning about the streams and rivers around her home, but now. . .now she could see how it would apply to people as well.

Sean Galen was still water, and there was no knowing where the depths ended.

"Will you teach me?" she asked suddenly, her face heating at the boldness of asking such a thing. "Will you teach me to be like that?" Sean looked at her for a minute.

"It's not something you can teach, so much as it's something you have to learn," he said finally. "It's not as easy as someone showing you. And it takes time," he added. "It's learning by experience, not by instruction," he finally settled on.

Jessica considered that. As a student learning to be a teacher she had focused on that. Teaching. Learning something by doing wasn't a foreign concept to her, but it was different.

"I have a lot to learn," she said evenly, looking out the screen again. "I'm afraid that I've been sheltered a good bit. When I was at Beria, I didn't stray from campus often, and that was just on rare occasions to eat out or see a vid. I...I guess I don't really have much real world experience." she admitted, looking back to him.

"It's not impossible to learn," Sean encouraged lightly. "The first thing, the most important thing," he stressed, "is learning to see. Not just to look, but to *see*. There's a difference. Anyone can look. Seeing takes practice."

"What do you mean?" Jessica asked.

"Look at me," Sean told her, even though she already was. "Look closely. Don't speak, just look." She did as ordered, eyes scanning over him. He sat completely still for nearly five silent minutes. Suddenly he lifted a hand and spun it.

"Turn around." She complied, turning the chair to face the opposite bulkhead.

"Describe me," he ordered. "Tell me what I look like."

Jessica opened her mouth and stopped, her mind blank. What did he look like? How did she describe him? How did you describe someone to themselves?

"You're tall," she said hesitantly. "I don't know exactly how tall, but as a point of reference you're slightly taller than Faulks. I don't know how but you seem to be able to appear smaller even though you aren't. Your hair is short but not so short as hers, or even the Captain's for that matter."

"Go on," he urged.

"Your clothes are plain, not colorful or attention grabbing. Nothing to stand out or call attention to yourself. Good quality, just not flashy. A mix of grays and blacks with the occasional brown. Always different shades of neutral colors. Earth tones. It's almost as if you're connected to the land, somehow, but I don't know how that would work considering you live and work on a space ship."

"Your eyes rarely stop moving. You aren't nervous, just. . .observant. You appear relaxed but you're not, not really. You aren't really tense, not on edge, just prepared for whatever might happen. You don't seem easy to surprise." She paused, biting her lower lip slightly.

"That. . .that's all I got," she admitted finally. She spun back to face him.

"I missed so much," she said, looking him over again.

"Can you see what you missed that's important, now that you're looking at me again?" Sean asked. She could see that he was uncomfortable with this and felt a surge of gratitude to him for helping her learn a valuable lesson.

"You're armed," she noted suddenly, seeing a pistol at his side. "I...all this time and I never noticed it before. You're wearing a gun."

"Why didn't you notice it before?" Sean asked, head tilted to the side.

"It's like a part of you," Jessica said without thinking. "It's. . .you don't see it because it's supposed to be there. You don't wear it, it's a part of you. Like the knife in your hand and the one in your boot."

"Very good," he almost smiled. "I've been aboard this ship nearly three years and I bet no one on this crew could describe me in as much detail as you just did. After just five minutes." He looked out the screen again.

"Learning to see, that's the first step in learning to protect yourself. In being able to function and not get taken by surprise when the time comes." He paused for a minute and Jessica could tell he was considering something. Finally, he looked at her.

"Practice on the others," he told her. "Study them. We'll go over your observations at different times. Study the ship, too. Learn it inside and out in the areas you're allowed to be in. Remember, don't just look. Learn to see."

"After that, we'll see what we see."

CHAPTER FOUR

Meredith stretched carefully as she lay in the hotel bed. It was pretty comfortable. She had to be careful not to aggravate her back but stretching felt good. *Celia* wasn't cramped by any means, but it was still confined. Most times that wasn't a big deal but every once in a while it was nice to be unencumbered by bulkheads and airtight doors.

"Morning," Linc said easily from her side. "That's a wonderful sight to wake up to, by the way," he teased, running a hand down her naked side.

"Sweet talker," Meredith snorted. "How did you sleep?" she asked, rolling carefully on to her side to lay partially atop her husband.

"I slept fine," he smiled, brushing her hair away from her face. "How about you? If you had a nightmare it was quiet enough not to wake me. Of course, I was pretty tired," he added with a lecherous wag of his eyebrows.

"No, no nightmares," Meredith told him, laying her head on his chest. She idly traced his skin with her right hand, her touch light and teasing. "I slept soundly for once. Must have been all that extracurricular activity," she snorted. The two had made good use of their time. The hotel had included a whirlpool which Meredith had used to good effect, followed by a massage from her husband that had led to a very pleasant evening indeed.

"What time is it?" she asked, not wanting to move from her place.

"Almost six," Linc admitted. "If you want to keep the zero nine-hundred departure we should probably get up. We'll likely be late as it is. It'll take at least two hours after I turn the engines over."

"I know," Meredith sighed. "I was just thinking that we're a little ahead of schedule," she temporized. Linc stroked her back idly, waiting. If she wanted his advice he would give it to her, but she had to ask for it. That was the agreement they had made when they'd gone into this venture together. She was the Captain; he was the pilot. Only in their personal areas was he the husband and she the wife. It had been a good arrangement since the beginning.

"What do you think about delaying out departure, maybe just twelve hours?" she asked, raising her head to look at him. "Not another overnight, just. . .not rushing to get back into space. We're at least three days ahead of our schedule by my calculations."

"Three days and several hours," Linc nodded. "Almost eight hours ahead assuming the original departure time this morning. We can spare the time, I'm sure. We might even make some of it back," he added. "We're not carrying anything perishable or urgent that I know of."

"No, we're not," Meredith agreed. She reached over to the nightstand and picked up her handheld. Pressing a button, she waited until she heard Sean's voice, perhaps a little sleepy, pick up.

"Ma'am?"

"How could you possibly know it was me?" Meredith demanded playfully.

"No one else would call on this channel, ma'am," he replied. She made a 'duh' eye roll. She knew that.

"I've decided to delay take-off for twelve hours. Is the fueling complete?"

"Yes, Captain. We're set. I'm glad you called early, I would have turned the engines over in a few minutes."

"Well, you can hold off on that until Linc and I get back. If the others call in, let them know the deal. You and Jessica okay?"

"Just fine, ma'am," Sean answered. "If we're going to stay in port a little longer I may take Jessica off ship."

"Oh?" Meredith allowed a teasing note to ease into her tone.

"She's interested in learning as much as she can," Sean informed her, apparently missing the tone in her voice or choosing to ignore it. "Once she hits Gateway she'll probably never go back into space again, so this is pretty much her only opportunity."

"That's true," Meredith mused. "She seems like a good kid," she said without thinking.

"She's very smart," Sean agreed. "Should make a good teacher."

"Well, we'll be in after a while. I'll make sure the two of you have some time. But Sean, you watch after her, hear? She's a babe amongst demons in a place like this."

"I'll see to her, ma'am." The connection broke and she found Linc watching her.

"Sean and Jessica appear to have hit it off," she grinned wryly. "Since we're staying a bit longer he's going to take her off ship for a few hours and let her look around."

"That won't be a problem when we drop her off will it?" Linc asked.

"No, Sean will never stay planetside for long," Meredith shook her head. "Now, we may face Jessica wanting to stay with him, if they really have 'hit it off'," she grinned.

"It's not like we don't have room," Linc shrugged. "But it sounds like you might be jumping to conclusions."

"Oh, I'm teasing," she admitted. "Apparently she just wants to see what she can see before she's stuck on Gateway for the rest of her life. I can't say I blame her. I do worry about Sean being her escort though," she frowned slightly. "I'm not sure he would be able to protect her if anything happened. What?" she looked at her husband as he shook with laughter.

"Oh, wifey dear," he rubbed the back of her head with a strong hand, massaging her scalp. "Have you never looked in his eyes?"

"What?" Meredith sat up slightly. "What does that mean?"

"Meredith, Sean Galen is just about the last person on the ship that I would want to cross, honey bottom," he leaned upward and kissed her lightly.

"Why in the world would you say that?" Meredith was stunned. "He's so quiet that you almost don't know he's there. And Faulks is constantly giving him hell and he takes it without a word."

"Yes," Linc nodded. When he didn't say more, Meredith huffed slightly.

"What is it that you think you know that I don't?" she demanded, arms crossed beneath her breasts. A sight that Lincoln enjoyed immensely.

"Honey, I could write a book with the things that I know that you don't," he teased, kissing her nose. "Seriously, you've never noticed anything else about him?"

"Apparently not," Meredith was not mollified.

"Mere, Sean's a killer," Linc dropped his revelation with a calm that shocked Meredith. "Look into his eyes. He's not *taking* Faulks abuse. He's *allowing* it. Because it doesn't mean anything to him. He ignores her and goes about his business. I think that's one of the things that drives Faulks to keep hammering at him. Drives her nuts that he *can* ignore her."

"So he ignores her," Meredith shrugged. "So what? You ignore her, too."

"No, I don't," Linc told her flatly. "She. . .well, never mind," he cut himself off. "Meredith, Sean Galen ignores Faulks just like you would ignore a bug. Not worth worrying about. Not worth noticing. See what I mean?"

Meredith opened her mouth to object, then stopped, considering her husband's words. She tried to think of a time when Sean had reacted poorly to Faulks, and couldn't. Not once.

"How long ago did you notice this?" she asked.

"Took maybe a month, I guess," Linc shrugged. "When he first came aboard we were all pretty busy. As things smoothed out I began to see it." He looked at her, noting the doubt in her eyes.

"I'm a trained observer, Mere," he reminded her. "My job. Well, was my job," he corrected with a grin. "And I was pretty good at it, if I do say so myself."

"Do you regret it?" Meredith asked suddenly. Linc shot her a confused look.

"Regret what?"

"Leaving your job that you were good at," Meredith clarified. "Leaving that behind to follow me into space?"

"Of course not," Linc scoffed. "What a ridiculous question." He kissed her soundly and she responded to it. When they broke the contact he was looking directly into her eyes.

"I've never regretted anything to do with you, Mere, outside your injuries and your nightmares. I wish I could take them away; wish I could hurt for you. I'd do it in a heartbeat if I could find a way."

"I know," she reached up and stroked his face with her hand. "And I love you all the more for it." She kissed him again, and the conversation about Sean Galen was forgotten.

For now.

-

Tony walked back to the ship whistling slightly to himself. He had managed to take care of all his business without any problem and then spent the rest of his time enjoying a carousing time in Common Place. He still wondered who had named the place. It was catchy he admitted, but silly. He was so distracted by his own satisfaction that he almost missed Faulks.

He stopped short seeing the large woman exit an obvious brothel. Well, obvious to those who knew what to look for. She was actually leaving a very high-end establishment, one that catered to all sorts of. . .needs. He was about to grin when he saw Faulks turn around, apparently being called from within. The woman who came to the door behind her looked familiar, and it took Tony a minute to recognize her. Or at least recognize why she looked familiar.

She looked like the Captain.

-

"You forgot this, dear," Faulks heard from behind her and turned to see her entertainer of the evening holding her small bag. She took it, smiling.

"Thank you, Regina." The smile felt odd on her face. Unusual.

"You're welcome, Carol. Do come and see me again when you're in port. And be safe." With that the door closed and Faulks was on her way to the ship, unaware that one of her crew mates had seen her exit the building, or who she was talking to.

-

"Well, I'll be damned," Tony said softly to himself. "I should have seen that coming," he added a second later. "I really should have."

What he'd just seen explained so much about Faulks. Her attitude, her dislike (almost too mild a word) for the Captain's husband and so much more.

Not my business, he told himself firmly. *Not my business at all.*

Having told himself that, Tony resumed his walk to the ship, once more humming along happily. Just because it wasn't his business didn't mean that he was above tormenting Faulks just a bit, now and then. Just to get at her for all her bullying.

Yes sir, this was turning out to be a pretty good morning.

-

Unaware that her secret was out, Faulks had tromped back toward *Celia*, people parting in her path like the proverbial sea. She enjoyed that, seeing people give way to her. Recognizing her status. Her strength.

The night spent with Regina had been nice, but it hadn't felt like she'd hoped. It hadn't solved her problem, just made it worse. While the night and the company had been enjoyable and highly entertaining, it was *off*, somehow. It was wasn't *right*. And that had ruined the overall effect. She shook her head, trying to focus on her duties. If she didn't get her shit together she was going to be out and gone from the *Celia* altogether and then it wouldn't matter anyway.

She would never have what she wanted. What she had now would have to do. And if she wanted to keep what she had now, she had better straighten her act up. The Captain had made it clear that she was sick and tired of Faulks' antics. The large woman sighed, shaking her head.

So many things were habitual. Things she had done all her adult life as a Marine. As a woman in what was still a 'traditionally' man's world. She had made it, made a name for herself and been well known and respected. Feared even. But to do that she had become something very hard and unyielding. And that was hard to let go of after so long.

But she would either learn to do it or learn to get along without the Captain in her life at all.

And that just was not an option.

-

Jessica was a bit nervous as she selected what to wear. It wasn't like she had a huge wardrobe to choose from and most of that had been clothing suitable to either work or attend class. On this planet that was probably not the way to go.

Plus, she had decided she wanted to try and dress like Sean did. Not necessarily just like him, but using his habit of choosing clothing that didn't call attention to himself. She wanted to mimic him for some reason that she had yet to understand. He had a stillness and confidence about him that Jessica wanted for herself. Learning from him was a start on that.

She selected a brown skirt that she knew would fall just below her knees along with a beige blouse. She added a sweater that was just a shade lighter than her skirt. Satisfied with her look she grabbed her backpack and headed for the cargo bay. Sean would meet her there and they would depart when the Captain and her husband returned.

She stepped out onto the catwalk and saw Tony standing below talking to Sean. She grinned at the doctor's slightly disheveled appearance. He had obviously enjoyed his night out. She reached the bottom of the steps and headed in their direction. Her smile died as she approached the two men and could see Faulks coming down the gangway toward the ship.

"You're sure?" Sean was asking Tony.

"Absolutely," the doctor nodded. "I should have seen it sooner, man."

"Not my business," Sean shrugged.

"Well, mine either, really." Tony looked at Jessica as she walked up.

"Well, hello Sunshine!" he beamed. "How are you this great day?"

"Fine, thank you," Jessica blushed slightly as she almost always did under Giannini's scrutiny. "Seems as if someone enjoyed their night off," she teased.

"I did indeed," Tony promised. "Well, you two kids have fun," he turned to Sean. "This time of day's pretty quiet, all things considered. Might try the Bayside for lunch, they usually have a buffet that's awesome."

"I...I hadn't planned on eating out," Jessica broke in. She didn't have the money for something like that.

"I wanted to treat you to lunch," Sean told her gently. "My way of thanking you for sharing the watch with me. Would have been pretty boring without you." She looked at him but found nothing in his eyes or face other than honesty.

"You don't have to do that," she objected.

"I didn't say I had to, I said I wanted to," Sean almost smiled. He didn't, but it was the closest she had seen him come.

"All right," she nodded finally. "I'd like that."

"Where are you two going?" Faulks' voice cut across the conversation. "We're supposed to be getting ready to leave."

"Captain's delayed departure for twelve hours," Sean told her. "Since she's done that, Jessica and I are going to look around some. You and Tony have the watch, Captain and Linc should be back soon."

"She didn't say anything to me about leaving later!" Faulks objected.

"I can't do anything about that," Sean shrugged. "She called bright and early this morning, said to tell you two if you called in, or when you reported back aboard. Consider yourself told." He turned from Faulks to Jessica.

"Ready?"

Jessica nodded, eager to be away from the bullying Faulks. She didn't hate the woman, but that day was coming she was sure.

"See you guys when you get back," Tony smiled at her and slapped Sean on the shoulder.

"The two of you? Walking a place like this?" Faulks snorted. "Better watch it, Missy," Faulks told Jessica. "Old Gale will run at the drop of a hat and leave you standing there."

"I'll take my chances," Jessica found the nerve to say. Sean just snorted and held out a hand. He looked at Tony.

"I got a com if you guys need us back." Tony nodded.

"What would we need you for?" Faulks snorted, trying her best to goad Sean. The younger man just looked at her and then stepped off the ship. He and Jessica were off the ramp and moving away before Faulks could say anything else.

"What a pansy ass," she murmured. She snapped her head around at the sound of Giannini's chuckle.

"What're you laughin' at, you little Core fop?" she snarled.

"Better watch that tongue, Faulks," Tony told her, still watching the duo of Sean of Jessica disappear. "Might need me one day. Or something might find its way into your coffee." He turned to look at her. "As to what I'm laughing about? One day you're finally going to say the wrong thing to Galen, and he's going to mop the floor with you. If he doesn't just kill you first." He looked thoughtful for a minute.

"I'm not sure which I'd find more entertaining," he added finally before turning to walk on inside the boat and up to his bunk. Faulks watched him go without comment, still thinking about his threat to her food and drink. She didn't even consider what the man had said about 'Gale'.

-

Jessica looked around her as she and Sean made their way through the light traffic around the port.

"I expected to see more people," she noted.

"You would later in the day," Sean told her. "It's early, yet. Mostly all you'll see this time of day are shippers and people who make their living supplying them. The crooks and thugs are usually asleep this time of the morning."

"Oh. I hadn't thought of that."

"No reason for you to," Sean replied. "But remember what I said earlier. See, don't just look. What do you notice about the people you're seeing?" Jessica studied their surroundings for a few minutes before replying.

"You're right," she said finally. "Most everyone is either on their way to the docks or else working in some business or other. Most of the bars and what have you are closed. The only businesses I see open are restaurants and stores."

"Right," Sean nodded. "What else?"

"Um," Jessica looked around her again. "I don't see anyone who looks. . .well, disreputable. Everyone looks clean and neat. Even those who are working."

"Yes," Sean nodded again. "The usual thugs and thieves usually aren't too concerned about their hygiene. Now that's not to say that someone who's nice and neat and clean isn't a threat or a crook or worse," he cautioned. "And you never know when you're looking at someone on his or her way home from work. Some jobs are just dirty. But that's where experience comes into play. You learn to separate them by other factors."

"Like what?" Jessica asked.

"Well, look at a man's hands," he held out his own. "Are they calloused? Scarred? Grease under the nails, like mine? I washed my hands right before we set out but notice that my finger nails still look dirty? Some of that is engine liquids like grease and oil, but some of it is just stained. Eventually it'll come out, but soap won't always get it off."

"If a man is dressed like a working man and his hands don't show signs of work, then he might not be what he looks like or claims to be. By the same token a man in a suit who has working man's hands might have just worked his way up the ladder so to speak."

"One of the best indicators of someone's intentions is to look in their eyes. Are the eyes shifty, always looking around? Does the speaker seem nervous? Impatient? Does he have a tic that you can see, maybe an eye flutter for example? It's not any one thing, Jess. Not usually. It's a combination of things. It takes time to learn, but you have to start by seeing what's in front of you. By not overlooking something that seems minor."

"You can't make a decision without input," Jessica nodded.

"Exactly," Sean nodded in approval. "If you don't see then you won't factor that into your decision."

"I'll work on it," Jessica promised.

"Here's Bayside," Sean pointed to a restaurant just ahead on their right. "Tony is right about that, by the way. They do have good food. Hungry?"

"Well, yes," Jessica admitted.

"Then let's eat."

-

"I still don't see it," Meredith said as she and Lincoln returned to the ship, arm-in-arm.

"See what?" Linc asked.

"About Sean," she admitted. "I've thought about it since you brought it up. I just can't see him like that, Linc. He's always so nice. So polite. So quiet."

"Yes," Linc nodded. "I didn't base what I think on any of those things, Mere. I told you, it's in his eyes. I'd be willing to bet he's seen combat somewhere."

"At his age?" Meredith scoffed. "The war was pretty much over even when the *Celeste* was attacked, Linc, and that was over five years ago. Sean's maybe twenty-five, twenty-six years old. By the time he finished basic and AIT he would have been at least nineteen. The math doesn't add up. And besides, we ran his background, remember? He didn't show a military record."

"Or any record," Linc pointed out. "Two things you're overlooking. He could see combat, or at least conflict of some kind, without having served in the war. There are always small planetary conflicts popping up. He may have seen action in one of those before he came to us."

"Maybe," Meredith mused. "Not impossible, that's true. What's the other thing?" she asked, looking up at her husband.

"That he was Freeborn."

-

"Wow," Jessica noted, sitting back from the table. "The food here is good."

"Tony usually doesn't exaggerate about food," Sean nodded. "He's a good cook himself, you know."

"Yes, he is," Jessica nodded. "I was shocked at the quality of food when I first came aboard."

"He's a medic by trade," Sean pointed out. "The rest of us share his other ship duties so that he's the full time cook. No one ever complains about the extra work. Not even Faulks."

"I can't imagine her not complaining about everything," Jessica snorted.

"She's a whiner," Sean agreed. "Has been since I've known her. Acts like she's the only one who ever served anywhere other than the Captain, or seen anything bad."

"You really don't like her, do you?" Jessica asked. "Not that I blame you, considering how she treats you."

"I don't really think about her," Sean shrugged. "She's nothing to me, one way or the other. I don't pay attention to most of what she says anyway. You ready to go?"

"Yes, I don't think I could eat another bite," she admitted. The two of them left Bayside and headed back to the ship. Sean continued her 'education' along the way, pointing out things she should always be aware of, things to watch for.

"How did you learn all this, Sean?" Jessica asked. "I mean, who taught you what you're teaching me?" She noted an instant change in his demeanor and in his stance. He had just closed himself off.

"My Pa taught me some of it," he said evenly. "Few others, here and there. Some I learned on my own." She was looking at him when he frowned slightly and slowed down. She looked back in front of them.

"What is it?" she asked.

"Nothin'," he murmured. "Keep movin'." Jessica frowned at his speech. He was normally well-spoken but suddenly he had slipped into an accent that was more suited to a planet on the Frontier. She noted that his hands were hanging loosely at his sides, no longer animated.

"Sean, what's wrong?" Jessica asked, moving slightly closer to him. Suddenly there was a darkness about him that was completely out of place for the young man she had come to know on ship. Without looking at her his left arm came out and fell across her middle, pushing her gently back and slightly behind him.

"Stay behind me," he ordered her, his voice soft. "Don't ask no more questions, just do as I say," he added. As she moved she looked forward again and saw three men moving down the street toward them. Rough looking men.

"Sean. . ." she began.

"Quiet now," he ordered her again. His hand came behind him holding a com unit which he pushed into her hands. She took it without question.

"When things start, you run," he told her softly. "Soon as you light out, you call the ship, tell 'em where ya are and that you're runnin' home. Don't stop til you get there, and don't look back. Hear?" She noted that his accent was growing steadily stronger and that his voice was so soft she had to strain to hear him.

"I hear you," she acknowledged, unsure of what else to say. The three men before them slowed, spreading out.

"I'll make sure they can't follow, but you have to get around 'em," he told her. "Remember, you don't stop, no matter what." She nodded, then realized that he couldn't see.

"I'll remember," she almost whispered.

"Mornin' friend," the middle member of the trio smiled. She noted immediately that it was a greasy smile. One that made her feel like she needed a shower when it was aimed at her. She also noted that the other two gave her the eye before centering on her escort.

"Gentlemen," Sean said easily. "If you'll excuse us?" He moved to the left, placing Jessica more behind him while making it seem as if he was trying to get past the three men.

"Hang on now, hang on," Middle said, raising his hands in a placating manner. "We don't mean no harm, just wanted a word with a pretty lady, that's all."

"We're late for our ship, sorry," Sean shook his head. "We got to be gettin' on." He moved another step to the left and the man on their left lunged. Jessica jumped back in surprise, a yelp escaping her as she did so.

The man never made it to her.

Faster than the eye could follow, Sean's knife was in his hand, ripping into the man attacking her.

"Run!" he ordered, never looking at her. She ran, fumbling with the com unit as she skirted the now falling man who had tried to grab her. She ran and she never looked back.

Just like Sean had told her.

CHAPTER FIVE

"Hello? Can anyone hear me?" Jessica called into the com as she ran. She could hear shouting behind her, but never slowed. Never looked back.

"Hello?"

-

Behind her Sean had turned on the two remaining attackers. The man on the right turned to go after the girl. Sean's arm raised and let the knife in his hand fly toward her pursuer. The knife buried itself almost to the hilt squarely between the man's shoulder blades. He took another three, perhaps four steps before pitching face first into the street.

The last man took advantage of that to launch his own attack on Sean, hitting the engineer solidly in the face. Sean stumbled back then fell to the ground, rolling with the fall and coming to his feet in a crouch after his roll, his boot knife now in his hand.

His attacker was larger, but slower. He was also unobservant. He had seen his prey throw his knife and had not seen him draw another from his boot, the blade now held low, edge up. As the man lunged for him, Sean ripped the blade upward, beneath the sternum of his attacker. As soon as he hit resistance Sean twisted his wrist and pulled the blade to the right, slicing along the bottom of the man's rib cage.

If Sean had taken the time to notice, he would have seen the look of shock on Middle's face. He didn't. He withdrew the blade, allowing the man to hit the ground while he moved down the street. He paused long enough to see that the first man he had struck was still alive. A single knife thrust to the back fixed that problem. Picking up speed Sean crossed the short distance between him and the body of the man who had pursued Jessica, slowing just long enough to retrieve his knife from the man's back. That done he continued on his way down the street, fighting to keep himself from running and attracting even more attention.

-

"Jessica, this is Captain Simmons," Meredith keyed her mike. "What's wrong?"

"Three men attacked us!" Jessica called back, out of breath and still running. "Sean is fighting them right now. He told me to call you and run for the ship!"

"Where are you?" Meredith asked calmly, looking at Linc. Her husband was already on his feet heading for the cargo bay.

"We were on the main street heading back to the ship. I can see the docks from where I am!"

"Can you find the ship?" Meredith asked.

"Yes! But what about Sean?"

"Help is on the way," Meredith promised. "Just keep coming to the ship. Don't stop until you get here." With that Meredith started for the bay herself, though much slower than her husband. As she moved, Linc's words from that morning came back to her.

-

"Faulks, come with me!" Linc ordered as he hit the bay. The former Marine looked up from where she was working, frowning.

"Sean and the girl were attacked in town!" he told her, still moving. Faulks was on her feet in an instant. Personal issues had to be laid aside when the ship was in danger.

The two of them pounded up the gangway in silence. Neither cared much for the other, but both knew that the other could be depended upon. They had just cleared the docks when Jessica's running form came into view. Linc managed to stop her just before she bowled him over.

"Easy, girl, *easy*!" he told her. "You're all right!"

"Sean....he's still fighting!" she told him in between gasps of air.

"Get her back to the boat," Faulks ordered. "I'll see to Galen." With that she took off running in the direction Jessica had just come from. Linc watched her go, almost smirking. Meredith's 'Gunny' was about to get an education or he was badly fooled.

-

"Doc, we may need you!" Meredith called over the ship's IC. "Jessica and Sean were attacked in town. Jessica's on her way to the ship now and Linc and Faulks have gone after them."

"I'll meet you in the bay," he called back. "I wouldn't worry too much unless there was an army. Sean can handle it."

"Just be down there in case," she resisted the urge to snarl at him. She was getting tired of being told how much she had missed about Sean Galen.

-

Faulks was at a dead run when she saw Galen walking toward the docks. True, he was walking fast but still walking. She slowed, wondering now if she'd been the victim of a prank. Galen saw her and nodded, but didn't slow. She fell in beside him.

"Girl okay?" he asked.

"She's fine," Faulks shot back. "What the hell is going on?" she demanded. "Girl said you were attacked."

"It's done," Sean told her flatly. "Keep walking," he added.

"What'd you mean, 'it's done'?" Faulks growled.

"I took care of it," was all he said. "No problem. I just don't want to have to answer any questions about it, that's all."

"Who was it then?" she pressed.

"No idea," he admitted, his voice still flat. "They were after the girl. One of them made a dive at her. When she ran, another cut out after her. They didn't care about me other than I was in their way." For the first time Faulks noticed blood on Galen.

"You hurt?" she demanded.

"Not mine," he replied tersely. "Now let's get back to ship, all right? No more questions." Faulks huffed at that and was about to lay into Galen again when he turned to look at her. Whatever she was going to say died on her lips as Faulks looked into eyes that were suddenly very akin to the pits of hell she'd always heard about.

"No. More. Questions." The words were soft for all that they were biting. Faulks barely heard them, still trying to get away from the rage and violence lurking in Galen's eyes. She had never noticed that before.

"All right," she managed to reply, far more calmly than she felt. "Linc has the girl, she's fine."

"You said that."

"Right," she nodded. She was more shaken than she wanted to admit. She made the walk back to the ship in silence at his side.

-

"Everyone all right?" Meredith demanded as Sean and Faulks walked up the ramp. She noted blood on Galen's hands and clothes.

"Fine, Captain," he nodded.

"You take care of things?" Meredith asked Faulks.

"Nothin' to take care of, Cap'n," she admitted. "Gale . . . Galen said it's done." Meredith frowned at the response. Faulks was supposed to be her strong-arm. She looked at Sean.

"What happened?" she demanded.

"Three men made a play at the girl," he shrugged. "Didn't work." At that he fell silent and began moving toward the catwalk stairs.

"That's it?" Meredith demanded, moving to intercept him. "That's all you got to say?"

"You want a blow-by-blow?" he asked, his expression not changing. "I gutted two of them and got another in the back as he chased Jessica down the street."

"And no one noticed the gunfire?" she demanded.

"Didn't use a gun," he shrugged. "And wasn't many people about. No one in a town like this wants to know what's happening so no one looked. Simple as that."

Meredith looked at him agog, not really knowing what to say. This was a side of Galen that she'd never seen. One she'd never imagined. Her husband had been right, it seemed.

"I'd really like to get this blood off me, ma'am," he broke into her thoughts.

"Go ahead," she nodded, moving aside. "Get cleaned up. We'll need to get shut off this place pretty soon I'd imagine."

"Won't no one care about three slavers, ma'am," Sean shrugged, moving past her. "They're a dime a dozen on a world like this." With that he was moving up the stairs. Meredith watched him go then turned to look at Jessica.

"What really happened?" she asked, her tone harsher than she'd meant it. Jess drew back from her slightly and Tony placed an arm on her shoulder to steady her. She looked up at him and found him smiling back, encouraging her.

"Just like he said, ma'am," Jessica said finally. "There were three men came up to us on the street. Sean, he saw them coming and warned me, moved me around behind him. They blocked our way and Sean said 'excuse me' and tried to move around, which put him right between them and me. He had told me to be ready and to run when he said so. He tried again to get us around the three of them and that's when one of 'em lunged at me. Sean. . .I don't know what he did because I was already running, but that man didn't follow me. I can't tell you what happened after that because I did like he said and I ran." The adrenaline that had pushed her this far was fading by now and Jessica was starting to shake. Tony took her hand in his, his arm still around her shoulder.

"Jess, come on with me and let's get you laid down. You need to rest a bit. Doctor's orders," he added when she seemed about to complain. She nodded shakily at that and allowed Tony to lead her away.

"Well," Meredith let out a long breath. "I guess we better get turned over and ready to get the hell out of here."

"Engines are already warming," Linc informed her. "We can probably be ready to light off in an hour. Two at most."

"We're secure everywhere else," Faulks added. "Fueling was topped off late last night and we've already delivered what cargo was off-loading here. We didn't need supplies, so as soon as we're hot we can go."

"Then let's get that way as fast as we can," Meredith ordered. "We'll have time enough in flight to sort this out."

"What is there to sort, Mere?" Linc asked. "Sean protected the girl, that's all."

"I said we'd hash it out in the dark," she shot back. "Now let's get this ship into space."

-

Three hours later *Celia* was in the black of space, on her way to the next destination.

Sean Galen had cleaned up and gone to work without another word about the occurrence on Dry Common. Meredith was wary around the soft-spoken young man now, something she'd never been before. Neither Lincoln nor Tony Giannini had seemed in any way surprised, though Faulks still looked as if she were in shock. It was good to know she hadn't been the only one that was so badly fooled.

No lawmen had materialized looking for either her passenger or her engineer, for which Meredith was eternally grateful. Had someone seen the attack and been willing to testify. . .well, Sean had apparently been correct about that. No one on Dry Commons had any interest in three dead slavers.

Meredith Simmons, on the other hand, had a great deal of interest in her ship's engineer. Once they were safely off planet and on their way to the next stop, she had called the crew together in the galley, including Jessica at the last minute since the girl had been involved.

"Sean, I'd be very interested in knowing how you managed to deal with three men set on attacking our passenger," she said flatly.

"With a knife, ma'am," Sean replied. "I used a knife. Two knives, actually," he added.

"That's not what I meant," Meredith's voice took on a brittle edge to it. "You've shown no sign in the nearly three years you've been aboard that you had any interest in combat. How is it that you suddenly managed to defeat three men all on your own?"

"We haven't been in combat, ma'am," the young man replied evenly. "I signed on to be an engineer. I fought this morning because we were being attacked by men who probably intended to kill me and almost certainly intended a dark purpose for Miss Travers. It was simple self-defense, ma'am."

"I'm not arguing that you were in the right," Meredith shook her head. "I'm curious as to how you managed to do it."

"I told you, ma'am, I used a knife. How would you have done it?" Meredith blinked at having the question thrown back at her. Either Sean didn't understand what she was asking or he was deliberately trying to throw her off track.

"Sean, I think what the Captain is trying to ask," Linc shot his wife an amused glance, "is where you learned to so something like that." Meredith, though annoyed at the interruption, nodded her agreement.

"I learned from my father and from other men in my. . .family," the engineer shrugged. "Some of it I learned the hard way," he added.

"This is something your family teaches its children?" Meredith asked, wondering what kind of family did that.

"It did," Sean nodded, his eyes becoming guarded. Linc noted that Sean's voice had dropped a degree or two.

"So they don't anymore?" she pressed.

"They don't do anything, anymore, Captain."

Linc stirred slightly. It had gone from 'ma'am' to 'Captain'. His wife was treading on some very personal ground here. Too personal for his liking.

"Mere, can I talk to you a minute?" he asked. "In private?" he added. His wife looked at him, her eyes narrow. Was he questioning her?

"Wait here," she ordered the crew, standing with a wince. Her back was hurting. She and Linc made their way into the lounge where they could talk in private.

"Why are you interrupting me?" Meredith demanded as soon as they were alone.

"I'm wondering where this it going," Linc told her flatly. "Why are you grilling Sean over this, Mere? He didn't do anything wrong and you're treating him like the criminal instead of those goons that tried to grab the girl. Why?"

"Are you questioning me, Linc?" Meredith demanded, and Linc frowned.

"Yes, I am," he stood his ground. "I'm confused as to when Sean Galen became the bad guy in this equation. You're delving into his personal life, Mere, and doing it from some kind of misplaced anger or resentment that I don't see the reason for. And you've touched a nerve asking about his family, in case you didn't notice. I have to wonder why, and where this is going."

"He's obviously been hiding something from us and I want to know what it is!" her voice cracked across the room like a whip.

"There's a difference between hiding something and you not being aware of it," Linc countered. "So his father taught him to use a knife, so what? He just used that skill to defend a young woman from a very nasty fate. To my mind that rates a 'well done', not a third degree interrogation. He hasn't done anything wrong!"

"I thought we agreed I was the Captain of this ship!" Meredith shot back and regretted it the moment it was out of her mouth. She could almost see the impact of her words upon her husband as he rocked back slightly.

"So we did," he nodded, his voice quiet. "Thank you for talking with me, Captain." With that he turned and started for the door.

"Linc, wait!" Meredith called. He stopped, but didn't turn around.

"I'm sorry," she said, almost grudgingly.

"So am I, Captain," was all he said before leaving the lounge and returning to the galley. Meredith watched him go, her heart tearing. In their time together they had rarely argued and he had never questioned her decisions as Captain of the ship. Not once. Why he had done so now she didn't know.

Unless he wasn't questioning her as the Captain, but as his wife. She hadn't thought of that until it was too late. They had hired the crew together, as husband and wife. Maybe that was why. But this was an issue for the ship and crew, which made it her decision as Captain. Linc would just have to live with that.

Mind made up, she returned to the galley.

-

While Meredith and Lincoln were in the lounge, the talk around the table had continued, of a sort.

"This is my fault," Jessica said aloud to no one in particular. "This is because of me."

"That's bull," Tony Giannini said at once, his voice firm. "This is in no way your fault, Jess. It's Galen's fault. Always is. Man's a trouble magnet, I tell you. Never shuts up, always picking fights, it's all we can do to keep him out of trouble even at the best of times." Jessica was growing more angry by the minute until she noticed that Sean was struggling not to laugh and realized she was being pranked.

"Oh, you're horrible!" she told the doctor, but smiled.

"It's not your fault, Jessica," Sean told her, a rare smile gracing his face as he continued to fight off laughter at the medic's diatribe. "Those men have pulled that stunt no telling how many times and there's no way to know how many victims they have. You would have just been one more if I hadn't been with you."

"We wouldn't have been there if not for me wanting to go and look around," Jessica pointed out.

"There's no law in wantin' to go nowhere," Faulks surprised her by speaking up. "You ain't to blame for this, girlie. Galen's right about that. Those three likely pulled that little stunt many a time and figured it wouldn't be no less effective this morning. Only they won't be using it no more," she added firmly.

"Don't ever apologize for living your life, Jessica," Tony agreed. "Those men weren't forced to attack you two. They chose to do it. Just so happens they chose the wrong people, that's all." His look was one of self-satisfaction.

Just then Lincoln came back into the room and it was apparent that he was upset. He might have been angry even, but it was hard to tell. Linc's professional background made him difficult to read. He took his seat, wrapping his hands around his coffee cup. Faulks looked at him, her face completely neutral. She knew when to stay shut.

Meredith followed him out, taking her place at the head of the table again. She looked down the table at her engineer.

"Sean, I'm disappointed that you hid all this from us," she said evenly, and watched as the young man's face tuned to stone.

"I haven't hidden anything from you, Captain," he said evenly. "I've answered every question you've ever asked me, truthfully."

"Be that as it may, you misrepresented yourself to us," she nodded to Linc.

"Leave me out of this," he said at once, looking her straight in the eye. "I'm in no way unsatisfied with Sean's performance. Nor do I think he has 'misrepresented' himself to us in any way." Meredith fought to hide a wince, this time from a different kind of pain. She had screwed up and now Linc was almost furious. So much so that he wasn't backing her where normally he would have.

"Then to me," she amended. "I don't know..." she trailed off as Sean stood.

"I see where this is going, Captain, so let me save you the trouble," he said stiffly. "Our next stop is Hartley Station, correct?"

"Yes," Linc nodded, frowning.

“Then I'll leave the boat there, Captain,” Galen told her flatly. “Consider this my notice, I suppose. If I recall we're about three days out, maybe three-and-a-half. You'll have a parts inventory as well as a list of recommended maintenance that I'm aware of that will be needed along with a schedule of when I'd normally do them. If you'll excuse me,” he bowed ever so slightly and started down the passageway that would lead him to engineering.

“I never said anything about. . .we aren't through talking about this, Sean!” Meredith called out and Galen stopped but didn't turn.

“I am,” he said over his shoulder. “You can keep talking if you want.” With that he was gone, down the passageway and out of sight. In a flash Jessica was up a following him.

“Where are you going?” Meredith demanded.

“This is my fault!” Jessica called over her shoulder. “I have to fix it!” Her steps could be heard echoing down the passageway following Sean Galen.

“Are we finished, Captain?” Linc asked evenly, his gaze unblinking. “I have work I need to see to.”

“Time for me to start on lunch, as well,” Tony nodded, a look of shock on his face.

“Yes,” Meredith's voice was subdued. “We're finished.” Linc and Tony got to their feet at once and headed for their respective work stations. Faulks stayed behind, not moving from her spot.

“You don't have something to do?” Meredith asked.

“I can find something, Cap'n,” the woman nodded. “I just waited to see if you needed me for anything.” Faulks fought to keep the hopeful note out of her voice.

“No, that will be all, Gunny. I'll see you at lunch.” Faulks nodded and rose. Meredith left the table, walking toward the bridge. She had to try and repair the damage she had done to her relationship with Linc. Faulks watched her go, trying to figure a way to keep her there but nothing came to mind. Cursing under her breath the former Marine stomped to the cargo bay to work out.

-

“Sean, wait!” Jessica called as she pursued Sean down the passageway to engineering.

“You aren't supposed to be here,” he told her, his voice flat but not unkind. “This area's off limits to passengers.”

“I know that,” she told him. “I'm so sorry, Sean,” Jessica was nearly in tears. “This is all my fault.”

"No, it isn't," he told her evenly. "This is what Commonwealth scum do to Frontier people, that's all. It's all they know. You're in no way responsible for this. Don't blame yourself, and don't accept any blame for it, either. Now you need to get out of here and back to the common areas. This area isn't safe." And with that he was gone, disappearing into the engine compartment and closing the hatch behind him.

Defeated, Jessica returned to the galley and then into the kitchen to see if she could help with lunch.

-

Meredith walked slowly onto the bridge, finding Linc bent over the navigation computer checking their course. He didn't look up as she entered.

"Linc, we should talk," she said quietly.

"Of course, Captain," he turned to look at her. She didn't wince at the coldness in his tone but it was hard not to.

"That's not fair," she told him.

"It's what you wanted," he reminded her. "And you were just reminding me of it a few minutes ago. I had forgotten my place in all this, apparently," he waved his hand to encompass the ship. "It's your ship, and you're the Captain. I won't ever question you again, Meredith." His use of her full name wasn't lost on her either.

"Linc, that wasn't what I meant," she tried again.

"Sounded like it to me," he replied, moving to the pilot's console and entering a slight course correction into the auto-pilot. "I saw you making a mistake and tried to point it out to you, and got slapped down for it. That was *my* mistake. I won't make it again. We did agree that you were the Captain. My mistake was thinking that my being your husband would come ahead of being your pilot. I thought it did and I guess I took advantage of that. It won't happen again."

"Linc, I was trying to solve a problem with the crew and that's my job as Captain!" Meredith was getting angry now.

"No, you were *creating* a problem with the crew," Linc corrected her, refusing to allow any anger to show. "You were riding Sean Galen like a plow horse for absolutely no reason. That man has been with us from the beginning and has been a loyal crew member. He's done his job, and done it well, since the first day he reported aboard. He's been a far better member of this crew than Faulks has, and I can *guarantee* that had she been the one to kill those three you wouldn't have said a word to her."

"That's part of what we pay her for!" Meredith shot back. "It's part of her job!"

"So Sean should have called Faulks and waited for her?" Linc was incredulous. "For Christ's sake, Meredith, he stopped that girl from being abducted and sold into slavery or worse, not to mention protecting his own life which *everyone* has a right to do! And all you could think to do was be pissed off because he was able to do it! And then, to top it off, you start digging into his *family*! What the hell kind of shit was that?" He stopped, visibly working to calm himself. His use of such language was an indicator of how upset, how angry, he was.

"You don't even see it, do you?" he asked her finally after several breaths. "You can't even see that you're basically punishing him for *you* not realizing that he was a bit more than just a simple engineer. What has he done in the three years he's been with us that this one action has led you to doubt him like that? Has he ever not done his job? Ever caused you a problem with clients or passengers? You damn sure can't say that about Faulks, can you? But I don't see you dressing her down in front of the *entire crew* for any of that."

"But he does something that you already agreed Faulks could have done without much more than 'did you handle it', and you're suddenly all over him in front of everyone, including the girl *whose life he just saved*!" He stopped again, aware that his voice was louder than he intended.

"I don't understand and I tried to get you to explain it to me. All that did was earn me the same kind of treatment," he told her in a softer, more controlled voice. "That was an error on my part. As I said, it won't happen again." He turned away from her and sat heavily in his chair, suddenly very tired. What had started out as a good day had turned to this in just a few hours. All for no good reason that he could see.

"I'm accountable for everyone on this ship," Meredith told him, her own voice tinged with anger. "That means I have to know what they're doing. I deserved to know that he was capable of doing something like that!"

"Have you asked Tony what he's capable of?" Linc asked, not bothering to turn to look at her. "For all you know he could have done the same thing." He did turn to look at her then.

"That reminds me, do you want me to post a notice to Hartley for a new engineer? We might have a few likely candidates lined up for interviews by the time we arrive. We don't want to. . .sorry," he raised a hand as he cut himself off. "I was about to do it again. We're two days and twenty-two hours ahead of schedule for our next delivery. We had scheduled a twelve-hour layover at Hartley that's built into that because we have a delivery at Hartley anyway. I can print out the schedule for you if you like," he offered.

"No, I know the schedule," Meredith replied softly. "Linc, I don't want this to be a problem between us. I've always counted on your help."

"All you have to do is ask," Linc told her at once.

"I shouldn't have to ask," Meredith said.

"I shouldn't get my head handed to me for offering, either," he shot right back. "You can't have it both ways, Meredith. We're either partners, or I'm the pilot and you're the Captain. Because I can tell you right now that what happened in the lounge isn't going to happen again. Understand?" His voice had taken an edge that she hadn't heard in a long time. "I'm not going to be talked to like some hireling, pilot or no." With that he turned back to his console and went to work.

Meredith didn't say anything else, knowing that it was useless until Linc had calmed down. He wasn't being fair but he wouldn't see it as long as he was mad.

She'd just have to wait it out.

CHAPTER SIX

By supper time the crew was completely out of sorts. Jessica had offered to help with lunch and then eaten her meal in her cabin. Linc had simply taken a sandwich and returned to the bridge. Sean Galen had not come out of engineering since he'd gone back to work and lunch was no exception.

Tony served lunch to Meredith and Faulks, then retreated to the kitchen to work on the evening meal. The two women sat in silence, Meredith not wanting to talk and Faulks not knowing what was safe to say and what wasn't.

The rest of the day was strained to say the least. Linc spoke when Meredith spoke to him, or when he needed to tell her something or required her input. Jessica eventually went to the lounge to read while Tony watched a video waiting for the sauce he was making to reduce. Faulks alternated between weights and treadmill, working herself almost into a stupor.

Sean Galen left the engine room late in the day, covered head to toe in grime. He had been working all day cleaning the engine room and doing routine maintenance. Normally that work would have been spread out over five or six days when they were in space but if he was leaving he wanted things to be straight. Some men might be the opposite, but for Sean Galen he couldn't leave things in a mess. He certainly didn't owe Captain Simmons anything, not after today. But he had signed on to do a job and he'd keep doing until he walked down that ramp for the last time.

Hartley Station wasn't a bad place to look for work, either. There was a lot of traffic through the station. He'd be able to find something else with little trouble. Might even work on the station itself for a while if the right job came along.

He was thinking about that as he stepped out of the shower, clean for the first time since that morning. He dressed quickly, reminding himself to use the laundry on the ship the day before they put in. He didn't know when the chance would come again. He had pay coming and a good bit put by so it wasn't as if he'd starve before he could find work, but there was no sense in spending money he didn't have to.

He headed for the crew quarters but was stopped in the galley by Tony Giannini, holding a plate with a sandwich and a glass.

"You need to eat, Galen," Tony said evenly, placing the items on the table. "Mad or not."

"I ain't mad," Galen replied without thinking. "Just. . .I just am," he shrugged. Seeing the sandwich reminded him that he hadn't eaten though, so he sat down, placing his shower bundle in the seat next to him. Tony sat down with him, nursing his own glass and a small snack of some kind.

"You ain't really quittin' are ya?" Tony asked, chewing on something crunchy. "I mean, not really."

"Yeah," Galen nodded, taking a bite of the sandwich and then chewing wolfishly as his hunger hit home. "Reckon I am."

"Why?" Tony asked. "Why do that?"

"Were you sitting here this afternoon?" Galen demanded, looking up from his meal. "You saw that third degree, man. She don't aim to let this go Tony, and I can't undo what's done. I can't make them three not be dead. And I don't intend to listen to any more of that crap." He took another bite of his sandwich.

"I don't know what got into her," Tony admitted, "but it can't last, Galen. Don't make any rash decisions, okay? This is a good crew and we've been together for a long time. Let's don't go breaking it up over one bad time, right?"

"You really think this is gonna get better?" Sean asked, eyebrows raised. "You saw how she lit into me, Tony. If Faulks had killed them three she wouldn't have said a word outside worrying over getting off world before the law might take notice. For some reason the fact that *I* did it put a burr under her saddle that she aims to take out on me. I can stand that up to a point. Digging into my family business is beyond that point."

"That was wrong," Tony agreed firmly. "Man's family is his own business and no one else's. I agree she crossed a line there. But," he held up a single finger, pointed upward, "that ain't no reason to run off, Sean. Just make sure she knows that's a line you won't allow to be crossed, that's all."

"Cap'n's word is law on ship, Doc," Faulks said from the passageway. Tony looked up at where the Gunny was standing, leaning on the bulkhead, but Galen didn't bother.

"This ain't none o' your concern, Faulks," Giannini warned, his voice dark. "Shove on off somewhere else, hear?"

"I'm just pointin' out something you maybe ain't thought of," Faulks surprisingly didn't react poorly to being ordered about. "On a ship, the Captain is the law. The rule. He or she wants something, they get it. It's that simple."

"Not that," Sean said softly. "My family ain't no concern of no one on this ship or anywhere else for that matter. I don't care who they are, or what they are." There was a warning timber in his voice that neither missed. Faulks stood up but didn't come further into the room.

"I'm not saying it is," she nodded, though only Tony was looking. "I'm just explaining what might be in the Cap'n's head, that's all. You got to understand how she thinks. How military people think."

"I know all about how 'military' people think," Galen's voice was cold. Still. "And I don't care. You might want to keep that in mind, Gunnery Sergeant." With that he rose, his actions smooth and swift, so abrupt that even the cook moved back in his seat.

"Thanks for the sandwich, Doc," he said evenly. Gathering up his bundle he left for his bunk, never looking back. Tony watched him go then turned back to Faulks.

"You have a real talent for butting in where you aren't wanted or needed. You know that, Faulks?"

"You think what you want," the woman surprised him, shrugging. "I meant no harm in what I said. Like I told you, I was just explaining how the Captain thinks. She was trained to accept responsibility for everything and everyone under her command. No exceptions. And while she ain't in the Navy no more, she still thinks that way."

"None of that gives her the right or the *need*," Tony emphasized, "to dig into someone's family life, Faulks."

"I don't disagree," Faulks surprised him again. "But you think about this. Sean Galen has been on this ship for three years and no one had a clue that he was capable of anything like what he did this morning. Not. A. Clue. Don't that give you a little bit of a problem, knowing he's been sleeping next door down from you all this time?"

"You mean as opposed to you being two doors down and across the hall?" Giannini sneered. "Comes to that I'm a lot more concerned about a loose cannon like you than I am a controlled weapon like Sean Galen."

"I'm a known quality," she shrugged. "You know what to expect from me," she turned to go. "Can you say the same about him?" With that she withdrew.

The medic sat there thinking about her statement but he wasn't fooled. Faulks might act like she was trying to be reasonable, but the truth was that she was suddenly faced with a Sean Galen who was far more capable than she'd thought. A man she had continually taunted and teased and tried to provoke without success. Now she was worried that a sleeping killer had woke up and might take exception to her treatment of him.

Tony thought that was just too funny.

-

Supper was strained. Silence reined around the table where normally there was small talk, laughing and joking. Tony had made spaghetti, a crew favorite, and everyone dug in with gusto including Sean Galen. Meredith had been surprised to see the engineer at supper since he had skipped lunch, but he had reported as usual, taking his normal seat without saying a word.

For Sean's part, he was enjoying the meal since this was almost certainly the last time he would get to eat Tony Giannini's spaghetti and it really was one of his favorites. To say it was delicious was an understatement.

He had considered the cook's words that afternoon but was unmoved by them. He had stayed here too long. This always happened to him, no matter where he went, no matter how careful he was. He had thought this time was different. He had been so very careful here.

It had been the girl. She had been a weakness he should have ignored. He should have never let her come on the bridge, let alone talk him into taking her off ship. He grimaced mentally at the thought. She hadn't talked him into anything. He had seen her, wide-eyed and wondrous about the world outside her little sphere, and decided he would help her learn. That had been his mistake, so it was on him and not on her.

She was a good kid and he had tried to help her. *Had* helped her at least a little he was sure. She would always remember the lesson he taught her, and it would grow as she learned more on her own. She would be able to fend for herself he was certain. And for some reason that he could not understand that was important to him. He would likely never understand it.

And it was done in any case. No sense dwelling on it. He would move on, as he always did when the past caught up with him.

With that thought he helped himself to second helping of spaghetti and ignored the stillness at the table. It didn't bother him nearly as much as it did the others.

-

The silence bothered Meredith. It signified trouble on her ship. Trouble that hadn't been there this morning. Trouble that she was beginning to understand just might be her fault.

The day since lunch had been difficult for her. She had expected Linc to approach her with an apology for earlier, but that hadn't happened. Nor had his cold shoulder warmed any, either. She wanted to be angry about that but a niggling thought in the back of her mind kept her from saying anything in haste;

What if he was right?

She didn't want admit it. Admitting she was wrong in any kind of command decision was anathema to her. You made decisions and you stuck to them. Good, bad, indifferent, you had to be the Captain.

And it wasn't as if she had fired Sean Galen. He had made the decision to leave all on his own. Her conscience tried to make her feel responsible because of her actions but she resisted that. She had the right to know those things, she told herself firmly. She needed to know those things so that she could make proper decisions and avoid being caught by surprise. As she had been earlier today.

Of course Linc, and apparently Tony Giannini, hadn't been surprised at all. That was something that bothered her as much if not more than the fact that she felt as if Sean Galen had basically lied to her. He hadn't of course, save perhaps by omission, but still. She didn't like the idea that someone she had trusted had hidden something that important from her.

She observed her crew as they ate in silence, however, and realized that she had wrecked her ship's morale by her actions, justified or not. Linc had been right about one thing. She would never have dressed Faulks down like she had Galen with the entire crew and a passenger watching and listening. She would have met with the Gunny in private and made her displeasure known without involving the rest of the crew and certainly not the passenger.

And she should never have spoken to her husband like she had, either. He had never been anything but supportive of her quest to return to space and had in fact been the one to suggest and encourage her to pursue getting her own ship if she couldn't stay in the Navy. And had left his own career behind so that he could be with her.

She had not discussed what she'd planned to do in the meeting with Linc and she could tell now, again with the benefit of hindsight, that he had been surprised if not shocked. He had tried to tell her when they were still on the ground that pursuing this train of thought was out of line but she had been angry for some reason that she was still unable to completely grasp. There was no reason for it and yet there it was.

She still clung to the idea that she had been right, however, refusing to accept or even entertain that she didn't have the right to do as she had. It never crossed her mind in all her ruminations that she had crossed a line she shouldn't have when she started digging into Sean Galen's family life. His family had no bearing on his job or his dependability.

Even after Linc tried to point that out to her, she had failed to back up and see it. He had tried to get her to see that she was wrong, at least in that, and she had flatly refused to listen. Not only that but had spoken to him far more harshly than he deserved.

What a mess you've made, Meredith.

The proper thing to do was approach Galen in private and try to mend that fence. Explain why she had acted the way she had and ask him to understand her position as Captain of the ship. But her pride kept getting in the way of that decision, refusing to allow her to consider that course of action as acceptable.

So she would have to hire a new engineer and upset the balance of a good crew that had served her well for nearly three years. How would that change the way the ship ran? How would it affect the others?

And while she worried about that she still had a disgruntled husband to deal with. It was looking more and more as if Linc was firmly convinced that his stance had been the right one and that her response to his input had been out of line if not completely uncalled for. She fought the urge to sigh. It had been a long day and she was tired.

Surely tomorrow would look better.

-

"Dude, seriously," Tony was trying again. He had lured Sean Galen into the lounge with promises of dessert, in this case an apple crisp pie. "You can't just run off and leave me to fend for myself against Faulks. C'mon, now!"

"Tony, I appreciate the food, I really do," Galen replied. "And I'll definitely miss your cooking, but have you seen anything change in all this?" he asked. "Cause I haven't." He paused, setting the now empty dish on the table between them.

"Look, I'm not long on patience, Doc. I ignore a lot of things because if I don't then I'm prone to react poorly to them. One of the things I react most poorly to is any kind of denigration against my family. I don't really care who it is, either." Galen took a deep breath, almost as if he regretted speaking.

"You've been a good friend, Doc," he said finally. "I've enjoyed shipping with you and that's the truth. You're a laugh riot and it's never boring with you around. But," he stood, "I don't think there's a place for me on this boat anymore. That's my fault, but I can't change it now.

Honestly, if I had it to do over, I'd have stayed on the boat and let you take Jessica to see the sights, or maybe the Captain or Faulks."

"Well, let's see," Tony brought his finger to his chin, tápping it in a thoughtful pose. "I seriously doubt that I could have stopped those three. I will admit that I'm not as helpless or harmless as I may appear, but neither am I so capable as you seem to be, my young friend." Sean snorted at that. Tony might be a year older, but then he might be a year younger, too.

"Faulks? If, and that's a *huge* if, she had accompanied the girl she would have tormented the poor thing for the entire time and made her miserable. And that's if the Captain told her to take it easy on the girl to start with. Jessica is terrified of Faulks, Galen. I doubt she would have accompanied her anywhere."

"And I feel certain that the Captain would not have taken the time to escort the girl anywhere are all. So, that leaves Linc, who would have been tied up with the re-start, aaaannnnnd...you." The final word was said flatly. Matter-of-factly.

"Be that as it may, I still made a mistake. And now I have to pay for it. I'll be getting off at Hartley. It's a good spot to pick up work, so all things considered I'm pretty lucky this happened now rather than somewhere further along. I might have been stuck on the Fringe for no tellin' how long."

"Galen, please," Doc stood as well, pleading with his friend. "At least be open to changing your mind, okay? We're still two days and change out from Hartley Station. There might be a change of heart between here and there."

"Goodnight Doc," Galen smiled. "Thanks for the pie." With that he walked away, leaving his shipmate sighing in frustration.

-

The mood aboard the *Celia* didn't improve over the next two days. It didn't worsen any either, for which Meredith was grateful. She and Lincoln were still just barely speaking to each other and she was growing tired of that. He was being completely unreasonable and refused to see it. She had to make decisions for the ship based on what was best not just for them but for the entire crew. Sean Galen had become a wild card. After nearly three years he was suddenly someone they didn't know and she couldn't trust. At least that was how she saw it.

Linc on the other hand saw a man who had acted to save a young woman from a terrible fate and didn't really care how he had gone about it. To his mind Sean Galen had done a good job and that was all there was to say about it.

Since leaving the ground at Dry Commons Linc hadn't had more than ten words to speak to her that weren't work-related. She knew that had nothing to do with Sean Galen and everything to do with how she had dismissed his opinion about the situation. She had to admit, sooner or later, that she had been wrong.

Might as well start now, she decided. They were still a half-day out of Hartley Station.

"Are you ever going to speak to me?" she asked calmly as the two sat on the bridge alone.

"I've spoken to you all day," Linc looked at her, puzzled.

"About the ship, yes," Meredith nodded. "What about as husband and wife?"

"I'm the pilot right now," Linc's words weren't a surprise, but they did sting. "I'll speak as a husband when we're on the ground. Well, station," he amended. "I'm still working to get my head organized around this new dynamic," he admitted. "I'll work it out."

"There doesn't have to be a new dynamic, Lincoln!" Meredith snapped suddenly, her frustration boiling over. "Things have been fine up to now!"

"Had been, yes," he replied calmly. "The last time I tried to speak to you as a husband, a partner, I was reminded that you were the Captain. Remember that?" he asked, eyebrows raised. "Because I do, Meredith. And I remember what I told you later. That won't happen to me again. Firstly, because I've earned better, or at least I'd like to think so. And secondly because I just don't intend to put up with it. I put up with your poking fun at my abilities, mostly because it's true. I'm not a natural pilot, I have to work for it. For all of it. That's the price I pay for wanting to be by your side," he shrugged.

"I also put up with your trained ape," he continued. "Always giving me the eye, always disrespectful, and always protected by you. That's going to change too, Meredith. One way or the other. You can either reign her attitude toward me in, or find yourself a new pilot as well as a new engineer." He stood abruptly, obviously upset.

"I'll be in the guest quarters tonight," he told her suddenly. "I need some time to think. And my shift is over, Captain, so if you'll excuse me?" Without waiting for her answer Linc stepped off the bridge and out of sight down the corridor, leaving a stunned Meredith in his wake.

Was Lincoln leaving her?

-

Linc stalked through the ship to the passenger area, taking a change of clothes and his kit with him as well as a reader with several books on it. He was angry and despite all his attempts he couldn't seem to get over it.

He threw his stuff on the bed and sat down heavily in the single chair, head in one hand. He and Meredith had always clashed over Faulks and the former Marine's attitude, but Meredith had always had the final say and that 'say' was that Faulks was okay. It didn't matter to her that Faulks seemed to hate him. Lincoln didn't really care one way or the other for what Faulks thought of him to be honest, but it made for a lousy working condition that was made tolerable only by the fact that he was sharing his life with his wife, whom he adored above all else.

He'd always thought that Meredith had felt the same way but now he was starting to question that. Not for the first time he reminded himself there was a reason that professional ethics frowned on a counselor becoming involved with a patient. In their case it hadn't been nearly as big a deal since he wasn't an actual doctor but a trained psychological and social counselor. One of the things he had done in the service was assist service members with the often difficult transition from military life back to civilians. The rules were different for civilians and military thinking was deeply ingrained. The longer the service, the deeper the training ran.

He had helped Meredith over her addiction to painkillers, then with her survivor's guilt over the *Celeste*. He then counseled her about her injuries and the loss of a promising Naval career. In the process of all these things he had fallen head over heels in love with her. That hadn't been his intention, of course.

When serving as a counselor you learned a great deal about another person. Another reason for the strict rules about the relationship between counselor and counseled. Linc had crossed those lines because he hadn't been able to help himself. Meredith Trenton had completely bowled him over and left him breathless in a way he'd never experienced. His heart still beat faster when she walked into the room. She could make him speechless with just a look.

And she could rip his heart out with one snarled comment, he sighed. He had not intended to question her command, and didn't think he had. He had seen her making a mistake and tried to head it off before she finished it. Tried to keep her from crossing a line of her own. Linc knew all about the dangers of crossing lines.

Her reaction had been to slap him down. He realized that she was angry, but he had presented a calm and rational argument about her behavior. She was in error, and that error was going to lead to more problems. The best thing to do was to correct that error before the situation could worsen. So he'd tried to do that.

Unfortunately, he'd failed to realize how angry Meredith was at the time. Failed to realize it because there simply was not a single, rational explanation, not one worthwhile reason for that anger. She was angry about absolutely nothing. And in her anger had lashed out at the voice of reason who had tried to point out that error to her.

Lincoln had always tried to be a salve to Meredith. She was in almost constant pain and taking pain medicines on a regular basis was a risk because of her former addiction. As a result, she suffered without them until and unless she simply couldn't take the pain anymore. Lincoln tried to be her crutch for those times. He tolerated a great deal for his wife simply because he loved her beyond reason. So much so that he had given up his own life to follow her into space. Just to be by her side.

Her treatment of him over this incident wasn't justified and that angered him. And that anger made him dredge up memories of other slights and ill-treatment that he had ignored over the years they had been together. Things that he had simply waved away because he knew she was in pain, because she was still suffering mental, physical and emotional trauma due to her injuries and the losses her ship had faced.

Now those things were coming back to him and he was angry.

Unlike his wife, however, Lincoln recognized his anger and was working to isolate it before it caused yet another problem between them. He sighed as his initial thought came back to him.

Maybe it's time I went home.

CHAPTER SEVEN

Hartley Station was a true space station, hovering above an angry and inhospitable planet. A planet that resisted any and all attempts to establish any kind of permanent settlement on its surface. The air was heavy with the noxious gasses created by constant volcanic activity and acidic water that boiled in some places while frozen solid in others. Seismic activity kept the ground in a state of constant upheaval, making it extremely difficult to erect even temporary structures on the surface. In any other place that would be enough for even the most hardy, or fool-hardy, to leave Hartley behind without a backward glance.

Hartley though, despite all this, had two major attributes that made it worthwhile to brave the horrid conditions and isolation.

The first was a seemingly never ending supply of serenium, an incredibly strong ore used in the manufacture of ship hulls. The bonding properties of serenium allowed it to be alloyed with multiple other materials to create the incredibly strong properties needed in hull material for space-faring vessels. The discovery of serenium had led to a great many improvements in hull design and construction and the ore was highly sought after.

The Station itself had been originally constructed and intended solely as a platform to base mining operations on. Quarters for workers, support staff, entertainment modules and eventually sutler stores had slowly been added until the platform had become a true space station, orbiting above the planet. Over time Hartley Station had become more than just a mining platform.

As the station had grown the owners of the mining company had seen an opportunity to make the station pay for itself by taking advantage of Hartley's second redeeming feature; the station lay in an otherwise empty area of space that just happened to be along three major trade routes and numerous other transit lanes. Hartley began to add services of their own for traveling starships. Fueling, repairs, transient quarters and supply operations soon had the station expanding again. Eventually the fueling and repair operations grew into a full-fledged service center, transient quarters grew into hotels and supply operations grew into way stations and warehouses for shipping companies.

Passenger services opened terminals at the Station to facilitate passenger transfers. Shipping agents began operating offices on the station to manage cargo shipments and transfers. And the station continued to grow.

Pay for mining the planet was high owing to the dangerous environment. Businesses operating in deep space paid their employees better than average to keep them on the job so far from a habitable planet with earth and sky. Operations prospered and brought money to the station in ever increasing amounts. All that money drew shysters, hucksters, brothels, holo-theaters and numerous other endeavors all designed to give the miners and others a chance to spend all that pay. Or to take it from them in games of chance. Or outright theft.

The company hired a security force to serve as police of sorts in an attempt to keep things under control, but a station like Hartley, built over time and in fits and starts, had many places that were not on any kind of plan or schematic. Hiding places. Places where criminal activity could flourish unchecked.

Places where the security force didn't even know to look.

And that was how a place like Hartley Station came to be both a glittering, grand endeavor in deep space and a cesspool of some of the worst people the galaxy had ever spawned. A place where life was cheap but everything else was expensive. Where enough money could buy you anything you wanted.

This was the place that a strife-ridden *Celia* put in to.

-

"Are you still set on leaving?" Lincoln asked as he and Sean Galen sat at the table alone, each with a cup of coffee. "Before you answer, know that I am not happy that you're leaving, nor do I think it's necessary. As far as I'm concerned you were completely in the right, and I've said as much. For all the good that did," he added with a frown.

Galen looked at Lincoln for a moment before answering. He was a bit surprised at Linc's outright statement.

"Yes sir, I'm leaving," he nodded finally. "There's no place for me here anymore, I'm afraid. It was bound to happen sooner or later," he shrugged.

"I don't understand," Linc frowned.

"It's not important," Sean shook his head. "I was going to ask you if you'd like me to stick around to show the new engineer around the compartment," he continued. "I don't mind doing that, if you want. Might make it easier for him to get up to speed. Be a help to you, maybe."

"That's more than we deserve," Linc nodded. "I'd appreciate it, but it's been pointed out to me that I'm not in charge around here so I can't give you an answer." That tidbit surprised Galen even more.

"I'm sorry, sir," he said quietly.

"Really not your fault, Sean," Linc shook his head. "Really. You did the right thing. Meredith was out of line digging into your family like that, too. Something I made abundantly clear, just so you know. For all the good it did," he sighed.

"This is my fault," Jessica said from the passageway behind them. Both turned to see her standing there on the verge of tears. "I am so sorry."

"We've been over this," Sean told her flatly. "You aren't to blame. It wasn't your fault. Stop saying it is and let it go. You did nothing wrong."

"Neither of you did anything wrong," Lincoln emphasized.

"I still feel responsible," Jessica shrugged, walking into the room and joining them at the table. "If I hadn't wanted to go out, none of this would have happened."

"Completely beside the point," Lincoln shook his head. "You had every right to go off ship if you wanted to. And Sean had every right to protect you and defend his own life. Now no more of that talk," he said sternly, though he softened the words with a wink. "I for one am just glad he was with you."

"So am I," Jessica admitted. "And thank you, Mister Galen," she looked at Sean. "For saving me, and for teaching me to look at things differently."

"You're welcome," Sean nodded and stood. Before he could say anything else Meredith walked into the galley followed closely by Faulks. She looked at the three of them, stopping before she reached the table.

"Captain," Lincoln said formally, "Sean has offered to stay aboard long enough to show the new engineer around and familiarize him or her with the set-up if you'd like. I told him that was your decision, but it was a generous offer."

Meredith bit back a sigh at Linc's tone and looked at Sean.

"There's no need for you to go at all, Sean," she said evenly.

"I'm afraid there is, Captain," Sean replied flatly. "But I don't want to leave you in a lurch, so if you want me to wait for the new guy and give them the once-over before I go I can. It won't take that long and as I was telling Mister Simmons it might help you with the transition. If they're aren't learning everything on the fly it might help you stay up to speed."

"If you have the time that would be appreciated," Meredith settled for saying. "Thank you. But if you have to leave early I won't hold you to it."

"Not a problem," he assured her. "Until then I'll make sure that things are ready." Without another word he headed for the engine room to make one last check for anything he'd overlooked.

"I asked him not to go, but he feels like he doesn't have a choice," Linc said evenly still nursing his coffee.

"I just told him the same thing, but he's a grown man and has to make his own choices." Meredith fought to keep her voice calm.

"True enough," Linc nodded. "Will you be going into the station to look for an engineer?" he asked. "I didn't think to ask if you posted a notice."

"I was hoping we wouldn't need one," Meredith shook her head. "We'll have to see if the job office has anyone looking for work. I don't want to fall behind schedule, but I really don't want to head out onto the Rim without an engineer." She looked at Linc pointedly.

"Will you be coming with me?"

"If you want me to, of course," Linc replied at once. "When are we going?"

"Sooner the better," she shrugged. "We're on the clock."

"Let me get my stuff," was all he said and headed for their quarters. Meredith looked at Jessica.

"You want to go onto the station?" she asked.

"Considering how my last outing off the ship went, I think I'll stay on board," Jessica shook her head. "There's no telling what might happen this time."

"That really wasn't your fault," Meredith told her.

"Hard for me to see that, Captain," Jessica shrugged. "I've caused you a lot of trouble just wanting to look around. Including costing a good man his job," she sighed. "I'll just wait in my cabin unless Tony needs my help with anything."

"Suit yourself," Meredith nodded. She walked to the IC.

"Doc, we're about to head out looking for new help. You'll have the watch. Sean is still in engineering for the time being and Miss Travers will be staying aboard."

"Yes, Captain," Tony's voice came back. "I'll meet you in the cargo bay shortly."

"Very well, we're headed down now," she added as Linc returned. Without another word she headed for the cargo bay, Faulks close behind and Lincoln bringing up the rear.

Jessica watched them go, then walked into the lounge to read. She had done all she could. It just wasn't enough.

-

"We'll be back as soon as we can," Meredith told her cook. "Keep the ship locked down until we get back. We have a delivery in three hours, so we'll be back by then for sure."

"Yes, Captain." Tony nodded. He waited for the trio to depart and then secured the ramp.

"We could have made the delivery first if you wanted," Linc mentioned.

"No sense in wasting the time," Meredith shrugged. "We can't make the delivery any sooner, so we can use the time until then to get the word out."

"Makes sense," Linc nodded. The trio fell into an uneasy silence as they headed into the station interior. Meredith was uncomfortable for more than one reason. Her back was hurting something fierce for one, but her heart was hurting too. Linc had never been as distant to her as he had been over the last eighteen hours or so. He spoke to her only on business-related topics, and that only when necessary. She was growing tired of that treatment, though she acknowledged that it wasn't entirely undeserved.

She had considered leaving Faulks behind and using the trip into the station's job office as a chance for her and Linc to try and work out their differences, but Hartley wasn't entirely safe and she decided that Faulks' presence might be needed. The fact that Faulks was along was almost sure to serve as further proof to her husband that she valued Faulks more than she did him. She regretted that but couldn't see a way around it.

She also couldn't speak openly to Linc in front of Faulks about something so personal. It would just have to wait until later when they could try to talk in private.

The twenty-minute walk to the office was made in that same uncomfortable silence. Faulks was uneasy as well but knew that she was on thin ice with the Captain and also recognized that her antagonizing of Meredith's husband was becoming a major bone of contention between her and the Captain. As a result, she was careful to stay quiet and mind her manners.

-

The Hartley jobs office had actually started as a bulletin board years ago. As a transient station there were ships coming and going at all hours of the day and night and sometimes those ships needed crewers. Sometimes crew members left a ship they were on and would need to find work. 'The Board' as it had once been known had started as a simple posting of people looking for work and ships and other employers looking for employees. Over time that had expanded to a kiosk and finally a full blown office.

The board was still there in digital form and required only a search entry to spit out either job openings for a specific position or a list of people with specific skills looking for employment. Meredith had never used the Board before, but everyone who made regular stops at Hartley knew about it.

The three of them entered the small office, Faulks trailing slightly behind and keeping a lookout. Meredith spotted an open terminal and moved to it, quickly entering her information. A list of prospective engineers popped up, but it was a disappointingly short list. Several of the names had been there for two weeks or more, suggesting that they perhaps were not top quality personnel or they would have been hired already. Meredith selected three names, all less than a week in the system, then moved to the counter.

The woman working the desk looked a bit harried but managed a weak smile as Meredith presented her finds. The woman looked at the list and then called up a similar list on her own terminal.

"The second name, Fields, is on an interview at the moment," she informed Meredith. "The others are all showing available right now. I can set interviews for the other two, and add Fields if he doesn't end up taking the position he's looking at now." She looked up.

"What time?"

"We need about five hours, I should think," Meredith said after considering. "We have a delivery we have to make and I'd prefer to have that out of the way before we start talking to people." The woman nodded and made a series of rapid entries into her terminal, using Meredith's information to enter the location of the *Celia*.

"Done," the woman said after several seconds. "That's fifty creds, Captain," she informed Meredith. "If any of them are no shows then we'll provide another choice at no extra charge. I can't promise that for. . .Fields" she said after consulting the list again, "since he's on an interview. You can select another candidate now if you'd like rather than run the risk. Once I've taken your payment and entered the information it will be too late to change."

"No, he looks like a good candidate, we'll take our chances just in case he's still available."

"Very well, sign here," the woman indicated the PAD on the counter top. "And enter payment information here," she hit a button to change the screen after Meredith had signed. "*Celia*, huh? You're registered back toward the Sphere?" she asked.

"Yes, why?" Meredith asked, finishing the form.

"Improves your odds of getting a good crewer," the woman told her. "Even if you're headed out right now, knowing that you'll eventually head inward will attract a higher quality of personnel. You want to post for an open position as well?" the woman asked. "It's only another twenty-five creds since you're already taking interviews. If someone comes in after you're gone they'll see your posting and ask for an interview. That'll be charged to them and not you."

"That sounds like a good idea," Meredith nodded, looking at Linc. "What do you think?"

"Can't hurt," Linc shrugged. "This place looks busy. It's entirely likely a candidate will come in and register after we're gone."

"It is, sir," the woman nodded. "And yes, we're usually busy like this. Are you former military?" she asked, eyeing the way Meredith and Faulks were dressed.

"We are," Meredith nodded. "Commonwealth Navy."

"Add that to your posting, then," the woman suggested. "We get a lot of former military applicants. You might end up with someone that has a military background and a good skill set that prefers to work for someone with a similar background." Meredith considered that and decided it was a good suggestion.

"I appreciate that," she offered.

"Part of the service, ma'am," the woman smiled. "We appreciate your business." And with that the woman turned to help another ship owner, leaving Meredith holding her chits.

"Well, that was painless," Meredith observed. "I admit I didn't know what to expect."

"Me either," Linc agreed. "Nice place." The three of them exited the jobs office, looking around. Though they had all been there before, Hartley Station was a huge place and none of them had ever been this far inside the station.

"You can't really get a grasp of how large this place is from space," Meredith noted.

"I was thinking that myself, Cap'n," Faulks nodded. "This place is huge. Be a good place for triple R sometime."

"Might be at that," Meredith nodded, looking at Linc. He shrugged but made no comment otherwise. He clearly wasn't thinking about rest, refit and recreation at the moment. Biting back a frustrated sigh, Meredith continued to look around.

"I suppose we could find a place to get something to eat, since we were so quick in getting the list finished."

"Sounds good to me, Cap'n," Faulks said at once. Meredith looked again at her husband. Once again his reply was a shrug. At her raised eyebrow he added;

"Whatever you want to do is fine by me." That was about as good as it was going to get, she figured.

"Well, I'm hungry, so I can't see why we shouldn't sample the cuisine here. Not that there's anything wrong with Tony's cooking," she added. "But I doubt he'll have anythi..." She trailed off as two men appeared in front of them. Faulks started to move forward but stopped when she felt something hard pressed into her back.

"Come with us and don't make a scene," one of the men in front of them ordered. "If you do we'll kill you right here."

Linc risked a glance over his shoulder to see two more men behind them, one with a large handgun pressed into Faulks' back.

"What is it you want?" Meredith asked evenly.

"We'll discuss that somewhere more private." Meredith looked around her hoping to see a security detail or at least a military presence, but there was nothing. The three of them were on their own and had walked right into a trap.

"We'll come," she said finally. She felt someone behind her remove her small pistol. Other movement indicated that Faulks and Lincoln were being similarly disarmed. With little choice in the matter at this point the trio fell in behind the two in front and followed them off the concourse and into a dark back passageway, moving further and further away from the busy traffic of the station.

They had been taken without the least bit of trouble. She might as well have left Faulks behind after all she decided just as the world fell on her and things went dark.

CHAPTER EIGHT

Anthony Giannini was becoming mildly concerned. The Captain had planned to be back by now. Not only had she and others failed to return on time, there had been no message from them. And now the pick-up crew was here for the delivery.

"Just a sec and I'll have everything ready," he told the foreman. "Captain meant to be back by now but she didn't make it looks like."

"No problem," the man nodded. "Just don't make it too long, okay? We've got four other deliveries to make today."

"Won't even be five minutes," Tony promised. He made his way up to the galley where Sean was sitting.

"Dude, Captain's still out with the others and now the crew is here to pick up the delivery. I have no idea how to deal with that."

"I can get it," Sean offered standing. "Should be a manifest with them, so all we have to do is match it to the one on the ship's computer." He followed the doctor back to the cargo bay. The two just missed the com unit signal that rang into the galley.

Jess heard it from the lounge and decided to answer it. Just to help out.

-

"Thanks for waiting," Tony smiled. "I honestly didn't know what to do and had to go get the Engineer. I'm actually just the cook."

"No worries," the foreman nodded, signing the transfer for the balance due as he accepted responsibility for the shipment. "Nice boat," he commented.

"She ain't bad," Tony nodded. "Thanks again." The foreman waved as he and his crew departed with their cargo haulers now burdened with the *Celia*'s delivery.

"Thanks, man," Tony turned to Sean. "It's not like the Captain not to be back on time. She's pretty anal about schedules. All that military training I guess."

"They may have had some trouble," Sean shrugged. "Or they could be already talking to someone interested in the job and lost track of time. She might also have happened on a job. Can't pass up a chance to make money, man."

"True enough," Tony sighed. "Still, it's not like them."

"Well, it's not my deal, so. . .I'm not gonna wait around anymore, man," Sean told him. "Well, I'll wait a little bit, but I'm gonna start moving my gear down."

"Yeah, okay," Tony sighed. "This sucks, dude."

"It'll be good," Sean shrugged. "I get somewhere new; I'll send you my contact. You ever need me man just gimme a call. Okay?"

"Same here, brother," Tony grinned. "Same here." Before anything sappy and unmanly could happen Jessica ran out onto the landing above them.

"Guys! Guys you gotta come see this!" without waiting she turned and ran back down the passage way.

"There's no way that's a good," Tony sighed.

-

"Be careful with her!" Linc hissed. "Her back is in such bad shape you could cripple her like that!"

His answer was the butt of a pistol to the side of his face. The man who was dragging Meredith's unconscious form dropped her beside the pilot, sneering.

"Not my problem," he growled. Two others threw Faulks against the bulkhead as well, causing her to groan as she began to regain consciousness.

"What the hell do you want with us anyway?" Lincoln demanded, not the least intimidated by the blow to his head.

"You'll see," the man that had spoken to them first told him. "You're from a ship in B-Dock, yeah? *Celia*, it looks like?" he asked. "Sphere registration?"

"Yeah. So?" Linc replied, and received another shot to the face for his trouble.

"Tell you what's gonna happen," the man smiled again. "You're gonna call whoever is still on your boat and tell them to offload your cargo to my men. Once that happens and we're satisfied, then we'll probably let you go."

"Probably?" Linc replied. "If it's probably then why the hell should we cooperate with you?"

In reply the man knelt beside Meredith's crumpled body and began to open her shirt.

"Her back may be bad, but the rest looks pretty good," he sneered quietly. "You wanna rethink that attitude?" he asked, moving his hand inside Meredith's now open shirt.

"You son-of-a-bitch," Linc snarled, trying to tear the bonds that held his hands behind him. "Real man, aren't you tough guy?"

A casual backhand brought stars to Linc's vision as his head rocked back against the bulkhead.

"More than enough man for her, I bet," the man laughed darkly. "Now, all you got to do is send a message. You wanna do that, or you wanna watch me entertain your lady friend some more. I'm good either way."

-

". . .so when they get there, let them have the cargo still on the ship," Linc's image said. "If you don't, then we're dead." the message ended abruptly after that.

"Son-of-a-" Tony began.

"Yeah," Sean sighed.

"What do we do?" Jessica asked, eyes wide. She was concerned to say the least.

"There's no we," Sean shrugged. "I'm out. I quit, remember? I can't make decisions like that anymore."

"You won't help them?" Jessica asked, stunned. "I know you're angry Sean, but-"

"I keep telling you people I'm not angry," Sean shook his head. "If I was angry, you wouldn't have to guess at it. And I didn't say I wouldn't help. But I'm not a member of the crew anymore. In fact, the only person on this ship that is," he turned to Tony, "is you. So I'm afraid this is on you, man."

"If we give them the cargo, they'll most likely kill them anyway," Tony said after a minute.

"Almost certainly," Sean agreed with a nod. "No witnesses. Might even try to kill you."

"No, that would cause a scene here on the docks," Tony shook his head. "That's why they're going to all this trouble. It looks like a normal delivery, no cause for alarm or investigation. Cargo disappears into the station and by the time we realize they aren't going to release the Captain and the others, there's nothing to be done. No trail to follow." He rubbed his head as he thought.

"They'll be here in less than an hour," Jessica reminded them. "More like thirty-five minutes," she corrected, looking at the time stamp and then the ship's chrono.

"Well, I'm open to suggestions," Tony said finally. "I don't think we can just pretend that this bunch will release the others though, which means that whatever we do is probably their only chance to live."

"Agreed," Sean nodded. "I've only got one suggestion," he added.

"I'm listening."

"Kill them."

-

Tony watched as the four men approached the ship with a ragged cargo hauler. All of them were dirty, their clothing stained and their bodies too long unwashed.

"You get the message?" one of them demanded, standing on the ramp with a casual arrogance that made the medic want to shoot him in the face.

"I got it," he replied instead. "This is it," he waved to the remaining cargo in the bay. "All yours."

"Don't look like much," the thug complained.

"Can't help you there, I'm just the cook," Tony shrugged. "Your message said you wanted the cargo, this is it."

"You wanna watch that mouth, buddy," the man warned and Giannini snorted.

"What you gonna do, tough guy?" he sneered back, walking back into the ship. "Cause a problem for me? Make things worse? Be my guest."

"He needs an education, boys, don't you think?" the thug called over his shoulder. The other three left the cargo hauler and followed Thug One, as Tony thought of him, into the bay.

And out of sight.

Tony let them keep coming until they were well inside the ship, then stopped short. Caught by surprise, the four thugs jerked to a stop as well. Giannini raised his arms and then lowered them. As he did, a pair of semi-automatic pistols slid noiselessly out of his sleeves, settling into his hands.

"Well, look how this has changed!" he smiled suddenly. A completely unfriendly looking smile.

The thug to the rear turned to run but stopped when confronted by Sean Galen, now standing between him and his escape route.

Thug One turned at his subordinate's squawk and froze, a look of fearful recognition crossing his face as he looked at Sean Galen.

"Crow?"

Galen looked at the man, cold eyes studying him with apparent disdain. Slowly recognition came to him, though it wasn't a source of comfort to the man.

"Well, well," Sean's voice was soft and mocking. "How about that? Running into you after all this time, Ferris. What would the odds be, you reckon?"

"Now Crow," Ferris raised his hands in supplication. "We had no way o' knowin' whose ship this was. Just tryin' to make a livin' that's all."

"Oh it's too late for that, old friend," Sean smiled and even Tony Giannini felt a chill at the sinister-looking grin. "Far, far too late for sorry, or we didn't mean to. Now, you got one chance to make it off this ship alive. Wanna guess what that is?"

"What is this shit, Dale?" one of the others demanded.

"Shut up!" Ferris hissed. "Crow, we don't want no trouble," he tried talking to Sean again.

"You should o' thought o' that 'fore you started this, 'Dale'," Sean's voice was mocking as his hand fell to the knife on his belt. "You know what I wanna know. We can do this the easy way or the hard way. The ending is the same, only difference is how we get there."

"Crow, I can't do that," Ferris shook his head. "He'd kill me."

"You mean as opposed to how good I'm going to treat you?" Sean smirked, and again Tony Giannini felt a chill along his spine. Knowing something and seeing it proven were two different things entirely.

One of the other thugs had had enough and grabbed for a gun in his waistband.

"No!" Ferris tried to stop him, but the hilt of a knife was already protruding from the man's chest. He looked down at the blade in his chest then up at his 'boss' before falling to the deck without a sound.

Seeing their compatriot die galvanized the remaining two hirelings and both made similar grabs. From behind them Tony Giannini's pistols each barked once through built-in suppressors and Ferris was alone in the cargo bay. Sean slowly walked to the man he had killed and retrieved his knife, casually wiping it on the man's clothing before he stood.

"Well, 'Dale'?" he taunted. "What's it gonna be?"

-

Tony Giannini was a hard man, raised in a hard world. He had tried to leave that world behind and gotten nothing but heartache for his troubles. He had been fairly certain that he had seen pretty much everything. Observed most every harsh and unforgiving attitude that man was capable of exhibiting toward his fellow man.

But all of that had been before he'd met Sean Galen. More accurately it had been before he'd seen Sean Galen 'questioning' someone. It wasn't that he had a problem with anything Sean had done, because he didn't. It had pleased him far more than it should have to see the thug now known as Ferris squirm and suffer. He was a bully, a thug, and a common thief. Such people deserved anything life dished out to them so far as Giannini was concerned.

It was the raw fear visible on Ferris' face as he contemplated being at Sean Galen's mercy. 'Crow' he'd called him, and Tony wondered what that was all about. Maybe he'd find out eventually. Right now they had larger problems.

-

"Well, that was interesting," Tony remarked as they dumped the cargo hauler, complete with four bodies, at the edge of the giant docking platform. Behind them *Celia* was locked up tight with Jessica still on board. She had suggested contacting the authorities, but both men had been insistent that was not a smart move.

"So it was," Sean nodded absently. "Too bad 'Dale' didn't know where the others are bein' kept," he added.

"Did give us a name, though," Tony pointed out. "We know the man he works for is called Hawkins."

"Yeah," Sean nodded, a shadow passing over him at that.

"What is it?" Tony asked.

"This place is huge," he looked at his friend. "How are we gonna find them?"

Tony wasn't fooled. Whatever had caused that brief look of . . . whatever it had been, it wasn't concern over the size of Hartley Station. But it was a problem.

"Nice guns, by the way," Sean said, grinning at his friend. "Better not let the Captain see that or you'll be out of a job," he smirked.

"Most likely," Tony nodded somberly. He had dreaded this, but. . .he was almost sure he could trust Sean Galen. Sure enough that he decided to take a great chance.

"I may know a way we can find him," he admitted. "But to use it I'm going to have to reveal something to you, Sean. Something that I really, *really* don't want known. If it was, I'd have to go home and I don't want to go home. I like my life just like it is, you know?"

"Sounds bad," Sean frowned. "Do what you have to do man and don't worry about me. I'll wait here for you, or somewhere else if you want. No need for me to know."

Tony wanted to laugh at the irony. A few days ago his friend's life had been turned upside down by one of the people they were trying to save. He'd been constantly bullied by another for the better part of three years. His private life had been stepped on, his family dragged into a discussion that shouldn't have even happened.

But he didn't 'need to know' whatever it was that Tony wanted kept secret.

"It might not be a bad idea for someone to know," Tony admitted, not having considered it before. "C'mon."

"Where we headed?" Sean asked as the two left the dock.

"To see a lawyer."

-

"Tuttle?" Sean asked, reading the sign.

"Yep," Tony nodded. "You're about to learn my own deep dark secret, Sean," Tony warned. "Don't say anything and don't act surprised by anything that happens. Okay?"

"Okay," Sean shrugged and followed his friend into the office. Sean noted that the place spoke of money, right down to the cosmetically enhanced receptionist sitting behind the desk.

"May I assist you gentlemen?" the blonde asked. She'd obviously been to school somewhere.

"I need to see Mister Tuttle, please," Tony smiled. "It's rather urgent."

"Do you have an appointment sir?" she asked.

"No, but I'm sure he'll see me if you'll give him my name," Tony told her. "I'm Anthony Delgado. And I can't stress enough how important time is."

"Please wait here," the girl's demeanor changed at once as she rose and disappeared into the office behind her.

"Nice," Sean commented, looking around him.

"There's a Tuttle on every planet or station that's of any importance in the galaxy," Tony nodded. "Remember that," he added just as the blonde returned.

"He'll see you at once Mister Delgado," she said evenly.

"Thank you." He stepped into the office followed by Sean Galen. The man behind the desk was walking forward to meet Tony as he entered, hand already out.

"Mister Anthony, it's good to see you again, sir," 'Tuttle' said with a smile. "Rebecca says it's an urgent matter that brings you here," he continued, casting a quick glance at Sean Galen and then dismissing him.

"I need to find someone, Mister Tuttle," Tony said easily. "Someone who hurt a friend of mine. His name is Hawkins and he runs a theft ring around here somewhere. I want him." Sean noted the edge to his friend's voice but didn't react, just as he'd promised.

"I'll need a few minutes, sir," 'Tuttle' nodded. "Please, take a seat while I make a call or two. Can I get you anything while you're waiting?"

"No, thank you."

-

Meredith had slowly come around, her head hurting terribly and her back hurting much worse. As she came to full awareness she became aware that her hands and feet were bound and she was propped against a wall or a bulkhead. Her shirt was open and she wondered why. She slowly moved her head to see Linc sitting to her left, watching her through one eye, the other swollen shut.

"Linc!" she moved by instinct before remembering she couldn't.

"It's all right," he told her grimly. "How are you doing?" he asked.

"I'm hurting," she admitted. She turned to her right to see Faulks leaning against the same bulkhead, bound the same way. She turned back to Lincoln.

"Linc, what happened to you?"

"Just a misunderstandin' is all," a strange voice caught her attention and she turned toward it only to wince as the pain in her head worsened. She blinked stars out of her eyes as she tried to focus on the speaker.

"Meredith. . .Trenton?" the man asked, looking at her ID.

"Simmons," she corrected without thought and the man chuckled.

"Well, that explains his problem then," he laughed. "According to this you're Commonwealth Navy. That right?" he asked mildly.

"Not for a long time," she replied, almost shaking her head but catching herself just in time. "Years in fact. I'm disabled."

"Is that a fact?" the man raised an eyebrow. "Back I guess? That was lover boy's complaint when we brought you in."

"Yes," Meredith nodded, clenching her teeth against both the pain and her anger.

"Injured in combat?"

"What difference does it make?" she shot back. The man casually kicked her legs, hard, which pulled them to the side, wrenching her back.

"Damn you!" Lincoln seethed, trying again to pull his bonds apart. He got another blow to the head as a reward for that and fell over, semi-conscious.

"Injured in combat?" the man asked again.

"Yes, you bastard, I was!" Meredith ground out. "My ship was shot out from under me and I caught a piece of shrapnel in the back. Couldn't pass the physical so I was out."

"Too bad," the man said idly. "Well, it's good to know you're Commonwealth scum. Makes killin' you a lot more satisfyin'."

Meredith was about to make another retort when the impact of the words hit her.

"That's what this is all about?" she asked. "Because I was in the Navy years ago?"

"Nah, we're stealin' your cargo right about now," the man looked at his watch. "We'd o' killed you anyway, once that's done. Just business. Knowing you're Commonwealth though, well, that makes it more personal. More enjoyable." He turned away at that, leaving them with one guard who was openly leering at her open shirt front. She looked at Linc who was obviously injured despite his attempts to satisfy her otherwise. She turned to look at Faulks, but the Gunnery Sergeant was sitting still against the bulkhead and refused to look in Meredith's direction. Great.

The only person left for them to count on for help was Tony Giannini. And while a good guy, he wasn't really the kind of man you could depend on in a situation like this.

Not for the first time she regretted running Sean Galen away. They could use a killer about now.

-

"I'm afraid the news isn't good, sir," Tuttle said as he ended a com call. "Hawkins is likely a reference to Josiah Hawkins, a former Freeborn commando who has been linked to quite a bit of criminal activity here on the station. He's very good, however, and nothing can ever be made to stick. No witnesses. He's a killer, Mister Delgado."

"That's fine," Tony smiled. "Where can I find him?"

"Sir, I don't know that this is a wise course of ac-"

"I didn't come here seeking advice, legal or otherwise," Tony's voice cut across the room, his smile gone now. "Now, where can I find him?" Tuttle scribbled a note on a piece of paper and passed it over.

"I can arrange some help if you'll give me a few minutes," he offered.

"We don't need it," Tony replied, once more the smiling, good-natured cook. "Thanks anyway. We'll probably be leaving in a hurry after we complete our business, so if you don't mind make sure we're cleared to depart at our convenience," he gave 'Tuttle' the *Celia*'s name and docking berth.

"I'll see to it at once, sir," the lawyer promised.

"Then we'll be off I guess," Tony smiled yet again. He was very big on smiling, Sean noted. "Thanks again."

"We're here to serve."

Sean stayed quiet as he followed Tony outside the office, sparing a glance and nod for the blonde as they breezed out. Once outside Tony checked a small PAD, looking for the 'address' he'd just gotten.

"Here they are," he pointed.

"How can we be sure they're there?" Sean asked.

"Tuttle wouldn't have offered help if he wasn't there," Tony replied, setting off in the right direction.

"You think he knows this guy?" Sean asked, falling in beside his friend.

"Might," Tony shrugged. "No law against it."

"Reckon he might warn him we're coming?"

"He wouldn't dare."

-

"Dale and the others should be getting back soon," Meredith heard the man she took to be the leader speaking to the one she referred to as 'guard'. "Once they're here, be ready to clean this up."

"What about the woman?" 'Guard' asked and Meredith cringed.

"Sure, long as you get rid of her afterward," 'Leader' replied after a second. "No slip-ups."

"You got it."

Meredith knew that she was in for a rough time and that was if she was lucky. She glanced at Linc who was out cold, probably from a concussion. In a way she was glad. He wouldn't have to see or hear. She glanced at Faulks.

"You're awfully calm," she almost accused.

"Nothing to do," the larger woman shrugged. "I should have done something earlier, before we were helpless. Too late, now."

"What could you have done?" Meredith asked, though not unkindly. "Six of them, and Linc or I neither one are much help."

"Still my job," Faulks shrugged, or tried to. "I should have done something."

Before Meredith could speak again she heard a slamming sound coming from outside the hatch in the other room. Even as she felt hope swell for a second, 'Guard' raised his rifle and pointed it at her. His message was clear.

She could just see the one who had spoken to her, the one she'd pegged 'Leader' for lack of anything else, as he crossed to the hatch.

-

"Maybe we better be square with each other before we get into this," Tony said suddenly, moving to a small alcove out of the flow of traffic.

"Okay," Sean replied. "What about?"

"You know my real name," he said pointedly. "My father is Jerome Delgado."

"Okay," Sean nodded.

"That doesn't mean anything to you?" Tony asked.

"Should it?" Sean asked. "I mean, I don't know a lot about the Sphere, really. You're from back there, right?"

"Yeah," Tony sighed. "I guess it doesn't matter then," he shrugged. "But you recognized this Hawkins guy's name, didn't you?"

"May have," Sean nodded. "Not sure of course, but it's not a common name, Josiah."

"No, it's not," Tony agreed. "If it is the same man, what kind of man are we dealing with?"

"A dead one," Sean's voice was hard, flint-like.

"Ah, that's not what I meant," Tony replied. "I meant what can w-"

"I know what you meant," Sean nodded. "He's a killer, your man was right about that. And if it's the same guy, then he *was* a Freeborn commando. Right now he's doing something that one of us would never do, or so I thought. He's off the rez."

"What's that mean?" Tony asked.

"It means he's got to pay," Sean settled for saying. "When we get there let me take the lead, just in case it is him. He'll know me. He'll probably talk to me, at least at first."

"Like 'Dale' did?" Tony asked, eyebrows raised.

"Probably not just like that, but. . .yeah."

"Works for me." The two of them set out again in search of the almost hidden compartment.

"This should be the place," Tony said softly ten minutes later. "If it's not then I'm going to pay another visit to Mister Tuttle," he said darkly.

"Well, let's see if anyone's at home," Sean said, drawing his knife. Using the hilt, he slammed it on the hatch three times, paused then hit it once more. He slid the knife back into his sheath as they heard the hatch being opened.

-

"Well lookie here!" Meredith heard as the hatch opened. "If it ain't Stormcrow himself. What the hell you doin' here?"

Beside her, Meredith heard a sharp intake of breath from Faulks. Looking her way, she was shocked to see a look of fury cross the Gunny's face where seconds before there was just resigned acceptance.

"Hello, Hawk," a very familiar voice came to her ears about then. "Fancy seein' you again."

"C'mon in and let me close up. . .who's this?"

"Friend o' mine," she was sure that was Sean Galen's voice. "Doc, this is Hawk. Hawk, my friend Doc."

"Friend o' Crow's is a friend o' mine," 'Hawk' replied as the hatch slammed.

"What you got goin' on?" she heard.

"You're just in time, Stormy," 'Hawk' said enthusiastically. "I got a treat for you like you wouldn't believe."

Meredith looked up helplessly as Sean Galen followed her captor into the room.

-

Sean didn't react to Linc's condition but it was difficult. He honestly wouldn't have cared one way or the other about the Captain or her trained ape, but Lincoln Simmons was a good man.

"Three Commonwealth heroes!" 'Hawk' said with a flourish. "We got a crew takin' down their ship right now! Once we don't need 'em no more they'll be expendable. I know how much you like that kind o' thing Stormy, and I'm so glad to see ya I'll give 'em to ya!"

Sean didn't grimace but it was hard. Had he been like that? Back then? *Probably*, he admitted.

"Well, I got a problem, Hawk," Sean said easily, looking at a man he'd once rode with. "I need you to let 'em go with me," his voice was calm. "That one is my boss," he pointed to Meredith. "Don't really like her much, but he," he pointed to Lincoln, "is a good guy and a friend. This one," he pointed to Faulks, "you can keep for all I care. But I'm gonna need those two."

"What?" Hawk looked puzzled.

"Let 'em go, Hawk," Sean repeated, quieter this time. "Don't make this go bad. Just let me have 'em and go about your business, I'll go about mine."

"I can't do that, Stormy," Hawk's attitude changed suddenly. "My guys 'll be back soon with their cargo. Can't have 'em turnin' me in. Bad for business. You understand." He smiled.

"Ferris won't be comin', Hawk," Sean said gently. "Neither will the rest. They tried to take me when they came for the cargo. Didn't work out."

"What?" this time Hawk's face showed some indecision. "Ferris wouldn't do that."

"But he did," Sean kept his voice low. "And he knew it was me, too. His call, his choice. Just like you, right now. I came here to get them back, Josie. You can let me have 'em, or I can take 'em. Either way it ends the same. Only difference is how we get there and how big a mess there is to clean up."

"You killed Wheel Man?" Hawk looked as if he were trying to catch up. "How could you do that?"

"With a knife, Josie," Sean smiled. "I used a knife."

Those were the same words he had said to her, Meredith remembered. They sounded colder somehow, here.

"You killed one of us for *them*?" he pointed at the three bound figures on the floor. "Over the Commonwealth bastards that did for us?"

"They didn't do anything to us, Josie," Sean said patiently. "Been ridin' with 'em for three years, or close enough. They'd be long dead was they part o' that bunch and you know that."

"They're still Commonwealth!" Hawk snarled. "And you're sidin' with them ag'in *me?*"

"Is startin' to look that way," Sean sighed. "What's it gonna be, Josie? I got places to be."

"You turncoat son-of-a-bit-" Hawk grabbed for his gun but stopped as eleven inches of razor sharp steel sliced into this midsection, cutting its way up to his rib cage and then shifting to cut along the bottom of the ribs. At the same time Sean's left hand flicked out and another blade buried itself in 'Guard's' chest as the thug tried to bring his rifle to bear. Meredith winced at the gurgling sound he made, his lungs filling with blood as he sank to the deck plating beneath him.

"I'm sorry, Hawk," she heard Galen say softly. "I don't know what become of you but this isn't our way. It was never our way. Time for you to ride the lightning." He lowered the man gently to the floor, watching as the life slowly drained from his eyes.

"Good hunting, brother," he whispered, closing Hawkins' lifeless eyes before he stood.

"Doc, get in here!" he called. "Linc looks bad hurt." He crossed to the other dead guard and removed his knife, cutting the man's throat with a casualness that made Meredith shudder. Wiping both blades on the dead man's clothes, he crossed to cut the ropes holding Lincoln's feet and wrists while Tony examined him, checking his eyes for reaction.

Sean moved to Meredith next and she drew back from him as his knife lowered. He stopped and backed up a step.

"You want to stay here?" he asked, the coldness of his voice enough to lower the temperature of the room.

"No," she shook her head. "Sorry."

"I get that a lot," Sean shrugged and knelt beside her. He reached behind and carefully cut her wrists loose, then her ankles as she pulled her shirt closed and refastened it.

"How is he, Doc?" Sean asked and Meredith looked to where Tony was looking Lincoln over, ashamed that Sean Galen had asked about him before she had.

"I'm pretty sure he's got a concussion," Tony reported. "We need to get him back to the *Celia*, Sean."

Sean knelt to cut Faulks lose but stopped as he noted her glare.

"You got a problem?" he asked gently, but she wasn't fooled.

"No," she said thickly. He cut her loose as well, though far less carefully than he had Meredith. He stood and stepped back as Faulks got up and then assisted Meredith in getting to her feet. As soon as Meredith was standing Faulks lunged at Sean.

"Faulks, what the hell are you doing!?" Meredith shouted even as Sean casually clubbed the former Marine to the deck with the hilt of the massive knife still in his hand. The ease with which he put her down shocked Meredith as much as it did Faulks.

"Stupid bitch," the venom in Galen's voice surprised her. He started to kneel by the stunned Faulks, knife ready, but Tony's voice stopped him.

"Sean, forget her, man. We need to get Linc out of here and back to the infirmary!" he hissed. Galen paused, his eyes bright with what Meredith could only describe as a bit of madness. Even as she watched the glint left his eyes and he nodded.

"I'll get him," he said, moving to where Lincoln was still on the floor, sheathing his knife as he did so. "Okay to lift him?" he asked.

"Just try not to jostle him any more than you can help," Tony nodded. Sean pulled Linc into a fireman's carry and stood, Tony making sure that he was still breathing.

"Watch my back," he told the doctor, nodding at Faulks.

"I will, man," Tony nodded. He turned to Meredith.

"Captain, may I suggest we get the hell out of here? Just in case there are more of them?"

"Yes," she nodded. "Is Linc going to be okay?" she asked, looking to where Faulks was slowly getting to her feet again.

"We'll see," Tony told her as he followed Sean out and toward the hatch. "I just need to scan him to make sure it's not more than a concussion." He looked at Faulks as he walked by.

"You need to get your fucking priorities in order," he told her flatly and then was by her and gone.

"What the hell is wrong with you?" Meredith demanded as she shoved Faulks toward the hatch. "Has it escaped your notice that those two just saved our lives?" she demanded.

"Didn't you hear?" Faulks demanded, picking up a pistol from the floor when she couldn't locate her own.

"Hear what?"

"Stormcrow? Captain do you not realize who he is?" Faulks looked aghast.

"He's the man that just saved all three of our lives, not to mention a very unpleasant time for me before then," Meredith answered.

"Jesus Christ Cap'n, you don't recognize the *name*?" Faulks looked amazed. "He had the largest bounty on his head ever issued by the Commonwealth! Over a hundred grand!" When it was obvious that Meredith still didn't get it Faulks stopped moving and looked her dead in the eye.

"Sean Galen is The Stormcrow! The Freeborn assassin!"

CHAPTER NINE

Tony's worst fear was that they would encounter a security patrol on their way back to the *Celia*. If they did he could likely make a call and get them cleared, but Linc needed attention sooner rather than later and the delay could be costly.

His second worst fear was that Faulks would let her mental retardation show again and try to attack Sean while he was carrying Lincoln. Tony decided if she did then he would kill her, but that was sure to attract unwanted attention. With Sean covered in blood and Linc looking like he'd gone three rounds with a cargo sled there would be problems.

Neither fear came to fruition as the security forces seemed to be occupied elsewhere and Captain Simmons rode herd on Faulks all the way. Tony called Jessica as they made their way toward the ship, and the girl had the ramp open when they arrived. She gasped at the sight of Lincoln draped over Sean's shoulder but maintained the presence of mind to close the ramp as soon as everyone was aboard. She hadn't missed the fact that Sean Galen was covered in blood or that Faulks looked murderous, either.

There had to be a story or two there, Jess decided, but this wasn't the time to ask.

Sean carried Lincoln straight to the infirmary, depositing him carefully onto the bed with Tony Giannini's help. Meredith followed them in, limping now, and took a seat near the bed. Faulks hovered at the door, hand on the pistol she had 'borrowed' from their dead captors.

Tony moved his scanner across to position it over Linc's head while Sean helped raise the rails on the bed and lock it into place. When he straightened up he noticed Faulks watching him.

"You got something you wanna say to me, Commie?" he asked her, using a rather derogatory name for anyone who served the Commonwealth.

"Not now, dude," Tony interrupted. "I need your help," he added.

"Can't turn my back on her," Sean shook his head.

"Faulks, get out," Meredith said, her voice showing her worry. "Wait in the galley or in your bunk, whichever you prefer. I'll deal with you later."

"Cap'n," Faulks tried to object, but Meredith's worry boiled over.

"*Get out*!" she snapped. "I've had all of you I can deal with for now and my husband is lying here hurt. Whatever your problem is you need to get over it. Do it somewhere besides here!"

Glaring at Sean Galen ever more hatefully Faulks left the infirmary, heading up the passageway to the galley.

Tony activated the scanner then drew a hypo from a drawer and took a bottle from the small cooler he kept for medicines. Drawing up an injection from the bottle he approached the Captain with a swab.

"Get his boots off, Sean," Tony ordered then turned to Meredith. "Pants," he ordered brusquely, startling her.

"Analgesic," he said shortly. "Shot in the ass to help with the pain. Hurry it up!" he ordered when she hesitated. She struggled to her feet, lowering her trousers just enough to allow the shot. She felt a swipe and a sting then the doctor was gone.

"Sit," he ordered over his shoulder. She secured her pants and resumed her seat beside her husband. Galen was just setting Linc's boots along the wall by the door.

"Help me with this jump suit, dude," the medic ordered and the two of them carefully pulled the blood-encrusted outfit from Lincoln's prone form, leaving him in just shorts and a shirt.

"Toss it. No, wait!" Tony changed his mind. "I need to test the blood, I guess. You need to shuck those clothes, too. No telling what you picked up."

"I was just gonna wash 'em," Sean objected. These were good clothes.

"Not with all that blood," Tony was shaking his head. "Sorry, bro."

"It ain't like I never had blood on me before, man," the engineer pointed out altogether too casually. "I'll wash 'em somewhere on the station when I get settled."

"You can't stay here after that!" Meredith objected and shriveled slightly as he turned his gaze on her.

"I'm not gonna stay any longer than it takes to get a job," he told her flatly. "And I ain't tossin' perfectly good clothes 'cause they got a little blood on 'em, either," he turned back to the medic.

"You're going to let me test them then," Giannini's voice brooked no argument. "There's no telling what you've been exposed to with thei-" he stopped as the scanner beeped. Pulling the screen closer he examined the readout. He frowned slightly and Meredith felt her stomach flutter.

"What is it?" she demanded. The shot was starting to kick in already and Meredith was feeling better.

"He's got a concussion for sure," his finger traced a hairline crack along the image of Linc's scull. "See here? Right behind his right eye." He frowned again and enlarged the image.

"There's some internal swelling behind his eye," he mentioned. "I can't tell if it's pushing on the optic nerve or not. That would affect his vision if it is. No way to test it until he's awake and that swelling goes down and lets his eye open. You know how that happened?" he asked, looking at Meredith.

"He took several blows to the head, mostly from gun butts," she supplied. "Trying to protect me," she added. Almost against her will she looked at Sean Galen. He ignored her, assuming she would blame him for this as well. It was the way things were going lately.

"What else you need me to do, Doc?" he asked instead.

"I told you to get out of those clothes," the medic replied. "I need to test them. You need to get cleaned up," he pointed to the shower. "Use disinfectant. Toss your underclothes. Be sure and clean your gear-"

"Teach your grandmother," Sean retorted at that.

"-with disinfectant," Giannini finished, smirking. "To kill any blood borne pathogens. This place is a breeding ground for disease, man. Now do what I said."

"Like I'm going to stay on this ship, let alone shower, with that murderin' Commie sittin' up there waiting for my back to be turned!" Galen snorted in derision. "You're not as smart as I thought, Tony."

"She won't bother you," Meredith said. "Do what he says."

"I don't work for you anymore, *Captain*," Sean made the word sound like a slur. "And there's nothing in the last three years makes me think you can control that gorilla without a shock collar. There's no trusting someone like her, especially not for someone like me." He dismissed her, turning back to Giannini.

"Now, do you need anything else from me?" he asked again. The medic looked at him, sighing.

"No," he admitted. "Not right now. If I can't treat him, we'll have to carry him to the station hospital though."

"You need me to help with that?" Galen asked.

"No," Giannini shook his head. "I can call for a lifter. Probably be safer than us carrying him."

"Then this is where we part ways, man," Sean nodded, his voice kinder now. "You're good, right?" he asked.

"Yeah, I'm straight," his friend nodded. "Dude, don't-"

"Take care, Doc," Sean cut him off gently. "You'll do to ride with," he grinned slightly. With that he left the infirmary, headed to collect his gear. He *would* have to change clothes he decided. He probably wouldn't get far covered in blood. Maybe Tony was right and he should just ditch the clothes altogether. They were pretty crusty.

"Sean, wait," he heard the Captain say behind him. He turned to see her standing in the infirmary door, leaning against the door frame.

"Thank you," she said softly.

"I didn't do it for you," he said calmly.

"I know," she nodded. "You did it for Linc, because he's your friend."

"He's not my friend," he surprised her. "But he's always been good to me. I don't forget things like that." He turned his back to her again, heading to collect his gear.

"You don't have to go," Meredith said again. "I'm sorry," she added. "This is my fault. All of it."

"You're right, it is," he nodded, never looking around. "I killed a man today I've known for most of my life because of you. A man driven to be what he is by people just like you. You and Faulks. Wasn't for you, he'd still be alive. Might not ought to be," he admitted, "but he would be. And if he wasn't at least it wouldn't have been me that killed him."

He had taken another two steps when the ship lurched slightly. Even as he caught his balance he realized that the ship was leaving dock.

"What the hell!" he and Meredith said in unison.

-

As Jessica Travers had closed the ramp she had debated on what to do. She was an outsider here, just a passenger on her way home. While she liked Lincoln and thought he was a nice man, there was really no place for her in the infirmary, especially with Tony Giannini trying to treat the pilot's injuries.

She had remained in the cargo bay for a few minutes before deciding to go back upstairs to the lounge. There was nothing else she could do and being out of the way seemed like the best place for her at the moment.

She had drawn up tight when she entered the galley and saw Faulks sitting and fuming as she stared at the pistol on the table before her. Freezing for a moment, Jessica debated what to do. When Faulks ignored her, she resumed her movement. No longer wanting to be in the lounge as that was too near the hateful woman at the table, Jessica instead passed through and made her way to the bridge.

Technically she wasn't supposed to be there, but then again, *technically*, she'd been informed that when the ship was in dock there was no danger. And other than the cargo bay itself, the bridge was the most distant place she could be from Faulks. Avoiding the former Marine was almost a biological imperative at this point, so the bridge it was.

She took a seat at the navigation console to avoid the ship's controls, just in case Captain Simmons was angry at her presence. Jessica wanted to cry but she fought the urge down. This was all her fault.

Her simple request on Dry Common had left the ship in turmoil, and that turmoil had led the Captain and her husband to be in a position to be trapped as they had been. Lincoln Simmons was badly injured right now, the tension on the ship was thick enough to cut with a knife and all of that could be traced directly back to her asking to go ashore.

Why couldn't I have just sat here and enjoyed a good book? she asked herself, not for the first time.

So engrossed was she in her depression it took her more than a minute to realize that the com unit was lit up with an incoming message. The strident tone finally caught her attention and she turned to look at the screen.

The last time she'd answered a message it had been Lincoln telling them what had happened and that the cargo was being taken. Fear almost prevented her from opening the screen, but she realized that with everyone other than Faulks still in the infirmary there was no one else to answer. She doubted Faulks would even notice she was so intent on her anger. Reluctant, but wanting to be helpful in some way, she timidly reached out and opened the call.

A middle-aged man in a fine suit appeared on the screen.

"Is this the *Celia*?" he asked. "Transport vessel? Dock B, Slip. . ." he looked down then back up, ". . .Thirty-Four?"

"Yes sir," Jessica nodded.

"I'm looking for Anthony. . ." the man trailed off as if unsure how to continue.

"I'm terribly sorry sir but he's treating a member of the crew at the moment," Jessica replied. "I can forward him a message and ask that he return your call as soon as he's free."

"No, that won't be necessary," the man shook his head. "But please tell him that Mister Tuttle called. The Station Security Forces are currently investigating a series of rather brutal homicides, young lady. Please inform him that several witnesses have come forward to inform the SSF that a group of people, one of them covered in what appeared to be blood, were seen carrying an unconscious man near the scene of two of those incidents and that the SSF are now searching the station for those people. Officially they are wanting to question them in relation to the homicides they are investigating but I think it's safe to assume they are also suspects. I believe that is information he will want to have access to at once."

As 'Tuttle' had spoken Jessica had felt apprehension grip her. The situation she had created had led to all this, and now Sean and perhaps Tony were going to get in trouble because of it. In her mind's eye she could see grim-faced Security Police coming to the ship, questioning the two and perhaps attempting to take Sean into custody and maybe Tony as well. Even though they had not done anything that hadn't needed to be done.

Another image flashed into her mind as well. That of a gloating Faulks watching in complete satisfaction as Sean was arrested or perhaps killed in the attempt. The horrid woman would take pleasure in something like that. Jessica's eyes narrowed at the thought without her even realizing it. That simply would not do. She could not, *would not*, allow Sean Galen and Tony Giannini to come to harm or be placed in danger. Both had been far too kind to her on her voyage home after all these years.

Jessica felt a shift in her thinking, almost a series of movements within her brain as her mind processed all of this and suddenly she knew exactly what she must do and how to accomplish it. A flood of calm washed over the normally nervous young woman as she returned her attention to the screen.

"...approval to depart at your convenience...young woman are you listening to me?" 'Tuttle' suddenly broke off, looking at her rather intently.

"Indeed I am," Jessica smiled calmly. "Thank you, Mister Tuttle." With that she shut off the com unit and stood, striding purposely toward the pilot's seat, pausing only long enough to close and secure the bridge door.

Settling into Lincoln's chair, Jessica scanned the panel before her, at once completely aware of what she was looking at and what to do. She had never flown a ship before but suddenly is seemed absurdly simple to do and she found herself wondering how a man as intelligent as Lincoln Simmons obviously was had so much difficulty flying the *Celia*. She slipped the headset onto her head and keyed the mike.

"Hartley Station Control, this is the *Celia*, Slip B-34, ready for departure," she said easily, as if she'd done it a thousand times.

"*Celia* this is Control, you are cleared to depart, traffic is open at this time. Thank you for visiting Hartley and please come again." The controller's voice was that of someone who said the same words over and over, day in and out. What a boring existence that must be.

"Thank you Hartley and I'm sure we'll be back," she replied. Her hands flew over switches as if she'd been doing it for years, aligning, adjusting, setting, correcting. She felt the ship vibrate beneath her as the engines wound up. She keyed the PA system on the *Celia*'s hull.

"De-coupling," she said simply and slammed the plunger that would retract the ship's coupling connections, releasing the station's feeds and retracting the ship's intakes behind their sealed hatches. She watched as light after light winked from amber to green. Satisfied that all was in order, she increased power to the ship's thrusters and *Celia* began to move.

It was time to leave Hartley Station behind.

-

"Who in the hell is flying my ship!?" Meredith demanded.

"You can't leave yet; I need to get off!" Sean shouted at the same time. The two of them raced up the stairs, Sean propelled by anger and Meredith sustained by a pain shot that kept her back from stopping her. The two of them slid to a halt as the sight of Faulks still seated in the galley.

"Who's flying the ship?" Meredith demanded. Faulks looked up at her, her gaze instantly shifting to Sean Galen and filling with hatred. Her hand twitched toward the pistol laying on the table before her but stopped as she saw his hand grasp the hilt of the huge knife at his side.

I wonder if it's the same knife? she wondered idly.

"Dammit Faulks I don't have time for that shit!" Meredith bellowed. "Who in the hell is flying my ship?!" Faulks tore her gaze away from Galen and looked back to her Captain. As she did she realized they were moving.

"I don't know," she admitted, finally broken from her funk. "The girl," she almost breathed. "The girl come through here not long after I got up here. She. . .it has to be her, Cap'n, there's no one else on board."

"Jessica?" Sean looked puzzled. "She knows how to fly?"

"We'd damn sure better hope so!" Meredith snapped, moving toward the bridge. "Because she at least knows how to get us moving." The three of them ran down the passageway to the bridge door only to find it locked. Galen drew his knife and pounded on the door while Meredith keyed the I/C.

"Jessica are you up there?" she demanded. "Open this damn door and do it right now!"

"Dammit Jess, what the hell are you doin' girl?!" Sean demanded through the door itself, careful to keep his back away from Faulks.

"Jessica!" Meredith shouted again into the I/C.

"Patience, Captain," Jessica's voice came back finally though it sounded. . .off, somehow. "Please make yourself comfortable. I'll be done in a moment. Well, perhaps two." With that the I/C clicked off again. Meredith looked at Faulks, then at Galen.

"What the hell?"

-

On the bridge Jessica smiled calmly at the consternation she was causing. It wasn't intentional, of course, but it was highly amusing and entertaining to say the least. She watched as their distance from the station climbed until they were outside the 'envelope' where a ship's engines could be ignited.

Killing the thrusters Jessica aligned the ship for their next destination, a Frontier planet called Weytan, and allowed the navcomp to figure their course. Once it was prepared, Jessica punched it in, locked them on course and powered the *Celia*'s engines. Already warmed and ready, the massive power plants in the rear of the ship blossomed to power, propelling the *Celia* forward. The ship's inertial compensator increased its influence on the artificial gravity so that the crew barely noticed the ship's acceleration.

Satisfied that all was correct, Jessica activated the auto-pilot and checked to make sure the computer was responding. Seeing that it was, she stood up and crossed to the door, unlocking and sliding it open to face three very surprised people, including the ship owner.

"I don't know what all the fuss is over," she told them easily. "The police were after all of you and I had to get us off the station."

And then she passed out.

-

"What the-" Sean exclaimed as he stooped to catch the falling girl before she could hit the deck.

"Did she say the police were after us?" Meredith asked, stopping herself before she too tried to catch the falling girl.

"Something like that anyway," Galen agreed as he stood, cradling the limp girl in his arms. "After you, Commie," he nodded Faulks down the passageway. "You don't stand behind me. Ever."

"That's enough," Meredith bit back a snarl, realizing that it would not be the best way to deal with this problem. "Take her to the infirmary," she ordered.

"Not with her behind me," he shook his head slightly. "That's not open for debate, Captain," he added as Meredith looked as if she was going to object. His tone was flat and final. Pushing him would not end well.

"Faulks, head down to the cargo bay and wait there," she ordered, still looking at Galen.

"Cap'n," Faulks began.

"*Now*," Meredith stressed, her voice still calm. "I need your cooperation while I sort this out. I think I've earned that and more from you, Gunny."

"Cap'n," Faulks nodded and started down the passageway. Meredith let her get out of earshot before speaking again.

"I'm not going to keep being dictated to on my own ship, Mister Galen," she said flatly.

"You want to carry her?" was the easy reply, offering his burden to the Captain. "No? Well, consider this. I wouldn't still *be* on your ship if your charity case hadn't hijacked me. I'm now an *unwilling passenger* on your vessel. Running from a mess I wouldn't be in if not for you. So before you unship too much of that attitude on me *Captain*, you better remember those facts. Add to them the fact that when I freed you, your pet gorilla attacked me without provocation *despite* the fact that I'd just freed her as well *and* saved your lives. So allowing her behind me is not going to happen. And if she so much as sneezes on me I will gut her like a fish. We clear on that? Captain?"

The air of calm that fell over Galen as he spoke wasn't lost on Meredith. He had never shown this side of himself and a part of her realized that he likely never would have had she not pushed him. Again it was clear that her own attitude was to blame for this difficulty.

"Understandable," she admitted finally. "Let's get her to the infirmary." He nodded and walked by her. She followed carefully, wondering how long the shot Tony had given her would last. She was sure that once it was gone she'd be laid up for a while after today's adventures.

-

Carolyn Faulks paced the cargo bay in a rage. It was bad enough that she had failed the Captain when she had needed her most, but now she had learned that Sean Galen, a man she had dismissed so derisively for nearly three years was probably the most notorious assassin of the Border War. A Freeborn criminal responsible for no telling how many Commonwealth deaths, including some of her friends and comrades.

His presence on this ship was completely unacceptable to her and should be to her Captain.

If it had been a shock to discover that Galen might be The Stormcrow, learning that her Captain didn't even know who he was had come as an even ruder awakening. How could the commander of a warship engaged against the Freeborn not know about The Stormcrow? Where the hell had she been hiding during the war?

She made another circuit around the bay. The police had been behind them somehow at the station and that was the best possible outcome. Had the SSF came aboard and took Galen out, then he'd be gone and there would be no threat to her, her Captain, or the ship. Instead that little pea-brained girl had hijacked the ship and took them into space.

And there was another thing! Where did a slip of a girl, a school teacher of all things, learn to pilot a ship? And if she did know how, why bother going to school to be a teacher? Didn't rimrats like her take jobs aboard ship all the time to get away from the rim? Why would she want to go back?

None of this made any sense. Combined with the hate and fear she felt for Sean Galen, it was enough to drive Faulks to distraction.

-

"Now what?" Tony demanded as Galen brought the still unconscious girl into the infirmary. "And are we flying? How the hell did that happen?"

"Good question," Meredith nodded, following Galen into the room. "Jessica apparently knows how to fly. Well enough to launch us anyway and put us on the way to Weytan. She told us that the police were coming after us so she had to get us off the station and then she passed out. Sean only just caught her before she hit the deck."

"Put her on the other bunk," Tony sighed, moving his scanner across to the small gurney he kept as a back-up bed. "What a day," he shook his head.

"You should see it from where I'm standing," Meredith agreed. Galen lowered the girl onto the small gurney, then stood.

"I may as well get cleaned up, I guess," he sighed. "It looks like I'm stuck here. I use your shower in here?" he asked Tony. "You'll be here, right? I need someone around I can trust while I'm inside."

"I'm not going anywhere," Tony nodded. "I'll lock the door, too," he promised. "You really should ditch those things," he added. "At least the blood was dried and didn't get on Jessica."

"I know," Galen sighed again. "I'm going to. I just hate to throw 'em away. Nearly new."

"I'll replace them," Meredith promised.

"I'm rather do without," the bitterness in his voice made her cringe inwardly but she refused to let it show. She must have really hit a nerve with Galen to release all that hatred.

"Easy man," Tony chided. "She's trying to make it right."

"Good luck with that," came the retort as the engineer departed to get his kit and some clean clothes. Tony shook his head in resignation as he ran the scanner over Jessica.

"Thank you," Meredith said softly.

"For what?" he asked, not looking away.

"For that," she didn't have to specify what 'that' she meant. "And for coming after us."

"That was all Galen," Tony shook his head. "I helped a little bit, finding you, but you saw as well as I did. He's the one who managed to get the guy who came to steal the cargo to rat out his boss. He's the one to thank."

"I tried that," Meredith admitted. "He's not really being social at the moment."

"You blame him?" Tony asked. "I mean let's take a look at the last few days and see if we can find a place where being social has paid off for him." Meredith's face flushed at that but she nodded in agreement.

"He certainly hates the Commonwealth," she noted.

"Probably with good reason," Tony shrugged as he set the scanner in motion over Jessica's still unconscious form.

"Why would you say that?!" Meredith demanded.

"Have you seen him do anything *without* reason?" Tony asked, finally looking her way as he activated his medical scanner. "I haven't. You've watched Faulks treat him like shit for nearly three years without more than a 'Faulks, don't do that' in way of correction and he's done *nothing*. As you saw today, Dry Common clearly wasn't a fluke or a lucky shot. If he'd wanted to take Faulks down, it's obvious he could have any time he felt like it."

Meredith nodded at that, remembering how easy it had been for Galen to club Faulks to the deck back on the station. Almost as an afterthought.

And she had never really tried to make Faulks toe the line. She'd allowed the former Marine to berate Sean and her husband with rarely more than a simple admonishment that Faulks plainly chose to ignore. Still. . .

"His anger seems more concentrated than that," she observed. "He's hid that hate from all of us all this time, too."

"For fuck's sake, not this shit again," Tony rolled his eyes. "I have never seen anyone so determined to screw up a good thing," he threw his hands in the air. "Go ahead then, Captain. Keep on the path you're on. Don't let me interrupt your mission to destroy what was a perfectly good crew less than a week ago."

The scanner beeped before Meredith could get her angry retort out and Tony turned to examine the screen.

"What the hell?" he muttered, punching buttons.

"What is it?" she asked, trying to see what he was looking at.

"Something screwed up," he shook his head. "I scanned off center or something and picked up part of the deck, or even the gurney. I keep forgetting it's steel. I'll make another-" he cut off as Jessica groaned slightly and began to stir. Just then Sean Galen returned with his things. He looked at Tony as if to remind him of his promise. The medic nodded and moved to secure the door.

"Go ahead man, I got it," he promised. Galen disappeared into the shower, locking that door behind him as well.

"Do you really think that's necessary?" Meredith asked.

"Well, let's see," Tony mused. "Faulks has attacked him at least once right after he saved her life, and yours. And Linc's, of course. So, yeah, I think *he* thinks it's necessary for sure, and I'm prone to agree. It's obvious you either *can't* control her or you *won't* and either way he can't afford to take the chance."

Meredith bristled at the implication that Faulks was beyond her control, but before she could reply she was interrupted again.

"What happened to me?" Jessica asked, clearly still groggy. "Why am I in the infi...oh! How's Mister Simmons?" she asked seeing Lincoln still out on the bed.

"He's fair at the moment," Tony said, checking Jessica's eyes with a penlight. "How do you feel?" he asked, stepping back. He snapped his fingers at each ear and she flinched each time.

"What is that for?" she asked.

"Checking your reactions," Tony replied. "What's your name?"

"Jess T," she replied automatically. "Three-one-one-five-seven."

"What?" Meredith asked.

"Huh?" Tony said at the same time.

"What, what?" Jessica looked at them. "You asked my name, I told you. Jessica Travers."

"That's not what you said," Tony shook his head.

"Yes, it was!"

"No, honey, it wasn't," Meredith shook her head. Her gentle voice belied the anger she still felt. "And where did you learn to fly a ship?" Jessica opened her mouth to reply but hesitated, clearly remembering what she had done.

"I honestly don't know," she admitted finally. "I just looked at the controls and knew what to do. Knew what everything did. It seemed absurdly simple, to be honest," she shrugged. "A man named Mister Tuttle called for you," she told Tony.

"What did he want?" Tony asked.

"He said to tell you that a series of homicides were being investigated by the station police and that witnesses had seen a group of people, one being carried by a man covered in blood, and were looking for them. He believed that the police considered them suspects even though they were reportedly just wanting to see if the people in question had seen anything."

"And that led you to the pilot's chair?" Meredith demanded.

"Yes," Jessica nodded. "This was all my fault and I needed to find a way to fix it. I couldn't let Sean and Tony get in trouble and the only way to stop it was to get us off the station. Mister Tuttle had said we had clearance to depart and, well. . .I departed us," she finished with a frown. "That didn't sound right," she added. She looked at the medic.

"Am I okay? What happened to me?"

"You fainted," Meredith supplied. "Walked off the bridge pretty as you please after setting us on course for Weytan, said the cops were after us and then collapsed. Sean barely caught you before you banged your head on the floor."

"He's always saving me," Jessica shook her head.

"Not really something to complain about, it is?" Tony asked with a grin.

"Not complaining," she agreed. "Just hate that he has to do it."

"I promise he doesn't mind," Tony assured her. "He's a good guy."

"One of the best," Jessica nodded. "Am I okay to leave?" she asked.

"Stay off the bridge," Meredith warned, then seemed to reconsider. "Although. . .can I assume you can still fly? You seemed like you were in some kind of daze when you first came off the bridge."

"I don't know what caused that," Jessica admitted. "I felt a bit lightheaded, almost like I had been on a carnival ride, but. . .I have no idea why. And yes, odd as it may sound, I still know how to be a pilot. I have no idea *how* I know, though. I have no memory of learning how. I just. . .*know*."

"No one 'just knows' how to fly a starship," Tony objected. "You had to learn somewhere."

"Like I said, I looked at the controls and it just made sense," Jessica shrugged helplessly. "It was like a map laid out in front of me. I knew what each control was, what it did, how and when to apply it. I can't explain it either," she held her hands up in a gesture of helplessness. "It really was absurdly simple though. I don't know why Lincoln has so much trouble. He seems fairly intelligent."

"Go and rest for a little while," Tony said smoothly before a bristling Meredith could respond to the comment about Linc's intelligence. "Maybe get something to eat. There's leftover spaghetti in the chiller that you can warm. Don't eat all of it, though," he grinned. "You took off before Sean could get off the ship so he's a little upset at the moment. If you eat all the spaghetti he'll be worse."

"I...I didn't think of that," she admitted, her voice small. "All I was thinking about was making sure the two of you didn't get into trouble. You've been so good to me I...and this has all been my fault, and I couldn't-"

"Stop saying that and go eat and then get some rest," Tony shooed her away. "Nothing is your fault. Well, the fact that we're in the black again and Sean is still on board, that's kinda your fault," he admitted with a grin. "Still, it's okay. Just take it easy for a little while and come tell me if you feel another spell coming on. *Capiche*?"

"Yes," she nodded, moving toward the door. "Got it." Tony followed her to the door, closed it behind her and locked it again, then turned to look at his boss.

"So, how weird was that from where you're sitting?"

CHAPTER TEN

Lincoln Simmons felt as if he were swimming in a very deep hole, far from the surface of whatever body of water he was currently in. He kept trying to rise from the depths but for some reason he couldn't seem to swim his way out. That didn't make sense because he was a strong swimmer, the result of growing up on the ocean. He'd been swimming almost before he could walk.

That was one of things he hated most about living on a starship. No water. Nowhere to swim. In fact, there wasn't even a bathtub. Sometimes when he was alone on the bridge he would look out at the black before him and imagine he was in the ocean at night, the stars pinpoints of light back on the shore. It was the closest he could come to the real thing anymore.

So why couldn't he seem to get out of this deep hole he found himself in? And if he was stuck under the water, why wasn't he laboring to breathe? Nothing about this made any sense. It had to be a dream and if it was then he needed to wake up because he could hear Meredith somewhere and she probably needed him if he could hear her voice. Of course, Faulks would be somewhere close by so she might not really need him after all.

He hated Faulks. He tried not to because he knew Meredith liked the cantankerous and hateful former Marine, but. . .Linc knew that Faulks wanted very much for him to be out of the picture altogether so that she didn't have to 'share' Meredith with anyone. He snorted at the thought, shaking his head, or at least he thought he did. Meredith didn't swing that way but that fact didn't seem to settle in for Faulks. He didn't know how or why the stupid Jarhead couldn't or wouldn't see that, but it was becoming a real pain in his ass. Big enough that he was beginning to think that they could get by without Faulks. They had Sean after all, and Galen was way more effective than Faulks had ever dreamed of being.

Why was he thinking about Sean Galen? Didn't he quit? Linc remembered trying to talk him out of going but it hadn't worked. That was a damn shame, too. Meredith had backed him into a corner for absolutely no reason and Galen had felt like he didn't have a choice but to leave. Linc had tried to warn her that she was making a mistake but Meredith hadn't listened to him. In fact, she hadn't listened to him much at all lately. Somewhere along the way she'd decided that she didn't need or want his input. He didn't know which it was, and he wasn't sure he wanted to know. The answer might hurt worse than the guessing.

Meantime though, they had to find a new engineer. That's why they were on the Station after all. Galen was leaving and they needed a replacement for him. They were facing at least a three-month circuit on the Rim and no one wanted to be that far away from civilization without a skilled engineer. They had found a couple interesting prospects though, so one of them would prob-

Wait. Hadn't they been attacked? After leaving the office? They were being robbed. He had been hit twice already, once for trying to make their captors take it easier on Meredith's unconscious form, and then again when he tried to stop one of them from-

"Mere!" Linc yelled, or tried to, as he came awake. He struggled to get up, aware that someone was holding him down.

"Linc, stop!" Meredith ordered, helping hold him down despite the pain in her back, the shot Tony had given her having long since worn off. "Linc, you're alright! We're all okay!"

"Mere?" Lincoln sounded confused. He turned toward her voice and Meredith felt her heart break a little at how bad he looked. The right side of his face was blackened and swollen, his right eye still swelled shut.

"I'm here, Linc, and I'm okay" she promised, trying to keep her voice calm. "You're on the *Celia*, in the infirmary. You've got a concussion."

"Why can't I see?" he croaked, his throat dry as parchment.

"Here Linc, take a drink," Tony held a water bottle with a straw to his mouth. "Careful though. Can you see out of your left eye?" he asked evenly.

"Yeah," Linc mumbled after taking a sip of the water and allowing it to wet his mouth and throat. "Little blurry," he added.

"That's understandable," Tony nodded. "You can't see out of the right eye right now because it's swollen shut. Swelling should go down in a day or two, but until then it'll be hard to see if you can at all. That's going to throw your balance off, too, using just one eye. Mess with your depth perception."

"When can I get up?" he asked, trying to shift around. "Hey, why am I naked?" he asked, seeing that he'd been disrobed.

"You aren't naked, just down to your skivvies," Tony chuckled. "You were a bit bloody so your jumpsuit had to go."

"Go?" Linc frowned. "You mean you threw it out? That was nearly new!"

"You and Sean can cry over your clothes together," Tony snorted. "He lost an outfit himself."

"Galen's still with us?" Linc asked, looking to Meredith.

"For now, at least," she nodded. "He's getting cleaned up," she nodded toward the infirmary shower. "He carried you back to the ship but he was. . .he had blood on him so he's washing up."

"I remember we were on the station, and I can remember getting pistol-whipped and that's about it," he admitted. "What happened after that?"

"Sean and Tony came and got us," Meredith told him. "Sean knew the man who had taken us. He wanted the cargo, you remember that, right? And Sean and Tony found us after they dealt with the men who came to the ship. Sean asked the man holding us to let us go, but he refused and Sean killed him. Both of them."

"Good," Linc nodded in satisfaction. "I'd have done it myself if I was able. I owe him."

"It's a touchy subject, Linc," Meredith warned. "Like I said, Sean knew the man. He's. . .unhappy."

"Some of that is probably the fact that he wasn't able to get off the ship like he meant to," Tony reminded her wryly.

"Why couldn't he get off?" Linc asked. "Are we. . .are we moving?" he asked, realizing at last the timbre of the engines and the pitch of the ship.

"We are indeed," Tony settled for saying as he turned away looking over the blood samples he'd taken from various articles of clothing.

"Jessica pulled us out of the station and set us on the way to Weytan," Meredith told him.

"Jessica?" Lincoln probably tried to frown but with his face swollen she couldn't be sure. "When did she learn to fly?"

"She doesn't know," Meredith shrugged. "Said she looked at the controls and it seemed like everything just fell into place in front of her. She knew what to do and how to do it. A friend of Tony's had called from the Station and said that the police we probably looking for us so she decided the best thing to do was get us off the station. And she did."

"Any problems?" Lincoln asked.

"No, and she managed to set the auto-pilot for Weytan just like we needed. We're making good time because of her," Meredith admitted. "She's supposed to be getting something to eat and then resting, but she says she can fly if we need her to. It was odd though because she had locked us out of the bridge at first. Once she had us underway she opened the door, told us cool as a cucumber what had happened and then went into a dead faint."

"Had that little spell when she woke up, too," Tony added, frowning at the memory.

"What spell?" Lincoln asked.

"I asked her what her name was," Tony explained as he discarded one blood sample and began checking another. "She looks at me and rattles off 'Jess T, three-one-one-five-seven'. I think?" he looked at Meredith who nodded.

"Anyway," Tony continued. "When we looked surprised she said she had told us her name, Jessica Travers. She hadn't, but she was absolutely certain that was what she had said. It's odd," he shrugged, switching samples again.

"This whole day has been like that," Meredith sighed. She was hurting and it was starting to show. Tony pulled a hypo and began to fill it.

"No," Meredith held up a hand but Tony had a swab and was already moving.

"Doctor's orders," he told her flatly. "You're going to be in bad shape for at least a day or two, Captain, and probably more. You need this to help you get through it. I won't give you more than I think you need and never enough to endanger you, but you need to be able to concentrate. You've got more than one headache to sort out, don't forget."

"She does?" Linc asked. "You do?" he looked at Meredith. She was lowering her trousers again, very carefully as every move she made sent spikes of pain up her spine.

"I'll want to scan your spine later," Tony told her as he gave her the injection.

"Is that really necessary?" she asked, fastening her pants back and sitting down carefully.

"Yes," Tony nodded firmly.

"What are the headaches?" Linc asked. "Or should I not ask?" he frowned slightly. "I'm not trying to butt into your Captain's business, I just want to catch up," he promised. Meredith sighed.

"Tony would you excuse us a moment?" she asked. Enough was enough.

"Can't, Captain," Tony shook his head. "Promised Sean I'd be here until he was out. I'm not going back on that. Soon as he comes out, provided that Linc doesn't show any distress, you can have the run of the place."

"What does Galen being in the shower have to do with you being here?" Linc asked, puzzled. "I mean it's none of my business what you guys get up to, so just tell me to butt out if I-"

"Oh, God, no!" Tony almost howled with laughter. "No, one of us per ship is enough, thank you," he chuckled.

"What?" Meredith asked, frowning. "Are you telling me that Sean is-"

"Sean?" Tony frowned. "Hell, no. He's straight as an arrow. I'm talking about Faulks of course."

"What?" Meredith looked almost angry.

"Faulks?" Tony repeated. "Tall woman, terrible haircut, terribler attitude. Is terribler a word?" he frowned. "I don't think it is," he decided before Meredith could answer. "Worse attitude, then."

"Faulks?" Meredith scoffed. "You better be careful making those kind of accusations," she warned.

"Not an accusation Captain," Tony shrugged. "And I won't lose any sleep over the threat of Faulks," he added. "I saw her myself. Not my business of course, and I'm certainly not fit to judge anyone else on the company they keep."

"You saw her what?" Meredith asked, glancing at Lincoln.

"You know, I'm not really sure I should be talking about someone's private business like this," Tony decided.

"You started it, so finish it," Meredith ordered. "I'm getting tired of people on this ship taking my orders as 'suggestions'." Meredith was in pain, she had had a long and difficult day, her husband had been grievously injured, she had a man on her ship that was capable of tremendous violence that hated her security officer and maybe her as well, a passenger that shouldn't have been able to decide which seat was the pilot's had taken her ship into the black and then on course without knowing how she knew how to do that, the list rolled on and on and she had finally snapped.

Unfortunately, she had chosen the worst possible target and that *included* Sean Galen.

"Well, Captain, if you *insist*," Tony sneered. "I saw your *friend* Faulks coming from a well-known brothel on Dry Common the morning that all this *bullshit* of yours got started. She was in the company of a familiar looking woman and it took me a while to figure it out. The *whore* she was with looked exactly like *you*. Same height, same weight, same haircut, roughly the same age."

"Now, since I happen to know for a fact that you and Lincoln were going to stay in town that evening before, it obviously wasn't you. Since

I *also* know for a fact that it wasn't you because I could see the woman clearly as I passed by on my way to the boat, and since she was handing Faulks her bag which she had obviously left behind her when she left the brothel in question that morning, I just *naturally* jumped to the conclusion that Faulks played for the other team. But of course I could be wrong," he added, his voice scathing and practically dripping with sarcasm.

Meredith sat very still, stunned at the revelation. She looked again at Lincoln who was lying very still, giving her a neutral look that was impossible to read anything into.

"Be careful when you make demands," Tony finished quietly. "Be sure you want the answer." Once more Meredith was prevented from answering as Sean Galen emerged from the shower, hair wet and shirtless. He'd obviously not expected Meredith to be still sitting there as he hastily pulled the towel he was carrying around his torso but not before Meredith got an eyeful of the scars and markings on his body.

"Sean, what in the world?" she asked, aghast at what she'd seen.

"I didn't know you were still here," he said rather than answer. "I apologize." He stepped back into the bath cubicle and a silent minute passed before he emerged again, fully dressed this time.

"Good to see you awake," he said to Lincoln, ignoring the question that Meredith had almost asked. "How you feel?"

"Like I got kicked in the head," Lincoln snorted then winced in pain. "Man I think my hair hurts," he complained.

"You took a pretty good beating," Sean nodded. "You're tougher than you act, Linc," he added approvingly.

"Just hard-headed," Linc tried to grin. "I understand I have you to thank for keeping me from whatever end I was looking at. Thanks, Sean."

"Doc did most of the hard stuff," Sean nodded toward Tony. "I did tote you back to the boat, though."

"For which I am truly grateful," Linc nodded carefully. "Seriously, Sean. Thank you." Linc was quiet and sincere. For some reason that seemed to resonate with the engineer.

"Glad I could do it," Galen nodded finally. He looked at Tony. "Check all that blood yet? Am I gonna be okay?"

"Blood?" Linc asked.

"It's clean," Tony nodded. "Amazing. I would have assumed it would be crawling with pathogens. I'm glad it wasn't."

"Can't always make assumptions," Sean nodded.

"What blood?" Linc asked. "I'm so far behind," he added helplessly.

"I got blood on me at the Station and Tony was making sure he didn't have to innoc me against something or other," Sean told him. "Doctors love needles."

"Hey, man, I was looking out for your best interest," Tony objected.

"I guess I'll be in my room," Sean said suddenly. "I'm at loose ends at the moment so I'll stay out of the way," he said to Meredith. He gathered his gear and belongings and departed without further comment. Tony watched him go then turned to look at Linc's monitor.

"Well, I'll leave it to you as well," he announced. "You're looking okay, Linc. Your eye should start to ease down in a day or so." He took an ice pack and broke the capsule inside, wrapped it in a towel and placed it gingerly to Linc's head.

"Try and keep that in place as long as you can," he ordered. "Should help with the swelling. Call me if either of you need anything. I'll be in the kitchen." With that he departed, pausing only long enough to remove the gloves he'd been using and dispose of them. Soon it was just Meredith and Lincoln.

He looked at her, waiting for whatever she was going to say. He assumed she was going to bring him up to speed on the day's events.

"I've had enough of your treating me like I'm your boss," she said instead, surprising him. "I don't like it."

"Then don't act like it," he shrugged carefully. He wanted things to be like they had before, but he wasn't going to take any more crap. From his wife or her hired bully.

"I was doing my job," Meredith defended.

"You went way over the line of doing your job when you started delving into that man's personal life," he corrected gently. "His *family* life. That was completely out of line. You can defend it any way you want and it will still be wrong. I tried to stop you from making a mistake, Meredith. You slapped me down, ignored my warning, and went right ahead with what you were doing."

"That led to our engineer leaving the boat, which put us on the station to get hijacked the way we did. Which led to your being hurt and molested, and me laying here wondering if my vision will ever clear up again or if I'll spend the rest of my life looking at the world through a haze."

"You're tired of me treating you like my boss?" he went on. "Well, let me tell you what I'm tired of. I'm tired of you treating me like a hired hand. I'm tired of your tame gorilla being in my face and in my business all the time. I'm *especially* tired of her trying to create a wedge between us. You may not see it, but everyone else does. I've taken her shit all this time because I know she's close to you, but no more."

"You ever treat me like that again and I'm gone," he said finally. "I toted an ass-beating like I've never received today. . .it was today, wasn't it?" he paused to ask. When she nodded he continued.

"I toted an ass-beating that you keep Faulks around to prevent, or so you say. Now that you've got some independent confirmation, I expect an apology for doubting me in the first place, but I assume that hell will freeze solid before I get it, so I'll settle for you telling her that she either gets her shit together in one sock or she's gone."

"If you want to choose her over me then I'll accept that and go quietly," he finished, laying back on the pillow, winded by the long speech.

"Are you finished?" Meredith asked, her voice testy at best.

"It looks like it," Linc sighed, seeing that he hadn't made a dent in his wife's attitude.

"Sean Galen is apparently some kind of Freeborn assassin," she told him flatly. "The man who had us knew him. Knew him well, in fact. He called Galen 'Stormcrow'. I don't recognize the name but Faulks did and almost blew a gasket. She tried to attack him as soon as he freed us."

"Figures," Linc snorted, then winced.

"Galen's attitude has changed considerably since then," she went on. "He has become extremely difficult to deal with, especially where Faulks is concerned."

"Imagine that," Linc's sarcasm was easy to spot.

"Do you recognize that name?" Meredith asked, trying to keep reign on her own temper.

"Yes," he surprised her. "I had no idea that's who he was though. You seriously don't recognize it?"

"Seriously," she nodded.

"Well, if he really is Stormcrow, *The* Stormcrow, then he is definitely dangerous and Faulks should be sweating bullets about now," he smiled at the idea. "The Stormcrow was probably the most wanted Freeborn assassin there was during the war. The bounty on his head was somewhere around one hundred thousand creds at the end of the war, as I recall. No one was ever able to collect it. More than a few died trying."

"Is he still wanted?" she asked.

"No idea, but as far as I know all bounty warrants were recalled at the end of the war," Linc replied. "And if you're even thinking about trying to collect it after what he did for us then-"

"Can you at least give me the benefit of the doubt?" Meredith's voice was just short of scathing.

"What do you think I've been doing?" Linc asked tiredly. "What do you think I always do," he added. "You know what? I don't want you to answer that, because I'm not sure I can deal with the answer. The fact that you felt like you had to ask means that I've gone wrong somewhere as a husband. You are the one person I was sure would never have to ask me something like that. Anything like that." He closed his left eye, still holding the ice pack to his swollen right.

"I'm tired," he said finally. "I'm going to try and sleep, I think. Would you mind asking Tony to fix me something to eat when he gets time? I'm kind of hungry."

"Linc, I don't want this to keep hanging here between us," Meredith was alarmed by Lincoln's abrupt reversal. That wasn't his normal way of doing things.

"Well, I don't want to be laying here with the shit beat out of me, either," he told her without opening his eye again. "Just like I don't want to be on a ship with someone who snipes at me every chance she gets without a word from you to back me up. You made this mess yourself Meredith and got mad at me for trying to stop you, at least long enough to think about it."

"I've done all I can do," he added tiredly. "All I'm going to do. Will you ask Tony if I can have something for pain? I'm really hurting."

"I'll call him," Meredith nodded absently, still reeling. She was losing everything in spite of all her attempts to stop it. She left the infirmary without another word, going to the kitchen to relay Linc's requests. After that she visited the head, cleaned up, and went to the cargo bay.

It was obviously long past time that she and Faulks had a pointed conversation.

-

Meredith walked out onto the landing above the cargo bay, looking down to where Faulks was working out at her weight bench. Faulks had never liked the machine in the lounge, choosing free weights instead.

Meredith had just left Tony, informing him that Linc was in pain and was requesting pain relief as well as something to eat. Doing that had allowed her to think over what she was going to say to Carolyn Faulks. So far she was coming up short.

It was painfully obvious to her now that Lincoln's warnings had been completely accurate. He had told her time and again that Faulks had a 'thing' for her and she had ignored it, believing that the woman was just clingy because Meredith had saved her life. While saving her life might have been the root of the issue, it was becoming clear that 'clingy' wasn't the exact term to use.

She made her way carefully down the stairs, grateful now for the shot Tony had insisted she take. It made her walk easier.

Faulks saw her coming and practically leaped up from the weight bench, toweling off rapidly as Meredith approached her.

"How you doin', Cap'n?" Faulks asked.

"I've had better days," Meredith admitted. "And this has been a long one. Sit down," she pointed to the bench. "We need to talk. Actually I need to talk and you need to listen."

"Yes ma'am," Faulks nodded, taking her seat. She patted the bench beside her indicating that Meredith should join her and suddenly everything became crystal clear to her.

"Faulks. . ." she started, then paused. How to start this? Strong and stay that way? Try to be easy with it? No, she'd tried easy and it hadn't worked. Had in fact helped create the situation between herself and her husband. It was time to try something else.

"Faulks, things are going to change around here, one way or another," she said firmly. "I've allowed you pretty much free reign aboard this ship because of our service together. In hindsight I see that was a mistake. More than that, it's caused me a lot of problems that I've allowed to fester because I didn't pull you in before."

"Ma'am?" Faulks looked worried now.

"Your antagonizing of my husband ends now," Meredith said firmly. "It's become obvious that your reason for doing so, at least one of them, is some kind of attraction to me," she lowered the boom. When Faulks' eyes went wide Meredith knew she'd hit the mark and that Lincoln had been right all along.

"That's not going to happen, ever," Meredith said firmly. "I could say I'm flattered, but I'm not, Faulks. I'm married and what you've apparently been trying to do has hurt my marriage. Damaged my relationship with my husband. I'm the one to blame for not seeing it and not stopping it sooner, but I'm telling you now that it ends today."

"Your bullying of the crew stops today as well," she continued without let up. "I've tolerated much more of that than I should because of your loyalty, which I mistakenly thought was loyalty to me either from prior service or because of my helping you aboard the *Celeste*. Again it's apparent that while some of that might have contributed to your loyalty, it wasn't the true cause. I've asked you time and again to dial it back, to tone it down, and you've refused. So today I'm telling you flat out; change your ways or you're off my boat."

"I've made some serious mistakes over the last few days," she admitted. "Those mistakes are my own, but they were compounded by my slackness in dealing with you over the last three years. That put a strain on things that, had it not been there, might have kept this from blowing up in my face. I'm still to blame for that because I allowed you to keep treating people like shit, including the man I'm married to and love more than life itself."

"So you either get with the program or decide where you want to get off and I'll take you there," Meredith finished, her voice ringing with finality.

"Cap'n, Galen is-"

"I don't care," Meredith cut her off. "I don't care who he is, who he was or what he did. Today he saved your life, my life, and the life of the man who means more to me than anyone in the galaxy. That's what I care about. Your problems with Galen are yours. I don't want them on my boat. If you can't deal, I understand and will take you to whatever port of call you desire and provide references for you to get work somewhere else. Though I doubt anyone else will tolerate your bullshit the way I have," she added.

"This," she motioned between the two of them, "isn't happening. Ever. If I somehow gave you the idea that it was, it was accidental and I'm sorry. I don't think I have, but you may have read something into my behavior that wasn't there. If you did that's on you and not me. I've made it as clear as I can. All of it. Are we clear, Gunnery Sergeant Faulks?"

Faulks stood slowly, almost bracing herself.

"Ma'am, I do not want to get off the boat. I'll do my best to measure up to your expectations. But Sean Galen is a murdering bastard and if he's staying then I'll have to leave because I swore I'd kill him if I ever had the chance. I won't go back on that."

"You won't do it here," Meredith's eyes narrowed. "Galen is unhappy that we left the station like we did and is staying in his bunk until he can get off at a desirable port of call. I don't want him to go and I've tried to make that clear. I pushed him to this because he surprised me. Whatever he did was in the war, Faulks. It's behind us and you need to leave it there."

"He killed friends of mine," Faulks voice was gritty and her eyes were filled with tears that she tried to contain. "There's no way I let him live."

"You tried him once and he put you down so easy that I still can't believe it," Meredith pointed out. "And how do you know he killed your people?"

"He always left a sign," Faulks said. "A lightning bolt carved in the victims. All of them had it. Every one."

"A lightning bolt?" Meredith frowned, thinking back to something she hadn't been sure she really heard. '*Time for you to ride the lightning*' Sean had said as he lowered the leader of the group that had kidnapped them to the floor, his knife still buried in the man's chest.

"Yes, ma'am," Faulks nodded. "The Stormcrow. Harbinger of Storms. It was how he let us know he was around."

"Us?" Meredith asked, eyebrows raised.

"Recon, ma'am," Faulks replied. "I was Recon before I was shipborne. Red Devils," she said proudly. "I got wounded my third tour in and couldn't rotate back so they assigned me to ship duty. I also did a stint as a DI on Marshal. Before the *Celeste*," she added. Meredith nodded absently, knowing Faulks' history already.

"So you weren't around when Galen supposedly killed your friends, were you?" she asked gently.

"No, I wasn't," Faulks shook her head. "If I had been maybe it would have been different."

"Or maybe you'd be dead along with them," Meredith pointed out. "I want your word, Faulks, that there won't be any trouble on my boat. Sean Galen has never instigated any trouble with you and I have a feeling he won't even now, so long as you leave him alone. I don't want or need any more drama on my ship. If you don't think you can then you'll be confined to your quarters and the cargo bay until we make Weytan. I'm sorry about that, but I mean what I say. No more. No more lip, no more trouble, no more anything on my boat. I can't take it and I don't intend to."

"He'll still be on this ship," Faulks pointed out. "How do I know he won't come after me?"

"He'd have done it by now," Meredith said flatly. "Think about it Faulks," she added. "You've treated him like shit for three years and he's ignored you completely. Let you do it. Never said a word in his own defense, never complained to me or to Linc, never raised a hand against you or anyone else. The enmity he may feel toward you is entirely your fault, Gunny. You made this bed, not Sean Galen. If he was going to do something to you, don't you think he would have done it long before now?"

"That's not the point, Cap'n, begging your pardon," Faulks refused to budge. "He's a murderer."

"Faulks, my orders killed more than one person when I was in command of the *Celeste*," Meredith said softly. "Sailors and Marines under my command died, and certainly enemy sailors died under my guns. Does that make me a murderer?"

"That ain't the same thing, ma'am," Faulks shook her head stubbornly.

"It was *war*, Gunny," Meredith said, a tone of finality in her voice. "We all did things we wish we didn't have to. It was brutal and ugly. You know that as well as I do. Sean Galen was Freeborn and he killed Commonwealth. We killed Freeborn. It's what we did. For all you know, you killed some of his family or friends."

"It ain't the same," Faulks insisted. "It ain't."

"I'm through talking about this Gunny," Meredith sighed. "Toe the line or you're out. Only warning you get. Any trouble on my boat and you're gone." She turned to go at that, realizing that she was slamming her head against a brick wall that wasn't going to give.

"Ma'am, he's a killer," Faulks voice followed her. Meredith stopped and looked back.

"He never had a better chance to kill all of us than when he *rescued us*, Faulks," Meredith stressed. "He killed a man he said he's known all his life to free us. A man that he said was driven to be what he was by the war and the Commonwealth. You think you're the only one who lost friends or family in the war? Hell, I rarely encounter anyone who *wasn't* affected by the damn war. So suck it up, Gunnery Sergeant."

Faulks was still standing at near attention when Meredith made her way up the stairs and back toward the infirmary to check on her husband.

And apologize.

CHAPTER ELEVEN

The stress level aboard the *Celia* was epic, Tony decided. He'd never seen so much turmoil develop so fast. Less than two weeks ago this had been a great place to be. Happy ship, happy people, seeing new places, no one bothering him, it just couldn't have been much better.

And in just a few days all of that had come crashing down around them for absolutely no reason whatsoever. Just stupid people doing stupid things. He shook his head as he tasted the sauce he was making. *Not bad*, he decided.

He had learned to cook in his parent's kitchen, taught by an elderly woman who cooked with love as the main ingredient. She had been a loyal employee of his family through three generations. His father had taught him the value of having loyal people around you and it was a lesson that Tony had never forgotten. Maybe that was the reason that he'd been so bewildered by his Captain's actions.

Sean Galen, whatever might be in his past, had been a loyal employee to the Simmons. In Tony's world, that meant something. Hell, it meant everything. You simply did not turn on loyal people because of something you found out about their past. If it was family-related then that was different, of course. Family meant different rules. But other than that, whatever they had done, so long as they were loyal to *you*, it was in the past. You left it there. You allowed *them* to leave it there.

Meredith Simmons had apparently not gotten that lesson. He thought that being in the Navy would have taught her the value of loyalty. Maybe it was because that loyalty was taken for granted in the military and not really earned. He'd never been in the military so he had no idea how that worked.

His musings were interrupted as he heard someone enter his kitchen. He turned to see Sean Galen standing behind him, leaning on the frame of the entrance way.

"What's up?" he asked.

"Just roaming," Sean admitted. "And hungry," he added with a grin.

"Left over spaghetti, man," Tony nodded to the chiller and Sean grinned.

"You know me so well, brother," the larger man said and moved to dig out the wonderful leftovers. He pulled the container out and stirred it, placing the dish in the warmer.

"So, what's the deal?" Tony asked as Sean waited for the food to heat.

"What you mean?"

"You know exactly what I mean," Tony raised an eyebrow. "You and Faulks have got history somewhere, and I don't mean her bullshit since we've been on this ship. What gives?"

"Have to ask her," Sean shrugged. "Never laid eyes on her before I came aboard."

"She knows you, or thinks she does," Tony pointed out.

"I promise you she doesn't," Sean's voice was hard.

"No offense, man," Tony raised his hands in supplication.

"None taken," Galen promised. "You're my friend, Doc. I don't have many, but the ones I do have I treat like family."

"Good policy," Tony nodded. "And I feel the same way, brother. I wasn't prying so much as just asking. I can't stand the bitch, to be honest, but I've never made that a secret. She's always careful around me because she never knows when she might need me. Or when I might slip something into her food," he added with a sinister chuckle.

"You'd make a bad enemy, man," Galen snorted.

"Damn straight."

"Well, she may think she knows me, but I'd remember," Galen shrugged. "And she wouldn't have to guess, either," he added cryptically.

"So, you want to tell me why that guy called you Stormcrow? That was it, wasn't it?"

"It's nothin'," Galen shrugged.

"Okay," Tony nodded and turned back to his sauce. He wasn't going to pry. Unlike some people he was okay not knowing other people's personal business.

Galen ate in silence, leaning against the bulkhead at the far end of the kitchen. The *Celia* had originally been meant for a crew roughly twice her size, plus the occasional passengers. That meant that the kitchen was somewhat larger than a vessel actually intended for a crew of just five. It gave him room to work and create dishes that weren't found on most small freighters. He had always thought secretly that his cooking was one of the things that made *Celia* such a happy ship.

He didn't think his cooking could fix this mess, though.

-

"How are you feeling?" Meredith asked softly in case Lincoln was asleep. His good eye opened at her voice and she could tell it took him a minute to focus on her. Her heart felt like it was going to break.

"I've felt better," he admitted. "I'm sure I'll hurt for a few days," he added with a sigh. "How's your back? You should listen to Tony about the pain meds, Meredith. Let him keep you easy for a day or two. You know he'll be careful."

"I know," she nodded. "I spoke to Faulks," she decided there was no point in beating around the bush. "I laid the law down to her. She either shapes up and gets with the program or she's gone. I think she'd try except for Galen being here. She's convinced that he's this assassin named Stormcrow. And if he is, then he apparently killed some former shipmates she left behind when she transferred out of Recon after she was wounded. As far as she's concerned, he's a murderer."

"That's what war is," Linc shrugged, wincing slightly as he did. "You kill the other fella. That's all it is. If that's her problem, she needs to remember how many people she killed in the war."

"I pointed that out but she's convinced that's different," Meredith sighed. "We'll probably have to give her the boot on Weytan. I'll have to make sure she can get back to the Sphere if we do. I'm not going to strand her on the Rim." She was almost defensive.

"She's been loyal to you," Linc nodded. "You should be to her."

"I spoke to her about that, too," Meredith felt her face heat. "And I owe you an apology. I owe you more than one, but firstly I owe you one about her. You were right and I just wouldn't see it. Maybe I didn't want to, I don't know. I've made it plain to her that whatever she's thinking isn't going to happen. You're my husband, Lincoln, and I love you more than life. No one is coming between us if I can help it."

She should have felt better after saying it, but the single tear in Linc's good eye took that feeling away from her, and rightly so, she decided. If Lincoln had been forced to question her that much, then she didn't deserve to feel good just because she said 'I'm sorry'.

"Her bullying was another thing that had to end, as of today," she carried on. "What's wrong between us was my fault, but allowing her to get away with so much made it worse. No more. Not just you, either. If I catch her or hear of her doing it again, either to the crew or anyone else, she's gone." He nodded but stayed silent lest his emotions get away from him. He was under the influence of some strong pain meds and was still hurting.

"But she won't give an inch on Galen," Meredith sighed. "I've confined her to her quarters and the cargo bay for now. She'll have to eat alone unless she can get her act together. We're on shaky ground where Galen is concerned. Technically he could make a case for kidnapping I suppose since he'd already quit. He would have already been gone if not for us being in trouble and Jessica shot us off the station before he could get off."

"I think if you don't push him he'll never say a word about it and get off on Weytan," Linc finally spoke. "He's not a bad guy, Mere." She felt her heart ease at the pet name Linc hadn't used in days. Things might not be fixed, but they were healing. It was a start.

"I should have listened to you," she said sadly. "All of this is my doing, Linc. All of it. Others may have contributed, but my bad decision-making is what led us here. I am so sorry," she finally broke down, sobbing slightly as she looked at her husband lying there, possibly permanently injured from an attack that wouldn't have been possible if she had just listened to him to start with.

She felt him take her hand and held to it like a lifeline. He didn't say anything, but he didn't have to. Just the act was enough.

She sat down beside him and cried away the pain and the hurt and the bitterness. She needed to deal with all that before she faced Sean Galen.

-

"Is this a guy thing or what?" Jessica asked from the doorway. Both men looked up to see her standing there smiling at them.

"Come on in," Tony waved to her. "We're just sitting here talking about you."

"Really?" she looked both wary and pleased.

"No, not really," Tony smirked as he shook his head.

"Oh, you're mean," she laughed as she slapped his shoulder.

"I understand I have you to thank for still being here," Galen said, his face stern and his voice severe. Jessica instantly stopped smiling, on edge now.

"I'm sorry," she said in a small voice. "I was afraid you and Tony were about to get into trouble. I couldn't let that happen."

"It's okay," Sean smiled suddenly and winked. The girl blushed furiously and gave Galen a slap of his own on the shoulder.

"You two are a pair of jokers from a bent deck, you know that?" she declared.

"Hey, I had to get some back for you hijacking me," Galen laughed. "I'll just get off on Weytan. Probably be able to find something heading back in without too much trouble."

"Or you could just stay," Meredith Simmons said from the doorway. "You don't have to leave."

"This place is popular today," Tony chuckled. "Come on in," he waved to his Captain. "Fresh coffee," he pointed to the pot. When she nodded he grabbed a cup and filled it, handing it over.

"Thanks for the spaghetti, man," Galen almost mumbled as he placed the dish in the sink. "Think I'll head to my room." He started to ease by, but Meredith stopped him.

"I'd really like to speak to you," she said earnestly. He looked at her closely and could tell she had been crying. Probably a lot.

"I don't know if that's a good idea, Captain," he said finally. "I've used up most of my patience. It's probably better for me to stay by myself." He wasn't as unkind as he might have been, just distant. Cautious.

"All I'm asking for is a few minutes," Meredith promised. "It won't take long."

"You should listen to her," Jessica said suddenly. Galen gave her a look that warned her to stay out of what he considered his personal business. She didn't shrink away but she didn't speak again.

"Easy there, brother," Tony said softly. "Do it or don't, take it easy." Galen looked at him and nodded slowly. Finally, he turned back to Meredith.

"Alright," he said simply and stepped by her and out of the kitchen. He crossed to the lounge, Meredith following. He wasn't sure what she wanted, but he didn't want a scene or an audience. Once there he turned to look at her.

"Mind if I sit?" she asked, wincing as she took a seat. "I'm about stove up after all this today," she explained.

"Understandable," he nodded. "What did you want?"

"Will you sit with me?" she asked, pointing to another chair.

"No." Flat and final. She sighed.

"I wanted first of all to say I'm sorry," she told him, looking up at him from her chair. "To apologize for giving you a hard time at all, but especially for digging into your family life. I had no reason to do that Sean and I'm sorry. I can't even give you a reason why I did. I don't know other than it rattled me to have misjudged you so badly. But that was me and not you."

"Okay," he nodded but said nothing else.

"I know that you're determined to go but I'd like you to at least consider staying," she continued.

"No room for me and Faulks on the same boat," he said simply. "Anything else?"

"I've spoken to Faulks-" Meredith began but got no further.

"I've seen you 'speak' to her before," he cut in. "That always works so well. Now that the gloves are off, she'll be the first one I kill, Captain. And then you'll take up for her which means I'd have to kill you. Which means I'd have to kill Lincoln too, because he doesn't know how *not* to fight for you. It's just how he is and it's not in him to do otherwise. I like Lincoln and I don't want to kill him. So it's better for me to leave."

She didn't know that he'd spoken so much at one time since he'd been aboard. It startled her as she listened to his progression, realizing that he had said he didn't want to kill Lincoln but hadn't extended her the same courtesy. It went without saying that he wouldn't mind ending Faulks.

But as chilling as they were, his words were less important that their tone. His voice had about as much emotion as a rock. For the absolute first time she could see what Linc and Tony had seen in Sean Galen that she had missed. And she could see how he might really be the killer that Faulks thought he was.

"Faulks thinks you killed some of her friends," she said suddenly.

"Probably did," he nodded. And that was all.

"It was a war," she said gently. "We all did things we regret."

"I didn't do anything I regret except not kill all of you," his voice cracked across the room. "Her kind, if she was one of the Demons, they killed men, women and children who weren't a part of your war. Took no part in it, had no say in it."

"And yes, I hunted them down, as many as I could find, and I killed them. I made them suffer as much as I could for as long as I could and my *only* regret is that I couldn't make that suffering last much, much longer." His voice was a cold as liquid nitrogen and Meredith fought the urge to shiver.

"If she moves against me again, I'll gut her and leave her for you to clean up," he warned softly. "And I'll enjoy it. So like I said," he was suddenly less cold, "it's better that I go."

"Will there be anything else?" he asked, as if he hadn't just admitted to being exactly what Faulks thought he was.

"No, that about covers it," Meredith nodded. "Thank you."

"Welcome," he nodded and then left the room. Once he was gone she leaned her head back and closed her eyes.

God, what a mess.

-

Faulks felt almost numb as she made her way down the passageway toward her quarters. It was either there or the cargo bay and she was tired of waiting around in the cargo area. She needed to change and she still had the gun she'd picked up on the station to square away.

This day hadn't started too badly with the prospect of getting rid of Sean Galen and replacing him with someone she could bully a bit so long as she kept the Captain unaware. She didn't consider it bullying, really, just asserting her dominance.

The dominance that had been a horribly ironic facade for the last three years as she realized who and what Sean Galen really was. He could have killed her anytime he chose without breaking a sweat, but instead he had simply ignored her as someone not worthy of thinking about. Someone who simply wasn't a threat to him.

That realization hurt. And it was insulting.

It had been bad enough when she had failed to protect her Captain. She should have been more aware of what was going on around them instead of concentrating on her delight in the trouble Meredith was having with Lincoln. She told herself that she wasn't a bad person to want Lincoln out of the way so she could have a chance at. . .at whatever she could get with Meredith Trenton. It wasn't wrong to want something like that, right?

After all, if Lincoln couldn't handle Meredith being the ship's Captain then he shouldn't have signed on. That would have made Faulks' life so much easier. But no. Not only was Lincoln there, he was constantly undermining Faulks' position with the Captain. Just because he had taken advantage of her at a time when she was weak and alone he thought that somehow trumped her own connection to the Captain?

Only today she had learned that her 'connection' with the Captain only existed in that fantasy world she had created for herself over the last several years. She had known when she had erected that little private fantasy world that it was exactly that, but she had also harbored the hope that it would one day become real.

That hope had just been crushed under the foot of Meredith Trenton herself (she refused to acknowledge that Meredith used Lincoln Simmons' name). Faulks had felt her carefully constructed little world crumble beneath her at the Captain's flat declaration.

For someone like Faulks, admitting that she was responsible for any of the problems she was having was pretty much impossible. She had done everything right. She'd been protective, patient, supportive, all the things that she felt she was supposed to be. None of it had worked. Lincoln Simmons occupied a place that she, Faulks, would never have and she hated him for it. For a few savage seconds she wished that their now dead captors had hit the man harder, crushed his skull. Meredith might have been devastated by his loss, but Faulks would have been there to support and comfort her. She ignored the fact that without Sean Galen and Tony Giannini she would be dead right alongside him, as would her Captain.

Sanity rushed back to her after those few seconds, however, and she felt deflated. She would never wish or allow such a loss upon her Captain. If the marriage failed, through no fault of hers, then that was one thing. Allowing harm to come to her Captain's beloved, though? No, that was not her way. It was not something she could even contemplate for more than a few depressed seconds of anger and heartbreak.

While she hated and despised the fact that Lincoln Simmons occupied Meredith Trenton's affections, she could not actually bring herself to hate the man directly. He was a good man and he had assisted her Captain through a terrible time. The fact that she wished it had been her to do that didn't make him a bad man. Or worthy of her hatred either.

Her thinking came full circle and she was more depressed than ever, ashamed that such a black thought had ever entered her mind, even for the few seconds it had. She was better than that. Better than that butcher who was even now apparently more welcome on this boat than she was.

It was completely infuriating to her that Sean Galen was not only still on this boat, but alive at all. He *was* someone she could hate, and did for all she was worth. He had killed a number of her comrades in truly horrific fashion on his way to becoming the most feared and hated of the Freeborn assassins that had killed so many Commonwealth personnel. It was unconscionable that Meredith Trenton not only didn't know who he was, but hadn't ordered him off the ship the second they had returned from. . .

From Sean Galen saving the three of us, her thinking completed another circle as she realized she was back where she started. With her, the Captain and her husband having been taken because she hadn't been doing her job. Because she had let her Captain down.

She found herself hoping that Lincoln wasn't permanently injured, a long way from her vicious thoughts only a few minutes before that had shamed her. If he was then she was at least partly to blame because she could have prevented it perhaps, had she been more aware.

But her thoughts darkened once again as she returned to Sean Galen. His having saved her life did not negate the way he had killed her friends and comrades. It didn't mitigate the way he had mutilated their corpses and then left them to be found by other Red Devils. Mocking them. Taunting them.

The image of Master Gunnery Sergeant Thomas Kineer flashed into her mind as she recalled his laughing at some prank she had pulled. He had deserved better than to be left like that, so horribly disfigured that his family had to have his burial closed casket.

Whatever she might owe Galen for saving them, she owed him double for what he had done to Kineer and the others. And someday, somewhere, she would see to it that he paid. Not here, but somewhere.

With her determination reformed, Faulks almost stormed into the galley on her way to her quarters.

And literally ran right into Sean Galen.

-

Meredith heard it from the lounge where she was still seated, her back keeping her still for a little longer even as Sean Galen left the lounge, presumably on his way to his quarters. He would likely keep to himself, or congregate with Tony and Jessica until Weytan, at which point he would be gone.

On the one hand she would be a little relieved that he was gone since that would eliminate any future problems with Faulks, assuming Faulks straightened up and flew right. Meredith didn't know what to hope for in that situation. Until she had been slapped with the realization that Linc had been right about her all along. Faulks had been someone she could depend on in jam. Steady and reliable even if she was abrasive. With the new development, or more accurately with Meredith's acceptance of the facts, she wasn't entirely sure she was comfortable with Faulks being aboard anymore. She honestly didn't know which would be better.

She did know that she had to start thinking of what was better for her and Lincoln as a couple rather than just what was better for the ship. Or even the crew. That didn't mean she wouldn't try and think of the crew's best interest because that was as much a part of her as breathing, something that had been drummed into her since her earliest days at the Academy where she'd been on the Command Track from her second year. You always considered the effect on the crew. You might still make the same decision, but you didn't make it without that consideration. Even if your only thought was to regret the casualties you were about to risk among them.

She leaned her head back and closed her eyes, wishing she could go back just one week. Go back one week and listen to her husband when he tried to tell her she was making an error in judgment. When she was making a mistake.

She shifted slightly in the overstuffed chair trying to find a more comfortable position. More comfortable as opposed to actual comfort which she knew she wasn't going to find today, or for several days after all the abuse her back had encountered today. She hated to admit the weakness, but asking Tony for something to ease the pain and help her sleep was looking like a good idea at the moment.

Just as the throbbing in her back started to ease she heard a loud thud from the galley followed by startled exclamations, and then a short scream from Jessica Travers. A startled curse from Tony Giannini and a cry of outrage from Faulks followed before Meredith could get to her feet, but once she did she took the few steps to the lounge doorway to see Faulks on the floor with a gun lying beside her and Sean Galen perched atop her with that horrific knife to her throat.

CHAPTER TWELVE

"What the hell is going on here?!" Meredith shouted.

"I was on my way to my quarters Cap'n and he attacked me!" Faulks cried out. She was holding very still and Meredith didn't miss the fact that her outstretched hand was only millimeters from the gun on the floor.

"Galen, get off her," Meredith ordered, but the engineer didn't move. He was staring at Faulks with an intensity that was frightening.

"I said get off her!" Meredith repeated, more firmly this time.

"No," the word was flat. "I told you what would happen and I'm a man of my word. All I was doing was going to my room. She hit me as I rounded the corner, gun in her hand."

Meredith looked up to see Tony Giannini frozen at the end of the galley table. He looked at her and nodded once. Jessica Travers was behind him, almost back into the kitchen, wide-eyed. When she caught Meredith looking at her she nodded as well.

"Faulks, it seems there's a difference of opinion about what you were doing," she said carefully. "I'm curious as to why there's a gun lying next to you instead of in its holster where is should be, assuming you're telling the truth."

"It's not my gun and won't fit in my holster, Cap'n," Faulks replied, her eyes locked on Galen's, her hatred almost palpable. "It's one I picked up on the station." Meredith nodded, remembering that she had seen that happen.

"Mister Galen, I'm not going to ask you again to get off her," she tried to sound menacing and Galen just laughed.

"If I get off her it'll be with her throat cut," he warned, eyes dancing with violence. "All I wanted was off this boat. No trouble, no fuss. Wasn't for you, I would be. In fact, if it wasn't for you none of this would be happening. I'm not sure I want to give her another chance to kill me. She can't do it, but she might hurt me and there's no point in taking the chance."

"You have my word that won't happen," Meredith said firmly, resulting in another round of derision from her former engineer.

"Your word? About Faulks? We've had this conversation Captain. She doesn't do a damn thing you tell her to unless it happens to be something she wants to do. You know that as well we do." Meredith felt her face flush at the barb, more from its truthfulness than anything else.

"As I recall," he went on, "you just got through telling me how you'd had a word with Faulks and this wasn't going to be a problem, at least not on the boat. Yet here we are."

Meredith was losing control of this situation, had already lost control of her entire ship in fact. She reached behind her and drew a small pistol from beneath her jacket and leveled it at Sean Galen's head.

"Get off her, Mister Galen," she said firmly. "If you don't, I'll shoot you."

"That won't save her," he replied calmly without moving. "And if you don't kill me you won't get a second chance," he warned, smiling slightly. "All I wanted was to be left alone. And you people can't even do that. You take and you take and you *take* until there's nothing left but blood and then you take that, too. So go ahead, Captain," his slight smile bloomed into a broad one. "Give it a shot. One hundred and seventy-three of your best have tried and failed. You just might be able to get it done. But your gorilla won't survive," he promised grimly.

"Do it Cap'n!" Faulks said immediately. "It's worth it! So long as you kill him it's worth it!"

"Which one o' your lyin', murderin' 'comrades' are you so mad at me about?" Galen asked suddenly. "I'd run down a list but some of them I can't really remember that well. Byers, maybe? Short? Ramses? They were your kind of people, weren't they Faulks? Bullies and cowards. 'Course all of 'em turned out to be cowards in the end, didn't they?"

"Tom Kineer!" Faulks bit out. "That's who!"

"Ah, Master Gunnery Sergeant Kineer," Galen smiled again and Meredith had to fight not to shiver. She'd had no clue how utterly cold Sean Galen could be. None. Had Linc known this? She looked at Giannini to see the medic watching things closely. He might have known. Neither of them had said a thing to her.

"A raping, murdering skunk of a man and a child molester to boot," Galen sneered at Faulks, lowering his head until he was face to face with her. "I carved a lightning bolt on him after I cut his manhood off. Did you know that, Gunnery Sergeant Faulks? Did they put that into the report? A raping pedophile doesn't really need anything like that anyway, right?"

"You lying son-of-a-bitch!" Faulks moved slightly and stopped as the knife cut into her neck the slightest bit.

"Oh, I'm not lyin'," Galen told her. "Know it for a fact. Your friend you're so proud of? Killed innocent women and children and laughed while he did it. Raped some of them beforehand including a twelve-year-old girl. You know what I regret most about Kineer? He wasn't as tough as I thought he would be. He only lived four days while I was working on him, Faulks. Screamed like a baby with diaper rash at the end. I imagine that's what his rape victims sounded like. Kinda ironic, ain't it?"

"Tom Kineer was an honorable man, you rim scum!" Faulks snarled back. "As good a Marine as I've ever known in my life! If you took him it was from the back, I know that!"

"His back was to me," Galen shrugged slightly. "When you rape and kill children you give up the right to any kind of honorable end, you stupid Commie. Don't they teach you that when you learn how to murder innocent civilians? How many kids did you kill, bitch? How many pregnant women did you shoot in the belly and watch die?"

"Enough!" Meredith snapped. "I'll count to three, Galen!"

"She'll be dead at one," he never looked up. "And you'll be dead at two," he added. "It's always better to just shoot, Captain. Talking don't get it done."

"Sean," Tony spoke suddenly, though he didn't move. "Sean, how do you know this guy Kineer did all that?" This was bad. Of all the scenarios he'd run through in his mind, this had not been among them. The Captain's treatment of Sean Galen had scratched off the veneer that normally covered all that hate and bitterness and Tony felt like he was seeing his friend for the first time.

It was a definite learning experience.

"He doesn't know because it's a damn *lie!*" Faulks all but yelled. "*Shoot him Cap'n*!"

"I know because I pulled his DNA out of my dead sister," Galen's voice was almost a whisper. "My *twelve-year-old* sister who was left laying atop my pregnant mother, shot through the stomach so that it killed an unborn brother and then left to bleed to death."

"My mother had one of your Red Devil patches in her hand, you Commie *bitch*," he growled, his head twisting almost as if he was a wolf, growling over a kill. Tony decided that wasn't really inaccurate.

"And his DNA was inside my dead sister," he spat out. "So yes, Faulks, you pathetic, simpleminded, partially trained ape, I killed your friend. It took me two years just to *find* him and I killed all of you I could until I *did* find him and when I did, I made him *suffer*. You can't *imagine*, Faulks, what I did to him. The way I cut him, the pain I caused him. And all the time I was sorry that I couldn't make it *worse*. That I couldn't make him feel what I had to feel when I came home to find my whole family, my whole *village*, *butchered!* You heard of me? *Good!* That was what I wanted. For you and everyone like you to *fear my name*. And you *do* fear me, don't you, monkey girl? I can see it in your eyes. You think you're ready to die if it means I go too, but I see it in your eyes, Faulks, and you're scared." By now his voice was hardly more than a harsh whisper, yet it was all the more chilling because of it. "You want to live and you think that you will, somehow, but I promise you, no matter what else happens, no matter who else dies, if anything happens to me you don't get up from this floor. Get me?"

But Faulks was already beaten. Hearing what she did had taken the fight out of her. Still, she couldn't accept that Tom Kineer-

"How did you get his DNA to test?" she demanded. Carefully.

"From your Marine database," Galen told her calmly. "Your government keeps all your medical and personal information locked away on a computer. Including a sample of your DNA so they can identify you after someone like me gets a hold of you," he smiled nastily. "Only they don't keep it all that locked, and your people ain't all that loyal. Simple test, simple results, easy to load into a computer and run a search. Your friend Kineer came up. No doubt about it."

"He even admitted it to me, before he knew I was going to kill him. He thought I was going to turn him over to you people for a trial. Stupid bastard," he snorted. "You people really ought to learn who you're dealing with before you start murdering a man's family."

"I...I can't believe it," Faulks almost breathed. "I would never. . .I'd never have believed it. I'm still not sure I do. You can't prove it," she accused suddenly.

"I don't have to," he said simply.

Faulks lay there looking at death incarnate, wondering how well she'd truly known Tom Kineer. Had he been that kind of man? That kind of Marine? Faulks had never been so proud of anything in her life as she was of being a Commonwealth Marine. It was everything to her. If not for Meredith Trenton being the owner of a ship she would still be a Marine. Still be serving. Still thinking of Tom Kineer as an honorable man.

Thinking of him, of any Marine, being guilty of the actions Sean Galen had just described. . .it turned her stomach. She felt nauseous but fought it down. Gagging with a razor at your throat was bad.

"Galen, I'm sorry," she said suddenly, her voice flat. "I...if I had known I would have killed him myself. All of them. Maybe not like you did, but still dead. No *true* Marine would do otherwise."

"That's why you're still alive," he told her plainly. "That and I know for a fact that you weren't there."

"How do you know that?" she asked. "I was one of them, once," she admitted.

"They're all dead," he told her. Suddenly the pressure from her neck was gone and he was on his feet. She hadn't even seen him move he was so fast. He looked down at her for a handful of seconds before extending a hand to her, his face devoid of any emotion. She looked at him for several seconds before accepting it, and he hauled her to her feet.

"I didn't know," she told him softly. "No one I know knew it either," she added. "Or if they did, they never spoke of it," she added, thinking that she had known at least some of the men who had done this deed.

"Like I said, that's why you're still alive," he told her, sheathing that terrible knife. "Now if you'll excuse me?" He turned and continued on his way, disappearing down the passageway toward his own cabin.

Meredith watched him go, not even realizing she was still holding the pistol in her hand.

"Cap'n, let me take that for you," Faulks said easily, laying a careful hand on Meredith's and slowly lowering the drawn hammer down. She engaged the weapon's safety and returned it before picking up the gun she'd been carrying before.

"Well, I was on my way to put this away," she said with a sharp exhale. "Reckon I'll just carry on." With that she followed Galen down the passageway and disappeared into her own quarters.

"Ho-lee *shit*," Tony Giannini finally breathed for what seemed like the first time that day. "Did that really just happen?"

"Did you know all that?" Meredith demanded. "*Any* of it?"

"Not a clue," Tony shook his head slowly. "And I mean not a *hint*, either. Hell, if I *had* known it I'd have been helping him hunt them down."

"My God," Jessica whispered. "I'd heard stories, but . . . I never thought they were true."

"What stories?" Meredith demanded, wincing as she moved too quickly.

"Stories about Bloodings," Jessica said softly. "I thought it was campfire tales. Stuff that people made up to scare you. Especially Rim Folk. Frontier worlds. You tried to stand up for yourself, make things better for your people, and you get Blooded. That's what they called it." She looked up, eyes wet.

"They say a man's not a soldier till he's had a woman and shed blood," she quoted something she had heard once as a girl. "You can always do both on a Rim world. That was the saying."

"I've never heard that!" Meredith snapped.

"No reason you would," Jessica shrugged. "You're a woman. And an officer. You'd never be involved in something like that. It was used as an initiation of sorts we heard. No idea what for," she admitted. "I always thought it was bull."

"Apparently not," Tony Giannini said gently. "Man, I can't imagine," he shook his head. Of course, he'd never have to, but that was another story. He stood up, looking at Meredith.

"Let's go and check on your husband and get you something for that back," he ordered. "Supper is almost ready and I actually think it might be safe for Sean and Faulks to sit at the same table. Not next to each other of course," he added wryly. "But in the same room might be okay."

Meredith was surprised to find that she agreed.

-

"What's wrong with you?" Linc asked as Meredith limped back into the infirmary followed by Tony Giannini. "You okay?"

"Fine," she lied. "Just hurting. I'm taking your advice and letting Tony doctor me," she admitted. "I'm expecting the next few days to be pretty rough considering how badly we were banged around and I want to be here when you need me."

"Don't worry about me," Linc told her. "I'll be fine once my eye opens and my head closes," he smiled crookedly. He didn't tell her that his left eye was still cloudy. He didn't have to tell Tony.

"You let me worry about you if I want to," Meredith told him. "You're my number one worry, mister."

"Okay I'm going to gag in a minute here," Tony rolled his eyes as he prepped a syringe. Meredith once more lowered her waistband and felt the swab and sting as Tony gave her another shot.

"Supper will be on in a half-hour or so," he told them as he checked Linc's monitor. "I'll ask Jess to bring yours down here if you'd like. I think you can be okay not riding herd on Faulks and Sean after that."

"Okay," Meredith nodded.

"After what?" Linc asked. "What happened now?"

"I'll tell you all about it if Tony will get me a more comfortable chair to sit in," Meredith promised.

"Your wish is my command, Captain," he bowed, and went to get the desired furniture.

"So what happened?" Linc asked.

"There has been a reckoning of sorts," Meredith sighed, nodding her thanks as Tony dropped off a chair from one of the passenger rooms before bowing out to finish supper. Meredith settled gratefully into the stuffed chair, sighing in contentment as she did so.

"We know a lot more about Sean Galen than we did this morning," she began.

-

"That was a horrible story he told," Jessica said softly as she helped Tony with setting the table.

"And I doubt we got more than the highlights," Tony nodded.

"I have to wonder how he kept from killing Faulks all these years," she almost whispered.

"A great deal of discipline and knowledge that she wasn't one of the people he was hunting," Tony shrugged. "That and knowing that she just wasn't a threat to him. That man is dangerous like nobody's business."

"I…he scares me," Jessica admitted. "I don't mean I'm afraid he'll hurt me," she shook her head as Tony frowned. "I can't imagine, even knowing. . .even after seeing him like that, today, I can't imagine him hurting me. Hurting anyone that hasn't done something worthy of it. For all the things he did, he had good and great justification. Greater than anything I could ever imagine."

"Agreed," Tony nodded, letting out a long breath. "If I had been in his shoes I'd have done the same thing. Only I wouldn't have stopped with just the guys that did it. I'd want whoever was in charge, too."

The two worked in silence as they finished up. Tony dished up two healthy servings of food and Jessica carried them to the infirmary where she helped Meredith with the tray table before departing with a promise from Meredith that she would call if they needed anything. When she returned she stopped short seeing Sean Galen seated at the table. He saw it and while he didn't react she could see in his eyes that it hurt.

"Sorry," she said, continuing into the galley. "I didn't expect to see you," she admitted.

"I get that a lot," he shrugged. "If you're uncomfortable I can eat somewhere else," he offered.

"No!" she almost shouted. "It's not that," she went on normally. "I really didn't expect to see you after earlier. I was afraid you would just stay off by yourself the rest of the way."

A tilting nod told her politely that he didn't believe her but he appreciated it anyway. Frustrated because she had been telling the truth, she turned away to help finish putting the meal on the table. Tony crossed to the I/C.

"Faulks, get your dumb ass up here, supper's on the table," he growled into the pickup and then crossed to his seat. As he sat down they could hear Faulks coming down the passageway. She stopped short seeing Galen but then continued inside and took her normal seat.

"Captain?" she asked, looking at Tony.

"Eating with her husband," Tony told her. Everyone observed a moment of silence and then started eating.

To say it was strained would be an understatement, but everyone got through the meal without bloodshed. Once it was finished Faulks thanked Tony for supper and returned to her quarters. Sean Galen sat still for a few minutes, idly picking at the remains of his food.

"If you want more all ya gotta do is ask," Tony said finally and Galen looked up at him.

"Seriously dude, there's plenty," the medic nodded. Suddenly Galen burst into laughter and Tony grinned.

"What's so funny?" Jessica asked, assuming she had missed something.

"He is," Galen jabbed a thumb at his friend. "Sitting here trying to pretend nothing happened. Like it's all okay."

"It is okay, far as I'm concerned," Tony nodded. "You ain't done nothing to me, bro," he smiled. "I mean, you're hard to feed and all but. . .well, and you're always complaining about my medical practice, but it's not like that's my main job or anything. Seriously, why wouldn't everything be okay?"

"Because now you know it's all true," Galen shrugged.

"Don't care," Tony shrugged. "I'd have done the same thing," he said easily. "Maybe not with your style of course, but in my own debonair way."

"Fair enough," Galen mused, looking back down at his plate. "You're a good cook, man. I'll miss food this good," he said more to himself than anyone else.

"You ain't got to go, man," Tony reminded him. "Captain said it, Linc said it, I said it, Jessica said it-"

"Faulks didn't," Galen shrugged. "Not that I care."

"Made my point for me," Tony nodded. "No one else does either, including the Captain. She can get with the program or get off. I vote for 'off' but I'm a reactionary. Always acting without thinking."

"You don't go to the head without thinking it over," Galen snorted and Tony laughed.

"I might not plan that well," he replied. "But point. Seriously dude. Stop talking about this shit and admit that you want to stay."

"I've never denied that," Galen replied as Jessica got to her feet.

"I'll be back to help with the cleanup in a bit," she promised as she headed into the lounge. The two men sat there quietly for a minute.

"It's my real name," Galen said softly.

"What?" Tony asked, startled.

"Crow," Galen reminded him. "Crow is my real name. Galen Crow. Sean Galen Crow to be exact. My father called me Stormcrow when I was born."

"What's that mean?" Tony asked.

"Harbinger of Storms," Sean shrugged. "Herald of bad tidings and ill weather. Stormcrows ride the gust fronts ahead of large thunder storms. You can see 'em riding the winds long before the storm shows on the horizon, you know what you're looking at. My father called me Stormcrow. My mother called me Galen."

"Don't seem like a proper handle to hang on a kid," Tony mused.

"I was born just in front of the worst storm on record where I'm from," Galen chuckled darkly. "Guess it seemed fitting at the time. It was my truename," he shrugged.

"Your real name, you mean?" Tony asked, placing his elbows on the table.

"No, not really," Galen shook his head. "My people have a truename. A name known only to their family members. Clan members. It's how you're addressed during tr-clan business."

"You shouldn't be tellin' me that then, right?" Tony asked.

"Doesn't matter now," Galen shrugged. "I got no family anymore. Killed the last one I know of today." He got to his feet.

"I will miss the food," he said again. "And the conversation," he added as he turned to go.

"Wait a minute!" Tony exclaimed, though quietly. "You can't just drop a bomb like that and then walk away. What do you mean about killing the last one?"

"Hawkins," Galen didn't turn around. "Cousin on my father's side. Me and him were all that was left. Now, it's just me." With that he was gone, disappearing down the passageway.

"Son-of-a-bitch," Tony swore bitterly.

CHAPTER THIRTEEN

"You wanted to see me?"

Lincoln looked up from where he was still reclining on the med bay bed. Sean took in the swollen features of the pilot and hid a grimace. Hawk and his bunch had done a real number on Linc. Even now, nearly two days out of Hartley station, Linc looked bad.

"Yeah, Sean, come on in," Linc smiled slightly, wincing at the effort. "Take a seat."

"How's the eye?" the engineer asked.

"Still a mess," Linc admitted. "Tony is keeping me easy, but the swelling is still a problem I guess. Can't really see all that well at the moment."

"You gonna be able to fly?" Sean asked, taking the seat that Tony had provided for Meredith to sit with her husband.

"Don't know yet," Linc answered calmly. "Have to wait and see if my vision clears up. At this point, there's just no way to guess."

"I'm sorry we didn't get there sooner," Sean told him. "If we had, maybe it wouldn't be like that."

"And if Meredith hadn't started all that shit with you, we wouldn't have been there at all," Linc shrugged. "And you came for us even though you weren't under any obligation to do so, especially after all she put you through. Thanks for that."

"Welcome," Sean nodded.

"I understand you had quite a tale to tell up in the galley earlier," Linc decided to get to the point.

"Shouldn't have said all that," Sean shrugged. "I don't normally talk about it."

"That's not healthy," Linc said evenly. "Mentally or emotionally. You can't carry that kind of baggage around like that and not pay a price for it, Sean."

"I paid the price years ago," Sean replied flatly. "So did the others. It's long done."

"You can't tell me it doesn't stick with you, Sean," Linc said mildly.

"If it had, Faulks would be long dead," came the flat reply. "Like I said, it's done. Over with."

"Something like that's never over," Linc shook his head.

"Is this an analysis, Doctor?" Sean's voice went hard suddenly. "Because it's a few years too late for you Commonwealth people to take an interest in the lives you ruined, you know? And, not to be rude or anything, but this really ain't none of your concern, Lincoln."

"Not even trying to make it mine," Linc replied calmly. Sean Galen was not the first violent, angry veteran he'd spoken with. "You helped me. Save me and my wife from being murdered, and her from no telling what before that. If I can help you I want to."

"How you gonna help me, Linc?" Sean asked just short of derisively. "You gonna make it not happen? Fix it so you people never declared war on mine? So that your marine killers never visited my world and killed my family? How are you gonna manage that one?"

"I can't undo something like that, Sean," Lincoln's voice was gentle. "Can't undo anything once it's done, whether good or bad. But you have to be able to process things, deal with them on an emotional level. If you don't they can eat you up inside."

"Little too late for that," Sean shrugged. "There's nothing left to eat on. And there's no one left to punish, either," he added flatly.

"You feel any guilt over that, Sean?" Linc asked calmly. "Over all those people you killed so horribly?"

"I feel guilt that I wasn't there to defend my mother and sisters," the reply was chilling and cold. "I feel regret that I couldn't make the pain last longer for the animals I tracked down and exterminated for murdering my people. I feel hate for everything Commonwealth that allowed Kineer and people like him to do what he did to people who weren't even a part of your war. What did you do during the war, Lincoln? Did you try to stop things like what happened to my people from happening?" His eyes were almost glowing now.

"Or were you cheering your troops on for standing up to those rebellious Freeborn bastards who so blatantly didn't want to be like you?"

Lincoln almost answered automatically but paused at the last second, considering more carefully what to say. This was dangerous ground he was treading. He had seriously misjudged, completely underestimated the depth of Galen's bitter hatred of the Commonwealth.

"No, I was a counselor, Sean," he finally replied, keeping his voice neutral. "I helped veterans adjust to civilian life after their enlistment was up."

"Oh," Sean nodded slightly. "Helping them get over the trauma of murdering helpless women and children, I guess. I can see where that might leave an emotional scar for some people." His eyes were hard as he spoke. "I really don't think this is a road you want to go down with me, Lincoln," he added finally. "I don't want or need your help. There's nothing you can do to change what is. I had put it behind me as much as I could and had a pretty good thing going here until your wife decided that my being able to defend her passenger from slavery somehow made me untrustworthy." He stood abruptly.

"I can almost appreciate you offering to help, but it's far too little, too late. And I don't want to have this discussion again. You need anything else?"

That rejection was as firm as any Lincoln had ever come across.

"We can always talk whenever you feel like it," he offered in return. "It's not like I'm going to be very busy the next few days," he added with a wry grin.

"I'll be off and gone once we hit Weytan," Sean told him. "Until then I'm pretty much staying to myself. I can't always resist temptation, and the temptation to gut Faulks is a strong one."

"I can understand that," Linc sighed. "I've had the same dre. . .thought myself," he caught himself but not before Sean made a short derisive bark of laughter.

"Anyway," Linc continued. "If you do decide you want to take advantage of my services, I'm always available. And while you're deciding, I'd appreciate it if you would at least consider staying aboard as the engineer. I'm not asking for an answer right now," Linc help up a hand to forestall any arguments. "Just for you to think about it."

His answer was to see Galen's back as he disappeared out of the infirmary and into the ship somewhere.

"That went well," Linc said aloud as the door closed.

-

"Cap'n, you got a minute?"

Meredith looked up to see Faulks standing hesitantly at the bridge hatch. That was new. Before the events of the last two days she would have simply barged onto the bridge and sat down.

"Yes," she kept her voice as neutral as possible. Her back was killing her, just as Tony had predicted. She'd drawn the line at any more shots after one more that first evening to help her sleep, but right now she was leaning toward taking another one. If Tony or Lincoln either one knew that it would tell them a great deal about how much she was hurting.

Faulks remained hesitant as she made her way onto the bridge, stopping a respectful distance from the chair where Meredith was standing watch, another departure from her usual behavior.

"Cap'n, I wanted to apologize," Faulks almost mangled the word getting it out and Meredith figured it wasn't something the former Gunny had said often in her life. "I won't offer no excuses for my behavior, since there really ain't one. I just wanted you to know that I really am sorry for any hurt I caused you. I know you said I could stay but. . .if you'd be more comfortable with me gone I'll leave. If that's the case, I really do understand." She looked at the deck for a moment and then shrugged without looking back up.

"I guess that's it."

Meredith looked at Faulks for a moment, taking in the change in her. There was no doubt that Faulks' self-confidence was shattered. She had learned something horrible about someone she had admired and respected, had realized that a man she had bullied and mistreated for three years could have killed her at a whim, and that that same man was responsible for the death, the horrible, terrorizing deaths of many of her former colleagues. All in all, Faulks had had a rough two days.

"I don't necessarily want you gone, Faulks," Meredith finally replied. "You've been a steady hand in times of trouble and you work hard and help keep the ship in good shape. It's never been your work; it's always been your attitude. I ignored it thinking it was just a natural inclination to bully. That's not to say I approve, but I understand your mindset a bit better than the others, having shared some of the same experiences."

"But with all that's happened in the last few days it's apparent that it was more than that, and that I can't have. I won't have," she added more firmly. "Lincoln resigned his commission to come with me into space, Faulks. Did you know that?"

"Yes'm," the other woman was studying the deck very intently now.

"He went to pilot school while still fulfilling his obligations to the Navy so that he could help me realize my dream of getting back into space," Meredith continued. "He worked hard to get his license and it doesn't come natural or easy to him. Everyone, myself included, gives him a hard time over his flying, and he takes it because it's that important for him to be here with me. And I almost allowed what I thought was friendship and admiration to interfere with that, Faulks. It will never happen again," her voice hardened. "I won't allow it. That man, like him or not, is everything to me. He's the reason I get up in the morning and the reason that I'm not sitting somewhere on a front porch right now drawing half-pay and working some dead-end job or at best teaching at the Academy."

"You would have been good at that," Faulks interjected. "Beggin' your pardon, but you would."

"Except I don't want to do it," Meredith pointed out. "If I can't be on a ship, then I'm out of the Navy as far as I'm concerned. Did I appreciate Admiral Wallace's offer? Yes. Was even flattered by it to be honest. But teaching tactics is a far cry from commanding a ship in space. And it's not for me. I'd rather be right where I am right now, with Lincoln, than sitting at the Academy even as a Captain or Commodore."

"Yes'm," Faulks nodded.

"Your attitude is the problem, Gunny," Meredith concluded. "Fix it, and stay. So long as you change your ways and stop trying to drive a wedge between me and my husband, I have no problem with you staying."

"About that," Faulks looked up suddenly. "I can see where you might think it, but. . .Cap'n, that wasn't never my intention. I admit I wouldn't have cried had he left, but. . .I wasn't tryin' to separate you. I just. . .I just was jealous that he was there when you needed someone. That it wasn't me. At first because I owed you and I wanted to pay you back. Later it. . .well, you know," the woman was studying the deck again. "Anyway, any trouble I caused between you, it wasn't on purpose. That don't make it no righter, but I just want you to understand I wasn't actually tryin' to cause you to separate."

"You were just hoping to take advantage of it if we did," Meredith's voice wasn't completely unkind, but it was unyielding.

"Something like that," Faulks nodded. "Still wrong I know, but. . .not *as* wrong, maybe," she was almost hopeful, but stopped just short of it.

"Remember what I said," Meredith was suddenly tired of this conversation. "No. More. There won't be any more warnings or talks. You'll just pack your shit and be gone. Work it out and you're welcome to stay. You've been a good hand and I'd hate to have to replace you." She almost added 'too', but caught it at the last minute.

"Thank you, Captain," Faulks said formally. "I'll be in the bay, you need me," she spun on her heel and walked out as if she were on parade. Her pride had been wounded over and over again the last three days, but. . .it was still there. Meredith did admire Faulks in a lot of ways, especially her strength and resolve. She refused to quit, even when it looked as if *Celeste* was going down for the count. She had hung right there with Meredith when she'd been wounded, too.

Maybe she'll straighten out, Meredith half thought, half prayed. She could use something good happening for a change. She had caused herself so much trouble.

And her husband was paying a terrible price for it right now.

-

"What do you see?"

"I see a light, idiot," Linc bit back a snarl. "You're pointing a flashlight in my eyes."

"And two days ago you couldn't tell that," Tony shot back. "If you can see light that's a good sign. Very encouraging. I can't see any evidence of damage to the optic nerve itself, though I can't promise you that it isn't there. Still, that's also encouraging. What I do see is a severe concussion right alongside the optic nerve center. That caused all the swelling and put pressure on the nerve which is what caused your troubles with seeing. What about now?" Tony covered Linc's damaged right eye.

"Now I see a light in my *left* eye," Linc sighed.

"Sorry," Tony pulled the light away. "I wanted to see your pupil reaction. Can you read that chart on the wall?" he pointed to the wall behind him.

"Some of it," Linc admitted.

"Far as you can," Tony ordered. Linc sighed but dutifully read through the first three lines without trouble. The fourth line he got five of eight, but the fifth line was beyond him.

"I just can't make it out," Linc sighed. "How bad is that?" he asked quietly.

"About average for someone your age," Tony said mildly. Lincoln blinked for a minute and then his face reddened.

"What the hell does that mean?" he demanded.

"You're not a spring chicken, Linc," Tony smirked. "Seriously, you got about as far as the average man your age would make it without aids. Which I don't have," he admitted. "When we hit a planet with an optometrist we should get you a complete exam but. . .Linc I think you're gonna be okay, man. I can't promise about your right eye, mind you," he warned again. "But you can see light, you can make out shapes and you can detect movement. All good signs. Great signs, really, considering the ass whipping that was laid on you back there. I'm very hopeful that you'll recover completely in time."

"How much time?" Linc asked warily. "Will I be able to fly?"

Tony almost made a crack about it might improve his flying, but this wasn't a time for that. Not until he knew for sure.

"Not for a while," Tony tried to let him down easy. "You're going to be plagued with dizzy spells, headaches and blurred vision at purely random times for a least a week or ten days and probably longer. That's all normal for a severe concussion like yours, though, so none of that should be a surprise or be discouraging. It's just part of it."

"But I can maybe still pilot, once I'm better?" Linc asked.

"So long as your depth perception is okay and your balance and vision aren't impaired, I don't see why not. I mean, how much worse could it get, right?" He could only fight it so long.

"Har-de-har," Linc mock snarled. "If this vagabond, traveling snake-oil salesman thing doesn't work out you can always try comedy."

"Did I say something funny?" Tony asked, a look of mock confusion on his face. "All right, I've got to go and fix supper. You can get up and move around some, but use the cane so you'll have something to lean on if you get dizzy. I'd prefer you wear the patch another couple days as well," he handed the 'pirate' patch back to Lincoln. "It will help keep the headaches and dizziness down since your brain won't be fighting to make sense of your right eye's input."

"Okay," Linc nodded, willing to do about anything to leave sick bay. "How's Meredith's back?" he asked.

"No additional damage," Tony assured him. "Her scan was fine other than some bruising. She's hurting like hell, I'm sure, though she's trying her best to act like she's not. I've got a shot in my pocket already drawn up. I'm thinking she'll go another three hours tops before she admits she needs it. It's been twenty hours since she'd had one."

"She's stubborn about that," Linc nodded. "After what she went through, though..." He shook his head.

"I know," Tony patted Linc's shoulder softly. "She's got to learn to trust me, though. I won't let that happen to her again, Linc. I promise. I may only be 'almost' a doctor, but I take it very seriously."

"How 'almost'?" Linc asked. "I always wondered about that since you seem to know so much."

"Very almost," Tony sighed. "Three weeks, give or take, and four exams. What's that old saying? 'In all but name'? That's me. I got everything except the sheepskin."

"What happened?" Linc asked.

"Doesn't really matter," Tony shrugged. "I didn't do anything wrong if that's what you mean. I got caught in a scam that my roommate ran. Guilt by association. In this case by transformation," his voice was a tad scornful. "Anyway, I'll be in the galley if you need me." And with that Tony Giannini left to fix supper.

"This crew is a smorgasbord of nutty," Linc shook his head, though careful to do it gently. Then he took the cane Tony had left and worked his way to his feet. It was time for him to get moving.

-

"I'm mad at you."

Sean Galen looked up to see Jessica looking at him from the entry to the lounge.

"Why should you be any different," he shrugged and then returned to the list he was looking over.

"You act like I don't want to be around you and that's not true!" Sean thought for a minute that she was actually going to stomp her foot the way she was acting.

"I'm used to that, once people know," Sean shrugged as he continued to scan the list in front of him.

"I told you I wasn't. . .I was surprised to see you because I didn't think you'd come to supper!" Jess kept at it. "You could look at me when I'm talking, you know!" She grabbed his arm intending to make him turn.

Before it could register on her, Jessica was on her back, her arm locked in Galen's grip with Galen looking down at her. The look on his face was absolutely savage for an instant but then was replaced by horror at what he'd done.

He was about to let go when Jessica's right leg shot out, crossing over the hold of Galen's arms and locking around them. At the same time her left leg came beneath her, crossing under her body and following her around. Using the momentum of springing off the floor along with the leverage she gained from her leg hooking his arms, she continued to twist around in mid-air until her left heel swung completely around to very nearly make impact with Sean's temple.

Very nearly because at the last second Galen simply let her go and took a step back. Instead of terminating with a devastating kick to his temple that would have at least addled Galen, Jessica's motion now worked against her and the momentum she still had carried her over into a full twist, the end result of which was her landing with a hard *thump* as her butt hit the deck.

Again.

"Ow," Jessica sat up, rubbing her now sore bottom.

"Where in the hell did a school teacher learn that?" Galen demanded, his eyes narrowing.

"Learn what?" Jessica demanded, getting to her feet. "How to get thrown around by a mean old engineer?"

"I didn't throw you around," Sean shot back. "And you damn near kicked my head off!"

"I did not," Jessica scoffed. "All I was trying to do was get you to look at me for just a minute. To get you to see that I really was glad to see you, just like I really was surprised that you had come to eat with us. But when I grabbed your arm you threw me to the floor."

Sean started to object, but stopped before doing so. Technically she was right. He had flipped her onto the floor completely by instinct. He hadn't even realized he'd done it until he was looking down at her.

How could she not remember almost taking his head off? And where had she learned to do that?

"An apology would not go amiss here," Jessica said tartly, breaking him out of his train of thought.

"I am sorry," he admitted. "I didn't mean to do it. It's just conditioning. It sticks with you no matter what. Grabbing me is a trigger for me to act. I did it, *do* it, without thinking about it. I'll try not to do it again, I promise."

"It's my fault," Jessica sighed. "I know better than to do something like that. People where I grew up don't like being handled like that either. I'm sorry."

Galen wanted to laugh. She was apologizing for grabbing him, but not for nearly kicking his head off.

"You've got a mean set of moves on you," he said carefully. "You take some kind of self-defense class in college?"

"What?" Jessica gave him a look of puzzlement. "What are you talking about?"

"You really don't remember nearly kicking me in the head?"

"Now you're just trying to be funny," Jessica crossed her arms beneath her breasts, not quite glaring. "I would never kick anyone, especially you."

"Why especially me?" The statement surprised him so much that he forgot about her apparent martial arts prowess.

"You saved my life, silly goose!" Jessica replied. "Not to mention how nice you and Tony have been to me since I've been here. And how about the time you spent teaching me how to look out for myself?"

"Fair enough," Sean nodded, more to cover his confusion than anything else.

"What are you doing, anyway?" Jessica asked, nodded to the screen Galen had been looking at.

"Looking for work," he admitted, taking his seat again as she sat beside him. "This is a message board for ships and crewers to look for help or for work. Further out we go though, the harder it is to find something decent. I'd have had better luck at Hartley, but I still might find something here."

"I had to get us off the station," Jessica didn't quite roll her eyes.

"I know that," he replied. "I'm not fussing, just explaining. Hartley is pretty far out too, but because of all the traffic it's a good place to look for work. Finding real jobs gets harder the further out you go. Not as many ships, and a lot of the ships that work out here aren't what you'd call good employment opportunities."

"Like our friends from Dry Commons?" she asked.

"Just like that," Sean nodded. "Anyway, that's what I'm doing."

"You really should stay here, you know," Jessica said softly. "No one wants you to leave."

"I can't stay somewhere once people know who I am," Sean shook his head. "Doesn't work like that. And if it gets out I'm on *Celia*, then it puts the rest of you in danger if they come after me. When someone is after me they tend to shoot first and not ask questions at all."

"Why are they after you?" Jessica asked. "And who is 'they'? Isn't the war over?"

"Not for a war criminal," Sean's voice was hard. "See, the benevolent Commonwealth, in all its glory and wisdom, has decreed that because I killed so many of their 'heroes' and did so in such a violent fashion that I should stand trial for my 'atrocities.' For me, the war won't ever be over," he added, and for just a second Jessica could hear, almost see the loneliness and despair that followed this man everywhere he went.

"Why don't you just find an out of the way place and settle down?" she asked suddenly. "Somewhere far from the Commonwealth's Sphere. On the Rim, for instance."

"Because I'm not going to hide," he told her simply. "I'm not ashamed of what I did. I never killed anyone who didn't deserve it or wasn't trying to kill me or someone else. And I never killed an innocent child or woman, either," he added with bitter softness.

"I was just thinking if you were somewhere small, out of the way, you could get married, have a famil . . . what?" she cut off as Galen was shaking his head.

"I could never have a family," he told her. "Any wife or children I had would just become targets for some Commonwealth murderers. I can't go through that again. I *won't* go through it again," he added more firmly.

"I hadn't thought of that," she sighed. "I'm so sorry, Mister Galen," she said gently. "I wouldn't have put you in this situation for anything. If I could go back, I'd just stay in my bunk."

"That ain't no way to live," Sean shook his head and patted her hand gently. "You didn't do anything wrong. Stop worrying about it. Had the Captain just let it go none of this would be happening. None of it. This isn't your fault, so stop thinking like it is."

"I'll try," she smiled weakly. "I think I'll go and see how Mister Simmons is," she said suddenly. "I hope he gets better soon."

"I'm sure Tony 'll fix him up," Sean nodded as the young woman left. He waited until she was gone before shutting off the web feed and standing.

He needed to talk to Tony.

-

"That happened to me, too," Tony nodded. "I mean, not getting my teeth kicked in," he added with a grin. "But the Captain and I had a similar experience with her. When she fainted, remember? She came to and I asked her what her name was and she rattled out 'Jess T, Three-one-one-five-seven' just as smooth as silk."

"What?"

"That's what she said," Tony nodded. "Thing is, when the Captain and I asked her what that meant, she wanted to know what "what" meant?' Had no memory whatsoever of saying it. Swore that she had told us her name was Jessica Travers. But she didn't. We both heard it, too."

"So that's two strange occurrences that she doesn't remember," Sean mused. "Almost like she's operating on auto-pilot or something."

"Actually that's very accurate, considering what she told us," Tony nodded. "She said she took a look at the bridge controls and it was like a map unfolded in front of her. She suddenly knew what everything was, what it did and how to use it. She could fly."

"No one just 'knows' how to fly," Sean scoffed.

"I said the same thing," Tony nodded. "Still, she insists that's the deal, and she seems to honestly have no memory of learning how. She does appear to have the skills though."

"Well if I'd been a second slower she would have at least knocked me cold," Sean told him. "There was real power behind that move, too. Had it hit me head on it could have killed me."

"Damn," Tony whistled slowly. "What the hell is her deal, dude?"

"No idea, but. . .I think she's not just a school teacher. Not by a long shot."

CHAPTER FOURTEEN

Tony and Sean continued to discuss the issue of what to do about Jessica Travers for some time before electing to visit Lincoln Simmons. While neither thought the girl was faking her memory lapse, there was the possibility that she was dangerous. Lincoln deserved to know about that, and then he could share with Meredith or not as he saw fit. Sean wasn't overly eager to speak with the Captain and Tony still harbored a bit of ill will toward the woman for wrecking the ship he'd come to call home over the past three years.

Lincoln knew from the serious looks on their faces that this wasn't a social call. He was reclining on the bunk in sick bay, attempting to read with his uncovered left eye.

"How's that going?" Tony asked, nodding to the reader.

"Okay," Linc nodded. "Takes some getting used to, but I've got it. But I'm assuming from the looks you two are sporting that you didn't come down here to ask me about my reading," he continued, laying the reader aside. "What's wrong?"

"We're not sure anything is wrong," Tony admitted, then frowned. "Okay, we're *pretty* sure something is wrong," he amended, "but we can't figure out what. Or why. We decided it was time to talk to you about it."

"Sounds serious," Lincoln sighed.

"It could be," Sean shrugged slightly. He recounted his experience with Jessica in the lounge, then Tony repeated his own encounter. By the time they were finished Lincoln was frowning.

"I agree that it sounds like something is wrong," he nodded slowly. "Is there any medical reason you know of that she wouldn't be able to remember doing or saying these things? Or knowing how to do them in the first place?"

"A few," Tony was almost reluctant. "Some people suffer from a form of selective amnesia, where they block out unpleasant experiences. But that's usually associated with some sort of emotional or physical trauma and it's not widespread. At least not that I've heard of."

"Widespread?"

"It wouldn't be spread over time," Tony clarified. "Something like that would be limited to a specific event or experience. It wouldn't even register as a gap in the patient's memory. It would literally be like it never happened. Some patient's minds even create alternate memories for the affected time period. It's a self-defense mechanism more than anything else. A way to deal with a trauma that's too much for the patient's psyche to handle."

"I've dealt with things similar to that," Linc nodded again. "And I agree. Even those with long-term memory issues related to something like that are suffering from a single event, though it might be anywhere from a few minutes to a few days in length. No matter how much time is involved, it's a solid block of time."

"Yes," Tony nodded. "Meant to protect the patient from the traumatic event, whatever it might have been."

"So we can rule that out for Jessica, you think?"

"On a strictly diagnostic level, absolutely," Tony was firm.

"What makes you so sure?" Sean asked. He was out of his depth in this conversation and was staying quiet for the most part.

"How long would it take her to learn something like that trick she used on you?" Tony replied with a question.

"Depends on what she already knew," Sean shrugged.

"Assuming she had to learn from nothing, how long are we talking about?" Linc asked.

"Weeks at least," Sean shrugged again. "There's no true way to know since everyone learns on a different level. But. . .the skill she demonstrated would have to come from more than just training."

"Explain," Linc ordered.

"You don't get that good in just exercises," the former assassin said pointedly. "She's used that ability, that training, somewhere. More than once." His voice was as firm as Tony's had been about the medical diagnosis. Both accepted that the engineer knew what he was talking about.

"Then there's her pilot skills," Lincoln mused. "I went to school for months and took lessons on the side from military pilots and still barely passed," he admitted. "I know it's a joke to everyone but. . .I really do try. It's just not as easy as it may seem. Yet she did a first rate job by all accounts and doesn't seem to remember even learning how, let alone where." He looked at Galen.

"And like you, I'd have to say that she's flying on more than lessons and theory to have done as well as she did out of the blue like that. It's not something you just 'know' how to do, no matter how smart you are."

"So we've got a girl who is supposed to be a school teacher that knows how to fly a ship, how to fight like a soldier, and in a moment of mental unsteadiness replies on auto-pilot with a name and what sounds almost like an ID number," Tony added it all up. "I have to admit fellas; I don't like where this points."

"I don't either," Sean said quietly. This 'girl' knew far too much about him already.

"So what do we do?" Tony asked, looking at Lincoln. "It...I don't like to think of her as a threat, she's so darn nice and all, but this looks bad."

"It does," Lincoln sighed. "But this may not be her fault, either," he pointed out. "She may be the victim of some trauma or another that has caused her to create a completely false identity to cover up what she was before. The thing is, she's not really old enough to have led that much of a life of adventure and then turn around and become someone else."

"Unless she was raised that way," Sean said absently. The other two men looked at him and it took a minute for the engineer to realize they were scrutinizing him.

"What?" he asked.

"Raised what way?" Lincoln asked.

"To be able to do the things she can do," Sean replied calmly. "She could have been taught those things, all of them, from childhood. It's not like she had to wait until she was an adult to begin learning any of it."

Lincoln thought that over, nodding slowly. He was accustomed to dealing with people from a military background. All of them, no matter how specially trained they had been, had started that training at the minimum age of seventeen, usually eighteen. Most of them knew little to nothing of what they needed to know in order to survive in battle and were taught everything from the ground up, even the simplest things being regimented in their training.

Taking a child and beginning that kind of training at a much earlier age would explain a great many things about their wayward passenger. Come to think of it, the same could be said of the man standing before him.

"I suppose that could be it," the former counselor said finally. "But you think she honestly doesn't remember anything? Using those abilities or how she learned them in the first place?"

"I really don't think she does," Tony shook his head. "Her answers are too. . .too honest," he struggled to find the right way to describe it. "She's too forthright."

"I agree," Sean nodded firmly. "It's almost as if there's a switch that turns her on for a second, and then turns her off as soon as the trouble is gone."

"Why didn't it work on Dry Common?" Tony asked.

"She was never in any direct danger," Sean reminded the medic. "I told her to run and took out the first one to jump at her. She took off like I told her and never looked back. Had I not been able to stop one of them and he had gone after her, my money is on her turning 'on' long enough to kill the guy. Since she didn't have to, it didn't happen."

"That makes more sense than anything else I can think of," Lincoln agreed. "Which means that her responses are almost like programming rather than training."

"Say what?" Tony asked.

"Sean may have hit the nail right on the head," Linc told him. "Every time she's had one of these episodes, she's been under some kind of duress. Even the name and number she rattled off to you was on the heels of her passing out after getting us off Hartley Station. And if you consider how able she was to pilot the ship. . ." he paused, thinking. "You said she told you and Meredith it was like a map opened up before her, and she instinctively knew what to do, right?"

"More or less," Tony nodded. "I think her phrasing was she knew what everything was and what it did. That is seemed absurdly simple."

"And if you were programmed to do it I suppose it would look like that," Linc mused wryly. "Think about it. They use therapeutic hypnosis all the time to teach people to stop doing things. How hard would it be to reverse the process?"

"You think she was hypnotized?" Sean's tone showed what he thought of that idea.

"No, no," Linc shook his head, wincing as he did so. "No, that's not what I mean. But consider how that works is what I'm saying. You can see someone under hypnosis do things they shouldn't know how to do simply because the idea of what they need to do has been implanted in their mind. That's all. What we're talking about with Jess would be something much deeper than that, something almost like brainwashing to be honest. Probably using some kind of chemicals that affect the brain's ability to process and retain information."

"So her mind becomes like a hard drive on a computer," Tony nodded slowly, starting to see.

"Exactly," Linc nodded, wincing again at the effort. "When she's under duress, her mind accesses that 'hard drive', for lack of a better term, and gives her the information she needs to get herself out of a jam."

"Like flying a ship," Tony mused.

"Or escaping an attack," Sean nodded. "Okay, that does make some sense," he agreed.

"Even if that is what we're dealing with, it leaves a giant unanswered question, though," Lincoln reminded them.

"Who did it?" Tony offered, and Lincoln was careful when he nodded this time.

"Exactly."

-

Unaware that she was the subject of such a serious discussion, Jessica made her way to the bridge, having been asked to come there by Captain Simmons.

"You wanted to see me, ma'am?" she said as she halted at the bridge door.

"Yes," Meredith looked up, trying to suppress the pain she was feeling. She had been determined not to take any more pain shots, but she was almost to the breaking point now and admitted, if only to herself, that a few pain free or even pain *reduced* hours would be welcome.

"Come on up," she waved carefully and the younger woman stepped onto the bridge.

"I need a favor," Meredith told her and Jessica nodded at once.

"Whatever I can do," she promised.

"With Lincoln still down and Sean reduced to passenger, I'm down two watch standers," Meredith explained. "Tony normally doesn't stand a watch because he does all the cooking plus he's the ship's medic. He's going to stand one watch a day until Linc is back on his feet and I can find a replacement for Galen, but. . .I need some help," she admitted.

"I'd be glad to help, Captain," Jessica assured her. "I'm sure I can stand the watch for you, so long as you explain what I need to do."

"Honestly you just need to be here and keep an eye on the boards," Meredith pointed to the banks of indicator lights running along the walls and consoles. "The computer watches most things for us, and sounds an alarm and activates the warning light if something is out of kilter. The most important things are the proximity alert and the engine temperature warnings. Either of those could be deadly in a matter of minutes. Just as important but less time critical are the life support systems, including the carbon dioxide scrubbers."

For the next twenty minutes Meredith went over the various duties of a watch officer aboard the *Celia*, after which Jessica repeated them all without a bobble, impressing the Captain with her ability to recall it all.

"That's pretty fast," she commented. "Nicely done."

"I've always been fortunate to have a good memory," Jessica shrugged easily. "And all of this is fairly straightforward."

"Then you can stand the watch?" Meredith asked hopefully.

"Of course, ma'am," Jessica nodded. "I'd be happy to. It's the least I can do, surely."

"I really appreciate it," Meredith told her. "I've got to get some relief for my back before I go crazy. The last three days have been pretty hard on me," she admitted reluctantly.

"Then please go and get some rest, Captain, and leave it to me," Jess told her. "If anything happens I'll let you know at once."

"Faulks is doing some routine maintenance around the ship so if you have any problems give her a call and she can deal with them," Meredith ordered and Jess nodded hesitantly.

"She won't give you any grief," Meredith promised, not missing the hesitation. "I know she's been difficult since you've been aboard but I think that should be behind us. If it isn't then she's gone, and she knows it. If she does give you any difficulty, then let me know." Meredith stood carefully, wincing with the effort.

"Meanwhile I'll be in the infirmary for the next few minutes and then in my quarters. I really appreciate this, Jessica."

"I'm happy to be able to help," Jessica told her again. "It'll be an adventure I can tell my students about one day," she smiled.

"Let's hope not," Meredith grinned slightly. "We've had about all the adventure we can stand for a while."

"When you come from a tiny moon like I do, anything is an adventure," Jessica's smile grew.

"Well, in that case you can have all the adventure you want so long as it's boring," Meredith laughed lightly. "Thanks again."

Jessica waited until Meredith was gone before taking her seat in the pilot's chair. She slowly ran her hands across the console, careful not to touch anything, and smiled to herself. She might 'know' how to fly a ship, but other than the brief stint leaving Hartley Station she'd never done so. At least not that she knew of.

Now, here she was, sitting at the helm of a real starship, flying through space.

"Long way from Gateway, girl," she smiled to herself. "But not as far as it was yesterday." She looked forward to being home for the first time in so long. It seemed sometimes that she could barely remember how things had been at home. She would be glad for the opportunity to reconnect with her parents and her friends, and looked forward to beginning her work as a teacher. Educational opportunities were hard to come by on rim worlds like Gateway and she would be helping to change that. Someday there would be an entire generation of children on her world that she had impacted with her teaching.

As legacies went, that wasn't bad. Not bad at all.

-

Meredith was surprised to see Sean Galen in the infirmary as she approached. He had been pretty isolated since the revelation about his reason for hating the Commonwealth in general and Faulks' former comrades in particular. Tony Giannini was also there, and the two of them appeared to be in some kind of serious discussion with Lincoln.

"What's all this about?" she asked lightly as she limped inside. "And Tony, I give. I'll take the shot."

Giannini looked at his chrono and nodded.

"What?" she asked, seeing the self-satisfied look on his face.

"You held out twenty-two minutes longer than I predicted," he told her honestly. "I expected you as soon as your watch was over."

"Well, you were right, then," she told him. "I spent those twenty-two minutes and change going over how to stand the watch with Jessica."

"Oh?" Tony kept his voice neutral as he looked over at her from where he was preparing a syringe. She also noticed that Lincoln and Sean Galen both perked up a bit at the news.

"What?" she asked as she lowered the waistband of her trousers enough to allow Tony to give her the injection. Re-fastening her pants she sat down carefully, looking around her.

"We were just talking about Jessica," Lincoln said easily.

"What about her?" Meredith asked.

"Well, we were talking about how she flew us off the station," Tony said. "And the little episode she had when she woke up down here." Meredith nodded.

"And about how she almost kicked Sean's head off a few hours ago," Lincoln added nonchalantly. It took Meredith's pain-addled mind a few seconds to catch up to that one.

"Say what?" she finally asked, catching herself before trying to jump out of her seat.

Sean briefly explained the events in the lounge of just a few hours before, stressing that it had been his fault for reacting as he had.

"Sean, you don't have to cover for her," Lincoln told him. "She's not in trouble. If we're right, she really doesn't remember doing it. Or how she did it, either."

"Right about what?" Meredith demanded. "Let's get back on target here, since I just left Jessica in charge of the bridge of my ship!"

Lincoln carefully relayed to her what the three of them had come up with to explain the odd behavior patterns of their diminutive passenger. Meredith listened with growing alarm until finally she was on her feet.

"I've got to get her off the bridge!"

"Wait a minute," Tony held up a hand. "You aren't hearing us, I think."

"Oh, I hear you just fine!" Meredith shot back, trying to get past him. "I've left a ticking time bomb on the watch of my ship!"

"See, we don't know that," Linc said calmly, trying to soothe his wife. "We're absolutely guessing, Meredith. Postulating because we don't actually know anything other than a handful of facts. Strange facts I admit, but it's not really a lot to go on."

"So you think we should just leave her on the bridge?" Meredith's voice was incredulous.

"I think that if we are correct, then she only taps into this. . .knowledge, or hard drive as Tony put it, when she's under duress. She responds to threats or to outside stress that activate this learning, wherever it came from."

"Well, there's no stress on the bridge of a starship, right?" Meredith's sarcasm was biting.

"No more than there is anywhere else on the ship," Linc shrugged. "And she's already proven she can handle the ship, and do so in times of stress. Even emergency, really," he added. "I don't think it's a danger to allow her to stand the watch while there are others on the ship who are awake and able to take over in a pinch."

"So don't let her take the late watch," Meredith was starting to calm down some.

"Exactly," Linc nodded. "Let her work while we're under way. If nothing else, it might be good for her. And it gives us a chance to figure her out."

"Us?" Meredith asked, glancing at Sean Galen. "Does this mean you've changed your mind, Mister Galen?" she asked carefully.

The question caught Sean by surprise, though he didn't allow it to show.

"I hadn't given it any thought," he admitted. "This just happened. I told Tony because I thought it might be something medical and he told me what had happened with you guys, and I already knew about the piloting. We were just talking about it with Lincoln when you came in."

"She makes a good point, Sean," Lincoln didn't miss this opportunity. "And I was meaning to ask you something anyway, before this came up. This is as good a time as any," he glanced at Meredith.

"Go ahead, then," Sean nodded.

"We're starting a nearly three-month leg onto the rim," Linc noted. "That leg includes taking Jess home of course, but there are at least five other stops along the way before we're back even to somewhere like Halcyon. That's a long time for a ship to be without an engineer. There's a lot that can go wrong on the rim, you know that."

Again Sean nodded, but said nothing.

"I know that things are still tense on the ship to say the least, and I understand where you're coming from. Not your exact point of view," Linc held up a hand, "but your desire to put this behind you and move on. All I'm asking is this; stick with us until we get back to Halcyon. Don't make us take this journey without you. We'd be forced to take on someone we don't know and whose skill we can't really verify. I'm asking you to not make us do that. That's all. When we hit Halcyon again, if you still want to go then go. You're better off looking for new work there than a backwater like Weytan and we'll come nearer finding a decent replacement for you there than. . .well, a backwater like Weytan."

"And you can help us figure out what's wrong with Jess," Tony nodded, liking this idea just fine.

"Not to mention be with us when we see her home," Linc added to that. Sean almost frowned but caught it before it showed. Mentioning the girl was hitting below the belt a little.

He admitted that Lincoln made sense. He had worried a bit about how well *Celia* would get by without an engineer as she made this deep space run along the rim. He couldn't care any less about Faulks and the Captain, but Tony was a friend, which was the highest, closest association in Sean Galen Crow's vocabulary. While he didn't consider Linc a friend, he did like and respect the man.

And Jessica, though she had been nothing but trouble since she'd come aboard, just had a quality about her that made you want to like her, and help her. He didn't understand it himself, but there it was.

He considered his relationship with Faulks for a moment. The two of them seemed to have reached a truce of some sort after he'd revealed to her why he'd become who he was. And how. Sean believed he was a decent judge of character and he'd sensed in Faulks a real shame at the thought that her former comrades had committed the atrocities they had. And he had to admit that he believed her when she said she would have killed them herself had she known.

That didn't make them friends by any stretch of the imagination, but it might make them non-enemies at least. And that might be enough for the rest of this trip.

He was also fairly confident that the Captain's issues were behind her at this point and he would not have to endure any more of her intrusive behavior. She might not like him, but they didn't have to like each other to work together.

"Alright," he sighed a bit as he nodded. "I can do that."

Lincoln couldn't hide his relief at that and Tony grinned widely, slapping his friend lightly in the shoulder. Meredith nodded, her eyes showing her own appreciation even though she chose to remain silent, believing it best that she didn't speak.

"Sean, I really appreciate this," Lincoln told him. "I feel better knowing you're with us on this leg. I can't explain it but. . .something just feels off, that's all," he shrugged carefully. "I got nothing to base that on but a feeling, but there it is."

"Shouldn't ignore that kind of thing," Sean told him, nodding. "And this trip has already been a lot of trouble and we haven't really gotten to the Rim yet."

"Too true," Linc nodded.

"Well, since I'm working again I guess I better get down to the engine room," Sean told them. "Everything should be in order but. . .well, it's my job again, isn't it," he let out a half-hearted chuckle at the statement.

"I'm making spaghetti tonight man, just for you!" Tony told him, still beaming.

"You know what? I'll take that," Sean nodded. With that he left the infirmary, heading to the engineering section. Meredith released a breath she hadn't realized she was holding as the door closed behind him.

"That was well done," she offered quietly. "I would not have given you good odds on that happening."

"It was a gamble," Lincoln agreed. "I assume that was alright with you?" he asked, looking at her.

"Absolutely," came her firm reply. "Now, if we're satisfied that Jess is okay on the bridge for a while, I'm going to get some rest," she told them. "Before this shot wears off."

"You should let me medicate you more, Meredith," Tony told her firmly. "I know your concerns and I promise you I would never allow that to happen again. The thing is, we can alternate the drugs and use the minimum dosage that give you at least some relief, and that will allow your system to relax some as it adjusts to not being in pain at all times. There are also nerve blockers that might help. They're non-narcotic, non-habit forming. They aren't really pain killers; they just block the signals that tell you you're hurting." He held up a cautionary finger at her.

"If we go that route you'll have to be examined on a regular basis, especially spinal scans. The pain blockers will prevent you from feeling it if something is wrong. We'll have to keep a close eye on you. But it's an option."

Meredith cut off her usual reply as the words sank in. What would it be like, she wondered, not to hurt all the time? How long had it been since she hadn't been in pain? She couldn't remember not hurting anymore. She knew there was a time when she hadn't, but she couldn't remember what it felt like to be pain free.

"Alright," she said suddenly, shocking both her medic and her husband. Neither had expected her to agree to anything remotely like what Tony had suggested. "We'll try it," she continued. "It would be nice not be in constant and complete pain," she admitted softly. "I can't remember what it was like not to hurt."

"I can understand that," Tony said sincerely. "I've seen it before, usually in vets with war injuries but also from trauma victims who were injured in plain old accidents. Damage may heal, but that's no guarantee that it will be right when it does. That causes pain. If I had to guess, you're also suffering from some serious headaches, stiff neck and shoulders, and hip trouble."

"I...yes," her eyes widened as Tony ran down a litany of problems that she was suffering through. "How did you know?"

"All of those things are the result of your keeping yourself so stiff to avoid as much pain as you can," Tony replied. "Your muscles are bunching in all of those areas and they never get to relax. Even when you sleep, they're so accustomed to being that way they tend to 'learn' to stay like that. All of that stiffness leads to sore muscles and eventually slightly strained muscles. That tightness and tension leads to headaches and other pains, which just adds to the misery you're already in." He stopped suddenly, aware that he'd been lecturing.

"You sounded like a real doctor then, Anthony," Meredith's voice held approval. "Well argued. And like I said, I'll do it."

"Excellent," Tony nodded, choosing to ignore the 'real doctor' comment which he interpreted as a request for information. "We'll start out with a schedule of three, maybe four shots per day as needed. When you don't need it, don't take it, but don't allow things to get out of hand because that will just undo all we've managed to accomplish up to that point. Now," he took a breath. "I have spaghetti to make so I better get to it."

"You're happy he's staying, aren't you?" Linc smiled.

"I am," Tony nodded gravely. "He's my friend, and I don't have many. And he's damn handy to have around. I have a feeling similar to yours, and mine is telling me we'll need him somewhere down the line." With that the medic departed for the kitchen, leaving husband and wife alone in the infirmary.

"I would never have believed that would work," Meredith commented finally. "That Galen would stay."

"I would never have believed that Tony could talk you into taking pain meds on a schedule," Linc shrugged. "It's been that kind of day."

The two shared a pain-filled laugh in the privacy of the infirmary. It had, indeed, been that kind of day.

CHAPTER FIFTEEN

"Are you sure you can do this, Jessica?"

It was a fair question for all that it had been asked at least a dozen times.

"I'm sure," the young woman nodded firmly from the pilot's chair. "I got it."

The trip to Weytan had taken just over eight days. In that time a semblance of peace had settled over the ship once more, for all that it was a bit strained. Sean Galen kept to himself more than before, though he continued to interact with Tony and Jessica regularly.

Lincoln was finally out of the infirmary and back in the quarters he and Meredith shared, Tony satisfied that any lingering effects from the massive concussion would be minor at that point. While the swelling had at long last reduced to a simple knot just above his right temple, Linc's eyesight was still iffy at best. His right eye was subject to blur at any second and do so without warning or reason. Tony hoped that would stop as the damage continued to heal but he could not promise that it would.

Which left the *Celia* without a pilot. It had never occurred to any of them that someone other than Lincoln might need to fly the ship. That was an oversight that Meredith was only just seeing the magnitude of. She had never envisioned a time when Lincoln wouldn't be at the helm and that was a serious miscalculation on her part. Poor planning from the very beginning. They had been aboard for three years and not one time had anyone considered learning how to handle the *Celia* in the event Lincoln was indisposed.

Now they were in orbit over Weytan, about to set down to deliver the first of several cargoes on Frontier worlds in a run along the rim.

At least everyone *hoped* they were going to set down and deliver a cargo. For all of Linc's apparent ineptitude, he'd never actually crashed the ship. He'd come close many times to be sure, but they had always escaped unscathed other than a few quick trips to the head and some minor dishevelment.

Everyone knew that Jess had 'departed' them from Hartley Station without any difficulty, but leaving the station was a far cry from entering atmosphere over a planet and then landing on said planet. To say that some nerves were frayed was an understatement.

But Jessica was firm in her resolve that she could, indeed, land the ship. The crew was on pins and needles as she calmly lined the ship up for entry into Weytan's atmosphere with Lincoln assisting from the co-pilot's chair.

"Alignment set," Linc told her. "Nozzles locked and lined, straight board green for entry."

"Got it," Jessica nodded. "Check angle?"

"Angle check," Linc nodded, hiding a smile. Checking entry angle wasn't a requirement, but it was one of those unwritten rules of piloting; have someone besides yourself check your angle of approach. People made mistakes sometimes. Mistakes in space usually only happened once. The fact that Jessica knew this meant that she really had gotten some training, somewhere. Where was still a mystery, even to her.

"Initiating," Jessica said next and Lincoln keyed the I/C.

"May I have your attention please; this is your pilots speaking. That's plural, as in two of us. We are about to make entry into Weytan's atmo. Should we be lucky enough to survive that, we will attempt to set down on the planet below without crashing. Those of you who believe in prayer, now is the time. That is all."

"*Damn you Lincoln Simmons!*" Meredith's voice came back at once. "*That is* not *funny*!"

"Nag, nag, nag," Lincoln grinned at Jessica but carefully didn't key the I/C as he said it. "Let's go to Weytan," he added.

"We are on our way," Jessica nodded as she nosed the ship down a few degrees and initiated the thrusters for their entry sequence. Behind them *Celia*'s engines could be heard and felt throughout the ship as their timbre changed. *Celia* nosed over slightly and suddenly there was a flare across the screen before them.

"Friction heating," Linc called out to reassure Jessica.

"Really?" the sarcasm was thick in her reply. "I thought we had blown a fuse."

"Everybody's a comedian," Linc mock groused.

"No, not everybody," the dry reply made him chuckle as the school teacher gave as good as she got. *Celia* meanwhile was through the upper atmosphere and headed for the planet below. Unable to resist, Linc picked up the mike again.

"Attention crew and passengers, we are now inside Weytan's atmosphere, but I must caution against the opening of any outer hatches or lock doors at this time since the outside hull temperature is still a balmy two *zillion* degrees thanks to the incredible heat generated by the friction of the ship sliding into the atmosphere from space. Conversely, the temperature around the ship is roughly three hundred degrees below freezing at this altitude, so even if the heat of the hull didn't roast you, you would freeze solid in a matter of seconds. So just maintain you cras. . .er, landing positions while we try to put this ship on the ground. On purpose I mean."

Muted cursing could be heard coming up the passageway behind them and Jessica smiled as she shook her head slowly.

"Someone is definitely feeling better," she observed. "How many is a zillion?" she had to ask.

"No idea," Linc replied at once. "Of course, I also have no idea what the actual hull temperature is, either. There's a gauge that tells, but. . .I found that I really don't want to know that kind of thing. I have to assume that however hot we get the hull can handle it."

"Why?" Jessica asked. "I have the beacon," she added, flipping a pair of switches in front of her.

"Locked on," Linc informed her. "Because I can't imagine a much more horrible end than the hull melting with me right behind it, that's why. I asked one of my instructors if he knew how hot the hull would get and he told me if it got too hot, I'd know it right away."

"Can't argue that logic," Jessica observed calmly. "Three-quarter thrust, please."

"Three-quarters, aye," Linc replied, making the adjustments. "You know; I should have trained someone to help me like this a long time ago. I've been doing all of this by myself since we started. Three-quarters thrust set."

"That might explain why everyone is so down on your piloting," Jessica noted. "Ten degrees up-angle, relative," she ordered.

"Ten degrees up," Linc repeated as he adjusted the angle of thrust. "Braking thrusters are online," he added.

"One-quarter braking thrusters, reduce forward thrust to one-half, please."

"Done," Linc said a few seconds later. "So how locked in on that teacher gig are you?" he asked. "'Cause we may need a pilot full time if my sight doesn't heal. You're doing great."

"Sorry," Jessica smiled as she allowed the ship to flare slightly. "Slow to one-quarter thrust, increase braking to one-half. I'm going to be a teacher when I get home."

"Set. Got your heart set on it, huh?"

"For as long as I can remember," she said wistfully. "I've been gone from home a long time to make it happen and it was hard making it, but once I'm teaching the children on my world, helping them live better lives, it will all have been worth it. Landing sequence initiated," she toggled a quartet of switches.

"Sequence is active, computer has the beacon and is tracking," Linc told her. "Well, it's an admirable thing to want to help your people improve their lives. I'm sure your parents are proud."

"I hope so," Jess said wistfully. "I haven't seen them since I left home. Vid-calls are just too much money to spend no matter how lonely you are. I haven't gotten a letter in several months, but then I started home almost four months ago so that's not a surprise. There are probably several letters from them in the dead-end office at Beria Academy of Art and Science. I'll never be seeing that place again," she laughed lightly.

"I'm sure they'll put the paper to good use," Linc chuckled. "And we're locked on, in the pipe and looking good."

Three uneventful minutes later *Celia* settled onto the pad as graceful as a butterfly landing on a flower. The two of them went through the shut-down sequence and were finished by the time Meredith walked onto the bridge.

"You know, it's narratives like that one that make me wonder why I married you," she said at once, and Jess wasn't positive that the Captain was joking, either.

"Ah," Linc waved her complaint away. "It's a lot easier to do this job when someone is helping you, I've just discovered. Tried to lure the school marm into hiring on with us but she's determined to be an educator," he sighed with mock regret, shaking his head. "What a waste."

"Oh hush," Jess giggled at that. "It really did go well, ma'am," she said to Meredith. "And it really does seem to be a two-person job," she added.

Meredith nodded at that but didn't reply, thinking of all the times she had sat by and cursed, ridiculed and antagonized Lincoln as he tried to land the ship alone. More and more she was seeing how she had really failed in her duties. She was trying to make up for that now, however.

"Well, it was well done," she told the pair. "I could get used to landings like that," she decided to tease, but bent carefully down and kissed the top of Linc's head as she said it. "Now, I have cargo to deliver."

"Watch your back," Linc called out as Meredith disappeared down the passageway once more. She waved over her shoulder before stepping out of sight.

"Well, seems as if we've started repairing more than just your sight," Jess smiled brightly. Linc nodded, smiling a bit.

"It's been a rough few days but the last few have been better. It'll be fine, one way or another."

-

"Here you go, Captain," the dirty faced crew foreman handed the pad over to Meredith. She looked at it closely, recognizing the name and manifest number as being correct and scribbled an electronic signature on it, handing it back.

"All yours," she smiled and the man waved his crew forward to start manhandling the crates and containers from the hold and onto the sleds waiting below.

Weytan was a far cry from Hartley Station. There was no actual dock as such, Weytan rarely receiving enough traffic to warrant one even if the money had been available to build it. Instead ships landed on a designated pad outside Weytan's largest town, a collection of rough-hewn lumber buildings that was almost an insult to the word 'town'. The 'planet' was actually a moon orbiting a dead rock of a planet and lay outside most transit lanes. The moon had been ignored for decades after discovery because there didn't seem to be any redeeming value there. Discovery of high-grade deposits of platinum and a few other ores in smaller quantities had changed that quickly.

Weytan would never be a 'boom' moon, as some liked to joke, because the company that owned the mineral rights would not allow that. The miners were mostly indentured, working off debts that had been sold to a labor company and shipped in to work for room and board and not much else. Meredith didn't much care for the idea of forced labor, but she was in no position to change what was. No one in the Commonwealth hierarchy had ever asked her opinion of such things, anyway.

She caught more than one laborer looking at her ship with more than a passing interest and began to worry that someone might try to stow away and escape. She turned to see Faulks watching them closely, which was her job.

"Have you counted-"

"Yes, Cap'n," Faulks nodded, never looking away from the crew. "And all hatches are dogged tight. The ramp is the only way on or off the ship at this time."

"Good work," Meredith murmured. Just then she heard several cat calls and turned to see Lincoln and Jessica stepping out onto the catwalk above them. The cargo crew were eyeing Jessica with altogether too much interest, considering their brazen attitude.

Before she could say anything the whistles and hoots died away, the men falling silent as they looked toward the rear of the hold. Turning again, Meredith saw Sean Galen standing there, simply looking at the rowdy work crew. Even in his silence, or perhaps because of it, Sean Galen was intimidating. She fought off a grin as she turned back to watch the rest of the cargo off-loaded, wondering again how she had missed that aura around her engineer.

"Sorry about that, Captain," the foreman apologized as he signed for receipt of the cargo and transferred the information to her pad. "There's only so much I can do about their behavior, to be honest. There's not much to punish a man with here."

"I understand," Meredith said graciously. "We can usually look after ourselves."

"So I see," the man nodded, but was looking at Faulks rather than Galen. Meredith actually had to turn away to hide her grin at that one. Faulks was looking at the foreman as if he were an alien being of some kind that she was deciding whether or not to kill.

Taking his leave, the foreman was halfway down the ramp when a call from Sean Galen brought him up short.

"You forgot one," the engineer came forward nearly dragging one of the loading crew with him. "Found him behind some of the other cargo, Captain," he said to Meredith as he flung the attempted stowaway toward the foreman.

"Hefty penalty for trying to escape," the foreman said angrily.

"Imagine it's pretty steep for helping him, too," Galen said calmly and the foreman went slightly pale.

"We're not stupid, you know," Galen told him. "No one knows but us, so best thing to do is forget it happened. Savvy?"

"I...sure," the foreman thought better of whatever he'd been about to say. "Let's go, you," he said to the attempted escapee, dragging the man along down the ramp.

"I'm sorry Captain," Faulks said.

"Not your fault," Galen shocked them both. "That foreman? He was getting something for helping the stowaway. He was distracting you two with that excuse about their behavior while that stowie was slipping away. He's played that before, I'd say."

"I'm glad you were watching, Sean," Meredith said carefully. "Faulks it isn't your fault any more than it is mine. The important thing is that we didn't wind up with a fugitive aboard. Good work, both of you." With that she left the two of them, heading for the stairs.

"I'll get the ramp," Faulks said aloud, though to no one in particular.

"I'll keep watch," Galen offered in much the same way.

Neither spoke again, but. . .it was a start. Meredith listened as she walked away and decided she would take it.

-

"No one's going ashore?" Jessica asked as she and Lincoln made their way back to the bridge.

"Not here," Linc shook his head. "You heard all that commotion when you walked out onto the catwalk. Keep in mind those were probably the better behaved ones. This place doesn't have anything for us to look at, anyway. The stores we just delivered are enough to keep their people going for maybe five weeks, six at most. Everything here is company owned, and the workers are indentured, so they aren't getting any pay at this end. No stores to sell goods since there's only the company people to shop there and they bring their stuff with them."

"I see," Jessica nodded. "Seems harsh, indentured servitude," she added.

"It is," Linc told her grimly. "I'd say a good twenty-five percent of the workforce dies here. Indentured labor is one of those dirty little secrets in the Commonwealth that no one wants to talk about. We ignore it because it's bothersome."

"Makes sense," Jess nodded.

"Anyway, that's why we kept the engines turning. All we're doing is dropping the cargo and now that's done, we're gone."

And thirty minutes later they were, back in space and on their way to the next stop.

-

They had taken to meeting every evening after supper, discussing the day's events, or lack thereof. Tonight was no exception.

"She landed us without a bobble," Linc told Tony and Sean as the two sat in one of the empty crew quarters. "No sign of distress, none of that other stuff the two of you have seen, just. . .flying."

"She told me that all the hooting and what-not had made her a bit nervous, but other than that, nothing," Tony shrugged. "She didn't do anything about it, though. Right?"

"She was never in any danger," Sean pointed out calmly. "There was no threat, so there was no trigger. Assuming we're right about that, anyway," he added.

"The more I think about it, the more sure I am," Lincoln threw in. "Nothing else makes any sense, to be honest. But she told me today as we were landing that she's wanted to be a teacher for as long as she can remember. Basically her entire life. Whatever she may have gone through, wherever she may have been, she's convinced that she's a teacher, going home to teach."

"Where did she go to school?" Tony asked suddenly. "Do we know that? I mean, how hard would it be to check and see if she's really a graduate. See what I mean?"

"She mentioned Beria Academy of Science and Art today," Linc nodded thoughtfully. "I don't think I'd heard her mention it before," he looked up. "You two?"

"Not me," Tony said and Sean shook his head no.

"Well, I guess I can call them and try to bluff my way into getting what we need," Linc exhaled.

"Let me see to that," Tony offered. "I can make a call to a friend who can probably get it for us without attracting attention. No sense in turning over a hornet's nest if we don't have to."

"Well, that makes sense," Linc decided after a second. "It kinda feels dishonest to be doing this. Either of you feel that way?"

"If we meant her any harm I'd agree," Tony replied. "But we're actually worried about her and trying to help. To me, that's not dishonest. We're trying to do the right thing here."

"I agree," Sean nodded. "Plus it's a mystery that needs answering. None of this makes a lick of sense."

"Can't argue that," Linc agreed. "Alright Tony, see what you can come up with and let us know."

"Will do."

-

"What in the world are you doing?"

Meredith had been headed into the lounge to download a book into her reader before her bridge watch when she spotted Jessica in the corner, basically standing on her head.

"Yoga," came the serene reply.

"Really," Meredith's sarcasm was only slightly veiled. "Because it looks to me like if you make one wrong move you'll probably break your neck."

"Oh, goodness no," Jessica laughed and as Meredith watched the younger woman's legs came down one at a time to find a purchase on the floor. From that bent at the waist position she straightened with a sensual grace that had Meredith trying to remember when she could have tried something like that.

"I wish I could still do something like that," she gave the thought voice.

"No reason you can't," Jessica told her, smiling. "I mean, you wouldn't want to start out with that position," she laughed again. "But many people use yoga to help with injuries like yours. It's very therapeutic, both physically and mentally."

"Mentally?" Meredith raised an eyebrow.

"Yes," the girl nodded, wiping her face with a small towel. "Meditative states in yoga help to ease the troubled mind, Captain. And assist in dealing with the pain of injuries not unlike yours. It isn't medical assistance, of course, but it can and will improve your flexibility and strength. Want to try?"

"No, Jessica, but thanks for the offer," Meredith held up a hand as if trying to ward off a demon. "My spine is seriously damaged. Some days it's all I can do to get out of bed. Something like that might leave me in a bad way sure enough."

"Might help you too," Jessica pressed slightly. "You should at least talk to Tony about it. I'm sure he's got some information on it and could tell you if it was safe for you or not."

-

"Yoga?"

"Yes, yoga," Meredith nodded. "That face makes it look like you've just tasted something sour."

"Yoga?" the incredulous look remained, sharpened now by a raised eyebrow. "I mean, of course I've heard of it. Somewhere. I had no idea people still practiced that stuff," he admitted.

"At least one does, and she thinks it might help me with my back," Meredith stated. "I want your opinion before I consider it, but I have to say she's almost got me convinced. There are days I think I'd try about anything if there was hope of improvement."

"I'm not going to say it won't help," Tony raised his arms in a half-shrug. "As to your doing it, I'll need to do a little research and see what exercises are best for someone with your injuries. Give me a day or two to access the web and look around, okay? If Jess is doing it then there should be others, somewhere, doing it as well. Has to be a book or a manual or something that I can find and download."

"Alright," Meredith nodded as she got up. "Thanks for the shot," she smiled, already feeling better.

"You're doing very well, by the way," Tony told her. "When the shots kick in, what's your pain level, usually? Scale it one to ten."

"With the shot, after say ten minutes, let's call it a three, give or take," Meredith said after a minute of thought.

"Excellent," Tony nodded. "I'm sorry you're still hurting, but a three compared to a nine or ten-"

"I'll take it and be grateful," Meredith nodded. "Let me know what you find out. Thanks Tony."

"Welcome, Captain," he smiled as she left. He closed the door and locked it after her, moving to his own terminal.

He had a call to make, and the Captain had just given him the perfect reason for being on the net should anyone notice and wonder why.

CHAPTER SIXTEEN

"And that's all I could get."

Tony bit back his frustration as he spoke to Mister Tuttle, an entirely different Tuttle than the one on Hartley Station, about his 'background check' on one Jessica Travers.

"I appreciate it," he managed to smile despite his disappointment.

"Sir, I can always try. . .other means," Tuttle said cautiously.

"No, that's not necessary nor desirable," Tony shook his head. "If that changes, I'll be in touch, but until then we'll consider this matter closed."

"Very well, sir. If you need us, we'll be here." The screen went blank and Tony got to his feet. Soon he was in the engine room, where Lincoln was already waiting with Sean, having been alerted when the call came in.

"Beria School of Arts and Science, or Sciences, whatever," Tony waved an impatient hand, "can confirm that there was a Jessica Travers registered there at some point as a student, but otherwise refuse to budge in any way on releasing any information that might be confidential."

"Well, all we needed to know was if she'd been a student," Sean shrugged. "Now we do."

"No, we know that 'a Jessica Travers' was once a student there," Linc pointed out. "We have no way of knowing if our Jessica is her or not."

"Bingo," Tony nodded. "All attempts to get around their confidentiality rules hit a brick wall. No age, description, nothing. Not even the years she attended."

"So she could have just stolen someone else's identity, that what you guys are getting at?" Sean asked, frowning.

"I'm surprised you didn't think of it," Tony nodded. "You're pretty sharp."

"Never crossed my mind," Sean admitted, shaking his head as if to clear cobwebs away. "There's just something about her that makes me want to trust her. And I say that as a complaint," he added, looking at the other two men. "I'm not, by nature, a trusting person."

"Is it because you're attracted to her?" Linc asked. "You think that's it?"

"No," Sean's voice was firm. "It's not that she isn't attractive, but. . .there are plenty of reasons for me not to go down that road with anyone, so I don't think about it," he admitted. "Thing is, there's almost a compulsion for me to be protective. Trusting."

"I don't like the sound of that," Tony frowned slightly. "I have to admit I sometimes get the same feeling," he added. "And she's cute, I'll give you that, but I'm not all that swayed by looks to be honest. And while I've spent a lot of time with her, Jessica isn't really my idea of a dream girl, looks aside. I can't imagine being dirt-side all the time," he shook his head again. "I'd go insane seeing the same shit every day, man."

"Maybe it's pheromones," Linc chuckled. "You two are around her more than anyone else, so it's only logical for you to be affected." He meant it as a joke but suddenly Tony looked very serious and Sean looked almost angry.

"Hey, that was a joke, guys," Linc said, hands raised.

"No, I...I was just thinking about it, that's all," Tony shook his head yet again. "That's all," he repeated.

"You?" Linc asked Sean.

"I was just thinking about plants that can give off that kind of euphoric feeling," Sean admitted. "There are certain plants that can be used in salves and potions meant to soothe and relax. They're usually expensive to buy, so you don't run into them much unless you know someone who can make them."

"Where did you learn that?" Linc asked, interested.

"I used to know someone who could make them," Sean shrugged.

"Can you call them and see if..." Linc trailed off as he realized, too late, what he was asking.

"I'm sorry, Sean," Linc said softly.

"It's alright, man," Sean waved it off. "But no, there's no way to. . .no way to check," he finally settled for saying.

"I'll do some checking," Tony declared, getting to his feet. "I think from now on we only meet when something happens," he added. "It's going to start looking suspicious if we keep doing this."

"True," Linc nodded. "Okay, if one of us notices something we'll get together and discuss it but otherwise we carry on as usual."

"Whatever that is on this boat," Tony added with a snort.

"Amen."

-

Celia made her way through three stops over the next three-and-a-half weeks without any incidents. Deliveries went smoothly and there was no drama among the crew or between the crew and any cargo crews. The worlds they traveled to along the Rim were usually small and scarcely populated. Only one delivery contained anything that wasn't the bare basic vital goods that someone on a Frontier world would need, and that was to a man who had retired to a small moon orbiting a world almost entirely covered in water called Aqua.

"Is that the best someone could come up with for that?" Tony had asked in derision. "Aqua?"

"What's wrong with it?" Jessica had asked. "I've heard of this place," she added before he could answer. "You know, there are a lot of scientists who come here and spend years studying that place," she turned to look at the others. "He may have been one of them."

"Might," Meredith nodded as she raised her coffee mug. "There was some scientific-type equipment on the manifest. Burners, tubes, scope slides, that sort of thing. No telling what he's doing."

"Long as the check clears, who cares?" Tony pointed out.

Celia had two more stops on her list before Gateway and this moon was one of them. Jessica had been excited that her journey was almost over. She would miss the crew and the ship, but being home again, seeing her parents, was worth more than anything to her at the moment. Now, with *Celia* outbound, the girl's enthusiasm seemed to bubble toward the surface.

"Eleven days to Gateway!" she almost crowed as she spun around in the pilot's chair. She had just entered their course for Liberty Vale, a six day run from their present position. From there it would be no more than six more days, max, to Gateway, Jessica's home world.

"More like twelve when you count the change," Linc informed her. "But we are almost there. I know you'll be glad to get home."

"You bet!" she beamed. "Auto-pilot is set and we're on course, on schedule. I'm going to find me something to eat!"

"Okay," Linc laughed at her enthusiasm. "Go ahead." He watched the waif-like girl bound away from the bridge, shaking his head at her attitude and antics. She had really come out of her shell in the last month.

There had been no further episodes. No strange or unexplained behavior. No one had noticed anything unusual or out of place. It had the three men on the ship wondering now had they overreacted to earlier events. Linc didn't think they had, considering what they had thought, but he was wondering now if their alarm had been needed.

There was still no explanation of where she'd learned her pilot's skills, or that fighting move she had used on Sean Galen, and nothing could explain her 'Jess T' moment in the infirmary, but without anything else to go with it, there really wasn't much that could be done.

Tony's search for pheromones or pheromone type chemicals at least, had revealed a great many sprays and potions that could make a person highly suggestive, but all of them required either inhalation or injection, neither of which Jess could have accomplished. That was out.

Maybe she just caused men to be protective, Linc thought to himself. Something in her diminutive size and cheerful demeanor made males of the species want to protect her. Wasn't unheard of. Or even unusual.

"She's awful cheerful," Tony mentioned from the navigator station.

"She's almost home," Linc pointed out, returning to the present from his musings. "Make a person happy, getting to go home. Especially after so long away."

"Yeah, I guess," Tony said absently. "So, we got four more drops and two pick-ups," he added, looking at a computer screen. "We're going to Liberty Vale next, I see," he added, and Linc could almost hear the frown in his voice.

"What's wrong with Liberty Vale?"

"Nothing," Tony shook his head. "It is a rough place," he added suddenly. "Even for a Frontier world. Might be smart to think ahead, be ready for trouble."

"Been there before?" Linc asked. Liberty Vale was a new stop for them. Every other drop or pick-up was somewhere they'd already been at least once.

"Ah, I sorta dropped in there during a walkabout kind of thing," Tony said vaguely.

"Walkabout, huh?" Linc replied, an almost grin creasing his features.

"I spent a little while just roaming after I left school."

"Why did you leave?" Linc asked.

"Like I said, I got caught in the storm my roommate created," Tony shrugged. "Guilt by association, more or less."

"That's not right," Linc shook his head.

"Made that argument myself," Tony sighed. "Didn't help. I could have fought it I guess, but. . .well, there were extenuating circumstances, let's say. Making a public scene would have been counterproductive. So, I sucked it up and moved on."

"I'm sorry," Linc said earnestly. "But it was our gain, no question about that," he added sincerely. "Having you on board has been a great advantage for us. I'm sure you know that."

"It works for me, too," Tony nodded. "I get to travel and get paid to do it," he grinned. "And meet the damnedest people," he added with grim chuckle.

"That is true," Linc admitted ruefully. "Speaking of which, is it just me or do Sean and Faulks almost seem to be getting along?"

"I think 'getting along' might be too generous, but. . .maybe 'less hostile' would be accurate. Actually, if you think about it, Sean was never really hostile to start with. He mostly just ignored Faulks as not being worth bothering with. And Faulks got a serious wake-up call when she was laying there in the floor with Sean's knife at her throat and him snarling down at her. Man that was a scene, right there."

"I hate I missed it," Linc told him, a nasty smile on his face. "I'd have given a good hunk of my retirement to have been there."

"It sounds funny, I'm sure," Tony nodded. "But Linc, you had to see him. It was like watching a wild animal set free to do as he pleased. I knew he wasn't someone to mess with, but. . .damn," he shook his head.

"I hope he'll stay with us," Linc said suddenly. "Having him as part of the crew is a good thing from my perspective."

"I hope so too," Tony agreed. "We'll see, I guess."

-

"So do you think you'll stay, Sean?" Jessica asked. They were both sitting at the galley table eating a light meal. She was due to stand watch in half-an-hour and Sean had just finished a four-hour work session on engineering.

"Doubt it," he said simply. "I'll stay until we get back to Halcyon I guess. Linc was right about that, it will be easier to get work there. And I didn't like the idea of letting them jaunt along the Rim without someone in engineering. It ain't safe."

Space travel seemed safe and reliable to people who never stopped to consider how easy it was for a ship to be lost in the black without anyone ever knowing what had happened to them. Derelict ships would often be found adrift, the crew dead from asphyxiation or worse after losing power or suffering a catastrophic breakdown. That was one reason no one spent much time thinking about what could go wrong in space. If you started thinking about all the ways you could suffer and die, you'd be afraid to step foot on a ship.

"I'm glad you did stay," Jessica told him. "I would have missed you."

"Not for long," he replied. "You'll be home soon, and we'll move on."

"I know," Jessica said wistfully. "And I'll never forget this time, either. I've learned so much these last few weeks, and a lot of that was from you."

"Well," Sean stood abruptly. "I think I'm going to get a nap before I have to start my work detail. I have a lot to get done on this leg. We'll probably try and take on water and flush the gray water tanks at Liberty. I need to be ready for that."

She watched him go, wishing that she could fix the damage that her presence had caused. Had she not come aboard, the rest of the crew might never have known his secret and he would have no need of trying to find new work somewhere.

She stood as well and headed for the bridge. She would soon be home, but until then she was technically a member of the crew. She had work to do too.

-

Liberty Vale wasn't the typical Frontier backwater. It was a backwater to be sure, traffic sporadic outside of freighters like the *Celia*, but Liberty Vale was more developed than most worlds or moons in the outer ring.

There were many reasons for that, first among them the rich soil found there. Paired with a fairly constant climate, the fertile ground was ideal for planting and raising livestock. While passenger ships didn't often make landfall on Elvy (the name most residents used), freighter traffic was almost constant as ships picked up foodstuffs on an almost daily basis for transport inward to the Sphere. Those same ships often delivered equipment and supplies from the Sphere at the same time.

Prosperity often drew trouble, however, and Elvy was no exception to that. The people of Elvy had long since adopted some rather strict and stringent laws for dealing with troublemakers, but even so the lure of possible easy money was often too much for career criminals to pass up. Many sharp-talking shysters had made their way to Elvy over the years, thinking they could fleece the 'hicks' of a backwater population that had more money than brains.

Life on Elvy was not easy by any means. Indigenous wildlife was plentiful and there were many predators among them. Each year, big game hunters would pay handsomely for the privilege of traveling to Elvy to hunt the massive Catodons, huge feline beasts that were a close cousin in appearance to the old Earth Smilodon, right down to the huge 'saber' teeth. Those teeth and the pelts of the huge cats were prized by big game hunters, and the bragging rights of having stalked and taken one were worth the price of admission alone to many.

There was also the equally massive and sought after Cinnabears, or Cinnamon Grizzly as it was officially known. There weren't many of them compared to their Old Earth counterpart and acquiring a permit to hunt them was strictly regulated. Elvy's Wildlife and Forestry Ranger Corps worked extremely hard to protect the planet's ecosystem and that included the famous wildlife. While the planetary government was willing to allow hunting to help manage the population and to help pay for conservation costs, they were equally *unwilling* to allow any infringement on hunting regulations. Poaching was big business on Elvy and kept the Rangers busy year-round.

There were some massive areas that were privately managed game reserves, but even there the laws applied. Each reserve had a limited number of permits it could bid out each year, and the bidding was usually high. In addition, there were some less than scrupulous 'guides' that worked for hunters using public lands to hunt upon, or sometimes even trespassing on private property.

The citizens of Liberty Vale took a very dim view of such trespassing and it was not unusual for a guide and his party to meet with 'unfortunate' hunting accidents when they were caught on the wrong rancher's property. Most people on the planet turned a blind eye to those happenings, believing that the encroaching hunters and guides had gotten what they deserved.

In addition to less than optimal living conditions there was the dangers inherent with any agricultural pursuits where massive machinery with excessive moving parts was always inches away from flesh and blood. All of these factors combined to create a very hearty breed of folk that knew hard work and high risk and were far tougher than the populace of most other worlds, even along the rim of the Frontier.

And because they were hard working they had also had a dim view of those who chased the 'easy' dollar by running confidence scams or perhaps outright thievery. Tolerance was usually in short supply on 'Elvy', and no one made any bones about that to outsiders.

Life could end quickly on Liberty Vale and come from any number of directions. As a result, those who made their home on Elvy were quick to celebrate, to laugh, and to enjoy life while they could. They were equally quick to retaliate, seek retribution, and respond to affronts, insults or challenges.

All in all, as Tony had said, a rough place.

-

"Attention crew, this is your Dynamic Duo of Piloting Awesomeness and we are now entering orbit over scenic Liberty Vale. Liberty Vale is a prime vacation spot known throughout the galaxy for it's wonderful wildlife and flowerful fauna, and is home to two of the most high profile Apex predators currently in existence, the Catodon and the Cinnabear, both of which are highly prized by big game hunters and hated by the ranchers who unwilling supply both with food from time to time."

"We will shortly attempt to cheat death once more and enter the atmosphere of Liberty Vale, after which, assuming we survive, we will attempt to set down on the planet without incident. That means without crashing. Please prepare for reentry and hold on for dear life."

Jessica looked very pleased with herself as she replaced the I/C mike and looked over at Lincoln.

"*That's* how you do *that*," she said smugly.

"*Jessica, I'll need to talk to you after we make this delivery*," Meredith's too mild voice prevented Lincoln from replying right away, and killed the smug look on her face as well.

"Yes, Captain," she replied, the earlier confidence in her voice gone.

"And *that's* why you don't do it like that," Linc smirked at her as he began to go through his entry procedures.

"I thought it sounded okay," Jessica shrugged, turning to her own duties. Lincoln was going to fly this time, the first attempt he'd made at a landing since his injury, with Jessica assisting. Lincoln tried to hide his apprehension but he was worried to say the least. He had never been that good a pilot to begin with and if his eyesight suddenly relapsed into blurs then...

He shook the thought away. There was no sense in borrowing trouble. He'd know in a few minutes if his depth perception and other visual abilities were going to let him keep flying or not.

"It'll be fine," Jessica told him, almost as if reading his mind.

"Sure," he nodded, never taking his eyes from his instruments. "Entering now," he told her. The glow of reentry fires flared across the screen briefly and then they were in high atmosphere, on their way down.

Too steeply.

"Linc," Jessica said calmly. "Angle check."

"It looks fine," Linc said, checking. "I...how's that?" he asked, making an adjustment.

"Looking good," Jessica said firmly. "We're on the ball."

But they weren't on the ball, at least not for long. The ship kept drifting out of alignment.

"Linc," Jessica said again.

"Jessica, I can't. . .I can't focus on the instruments and the screen at the same time," he admitted finally. "I can't shift back and forth without my eyes going haywire."

"It's your depth perception," Tony surprised them both from behind, having joined them without their realizing it. "Lincoln, concentrate on one or the other, let Jessica take the rest. I need to see if it clears up."

"We don't need to see it so bad that we crash!" Linc shot back.

"We aren't going to crash," Jessica assured him, and Tony caught the timbre in her voice that said 'Jess T' was present once more. Instantly he shifted from watching Linc to watching her.

"Ten degrees up angle, Lincoln," Jess ordered in a flat voice. "Hold on this heading after that. Applying braking thrusters at one-quarter in five. . .four. . .three. . .two. . .braking now." The ship shuddered ever so slightly as it began to slow. "Cutting forward thrust to one-half. . .now," Jessica continued to roll on, flipping switches as she spoke. "Angle is good, rate is good, beacon locked on. We're in the pipe, Mister Simmons."

"Thank you Jessica," Linc replied finally as he watched the world growing larger in the screen before him. "Brake on your say so," he added, afraid to look away again.

"Increasing brake to one-half in three. . .two. . .one. . .now," Jessica's voice was still devoid of any real emotion as she increased the braking thrust for the *Celia*. "Cutting forward thrust to one-quarter in three. . .two. . .one. . .now," she continued, and the ship again bucked slightly as her forward momentum began to stall.

"Check stall," Linc said quickly.

"Plus ten percent," the girl told him calmly. "We're green."

Five minutes later they were on the ground without further incident and Lincoln Simmons was looking through the view screen with a stricken look on his face.

"Linc, it's okay," Tony told him. "It's your first time back. There's bound to be some trouble."

"I couldn't focus," Lincoln replied idly. "I couldn't shift my vision back and forth without it being a blur. I…I can't fly." He turned to look at the medic and the look in his eyes was almost heartbreaking.

"I can't fly."

CHAPTER SEVENTEEN

"Concentrate on this dot."

Linc bit back a sigh and focused on the black dot Tony had painted on the wall of the infirmary. After a few seconds, Tony spoke again.

"Now look at the yellow square, and tell me what you see."

Lincoln shifted his gaze left to a two-foot square patch of yellow on the same wall.

"I see a black dot inside a yellow square," he said softly.

"Tell me when it fades," Tony ordered, watching Lincoln carefully. It was a long ten seconds before Lincoln finally spoke.

"It's fading. Slowly, but it's going."

"One more thing," Tony said, standing. "Let's go to the cargo bay. Sean has set up something for me to test your depth perception but we need more room than we can get in here." The two of them walked in silence to the cargo bay. Sean was waiting there along with Meredith and Jessica. Faulks was on the bridge.

"Good work," Tony nodded as he surveyed the rig he'd asked Sean to create. "This is just a rough test, so don't read too much into it. All we need from this is to check and see if your depth perception is the problem or not. Stand there," he pointed. Lincoln moved to the indicated spot, examining the 'contraption' as he did so. Two rails, side by side, each with a pulley driven block on it sat along the floor. Each pulley had a rope with a handle attached at the head of the rails where Tony had ordered him to stand.

"Lincoln, I want you to stand with your back to this get-up, bend at the waist so you can see the blocks, then take the ropes and pull the blocks to the blue markers along the rails. You should pull them at the same time. Just draw them up and stop them when they hit the blue marker. Got it?"

"Got it," Linc nodded, doing as he was told. "Ready," he said, taking the ropes in hand.

"Now," Tony said simply and Lincoln pulled the two blocks forward, stopping them both at the same time. Lincoln waited but no one spoke.

"Well," he asked finally?

"Green next," Tony ordered rather than answer. Biting back his frustration Lincoln again pulled the ropes and stopped the blocks in unison.

"That's enough," Tony said gently and Lincoln stood. As he did his head spun slightly and Sean reached out to grab the pilot's shoulder as the man appeared to be going to topple.

"Thanks," he nodded and the engineer nodded back in silence. Lincoln turned to look at Tony.

"The verdict?" He followed Tony's nod to the rails and froze. The blocks were at least a foot apart. To him they had looked even. He looked back to the medic.

"That can't be good," he settled for saying, fighting to keep his voice calm.

"It's not," Tony agreed, "but it's not the end all, either. All this was designed to do was help us see what the problem was. Now that we know, we can work on it."

"How can you fix something like that?" Lincoln asked as Meredith wrapped an arm around his waist in silent support. He draped an arm about her shoulders and squeezed gently, grateful for her presence.

"Depends on what's causing it, Linc," Tony told him. "I know what's wrong, at least partly anyway. Now I have to figure out what's causing it. Once we're back to the Midterior we can consult with an optometrist. You may just need glasses or corrective surgery."

"In the meantime, I can't fly," Linc stressed.

"Well, you can fly," Tony hedged. "You'll just need someone to help you with the instruments, that's all. You know, not to be funny, but . . . Linc, this may have been part of your problem all along."

"What's that supposed to mean?" the pilot demanded.

"If your depth perception was already off, then it would explain the trouble you had in landing the ship. Coupled with the fact that it's really a two-person job anyway, that's more than enough to keep you from being able to handle everything on your own. This," he indicated the test, "slows your reaction time. Not by much, but it's cumulative. You lose a second here, another on the next step, and so on until by the fifth or sixth step you're five seconds behind where you need to be. Five seconds is a long time for a pilot I'd think."

"Well, yes," Linc agreed, clearly thinking it over. "Maybe you're right. Can it be fixed; you think?"

"Depends on what 'it' is, but probably," Tony nodded. "May take surgery but it would also probably be fairly simple and straightforward."

"Whatever it takes, we'll get it," Meredith spoke for the first time, her voice taking on that command edge that she usually tried to avoid using these days. "Until then, we'll make do with someone helping you like today. We've only got a few more stops before we come around to Halcyon again. Once we're there, we'll see what can be done."

"All right," Lincoln nodded, not knowing what else to do or say. Maybe there wasn't anything else. He didn't know that, either.

"What do we do in the meantime?" he asked, looking from Tony to Meredith.

"We'll have to do the best we can," she shrugged. "We've all learned enough over the last few weeks that we can help you get up in and out of atmo, so we will. Once we're back on Halcyon, we'll see an eye doctor and go from there. If we have to hire a pilot for the short term, then we will. We will do whatever it takes," Meredith said firmly, her command tone again showing through. She might as well have added *and that's all there is to it.*

-

"I didn't want to bring this up earlier, what with everything else, but Jess had another bout of 'Jess T' syndrome today."

Sean looked up from what he was doing to see Tony standing over him in the engine room and frowned. He hadn't heard the medic walk up on him. Was he that far out of practice?

"It wasn't a bad one," Tony added, misinterpreting the frown, "When Linc started having problems she went to that 'cool as cucumber' voice of hers and talked him right down to the ground while still doing her own job. And you know," he sighed, sitting down on a crate nearby, "I really owe Linc an apology. He's been doing this all by himself all this time and it really is a two-person job, looks like. I mean, even with two of them there's so much going on I don't know how they manage."

"Training," Sean shrugged. "How do you manage a bleeder who's gunshot and has trauma besides the bleeding? How do you know what to do?"

"I practiced over and over," Tony nodded absently. "You realize what that means, right?" he asked, looking at Sean again.

"It means Jessica didn't just 'learn' how to fly," Sean nodded, setting the part he'd been working on down with a sigh. "It means she's spent a while doing it."

"If she were staying I'd say we need to keep on this, but. . ." Tony held his hands up in silent wonder. "She's going, man. Next stop is hers and she'll be on Gateway. Like as not we'll never see her again."

"Like as," Sean agreed, resuming his work. "So long as she's not a threat to us, and I seriously don't believe she is, then it's not our business."

“I do wonder about that 'protective' thing, though,” Tony admitted suddenly. “I mean, if that's something she can do, and do at will, there's almost nothing a...well, a spy, an assassin, a politician, you name it and they could use that to change things in a big way. Influence important people to do things the way they want.”

“That is true,” Sean mused. “Be a very good weapon to have in your arsenal.”

“You know, I can't stand to think of her as some kind of weapon,” Tony shook his head. “She's such a sweet kid, you know?”

“I do,” Sean nodded. “And it bothers me that she can have even the slightest bit of influence or control over me. I don't like that.” His voice took on a flat edge that Tony didn't miss.

“I don't think it's like that, man,” he said gently.

“I'd like to think it's not,” Sean agreed. “But I can't afford to think like that. I have to think like the people that are after me.”

“People like Faulks?” Tony snorted, but his mirth died when Sean turned to look at him. The look in his eyes startled the young medic.

“People who would step on Faulks and not notice she was there,” he said evenly. “Faulks is pretty good at what she is; a fighter. She's a soldier, and a good one at that, though I'd die under torture without admitting it. She meant what she told me in the mess that night, man. If she'd known about Kineer, she'd have done him herself. Faulks is a bullying ass, but she has honor. At least in her own way. And she wouldn't make war on someone who wasn't capable of replying in kind. Not her way, man.”

“The world may be ending,” Tony's eyes crinkled slightly. “You've complimented Faulks.”

“Just a statement of fact,” Sean shook his head, unruffled by the comment. “Anyway, I will most likely always be a wanted man, Tony. Hiding like I was doing here is okay until someone knows who I am. Sooner or later they let slip, not meaning to, and then Very Bad People start looking for me. People who couldn't care less about who else gets hurt so long as they get what they want.”

“And what do they want, Sean?” Tony asked, leaning forward.

“My head, for starters.”

-

“Sorry we were late, Captain,” the cargo chief apologized as he handed over the EDOC for Meredith to sign. She scribbled her name after reading the manifest.

“No problem, Chief,” Meredith smiled. “We had a few things to take care of anyway so it wasn't wasted time.”

"I'm glad to hear that," the Chief nodded. "I had orders to ask if you're interested in outbound cargo? Not a rush delivery since it's freeze-dried, but it needs to get Sphere-ward. To Halcyon to be exact if you happen to be going near there. Good pay, too," he added.

"We happen to be going to Halcyon," Meredith smiled. "We work out of Halcyon a good bit. This leg started there, in fact. If we have the room I'm always interested in good pay," she smiled a bit brighter.

"Outstanding," the Chief laughed, pulling up another page on his PAD. "Here's the manifest and rate offer. The only catch is I can't deliver it until dark thirty tomorrow, local. I'm behind already, as you've seen yourself. I can have the late crew make it their first job, though, if that's okay?"

"How long is that, local?" Meredith asked, looking at the dark sky outside her ship.

"Another eight hours, ma'am, tops. That's assuming there's no trouble with loading, of course," he added. Meredith nodded as she gazed at the manifest. It looked like a good haul, but nothing they couldn't handle. She waved Faulks over to her.

"Gunny, can we manage this with our other jobs? It's bound for Halcyon and it's a good rate."

"I'll make it work, Cap'n," Faulks nodded after a minute spent in study of the manifest. "I'll need a few hours to re-arrange, though."

"That works out great then," Meredith nodded, looking back to the Chief. "If the payment clears, you've got a deal, Chief."

"Payment's up front, Captain," the man smiled again. "Most of our shippers prefer cash on the barrel."

"Cash is always accepted aboard the *Celia*," Meredith laughed lightly.

"Captain, if you guys get this way often, there's a wealth of work here for a ship your size," the Chief offered after a minute. "We literally have cargo sitting on the docks around the clock waiting on shipping. You might want to consider that if you'd like a regular run. Not all do, I know," he raised a hand. "Just a mention. But I think I can safely say that anytime you're in our neck of the woods, we can scare up a cargo for you. Probably more than one. Just something to keep in mind."

"Thank you, Chief," Meredith nodded, thinking. "I didn't know the work was that plentiful here."

"We're off the beaten path, Captain, but the products from here are in such high demand that we can afford the shipping. I say we as if I'm a part of it," he chuckled. "I make my money running the docks and doing a little brokering on the side, as you've just seen. It's not a conflict of interest," he assured her without prompting. "I'm just always looking for respectable shippers who seem dependable."

"How do you know we're dependable?" Faulks demanded, though far less gruffly than she once would have.

"You arrived three days ahead of schedule, the cargo is intact and unmolested, you didn't raise hell when we couldn't get to you right away, and you looked over the manifest to make sure that you could actually haul the cargo safely before accepting a high paying job," the Chief rattled off. "I think I'm pretty safe in assuming you're dependable." To his credit he managed not to look too smug.

Meredith was about to reply when Faulks broke out laughing. Amazed, the Captain turned to look at her cargo Chief only to see Faulks' eyes damp from laughter.

"Now *that,* by God, was spoken like a real Chief!" Faulks finally managed to get out. "COB?"

"Yep," the Chief nodded, grinning back. "Been out a long time, but I guess some things stay with you."

"I'll say," Faulks was more serious now. "Well, we'll be ready when your yard apes get here."

"I'll make sure they're at least close to on time," the Chief promised as he departed.

"What?" Faulks asked, as Meredith was still looking at her.

"Who are you, and what have you done with Gunny Faulks?" Meredith asked.

"Gunny Faulks don't live here anymore," Faulks shrugged. "I ain't a Gunny no more. I guess I'll always be one in a way, just like he's always gonna be a COB, but. . .this ain't the Navy, and I ain't a Marine anymore. Got to start acting like it."

"Well done, Gu. . .," Meredith paused, then grinned slightly. "Well done, Chief."

She managed to get the last laugh as she walked away leaving a stunned Faulks in her wake.

-

"Anyone want to go into town?" Meredith asked the assembled crew. "We've got a minimum of seven hours to kill before we'll need to be back. We're picking up a new cargo."

"I'll need to re-work the load, Cap'n," Faulks shook her head.

"We're still taking on water, ma'am," Sean shook his own head. "I can't leave until that's finished. Grey water tanks are already dumped and flushed though," he added. "I'll help you with the load while we're taking on water, Gunny," he added, looking at Faulks.

"Just Chief, from now on," Faulks shook her head. "Ain't a Marine no more. And I'd appreciate the help."

"Well, I think I'll meander into town, myself," Tony sighed, a grin on his face as he sat back. "You know, just to rehash old times."

"Been here before?" Meredith asked.

"Long while back, but yes," he nodded. "No idea how much has changed, but for anyone getting off, this can be a rough place, so mind your P's and Q's, okay?"

"Looks like no one is going anywhere," Meredith shrugged but Linc shook his head as he stood.

"No, we're going out," he declared. "I'm assuming that there's nothing you three need us for?" he looked from one to the other of the 'regular' crew.

"I'm sure we'll get by," Faulks grinned slightly. "Girl, you going into town?" Again, the comment/question didn't come close to Faulks' original gruffness.

"No, I think we all know it's best if I stay on board," Jess sighed. "And I'm tired, anyway, so I'll just take a nap."

"We'll be at the Silver Dollar casino and restaurant," Linc told the others. "There's a theater there, and they are supposed to have some of the best beef in the known universe. I intend to inspect that claim." The others laughed as he and Meredith went to get ready. As soon as they were gone, Faulks looked at Tony.

"Where you goin'?" she asked suddenly, but with none of her usual rancor.

"Don't know, really," he admitted. "Got one or two stops I'll make, but otherwise that's it."

"How 'bout you make sure they get where they're goin', then, 'fore you start meanderin'?" Faulks suggested. "Have any trouble, you call us."

Tony nodded, impressed with Faulks in a way he'd not been before.

"I can do that."

"Good deal," Faulks stood. "Missy, if you're going to sleep, how about keeping a com on where we can wake you if needed. I don't think we'll need a quick getaway, but you never know."

"Sure thing," Jessica smiled. She was almost starting to like this version of Faulks. If it was real, anyway.

"I'll be in the cargo bay," the 'chief' said, heading that way.

"Let me check on the water and I'll join you," Sean called after her, heading to do his own work.

"I guess I'll just be an annoying third wheel," Tony winked at Jess. She smiled at him before heading to her own room. Tony shook his head and went to get ready for a night on the town.

-

"I assume Faulks appointed you as our guardian, Mister Giannini?" Meredith asked idly as the trio walked along the boardwalk toward the sprawling metropolis that was Liberty City.

"I make it a point never to do anything that Faulks asks me to do, Captain," Tony grinned broadly. "As it happens, I'm on my way to see an old friend, and by the most fortunate of coincidences, my destination lies some little way beyond your own. As I recall, the Silver Dollar is a pretty nice place for a backwater world like this. There are some very wealthy people on this rock, mostly ranchers and big time planters, and they can afford the best in accommodations and entertainment. Already got the best food," he admitted.

"I'm glad to hear that you approve of our destination," Linc smiled. "It looked good when I viewed their net page."

"Almost fancy, even," Tony nodded. "Hotel ain't bad at all, either. I mean, if you was of a mind to stay overnight, that is," he added with yet another grin.

"That had crossed my mind," Linc nodded, hugging Meredith closer.

"You'll be safe enough on their grounds," Tony grew serious. "Do us all a favor though and *stay* on their grounds, okay? Once you get away from the lights around here you're in dangerous territory."

"We'll mind it," Meredith promised, not wanting a repeat of their 'stay' on Hartley Station. "What about you?"

"I'm as safe as if I was in my mother's arms," Tony scoffed. "Everyone loves me. Haven't got an enemy in the world!"

"I'm sure," Linc snorted lightly. "Just ensure you take your own advice, Tony," Linc ordered as he and Meredith came to a halt before their destination. "We've become accustomed to your being around."

"Yes, dad," Tony sighed. "You two behave," he laughed, and headed on down the boardwalk, deeper into town.

"There are times I wonder about him," Meredith admitted, watching the younger man depart.

"I do too," Linc admitted. "But I'm not prepared to look a gift horse in the mouth. His presence is a real comfort sometimes. And his cooking is a comfort *all* the time."

"I can cook," Meredith protested mildly.

"Of course you can, dear," Linc nodded smoothly. "It's just that your time is far too important to be wasted slaving over a hot stove. That's all."

"Lincoln, I think you've just insulted me," Meredith's eyes narrowed slightly.

"If you have to think about it, it probably isn't accurate," Linc told her. "Now, let's investigate the famous Silver Dollar rib-eye buffet."

"That's a real thing?" Meredith asked.

"On a moon where the cows grow, it apparently is."

"Then lead on, sir," Meredith ordered, insults to her cooking forgotten.

"This way, my lady."

-

"You think Cap'n's husband 'll get his sight back?"

Sean had to think a minute before he realized that Faulks had just asked him a question. They hadn't spoken more than was absolutely necessary since The Incident, which is what everyone had settled on calling it apparently, capital letters and all.

"What?" he looked up, managing to hide the surprise on his face.

"Think Lincoln will get his sight back?" Faulks repeated, still laboring to move another crate into position.

"Uh, he can see now," Sean temporized, moving to get another load. "Just can't focus is all. Not like he should be able to anyway."

"What I meant," Faulks nodded, sliding the crate into place finally. She stood and stretched her back, then moved to get another. "He can't get that fixed, what happens?"

"I don't know," Sean admitted. "I mean; I guess they'll need to hire a pilot."

"Still set on leavin' then?" Faulks asked, catching him by surprise yet again. He looked at her for a moment, wondering what angle she was working.

"Yes," he admitted finally. "I'll wait until we hit Halcyon again, though. Leave there."

"You know, there ain't no real need o' you goin', right?" Faulks didn't quite hassle with exertion as she moved a heavy crate by hand.

"Faulks, what the hell is this?" Sean demanded, stopping to look at the former Marine askance.

"What you mean?" she replied. She didn't stop, in fact wasn't even looking at him as she levered another crate into place. "Just sayin'."

"There's no real way I can stay here," he finally answered, returning to work. "Someone will let slip who I am, sooner or later. When they do, people will be after me. Anyone around me will be in danger."

"Who's after you?" Faulks did look at him this time, puzzlement on her face. "I know I was," she raised a hand to forestall his comment, "but that was personal. There's no reward out for you anymore."

"You think you're the only one who'd like to take down The Stormcrow?" Sean asked her flatly. "And reward or no, I'm still considered a war criminal as far as I know."

"I hadn't heard that," Faulks frowned. "Are you sure?"

"What I heard, anyway," Sean shrugged as if it made him no difference, which it didn't.

"Where did you hear that?" Faulks pressed slightly. "Just 'cause someone said it don't make it real," she pointed out.

"Ah. . ." He paused. There was no good way to explain how he'd come across the information.

"Oh," Faulks got it at once. "Well, I guess there could be some want on you somewhere, but I try, or tried, to keep up with that sort of stuff, and I ain't never seen it. And no one on this ship will rat you out, either," she added, fighting to keep the defensiveness out of her tone.

"Wasn't an accusation that someone would do it deliberately," Sean shook his head. "Stuff just happens to me, that's all. And accidental or deliberate, someone figuring out who I am will elicit a negative response. One where some of you could get hurt, or killed. I don't put others in a place where harm could come to them because of me."

"That's well and good," Faulks agreed, grunting as she hefted another container. "But you run that risk no matter where you are or where you go. Ain't no point in trading the devil you know for one you don't. You're as safe here as you would be anywhere else. Maybe safer in a way, since we'll all be more careful what we say on account of we know who you are."

Sean considered that for a minute before answering. It was a point he'd not thought of before. Of course, he'd never been in a position or place where people knew who he was and could be trusted not to sell him out. Did he have that now?

No, he didn't think so. Faulks might be okay right now, but eventually she'd revert to type and when she did she would turn him in. She knew she couldn't take him herself, but she would call someone else. That might result in someone he liked getting hurt. Tony had become a good friend, something Sean had precious few of. The thought of either him or Lincoln being hurt or killed by a team sent to capture or eliminate him didn't sit well in any way. Faulks or the Captain he honestly couldn't say he'd shed any tears over, though he didn't want Lincoln to have to go through that kind of pain.

"That sounds nice, but things rarely work out that well in real life, Faulks," he replied finally. "Something usually goes wrong, down the line."

"Yeah, Murphy has a way of showing up when you least expect it, that's for sure," Faulks nodded. "But think about this, okay? Now that I know what I know, I agree that what you did was called for. I admit I might not have done it that way, but it wasn't my family. I ain't really got no family, to be honest," she admitted suddenly. "That was why the loss of some of them hurt so much I guess. The Corps was all the family I ever really had. I only left to follow the Cap'n. You may or may not know, but she risked her life to save mine on the *Celeste*. Compartment I was in vented into vacuum and by rights she should have slammed the hatch in my face. Instead, she hooked herself to a gear line and came inside to haul my big ass out of there and onto the bridge." She paused, looking at him.

"You don't forget something like that."

"No, I'd say not," Sean nodded. "And I don't blame you for being loyal to her for that, either. My people understood loyalty. Family. None of us would ever need an explanation beyond that for whatever you'd done."

"Anyway," Faulks returned to work, "all I'm saying is that here, you already know the people. You know you're appreciated, too. I know me and you ain't been friends, but I figure that's more me than you. I'm an asshole. Always have been. Always figured I had something to prove I guess. So I act domineering and lord my size and ability over others as a way of hiding that need to prove myself, I suppose. I imagine a shrink 'd have a field day with me," she snorted.

"You know the ship, know the kinks of the engines and the systems in a way that would take a new man months to learn. And you already proved you're handy to have in times of trouble. Thing I'm saying is that everyone here appreciates that, including me." She stopped again, looking at him.

"I let the Cap'n down, Galen," she admitted flatly. "She depended on me, or tried to, and I flat out let her down. She should have been able to depend on me keeping this bay and the cargo straight, and having a good workin' relationship with the folks we see regular, and just generally helping her run a taut ship. Instead, I was my usual self and made things hard on me, her, hell the whole ship and crew."

"I'm tryin' to make up for that," she continued. "That means I do things that's best for the ship and the crew, period. And the best thing for this ship, and this crew, is that you stay aboard. So I'm tellin' you, flat out, that I'd never sell you out or rat you out. It would hurt the ship, and the Cap'n. More than that, I'll tell you this; anyone ever does come for you, I'll be right there beside you fightin' 'em. Don't really figure you need the help, mind you," she chuckled darkly, "but I'm the crew chief. That makes every single person on this boat my responsibility. And I don't aim to let that slide no more." She hefted one of the last crates up into her arms and started moving away.

"Just something for you to think on, okay?" she said over her shoulder.

"Okay," Sean replied, more from a lack of knowing what else to say than anything else.

But his mind was working. Could he stay and still be reasonably safe? Was Faulks on the up and up? If she was, then staying here would be much better than trying to start over somewhere else. He really did like the ship and the people, for the most part.

Maybe he'd talk to Lincoln about it. And Tony.

He needed the opinion and viewpoint of someone else for something like this.

Meanwhile, he still had work to do.

CHAPTER EIGHTEEN

"Mister Anthony, you have some messages from home," 'Tuttle' said with a smile. "There's a private terminal in that room," he pointed to a door off of his private office. "It's completely clean, sir. Is there anything else I can do for you this evening?" The dapper man showed no sign of irritation at having been called out in the evening time. 'Mister Anthony' and his family were his sole client, after all.

"Yes, there is," Tony avoided sighing in resignation at the thought of 'messages from home'. "I need you to do some research for me if you don't mind. There's no rush, I won't need it for at least a few days, maybe a week. I won't be here that long, but you can reach me here," he handed over a card with his own private netmail address.

"Of course," 'Tuttle' nodded, accepting the card and placing it in a small brief on his desk. He took a pen and waited.

"I need you to see if there are any ophthalmologists, and I mean good ones, on Halcyon. They'll need to be able to repair damage to the optic nerve caused by swelling in the occipital lobe due to blunt force trauma that resulted in a Grade Three concussion. The patient is suffering from advanced depth perception problems and a degradation of visual acuity. It's possible the problem was pre-existing and simply aggravated by the injury. I need to know if there's an ophthalmologist on Halcyon capable of diagnosing and treating that kind of problem. If there's more than one, I want the best one. And by best I mean I want the absolute best, regardless of what it takes to get him. Got all that?" Tuttle was scribbling furiously, nodding as he did so.

"Yes sir," he said as he finished. "You require the services of a first rate ophthalmologist that can diagnose and treat a visual acuity problem that may or may not have been caused by mild TBI, or that was aggravated by the injury to the point of realization. You want top quality only, and will do whatever it takes to have the best possible physician."

"Outstanding," Tony smiled. "I can forward them scans and records of the injury and the progression of recovery up to this point. When you have it, just message me with the information and I can contact them myself if they require it. In fact, that might be best, all things considered, once your firm has laid the groundwork for me. Can do?"

"Of course, sir," Tuttle made some additional notes. "We'll take care of it."

"Thanks," Tony smiled. "Now, I'll take care of the messages."

"If you need anything, let me know," 'Tuttle' replied. "I'll be here as long as I'm needed."

"Appreciate it," Tony nodded, moving to the doorway and entering the small but comfortable room. He accessed the portal there and made himself comfortable as the messages loaded and went through decryption. The first one was from his mother.

"Anthony, you could at least take the time to let your mother know that you are well," she said at once, a frown marring her normally beautiful features. "I realize that you need your space and all that, but I don't think it's asking too much of you to call me once in a blue moon just to tell me you're okay and that you love your mother," she smiled finally. "I worry about you, my sweet boy. Please don't bother telling me not to. I'm fully aware that you are a grown man, but you are still my *bambino*, and I will always worry for you." She paused for a moment before continuing.

"I know that you were upset by what transpired my son, and I assume you still are," she said in a softer tone. "Your father still reacts poorly every time it's mentioned and I...I think he has taken some retaliatory steps because of the poor treatment you received. I tried to tell him you would not want that, that you would prefer to deal with it on your own, but. . .he feels responsible, and I suppose in a way he is. You know he would never purposely do anything to hurt you, Antonio. I know he was never good at saying so, but he was so very proud of you for striking out on your own. He admired you greatly and still does for making your own way." She grinned slightly suddenly.

"I think he wishes he had done the same, to be honest. He lives vicariously through you, I sometimes believe. And, strictly between you and I, I sometimes think that he wishes your brothers and sister would act in such a manner."

"At any rate, please let me hear from you on occasion, would you? Surely it's not too much to ask. I promise I will not implore you to return home or any other such thing. I simply want to see your face, hear your voice, and go to sleep at night knowing that you are safe and happy. I love you Antonio." She placed a hand to her lips and then blew a kiss at the camera before killing the feed.

Tony wiped at his eyes to dispel a sudden dampness there. He hadn't realized how much he missed his mother. He never did until he saw her like this. He resolved that he would record a message for her before he left the office and then opened the next one. From his father.

"Antonio, I hope you are well," his father said, perhaps not as stiffly as he normally would have. "Your mother misses you, my son. You should at least send her a message even if you can't take the time to call her direct." Unspoken was the condemnation that he should certainly be able to spare the time to speak to the woman who had given him birth and nurtured him.

"I've never said I'm sorry for what happened to you, but I am," his father continued after a minute. "I've also never told you how very proud of you I am for being your own man. I've often wished I'd had the same courage. Alas, I did not and so here I am," he smiled sadly. Tony almost smiled as his father admitted to exactly what his mother had just said in her own message.

"I have. . .taken steps to rectify the situation you were faced with," his father's voice turned business-like. "I am aware that you are capable of dealing with your own issues," the older man's image raised a hand as if to forestall some comment his son might make. "That is irrelevant to this situation because it was because of me that your problems arose." He leaned forward, placing his elbows on the desk before him.

"Should you desire to do so, my son, you will be able to return and complete your studies without further interference. I will not presume to tell you what to do, or what you should do. That decision is your own to make, as it ever was. I simply wanted you to know that door was open for you should you desire to go through it. I realize, based on your travels, that you may no longer have such a desire, and I will respect and honor whatever decision you should make."

"Know that I am proud of you," Jerome Delgado drew himself up straighter in his chair. "I am proud that you are my son, and I am sorry that being my son has ever caused you a moment's heartache. Could I change it, I would, regardless of the cost to me. As I cannot, I have done what I could to rectify the situation, and ensure that it will not happen again."

"Call your mamma, son, and let her know you are well. You may always call me as well," he added with a genuine smile. "I will always be glad to hear from you. I will always love you. Good travels to you, my boy."

Again Tony found himself wiping at his eyes. His father had rarely spoken to him so frankly before. The other messages were from various women he had known, one from an old classmate who wanted to know how he was, and one from his broker concerning his trust. He returned that one, left a message for two of the several women, the only two he cared to ever see again, and ignored the rest.

He then spent a half hour recording a message for his mother and father, assuring them that he was in fact well, that he was not only in good health by but good company, and had found a place where he was happy. He also promised to keep in better contact and to visit at some point when he was closer to the Sphere than he was at the moment. Finally, he signed off and stood, his legs stiff from having sat for so long. He made sure he had everything and then left the small room, back to 'Tuttle's' office.

“Everything satisfactory, sir?” the attorney asked.

“Fine,” Tony nodded amiably. “I've another favor, though it may not be one you can help with. If not that's okay, just let me know. I want to find a cargo heading from Halcyon into the Sphere. As near Lucia as possible, but it doesn't have to be there specifically. It needs to be a good job, but. . .you know what, just see what you can find and then message me. I'll take care of the rest. Is that something you can deal with?”

“Of course,” Tuttle was scribbling again. “I manage shipments for the family all the time, leaving here for. . .well, everywhere.”

“Do we have actual holdings here or simply acquiring and reselling?” Tony asked, aware that he should already know that. “I've been out of touch for a bit,” he admitted with a shrug.

“The company does maintain a facility here for processing beef and finer pork products,” Tuttle supplied. “There's also a ranch among the holdings, though it's nothing like as large as most here. It's primarily a breeding facility, specializing in prize-winning breeding stock for others.”

“I wasn't aware of that,” Tony shook his head with a wry grin. “Last time I was here; I was more interested in the night life.”

“It is lively here at times, sir,” Tuttle smiled knowingly. “What else can I do for you this evening?”

“Nothing, Mister Tuttle, and I sincerely appreciate your taking time to meet me here off hours,” Tony offered his hand. “I can't say what good it will do, but I will put in a good word for you after the courtesy you've shown me this evening.”

“I appreciate that, sir,” 'Tuttle' beamed, shaking Tony's hand. “We're here to serve.”

“Good evening, then,” Tony took his leave. Stepping out onto the street he took a deep breath and let it out slowly. The air here was cleaner than anywhere in the Sphere, save maybe his home of Lucia. His father maintained a strict management policy of clean air and water that was rigidly enforced. After some of the things he'd seen in his travels, Tony was more appreciative of his father's efforts.

He needed to tell his father that, it hit him suddenly. He needed to tell his father many things, in fact, as well as his mother. He might even talk to his siblings, though at the moment that was still out.

Whistling happily, he set out to find himself some entertainment among Elvy's not inconsiderable night life.

-

"That's it," Faulks said tiredly as she placed the last cargo-tainer in place and strapped it down. "Thanks, Galen," she added while she worked. "You hadn't helped; I'd have been down here all night."

"Glad to do it," Sean told her, surprised to find he meant it. "I need to check on the water," he added. "You got this?"

"Already done but for sweeping, and I got that," Faulks nodded. "I'm just gonna check the tie-downs first and then clean up and square away. We'll be getting a load before morning."

"Gotta love steady work," Galen nodded.

His mind was turning over what Faulks has said, weighing the pros and cons. Working with Faulks tonight had been an eye-opening experience. While it might be an act, she appeared to have had some kind of revelation. Maybe this time the Captain had really gotten through to her, he didn't know.

He did know that she was right about one thing. Staying here was preferable to starting over somewhere else yet again. Especially if he could trust the rest to stay quiet about his past. And it was in their best interest to do so.

He decided again that he'd talk to Tony and Lincoln about it before he decided one way or another. He trusted Tony as much as he did anyone in the galaxy, and he liked and respected Lincoln. Their opinion would be weighed into what he already knew before he made a decision.

-

"Good grief," Meredith groaned as she pushed her plate across the table from her and leaned back. "If we lived here I'd weigh three hundred pounds in a year."

"And I'd still love you," Lincoln promised, still working on his last steak. Last as in 'last of three' wonderfully cooked rib-eye beef steaks. Accompanied by fresh fried potatoes and preceded by a salad with all fresh ingredients and an in-house dressing.

"Liar," Meredith grinned. She was very happy at the moment. Having an issue, any issue, hanging between her and her husband had been worrisome to her. So long as the two of them were on the same page, the rest of the world could be collapsing and she could deal with it.

"Am not," Lincoln looked mildly offended, though it wasn't enough to stop him from taking another bite of steak.

"How can you still be eating?" Meredith demanded, eyes wide.

"I'm hungry," Linc replied easily, as if that explained everything.

"Well, assuming you ever get done eating, what's next on your agenda?" Meredith asked, leaning forward again and resting her elbows on the table.

"There are two options," Linc smiled. "We can go to their theater, where there is a production of Swan Lake, of all things, being performed by a local amateur group, or. . ." he smiled then popped the last piece of steak into his mouth, "or, we can go to our room and make out. After a soak in a spa tub. A private spa tub with water jets and whirlpool."

"Really?" Meredith asked, eye brows raised.

"Really," Linc slid his own plate away. "Just for you my queen," he added with a smile.

"I don't deserve you," Meredith said softly, her left hand moving to stroke his cheek gently.

"You really don't," Linc replied deadpan, "but since you have me, there's no point in worrying over that. Your choice, milady. What's it going to be?"

"I've never been a fan of theater," Meredith said, standing slowly and holding her hand out to her husband. "I think I'll take option two."

"Door two it is," Linc took her hand as he stood. He paused long enough to leave a tip for their waitress and then the two of them walked toward the room he'd already reserved.

It was looking like a pretty good night after all.

-

Jessica Travers tossed once more on her bunk as she tried unsuccessfully to get to sleep. There was no good reason that she couldn't sleep other than. . .well, that she couldn't. It didn't make sense considering how tired she was.

She tried fluffing her pillows and re-situating herself on the bed, but with no more luck than before. While comfortable, sleep simply was not going to come. Finally, she got up, put on her night coat and stepped out into the passageway, moving quietly down to the galley.

She stopped in the doorway when she saw Sean Galen sitting at the table, reading. He looked up as she entered and frowned slightly, though it disappeared in an instant.

"Something wrong?" he asked, closing the book and marking his page with a finger. The move was oddly familiar to her.

"My father used to do that," she said wistfully, nodding to his hand. "And no, nothing's wrong, other than I can't sleep." She came forward and sat down at her usual spot.

"Excited to see your family I'm sure," Galen nodded, laying the book aside after placing a book mark. "You've been gone a long time."

"Yes, I have," her voice took on that wistful tone yet again. "But it will be worth it."

"Five years is a long time," Galen nodded again, his mind working. Was he under her influence somehow? If so, was it chemically induced? Or had she slipped something into the food while she was helping Tony in the kitchen. Why hadn't that occurred to him before now?

"Is sure is," Jessica didn't notice his ruminations. "But there was no other way, you see? I had to go into the Mid-terior in order to get my teaching degree. That was the only way for me to get where I wanted to be."

"Always wanted to be a teacher?" Galen asked, his senses working overtime as he asked simple questions.

"I don't know about always," Jess smiled. "For a while I wanted to be a pirate, until I realized what that actually meant. Then I wanted to be miner, like my father, so I could have a helmet with a light on it. Then, once I was along in school, I saw how not having a proper education was hurting people on my world. Keeping them down, you know? That was when I decided I could help more people as a teacher than I could as a miner, or certainly as a pirate, even one like *RazorRick*," she laughed.

"I don't know who that is," Sean admitted, frowning. "Is he an outlaw where you hail from?"

"You're kidding, right?" Jess looked shocked. "*RazorRick* was only the most handsome and debonair space pirate ever in the history of the known universe! Always helping the oppressed, stealing from powerful barons and thieves to help those less fortunate. How could you not know who *RazorRick* is?"

"Wait, are we talking about some kind of vid show?" Sean asked.

"Well of course!" Jess smiled.

"We didn't have anything like that," he shrugged, realizing finally why he didn't recognize the reference. "We spent our time learning and doing. He sounds like a nice enough fellow," he added as Jess continued to frown.

"Wow, I can't imagine how boring it must have been without *RazorRick*," Jessica shook her head.

"Trust me, it wasn't boring," Sean laughed lightly. "We worked, we played, we had lessons of all kinds every day and most every night."

"What kind of lessons?" Jessica leaned forward, interested.

"Hunting, tracking, other skills," Sean shrugged. "And we had school lessons of course," he added. "We were well trained."

"You make is sound like a rite of passage, the way you say that," Jessica laughed.

"Just the ways of our people," Sean replied carefully. He had been about to say 'that comes later on', but caught himself. He was more and more convinced that Jessica had some kind of hidden ability to influence other people. Whether she was aware of it or not he still wasn't sure. But now that he knew it, he could guard against it.

"Well, I'm going to get some warm milk and then try again to get some sleep," Jess said suddenly, standing. "Good night, Galen."

"Night," Sean nodded, watching her go into the galley. "I'm turning in myself," he added, getting to his feet. He went to his own cabin without waiting for her to return.

-

"*RazorRick*?" Tony looked confused.

"That's what she said," Sean nodded absently as he continued to work on a water valve that had become stuck while the water tank was being filled. It was still early but Tony had returned just after sunrise. Faulks had already supervised the loading of the new cargo and they were only waiting on Lincoln and Meredith to get back into space.

"I never heard of it either," Tony admitted with a shrug. "Sure it wasn't a local thing?"

"No idea," Sean shrugged, finally succeeding in closing the valve to the water circulation unit. "I never watched any of that stuff, so I got no clue."

"Well, I watched some shows, but I don't recall that one."

"Which one?" Lincoln's voice floated down the passageway. The two looked up to see the pilot saunter into the engine room. "What one, for that matter?" he asked with a smile. "How are you two doing this morning?"

"Good here," Tony answered with a grin of his own.

"Same here," Sean agreed, sans grin. "We were talking about a show that Jessica said she used to watch as a kid that made her want to be a pirate before she was a teacher."

"Yeah?" Lincoln's eyebrow rose. "Which show?" he asked, leaning against the hatchway.

"Something called *RazorRick*?" Sean said over his shoulder as he put his tools away. He wasn't looking so he missed the color draining from Lincoln's face. Tony didn't.

"What is it, bossman?" Tony asked, frowning.

"Are you sure that's what she said?" Lincoln asked. "*RazorRick*? Stole from the rich and gave it to the poor? That kind of thing?"

"Yeah, as a matter of fact," Sean had turned around. "Why? You heard of it? Neither of us have."

"That's because the show is at least forty years old," Linc said softly.

"Say who now?" Tony looked confused.

"*RazorRick* was on when I was a kid," Linc told them flatly. "And I'm a hell of a lot older than Jess Travers. The show has to be nearly a half-century old. And it wasn't on that long. Maybe three years, if I remember right."

"She must have seen it on a rerun, then," Sean offered, despite the hair rising on the back of his neck.

"No," Linc shook his head. "The reason it went off the air was that someone complained that it was anti-government, which it was, really. *RazorRick* was based on a number of other tales that all traced back to earth and the story of Robin of Locksley. Robin Hood, you probably heard him called."

"So, it got canceled for that?" Tony asked.

"And destroyed," Lincoln nodded. "It was overreaching by a long mile, to be honest," he said grimly. "Led to a series of court decisions that limited the central government's power for the next quarter of a century. Probably held off the Frontier War by at least that long, too, since it put a halt to the moves the Commonwealth was making on the Frontier Rim and among even some Mid-Terior worlds. One of the decisions involved the Commonwealth's seizing all of the *RazorRick* material and destroying it as subversive because it was teaching children to defy the government."

"So how could she have seen it then?" Tony asked.

"She shouldn't have," Lincoln said softly. "No older than she is, there's no real way she could have seen it on any legal station."

"Maybe someone had it recorded from home and she saw it there," Tony offered.

"That's possible, but not likely," Lincoln shook his head. "Possession of anything the Commonwealth labeled 'subversive' back then carried a hard penalty with it."

"Fines? Imprisonment? What?" Tony asked.

"Death in some cases," Lincoln's answer surprised both younger men. "Like I said, it was a bad time. The case concerning *RazorRick* set the Commonwealth back on its ass for a long time, but they'd already destroyed the show and its creators. At the time anyone caught in possession of the show would have automatically been declared subversive and arrested. It's unlikely anyone would have chanced it. Too risky."

"Then how could she have seen it as a kid?" Sean asked. "She was young, maybe five I guess, the way she talked about it. And she was pretty adamant about it being the show that made her want to be a pirate when she was a kid."

"She couldn't have," Lincoln said flatly. "I mean, there's always the possibility that someone had a bootleg copy, but. . .I really can't see anyone taking that chance, guys. It was a different time and people were afraid of the government."

"With good reason, apparently," Tony's voice was hard. "That's a bunch of shit, right there, Lincoln!"

"I agree," Lincoln raised his hands in supplication. "Hell, I liked the show, myself."

"The show being confiscated ain't the problem, Tony," Sean's voice took on a hard edge. "The problem is how the hell she saw it as a kid, as if it was a current show. According to Lincoln, the show was destroyed before she was ever born!"

-

Unaware that she was once again the subject of an intense discussion among the male members of the crew, Jessica Travers sat in the pilot's seat on the bridge of the *Celia*, preparing for the ship's departure. As she ran through the pre-flight check list she became aware of a presence behind her and turned to see Meredith Simmons looking at her from the hatchway.

"Good morning, Captain," she smiled easily. "Did you have a good evening?"

"I did indeed," Meredith nodded, walking onto the bridge. "Did you manage to get any rest?"

"Finally," Jess sighed, returning to her work. "I tossed and turned for a long time but finally got to sleep."

"One more lift-off and re-entry and you'll be home, Jess," Meredith said softly, a slight smile gracing her lips. "I know it's taken a long time, but you're almost there. And I have to admit I'm glad you were here. I don't know what we'd have done without you."

"Without me, you wouldn't have needed me," Jess pointed out at once, though she didn't stop working this time. "All of the trouble you had was caused by my presence, Captain. And I cannot tell you enough how sorry I am for that, either."

"That's not really accurate, Jessica," Meredith said evenly. "That could have happened to any of us, at any time. The real problem was my attitude toward Sean Galen. I had no business being upset to start with, let alone pushing him so hard. That was entirely on me. If I hadn't done that, he wouldn't have been leaving the ship, we wouldn't have needed a new engineer, and we wouldn't have been on the station to be taken in the first place."

"And the irony, of course, is that Galen offered to stay aboard to help get his own replacement situated before leaving, so he was still here when the call came to the ship. If he hadn't been, I don't like to think about our chances of being rescued."

"He never suggested not doing it," Jessica nodded. "He left the decision in Tony's hand because Tony was technically the only member of the crew on the ship since he'd quit, but he was ready to lend a hand to whatever Tony wanted to do."

"I know," Meredith nodded, staring out the screen without really looking at anything. "And, like you, I can't tell him I'm sorry, or thank you, enough times for it to be sufficient. He saved all three of us when we had no right of any kind to expect his help. Especially me," she added ruefully.

"Or Faulks," Jessica reminded her, but grinned over her shoulder to rob the words of any sting. "And it seems as if the two of them have buried the hatchet. I mean, without actually burying it in each other's heads," she added with a laugh.

"That is something else to be thankful for," Meredith gave a similar chuckle. "And I'm glad for it. Maybe between here and Halcyon Galen will decide to stay after all. That would make me very happy."

"You should tell him that, then," Jessica suggested.

"I have, more than once," Meredith reminded her.

"Doesn't hurt to get another plug in whenever you can," Jessica shrugged.

"I suppose that's true," Meredith sighed. "I'll look for an opportunity to try again. Meanwhile," she turned business like, "how close are we to lifting off?"

"About another ten minutes or so and we'll be a ready fifteen, once we get our clearance," Jess replied absently. "That shouldn't take too long, I should think," she added.

"The new freight is already secured, so once you've finished, go ahead and request clearance. Once you get it, make the announcement and prepare to get us airborne. Sooner we're on our way, the sooner you're home again."

"Yes, ma'am!"

-

Faulks happened to be at the ramp when the vehicle drifted by the *Celia*. Five men were in the open air hover bed, scanning the ships along the pad. There weren't many, but she knew two had already departed with the morning and from the chatter on the radio there were at least two more in the queue on their way in. A place like Liberty Vale had ships in and out and at all hours pretty much non-stop, ferrying foodstuffs all over this side of the galaxy.

The former Marine's eyes narrowed as she took in the five men. They were so obviously up to no good that they may as well have been wearing signs declaring 'we steal shit'. Without taking her eyes from the vehicle she reached for the I/C unit near the ramp.

"Cap'n, we maybe got a problem comin'," she said calmly. "There's a truck out here with at least five men in it, giving all the ships a once over. No sign of any business markings or uniforms, either. If I was a gambler, I'd say they're lookin' for someone or something to roll."

"Close the ramp, Faulks," Meredith ordered at once. "We're about ready to lift, in any case." Even as the Captain issued the order, Faulks knew it was too late. The hover bed whirled around, heading straight for the *Celia*.

"May be too late, ma'am," Faulks informed her Captain, though she activated the ramp anyway. "They're headed this way at a good pace."

"I'm on the way," Meredith said.

"Ma'am you should stay put," Sean Galen's voice came across the channel before Faulks could suggest the same thing. "Me and Tony are almost there, Faulks," he added for the 'Chief's' benefit.

"Better get a move on or you'll miss it," Faulks told him lightly, though she hoped the other two would arrive before the truck. A show of force might be enough to stop whatever thoughts that bunch had.

The ramp closed slowly. It seemed to Faulks as if it closed far slower than was normal, but there was absolutely nothing she could do to speed things up. The ramp was only half closed when the hover bed zoomed up the *Celia* and the thugs jumped out, brandishing weapons.

"Hold it right there!" one of them called, aiming a shotgun in Faulks' general direction. She cursed herself for not having a gun on. She had decided against it because they were leaving soon. Too late, she realized that was a mistake on Liberty Vale.

"Sorry, can't stop it!" Faulks called out, moving away from the opening to put distance between her and the attackers. "Best stand back, we're lifting!" she added, hoping that fear of being caught in the engine's wash would hold them back.

"You're not lifting anywhere before we che-"

The man had been in the process of raising a shotgun to his shoulder, intent on shooting Faulks if he couldn't intimidate her into holding the ramp. So intent, in fact, that he failed to realize it when two other figures joined her near the cargo ramp.

Faulks jumped at the sound of a gunshot in such close confines and her head snapped around to see Tony Giannini standing nearby with a pistol in hand, smoke rising lazily from the barrel. By the time she looked back to the shotgun wielding thug, he was on the ground, already dead.

Another shot followed, then a third, and then there was a volley of fire and Faulks sought cover as bullets pinged off the hull and the ramp. By the time she had gotten out of the line of fire, it was over.

All five would-be attackers lay dead or dying on the ground behind the ship. Sean Galen was beside the medic, a pistol in his hand as well as both men covered the ramp until it sealed.

"Green light, good seal!" Tony shouted into the com unit. "We're clean!"

"We're moving," Jessica's voice came to them at once. "Find a seat, this might be bumpy."

"I have to get back to the engine room," Galen told his friend, heading that way at a run.

"I got this," Tony nodded. "Go!" He turned to Faulks.

"You hit, Faulks?" he asked, extending a hand to her to help her up.

"Just my pride," she shook her head, accepting his hand and allowing him to pull her up. "I should have had a gun on, but didn't because we were leaving. Didn't think I'd need it," she shook her head again, this time in chagrin. "What I get for thinkin'," she added wryly.

"Ah," Tony waved her comment away. "Stupid *cazzos*," he murmured. "What the hell were they thinking, trying to board a transport about to lift off?"

"They were just thieves, I think," Faulks shrugged. "They drove down the line looking around and saw the ramp open, then headed straight for us. I should have already closed the ramp," she sighed, shaking her head once more. "This was on me."

"Like hell," Tony shot back. "Those dumb shits shouldn't have been out tryin' to steal to start with. You sure you ain't hit?"

"No, I'm good," Faulks assured him. "Just embarrassed."

"What the hell happened?" Meredith's voice cut across the bay. Both crew members looked up to see their boss standing on the landing overlooking the cargo bay, hands on her hips. Lincoln appeared behind her just seconds later.

Faulks quickly and concisely ran through the encounter just as if she were making an after action report. Meredith listened without interruption until Faulks ended her report by taking responsibility for the attack.

"That's bullshit," Lincoln said at once and Meredith nodded her agreement. "They were here to steal or worse and no one on this ship is responsible for that. You stow that, right now, Faulks. This was not your fault."

"See?" Tony gloated, turning to look at Faulks again. "Tony is always right. Always listen to Tony."

"Don't be a wiseass," Faulks muttered, but smiled slightly as she said it.

"Faulks!" Tony feigned shock, grabbing his chest theatrically. "You smiled! Captain, we should land immediately!" he turned to Meredith.

"Why is that?" Meredith asked, fighting a grin.

"If Faulks is smiling, the world may well be ending. We don't want to be in space for that. We need to be on the ground. Where there are bars!"

Meredith lost her battle with the grin at that point and laughed, Lincoln's laughter echoing her own. Faulks' face reddened slightly, but soon she was laughing as well.

"Now that we've established that Tony is always right, I need to get to the kitchen," the medic declared. "You're sure you're all right?" he checked, turning to Faulks one last time.

"Positive, you nutter," Faulks nodded. "Thanks."

"Hey, just doing my job," Tony raised a hand as if to ward off her 'thank you'. "Anyway, I got grub to work on, if you lot will excuse me."

He was already climbing the stairs and soon disappeared down the passageway toward the galley. Meredith waited for Faulks to follow him up to the landing.

"You okay?" she asked, checking on more than Faulks' physical well-being.

"Just embarrassed at being caught out," Faulks promised.

"Well, it's a reminder that we can't be too careful next time we come back here," Meredith shrugged. "Don't let it bother, and we'll all learn from it. That's all."

"So we're gonna come back?" Faulks asked.

"We may well," her Captain nodded thoughtfully. "It's a good run with good pay. A regular route with solid, dependable income. There's not many downsides to that arrangement, attacks by stupid thieves aside."

"Agreed," Lincoln nodded. "I'll contact the Port Authority and tell them what happened." He left, heading for the bridge.

"Call the broker instead!" Meredith called after him. "He can probably take care of it, and he works for the port and most of the shippers. There shouldn't be any trouble for an attempted act of piracy."

"Will do," Linc's voice drifted back to them.

"I'm sorry, Cap'n," Faulks took a deep breath. "I should have already had us closed up, and should have been armed. Won't happen again," she promised.

"Good enough," Meredith nodded simply. "Get yourself cleaned up and get some rest. I know you worked late into the night. We're well away now so there's nothing that needs doing that can't wait."

"Aye, Cap'n."

CHAPTER NINETEEN

"I'm still not seeing the significance of the cartoon thing," Tony admitted. He and Lincoln were sequestered in the infirmary where Tony had just finished running a scan on Linc's concussion site.

"What do you mean?" Linc asked.

"Why destroy a cartoon? What the hell kind of threat can a cartoon be to anyone?"

"Children shows have always been a good way to indoctrinate future citizens," Linc pointed out. "If they grow up believing in truth, justice and all that goes with it, then it's harder to convince them to go along with something that's not really legally or morally right."

"You mean the Frontier War," Tony said evenly as he put his tools away.

"Among other things, yes," Lincoln sighed. "The Frontier War shouldn't have happened. More than that, it shouldn't have been *able* to happen. The Commonwealth violated almost every article in the constitution to fight it and bring the Frontier Rim worlds 'under' Commonwealth dominance again. There were so many laws broken I wouldn't know where to begin in listing them."

"So why do it?" Tony asked, leaning against the counter now that he was finished. "Why not just refuse?"

"Some did," Linc surprised him. "Some retired, some were conscientious objectors, a term left over from the days before Earth even had a planetary government. Others refused orders to lead men, and some enlisted refused to participate. More than one good man was dishonorably discharged over it. Many a life ruined."

"Yeah, well, I'd say it went easier for them than it did for Sean's people," Tony's voice was acidic. "If the war wasn't legal, then why was if fought to start with?"

"Money," Linc said simply. "Most Rim worlds are settled by corporations or consortiums. They spend money, a lot of it in some cases, to settle worlds hoping they will be profitable. They exercise ownership rights over the whole world, which includes the people who settle there. When those people try to break away, form their own governments and enforce their own laws, the companies who have paid to settle those worlds start to lose out. They don't like that."

"So the conspiracy nuts are right," Tony looked shocked. "Corporations really do run the worlds. Run the government even."

"Not quite, but close in some cases," Linc admitted. "Money buys a lot of influence. And they have a lot of money."

"Well that's just dandy," Tony almost spat.

"So it is," Linc nodded. "And it's why I didn't hesitate to take my early retirement and follow Meredith. There's no honor in serving anymore."

"Then why did she fight so hard to stay in?" Tony asked.

"Meredith is an idealist," Linc shrugged. "She doesn't see how corrupt the Commonwealth is because she hasn't experienced it. She was doing what she had always dreamed of doing; commanding a naval vessel. It was her only dream as a kid and all she ever wanted to do with her life. The Commonwealth has the only real navy anywhere. A few of the larger, wealthier worlds have their own Defense Forces, but they're not much more than anti-smuggle or anti-pirate forces. That's not what she wanted."

"So she turned a blind eye to all that corruption because she had what she wanted?" Tony frowned. That didn't seem like the Captain he knew.

"No, she honestly doesn't see it," Linc was shaking his head. "Meredith believes in proof. If you can prove something, then she'll see it. Otherwise, she's not interested in what she considers 'gossip' and 'back chat'. Back room talking," he explained the term. "It's a military term mostly, used to describe back room deals and rumors of such. If she can't see proof, she ignores it as either unimportant or untrue."

"Convenient," Tony snorted lightly.

"No, just focused," Linc didn't take offense. "She worked hard to get where she was, and that took focus and determination. She had to keep focused on what was going on. It takes a lot of work to reach a point where you command a warship, even a corvette."

"Suppose so," Tony admitted, nodding. "Still, surely she can see it now," he added.

"If she looked, she probably could, but she's just as focused on the *Celia* as she was the *Celeste,*" Linc shrugged. "She doesn't have time to delve into speculation or chatter. At least the way she sees it she doesn't."

"Back to convenient, then," Tony sighed. "Well, I suppose it doesn't affect us, does it?"

"Not directly," Linc admitted. "Still leaves a bad taste in the mouth, though."

"Yeah."

-

Gateway was, as Faulks had so indelicately put it, a backwater dumping ground for those with strong backs and little education. For people who had questionable morals and a desire to avoid the more Law and Order interior worlds.

Alongside those less desirable however were people like Jessica's parents and the people they worked with. Some original settlers along with a large second generation, they worked the mines and smelters that accompanied them, delving deep into the ground to pull ore from the ground. That ore was then refined right there on the spot before being shipped inward.

Gateway made a tidy profit literally by the day for the conglomerate that had financed the exploration, terraforming and settlement of what so many, like Faulks, considered a dump.

But to Jessica Travers, Gateway was home. Her parents, her friends, her life, were on Gateway. She had been away for years, but now, seeing her home world growing in the screen before her, she felt a thrill she could not suppress.

"Home sweet home!" she breathed enthusiastically. "I'm almost home."

"That you are," Lincoln nodded from the navigation stations. "Ready, Mere?"

"Yes," Meredith nodded from the co-pilot's seat. She would be taking the *Celia* in to land this time, trying to make sure she could do it, or at least assist Lincoln with it, for the remainder of the trip. Tony had already learned a good deal and could assist Lincoln handily, but they needed more than one, as experience had taught them all too well.

"Anytime then, ladies," Lincoln said, leaning back. He wouldn't have much to do this time, unless something went wrong.

-

"So, Captain's gonna try and land us this time," Tony said as he sat at the table, sipping a cup of what he'd called 'Irish Coffee'. A brew of very strong coffee liberally laced with Irish cream liquor. Tasty and soothing for these trying times he lived in.

"She had pilot trainin' at the Academy," Faulks was confident as ever. "She'll do fine."

"Ever see her fly anything in the Navy?" Tony asked, both to create conversation and because he was interested.

"No, she was the ship's Captain by the time I came aboard," Faulks shook her head. "But she had the wings. Meant she'd qualified as a pilot. She can do it."

"I have no doubt," Tony smiled thinly as he lifted his cup to take another drink of liquid courage. "None at all.

-

"Looking good, Captain," Jessica nodded as she initiated the braking thrusters. "We're on the ball."

"Roger that," Meredith said tersely, concentrating on the job at hand.

"You're doing fine, hon," Linc encouraged from his station. "Way better than me, that's for sure."

"So long as we land without breaking anything, I'm happy," Meredith squeezed out as she fought the controls slightly.

"Thermals," Jessica said tonelessly. "Nothing to worry about, Captain. Let your grip loosen a bit and allow the ship to ride them out. You have the altitude and speed not to worry about them, so just let them roll over us as we move through. Ambient temperatures make solar wind conditions pretty harsh at times here in our little piece of heaven."

"So I noticed," Meredith gritted, continuing to fight the controls despite Jessica's admonition not to.

"Captain, loosen up and let the ship ride them out," Jessica repeated calmly. "There's no sense in fighting them because you can't win."

"It's easier to say it than do it," Meredith fought the urge to snarl, but managed to relax slightly. "How long will this last?" she demanded. Before Jessica could answer the ship seemed to steady.

"About that long," Jess smiled brightly. "We're slightly off track but within parameters. Come left ten degrees and steady up." Meredith made the required correction carefully.

"Excellent," Jessica nodded. "We're on the ball, Captain. Braking thrusters ready."

The rest of the trip down went far smoother than Meredith had anticipated as she managed to land with only a slight jolt to indicate she didn't have the feather touch that Jessica seemed to have.

"And that's it," Jessica said simply as she helped Meredith place the ship's systems into stand-by. "You know," she said wistfully as telltales began to indicate the ship was idling properly, "I'm going to miss this."

"Not too late to hire on," Lincoln told her seriously. "We definitely need a pilot. Hopefully just short term," he added with a wry smile. "We can make a run back here to get you home after say, a year?"

"No," Jess shook her head. "I've been gone too long as it is. As much as I'd love to do it, I want to be home more. There's so many people I haven't seen in so long I hardly know where to start."

"Well, let's start with getting our cargo delivered and then we'll see you home," Meredith stood. "You'll need help with your things, anyway."

"Thank you, Captain."

-

"Anywhere we can hire a lifter or pax sled around here, sir?" Lincoln asked the surly dock manager as the last of the Gateway bound cargo was off-loaded.

"What 'n hell ya wanna sled for?" he demanded, spitting a stream of brown liquid into the dust at his feet. "Ain't no tourist sites roun' here."

"We have a passenger who's from here to get home," Lincoln smiled easily. He had an easy way with people and his height made him hard to intimidate when there wasn't a gun to his back. Or head.

"Try the passenger terminal, then," the man waved vaguely toward a collection of ramshackle buildings in the distance. "They usually keep something around for that sort o' thing. Don't 'spect nothin' fancy, mind. We don't run to that roun' here."

"I'll keep that in mind, thank you," Linc nodded. He walked back up the ramp to the waiting collection of crew.

"We need to head over to the somewhat grandly named 'passenger terminal'," he pointed to the collection of buildings, little more than huts really, in the distance. "Our esteemed dock manager assures me that we can find some non-touristy, non-fancy transportation available there."

"Sorry," Jessica grinned nervously. "I know it's not much," she semi-apologized.

"Can't see how that bears on you," Tony shrugged. "One of us should go with Lincoln," he looked at Sean and Faulks.

"Sean," Meredith ordered calmly. "You go. Faulks will be in charge of the boat until we return, anyway. I don't want the ship unmanned here for any reason. We'll be on com the entire time," she told the boat 'chief'.

"Aye, Cap'n," Faulks nodded. If she was disappointed by not going along with the rest, it didn't show. "Girlie, it's been nice havin' ya aboard," she surprised everyone by telling Jessica. "I hope you can make a difference for your kids."

"Thank you Faulks," Jess smiled. "I really appreciate that."

"Mister Galen, let us away to the rental agency and secure transportation," Lincoln said lightly.

"Okay," was the simple reply as the engineer stepped off the ramp behind him.

"We'll be back shortly," Linc promised.

"Careful," Meredith ordered, receiving a wave in reply as the two headed off.

"Jess, I'll help you with your things," Tony offered.

"I don't have much," she reminded him shyly.

"That in no way negates my obligation to assist a lady with bearing her load," Tony bowed gallantly.

"Thank you," she smiled again, brightly, and the two headed away.

"I think she'll find she's got more'n she thought she did," Faulks commented once the two were out of ear shot.

"What do you mean?" Meredith asked, her gaze roving the outside visible from the ramp.

"Doc bought her some stuff," Faulks shrugged. "Pretty sure Galen did too, but I know Doc did. Got here a tablet and a nice satchel for it and to carry her schooling things in. I think Galen bought her a new dress or two, and at least one of 'em got her a new pair of shoes."

"Those two never stop surprising me," Meredith shook her head slowly. "I wish I'd thought of it," she admitted. "Jessica's been a lifesaver with Linc hurt."

"You gave her a ride home, ma'am," Faulks pointed out. "Free of charge for the most part. That ain't no small thing. She's likely still be trying to get here, not for you. And that assumes that nothing bad didn't happen to her on the way."

"I suppose," Meredith mused. "I hope she does well. And finds her parents okay."

-

"Hello," Lincoln said to the very unfortunate looking woman behind the grandiosely named 'travel counter' in the dock station. "We need to rent a conveyance, please. As many as five passengers and a small amount of baggage. We need it only for a few hours I think, but will pay for overnight rental to be sure," he smiled.

As he spoke, Galen was surveying the area around them. This place was about as rundown as it got, even for the Rim. He hadn't expected much of course, knowing it was a Frontier planet, but still. . .this was pretty bad.

It looked as if the planet was either arid or in the middle of a harsh drought, but he couldn't tell which. The fact that there was dust instead of sand suggested drought, but every planet was different in that regard, so even that fact wasn't an absolute indicator.

The one thing he was sure of was that this place was suffering from bone-crushing poverty. Again, he hadn't expected it to look like even a Mid-terior world like Halcyon, but. . .he had expected better than this. Jessica hadn't described things as being this bad. According to her the mines were fairly productive and while the people weren't getting rich, they weren't starving. He had already caught a few toughs eyeing him and Lincoln as if wondering if it would be worth it to try and take them for whatever they were carrying.

"We look like a rental agency to you, buddy?" the woman demanded from behind the counter.

"No ma'am, I understand there's no such facility here," Linc smiled broadly. "The dock manager simply said you might have something we could rent from you to deliver a passenger home. As I said, we'll pay for overnight use, just in case. If we get back today you can consider the extra as a surcharge, can't you?"

The woman glared at Linc for another minute before demanding to know where they were going.

"Ah, Sean, where are we going?" Linc asked, having neglected to ask.

"Shaletown," Sean said without looking around. "Place called Shaletown. Just outside it, I think, actually."

"Shaletown?" the woman frowned. "What in hell you want to go there for?"

"Our passenger is from there," Lincoln replied. "We're taking her home."

"Ain't hardly no one lives there I know of," the woman shook her head sadly. "Mine over there played out seven, maybe eight years back now. Ain't a tithe o' people left there now."

"Well, our passenger is one of them, or was," Linc shrugged, missing how Sean Galen came to attention at the news. "And will be again as soon as we can get her home."

"Ain't got nothing that can get you that far 'thout refueling, which ain't available nowhere 'tween here and there," she informed them after a moment of looking through the papers on her desk. "Best bet would be to just fly over there. Be there in ten, twenty minutes on your ship. Take near two days to drive it, the route you'd have to go to get fuel."

"I see," Lincoln nodded. "I confess I hadn't considered that. Do we need to file a flight plan in order to do that?"

"Here?" the woman snorted in derision. "Not hardly. Just don't hit nothin' on the way out. Or back in for that matter. You'll be fine."

"Thank you ma'am for you kind assistance," Lincoln bowed slightly. "I hope you have a day as lovely as you are." He turned and left with the woman still sputtering, Galen close behind him.

"This is all wrong," Galen said once they were outside and on their way back to the ship.

"I admit she might be the ugliest woman I've ever encountered, but I'm not-"

"I don't mean her," Galen cut Linc's sarcasm off in mid-stride. "This place look like what Jessica described on the way here?"

"Well, no, but this isn't where she's from, either," Linc reminded him.

"And the mine played out how long ago?" Galen pressed. "Jess said she's been gone five years. If that mine played out seven or eight years ago, then she would have known it. Her old man's a miner, remember?"

"Hmm," Lincoln mused, seeing Galen's point. "That does make sense. What do you suppose?"

"Either I got the town wrong, or she lied," Galen shrugged. "Can't really see another option."

"Lie is a strong word, Sean," Linc said easily. "Maybe she's just confused. Or she isn't keen on letting us know just how hard things are for her and her family. Wouldn't be the first person to do that."

"Point," Galen nodded after a moment. "Still."

"Yes," Linc nodded. "We'll see what we see."

-

"No, I'm not from Shaletown," Jessica shook her head. "I mentioned it several times because my mother's family was from there, but I live several miles north of Shaletown in a town called Deaver Mills. We have two mines there as well, but our chief industry is the ore mills. Three of them and two smelters, actually."

"I'm sorry to hear about Shaletown," she said sadly. "I had family there, still."

"According to the woman at the office the mine went down over seven years ago," Sean said calmly.

"That can't be right," Jessica shook her head. "Even if I wouldn't have known, my father would have. And my mother would have mentioned it, too. Her brother was a shift foreman in the Shaletown shaft."

"Well, that woman didn't strike me as an absolute fount of accurate information," Linc assured her. "And I think we interrupted her. .

.whatever she might have been doing, by trying to do business with her, too."

"So we fly there," Meredith shrugged. "Shouldn't take long. Another half-hour, maybe?"

"What I figure," Linc nodded. "And has to beat a dusty, all day drive any day," he smiled.

"That is true," Jessica nodded. "I'll just get home that much faster!" she smiled suddenly. "And the ship landing there to let me off will be the talk of the town for ages!"

"Well, let's go give the good folks of Deaver Mills something to talk about, then."

-

"There she is," Jessica smiled once more as her home town came into view. "It's grown!"

"Well, five years is a long time," Lincoln said as he concentrated on the screen while Meredith watched the instruments for him. So far everything was fine.

"You can land east of town," Jessica pointed for him. "There's a large field there that my family owns. Shouldn't cause any damage to it. There's no crops planted there that I can see."

"I see it," Linc nodded. "Long as you're sure it's okay."

"Ships land there fairly often, or did when I was a girl," Jessica nodded. "I'm sure it will be fine. You may draw a crowd, of course."

"Well, we can deal with that, I'm sure," Linc grinned. "Here we go."

Landing was far simpler when you weren't entering atmosphere from space. Linc had never lost sight of the ground detail and so didn't have to work to reacquire it. He managed to set the ship down without a jolt.

"Smooth as a baby's bottom," he grinned, obviously relieved that he'd been able to do it.

"So it was," Meredith nodded, relieved at more than just a good landing.

"I want all of you to come and meet my folks!" Jessica entreated suddenly. "I promise it won't take long, but I want them to meet you. You have all been so nice to me and I might not have made it home without you. Please?"

There really wasn't any way to refuse such a plea. Twenty minutes later the crew, including Faulks, was leaving a secured ship and headed into town, Tony, Sean and Lincoln sharing Jessica's things, including the new items that she had only just discovered.

"I can't believe you guys did that!" her face was still blushing. "I can't possibly pay you back!"

"Ah," Tony waved it away. "I got plenty o' money," he said without thinking.

"I'll remember that next payday," Meredith said caustically, though her eyes were glinting with good humor.

"Hey, I earn every nickle o' that money putting up with Faulks' attitude, Lincoln's flying 'skills' and Sean's bottomless pit of a stomach!" Tony shot back, a mock look of offense on his face.

"Hey!" all three of the named offenders chorused at once.

"What about me?" Meredith asked far too calmly.

"Oh, Captain, you are a treasure to work for and a saint to take care of," Tony piled it high. "I couldn't ask for anyone more genteel, understanding or-"

"Oh, shut up!" Meredith lost her battle with her laugh and erupted, the others joining in.

"There it is!" Jessica said excitedly as they approached a small adobe house right at the edge of town. "Wow, they painted the shutters and the fence a new color," she said wistfully. "Doesn't it look good?"

It did look good, the others admitted. The small house was well maintained and far better quality than they had expected on a world like this.

"I wonder what they've done to the interior?" Jessica mused aloud. "I can't wait to see my mother and father!" she enthused.

"Are we sure they're going to be home?" Lincoln asked, eyeing the house as they approached.

"My mother should be, but my dad is probably at work still," Jess nodded. As they made the gate entering the yard a woman walked outside with a basket, heading for the same gate. She slowed and then stopped as she saw the collection of people standing before her house.

"Can I help you?" she asked, maybe a bit hesitantly but friendly enough considering she'd just found a bunch of strangers on her front stoop.

"Who are you?" Jessica asked, her face scrunched.

"I'm Susan Vanover," the woman replied, a little uneasily. "Who are you?"

"We're looking for the Travers' residence, ma'am," Lincoln said as Jessica seemed lost for a second.

"Travers?" Vanover frowned slightly. Recognition dawned on her after a moment. "Oh, the old couple that used to own this place! Lord, they've been gone for. . . must be ten years now!"

"Gone? What do you mean gone?" Jess demanded, taking a step forward.

"Why. . .they passed, miss, some years back," Vanover's unease returned. "The Mister had the Lung Ails, but I always heard the Missus died of a broken heart over their daughter," she confided.

"What do you mean?" Meredith asked. "Over their daughter?"

"What's the Lung Ails?" Tony asked at the same time. Vanover seemed buffeted by the multiple questions.

"Sorry," Tony asked, deferring to Meredith.

"The way I heard it, their daughter went Core=ward for schooling," Vanover was a bit hesitant. "She was one of the first people around here to be able to go off world for her schooling, and everyone was really proud and happy for her. But she went and never came back!"

"I was gone for five years, but I came back!" Jessica bit out suddenly, but Vanover didn't hear as Meredith was asking questions while Vanover was still talking.

"What happened to the daughter? Do you know?" Meredith was asking.

"She apparently made it to school on Beria, but then disappeared without a trace," Vanover was already saying, even as Meredith asked. "She was their only child, too," the woman added sadly.

"When did they die, Miss Vanover?" Lincoln asked as Tony tried to keep Jessica from interrupting. She was in shock but also angry.

"Oh my, it must have been. . .fifteen years or more, now," Verona replied. "It was so sad. They were so very proud of her."

"Fifteen years!" Jessica almost screeched. "I've been gone five years! That's all!"

"What?" Vanover looked startled by that declaration.

"Our young friend has been away a long time," Lincoln soothed. "She was looking forward to seeing old family members, but she's been out of touch and wasn't aware that her extended family members had met with such misfortune. I'm afraid she's taking it rather hard."

"Poor dear," Vanover was instantly sympathetic. "I'm sorry, but as far as I know they didn't have any other family. At least not here in the Mills. They were very well thought of, though. The town buried them together in the city gardens," she pointed toward the center of town. "They were part of the original founders here. Did you know that, dear?" she asked Jessica.

"Of course I knew that!" Jess almost spat before Tony grabbed her again.

"I'm afraid this has really overwhelmed here," Lincoln sighed. "We better see to her. Thank you ma'am for your help. Have a good day."

"I'm sorry," Vanover was sympathetic. "I wish I could have given you happier information."

"What the hell is going on here?" Meredith asked to the crowd in general.

"We need to get back to the ship," Lincoln said quietly. "Something is very, very wrong here."

"You can say that again."

-

"Jessica, try and calm down, okay?" Sean attempted to sooth their young passenger. "Just get it together and then we can try to see what's really happened."

"Something is really wrong here," Meredith was saying.

"Really?" Tony's sarcasm came floating down the table.

"Tony, please," Linc raised a hand to forestall the oncoming storm.

"Sorry," the medic cum chef relented. "This is really screwed up, though."

"I have to find out what happened to my parents!" Jessica exclaimed. "That woman has to be wrong!"

"That's our first step," Lincoln agreed. "Do you know where this. . .this Garden place is?" he asked Jessica.

"Yes, it's the garden in the middle of town," Jessica had finally lost the battle with her tears. "Sometimes it's called Founders Garden, after the original settlers to this area."

"Would someone be buried there?" Meredith asked.

"Only someone from the original group who came here and founded the town," Jessica nodded. "My p-parents were original settle-settlers," she tried not to sob but clearly it was difficult.

"Why don't Sean and I meander up through town and see what we can see, and what we can find out?" Tony asked calmly. "Jessica, you need to take it easy and get your feet under you while we try and suss this out. Something in clearly amiss and you getting more upset before we really know what it is, well, it's not doing you any good or helping us find out what's going on."

"I want to go see," Jessica shook her head, crying openly now.

"You can, sweetie," Meredith placed an arm around the girl's shoulders, wincing slightly at the twinge in her back as she did so. Tony noticed it and rose without a word, headed to the infirmary. He returned a moment later with a syringe and quickly gave Meredith a shot for her pain. The stubborn woman tried to send him away with a shake of her head but the medic ignored her.

"You're going to need to be clear-headed today, ma'am," he almost whispered as he leaned in. Relenting in the face of his calm argument, Meredith accepted the injection, and soon felt the welcome relief it brought.

"I think it's a good plan," Lincoln said as Tony finished up. He had been pondering the situation while the medic was seeing to Meredith. "The two of you investigate this Garden, see what's there. Write down the names of whatever you find. If someone's there and you can casually question them, do so. Meanwhile, I'm going to hit the net and look for a source of local news. Maybe there's a library somewhere. Look for one while you're in town, for that matter. If there is a local paper, there may be back copies stored there."

"Right then," Tony nodded, looking to his friend. "Let's hit it, amico."

"All right," Sean was clearly dubious, but escaping the ship and the crying female seemed like the thing to do at this point. Faulks followed them down to the cargo bay.

"You two get the feeling something's hinky with this place?" she asked.

"Seriously?" Tony looked amazed. "You're seriously asking this, after what we've seen today?"

"Yes, I'm asking," Faulks growled back. "Look, I know the situation with the girl is a frakin' mess, but I'm talkin' about the town. The *people*. That woman didn't seem off in any way to me. Did she to you two? I didn't see or feel anything out o' place in town, either."

Tony froze with a sarcastic reply on his lips and looked at Sean. Galen looked in thought, clearly thinking back over the events of the past two hours or so.

"No," he said finally with a shake of his head. "No, everything seemed okay, so far as I could tell. Woman wasn't nervous except about finding us on her doorstep. And she wasn't fishing for a tale, either."

"Exactly," Faulks nodded firmly. "All I'm sayin' is that whatever's wrong here, it's the girl, not the town. That's what I'm seein' right now."

"Where is the profit in lying about being a college student on her way home?" Tony pondered. "I mean she did get a free ride, but-"

"To the ass-end of the universe," Faulks pointed out. "Who the hell wants to visit a place like this unless they have to, or they have a reason to be here? Family is a reason. And I didn't say she's lyin'."

"But you said-"

"I said that it wasn't the town," Faulks corrected the flustered cook and medic. "Just because she's telling us something that doesn't make sense don't make her a liar. That's why I asked you two what you thought about the folks we did see. Keep an eye and ear open while you're out. We find out if that Vanover woman's story is straight, then we can narrow it to the girl. Maybe she don't remember right. I've seen people block out traumatic shit that happened to them."

"Forget their parents died?" Tony raised an eyebrow.

"I've seen troops keep talkin' to mess mates that was killed weeks before," Faulks shrugged. "It happens. Nothin' says it can't happen to her. Or that it ain't, for that matter."

Both men were impressed by Faulks' reasoning, though both would take that to their grave rather than let her hear them say it.

"We'll mind it," Sean settled for saying. "We'll be back soon as we can."

"Watch yourselves, just in case it ain't the girl."

CHAPTER TWENTY

Sean Galen and Tony Giannini walked slowly up the main street of the small town, casually taking in the sites along the street. Neither wanted more attention that two obvious strangers from a ship that landed nearby would bring, which was plenty, and they tried not to attract any extra.

"Faulks made a sound argument," Tony noted as the two walked. His tone might have been the same if he'd said that a gorilla had rubbed two sticks together to make fire.

"You make it sound like she can't," Sean chuckled.

"Didn't think she was equipped for it," Tony shrugged. "But she does make a point. Unless this entire town is in on the biggest surprise ever pulled off, Jessica is either lost in time, lying, or she was. . ." he trailed off.

"Or what?" Sean demanded after a minute.

"I can't think of anything else at the moment," Tony admitted. "I'm working on it."

"You do that." Sean was feeling more uneasy by the minute with the entire situation.

Jessica Travers had been adamant during the weeks she had spent aboard the *Celia* that she was on her way home after five years away for school. Her story had been consistent every time she had relayed a part of it, whether to him or the others. Now they were on her home world, yet according to the woman living in what Jessica was sure had been her childhood home, her parents had been deceased for some time, and their daughter had gone away to school over two decades ago and hadn't returned, or been heard from ever again.

"Take it easy, bro," Tony soothed his friend. "I know it's weird."

"It's spooky is what it is," Sean replied just short of tersely. "That girl was absolutely positive that she was on her way home to be with her family. Every time she's told us her story, it's been consistent and I haven't found or heard of a single discrepancy, yet here we are."

"Here we are," Tony nodded, looking to their front. Sean followed his gaze and found they were standing at the entrance to the Founder's Garden.

"Well, let's take a gander, shall we?" Tony said.

The two walked into the walled area not knowing exactly what to expect. What they found was a beautifully maintained garden with flowers, trees, a few small structures and signage explaining the significance of everything inside. Near the center of the area was an old well, complete with a brick walling around the mouth and a cover over the top. A pulley and well bucket were suspended from a cross beam in the small roof and looked well maintained.

"According to this," Tony was reading the sign while Sean continued to look around them, "this well was the sole source of water for the first two years anyone was here."

"Harsh living," Sean nodded.

"No kiddin'," Tony nodded. "Hey, look there," he added, pointing. Sean followed the gesture with his eyes to find another wall, much smaller this time, encompassing a small area of the garden.

"That might be the cemetery," Sean decided.

"What I was thinking," Tony agreed. "Let's go have a look, shall we?"

The two entered the small burial ground respectfully. Tony watched as Sean stooped to pick up a handful of soil and spread it about him, his mouth moving silently. When he finished he noted Tony's stare.

"Just a prayer," he shrugged. "This is a burial ground," he added, as if that should explain it all.

"My people use crypts and vaults," Tony shrugged. They moved through the small garden of stone, until they were standing before a large rock bearing two names.

Daniel and Amanda Travers.

"Dude," Tony pointed to the dates on the rock.

"So, it is true," Sean breathed out. The dates for the deceased were nearly twenty years old.

"Man, this is creepy," Tony said softly. "Hair on my neck is standing up, Sean."

"I know the feeling," his friend nodded.

"You knew the Travers?" a voice made both jump slightly and they turned to find a short, wizened man with sun darkened skin standing behind them, a shovel in his hand serving at that moment as a staff.

"Sir?" Tony said, still startled by the man's appearance.

"Did you know 'em?" he indicated the rock.

"Just knew some of their people is all," Sean replied. "We were. . .we were supposed to deliver a message but. . ." he trailed off, indicating the rock.

"Long time late in deliverin' anything to Dan and Mandy," the man shook his head. "Been gone nigh twenty years, I guess. Longer for Dan I guess," he said after a pause. "Memory ain't what it used to be."

"We had heard he had the Miner's Lung," Tony nodded. "Miss Amanda though, she died after Dan?"

"Probably of a broken heart," the man nodded, his eyes starting to water slightly. "They had a daughter, Jenny. . .no, Jessica. Yeah, that was it," he nodded firmly. "Called her Jess, mostly if I recollect. She left, oh, must be twenty-five years and gone, now. Pretty thing as I recall," he smiled. "Smart too. Won some kind of scholarship for it and went Sphere-ward to school. Man, ol' Dan was so proud he was fit to burst."

"She never came back?" Sean asked, feigning polite disinterest.

"Dropped off the face o' the world, seemed like," the man shook his head sadly. "Never seen or heard from again. Broke their heart. They spent years trying to look for her. Everyone pitched in to buy Dan a ticket to wherever she went to school, can't recall where that was just now, but he went and tried to find what happened to her. Never could. Came home a broken man. I always did think that was how the Lung got him so fast. Usually a man hangs on a while if he's got medicines."

"Did he?" Tony asked.

"He did, for all the good it did," the man nodded. "We had a doc by then, and he was good, is good I should say. But wasn't nothin' he could do for Dan, seemed like. Man just lost the will to live, I always thought. Amanda maybe lived a year after he died," he pointed to the date on the rock.

"That's a shame," Tony sighed. "I'm sorry to hear that."

"They was the last o' the founders, too," the little man continued. "Always heard tell Dan was maybe seventeen and Amanda just turned sixteen when they came here with the company's forward team. Didn't even have a shaft started. Dan worked his way up to shift foreman and then finally took over runnin' the mill, but it was too late for his lungs. Didn't always have the best safety equipment in the old days. Better now."

"I'm glad to hear that," Tony said sincerely. "Well, I guess we'd better get going. We appreciate you talking to us, Mister. . .?"

"Poole. Willie Poole. Pleasure was mine," he smiled. "Don't get as many visitors here as we used to. People always in too much of a hurry. I've been caretaker since I was hurt in a cave-in back, oh, twenty-years or so ago, maybe. Give or take. Don't really keep up with the time much, these days," he admitted.

"I know that feeling," Sean nodded. "It's a beautiful garden Mister Poole."

"Thank you, son," the older man nodded gratefully. "You two take care. Come back if you're in the area again. I'll try and tell you something a bit more uplifting, next time."

"We'll do just that."

The two made their way out of the garden and started back toward the *Celia*. Half-way there the two had spotted the local paper's office, conveniently beside a small library. Apparently the two were run by the same people.

"Want to go in?" Tony asked, nodding that way.

"No," Sean shook his head adamantly. "I want to get the hell off this rock and never come back. This is wrong on a dozen levels or more."

"It's weird, I agree," Tony nodded. "If she wasn't so young, I'd say she's just suffering amnesia and started to remember where she belonged," he mused as they continued along their way. "Thing is; her age fits her story. At least until we got here it did."

"She is so certain," Sean shook his head again, more slowly this time. "Whatever the truth may be, she is absolutely convinced that she's from here, and those two," he jerked his head toward the garden, "are her parents. That she's been gone five years and that's all."

"You know, we should have asked if they had any other family," Tony snapped his fingers suddenly. "What if that was her grandparents, man?"

"Names fit the story," Sean shrugged. "We'll ask Jess what her parent's names were when we get back. If she says Dan and Amanda, then. . .well, I don't know what exactly," the engineer admitted helplessly. "Got no idea, in fact."

"Linc will figure it out," Tony said confidently.

-

"I can't figure this out," Linc shook his head slowly. He and Meredith were on the bridge looking at local news stories from two decades in the past. "Everything is so. . .so normal."

"What did you expect?" Meredith asked, leaning against him slightly.

"Well, I thought there'd be something weird, you know?" he admitted. "I mean, this has got to be the strangest thing I've seen, ever. Things like that don't usually happen in a vacuum. There should be something else."

"Maybe you're looking in the wrong place," Meredith suggested.

"What do you mean?" Linc looked up at her from his seat before the ship's computer.

"She went missing after she left, according to the Vanover woman," Meredith pointed out. "On Beria, apparently. Maybe you should be looking there."

"We're too far away for that," Linc sighed, shutting off the screen and standing. "Maybe when we're back closer to the Sphere we can do that. I mean, if we want to try and find out what happened."

"Why wouldn't we?" Meredith asked.

"It's not really our business, I guess," Lincoln shrugged. "I mean, if she asks us to find out what we can and send it to her, then that's different. Otherwise, it's like we're digging into someone's life. Prying, sort of."

"You're assuming she's going to stay here," Meredith said evenly. "Why should she? Where would she, for that matter? And what will she do? Her name will start ringing bells the minute she uses it. The best she can hope for is to be accused of identity theft. And her teaching cert will be in Jessica Travers' name, too. I'm willing to bet that's going to be useless to her."

"Hadn't thought of that," Lincoln admitted. "Poor kid. What's she going to do?"

"We'll see," Meredith shrugged. "Meantime-"

"*Cap'n*," Faulks' voice across the I/C speaker cut off whatever Meredith was going to say. "*Galen and the Doc are back.*"

"We'll be down in a second," Meredith called back. "Let's get everyone into the mess, Gun. . .Chief, and see what they've found out."

"*Aye, Cap'n.*"

"Let's go see what they learned."

-

"Yes," Jessica nodded. "Daniel and Amanda. Why?"

Tony blew out a long breath, fidgeting under her stare.

"We found a grave with their names on it," Sean lowered the boom calmly. "Dated between twenty and twenty-five years ago," he added. "We also met the caretaker of the gardens. He knew them, at least slightly, and told us pretty much the same story the Danover woman did, though he had a bit more detailed information." He looked at Lincoln and Meredith for a second before turning his gaze back to the distraught girl.

"The caretaker's name was Poole. Willie Poole. He said that the Travers' daughter, Jessica, went off world to study. She was smart, he said. Won a scholarship for an off-world school and left to study, but was never heard from again. He said Dan went to whatever world

Jessica went to study on to look for her, that they all pitched in to pay for his passage. But he never could find out what happened."

"He passed a bit later from an ailment called Miner's Lung," Tony took up the narrative, though with reluctance. "Amanda died about two years afterward. Poole reckons she died from a broken heart more than anything else. Jessica, I'm sorry but. . .everything we've found checks out pretty good."

"I don't understand," Jessica shook her head. "I can't understand. I've only been gone a little while, just five years and a few months. I did win the scholarship," she confirmed. "I couldn't have gone to school without it in fact. Far too expensive. As it was I worked almost a year at whatever I could do in order to pay my passage to Beria. And I had to work while I was in school to pay my living expenses. The scholarship only covered tuition and books. Nothing else."

"Look, we're all exhausted," Meredith said suddenly. "And Jessica you've got to be near the end of your tether after all this. Let's get some rest and then we'll see what else we can learn. There has to be a reasonable explanation for this, we just have to figure it out. That's all."

Tony and Sean exchanged looks, then both looked at Lincoln, who only shrugged in return. He didn't have any better ideas at the moment.

"Faulks, you have first watch," Meredith ordered, standing. "We'll stand four hour watches so that someone is always awake. We're not in a port so someone may come wanting the ship gone. For the moment I think it best if we kept your name and story to ourselves, Jess."

"Why?" the girl asked. "I don't understand."

"If we can't prove who you are, that you are who you say you are, then your name might cause a stir among the locals. You might be charged with identity theft, for starters. We want to avoid that. In fact, we want to avoid bringing any attention to you at all if we can. It will only interfere without getting to the bottom of all this. See what I mean?"

"Yes, ma'am," Jess nodded, sniffing. "What name do I use if someone wants to know who I am?"

"Jessica Trenton," Meredith said flatly. "That's my maiden name," she reminded everyone. "You're my younger sister, for now, riding with us and learning the business. Keep it simple, and remind anyone who asks too many questions that it's rude to do so. I'll leave that to you two," she looked at Sean and Faulks, both of whom nodded.

"We can do that," Faulks said, and Sean again nodded in agreement.

"All right then," Meredith said, satisfied for the moment. "We'll rest, refit, and start fresh after everyone has had some sleep and at least one good meal. There has to be an explanation," she repeated. "We'll find it."

-

"I can't think of a single reasonable explanation for any of this shit," Tony said quietly as he and Sean huddled with Lincoln in the engine room a few minutes later.

"Neither can I, and I've worked on it since you two left," Linc agreed.

"We found a paper," Sean told him. "Their office and the library are beside each other. Looks like the same people run both. Might be a good place to get some information."

"Might be, but I think we've got all the local information we need," Linc mused. "We've got pretty much the same story from two sources, and there's physical evidence to support that story."

"The girl is convinced she's telling the truth," Sean stated firmly. "She is absolutely sure that she's telling the truth as she knows it."

"I think so too," Linc agreed. "Which means the problem is a lot deeper than we know. But we can't rule out that she's running a game of some kind, either," he warned. "Remember our earlier discussion about how we all felt so protective of her."

"True," Tony murmured. "I hadn't added that in."

"I'm not saying that's how it is, either," Lincoln stressed. "I'm saying that this is the weirdest shit I've ever even heard of, let alone come across myself. We can't rule out anything at this point except maybe alien abduction."

The joke fell flat as the three of them went to get some rest.

-

"*Galen, you're up for watch*," Faulks' voice drifted across Sean's cabin. He was instantly awake and keyed the I/C without conscious thought.

"Be right there."

He stood and went to his sink, washing his sleep away. Five minutes later he was dressed and on his way down the passageway. He met Faulks in the galley.

"Nothing happening at the moment," she told him tiredly. "I took the Cap'n's shift myself so she could rest. Lincoln is up next."

"I'll cover for him, then," Sean nodded. "Let them get a good night's sleep since most of this is on them."

"Is this not some freaky mess?" Faulks asked, fighting off a yawn.

"Most I ever seen," Sean agreed.

"Well, I'm beat," the former Marine told him. "I got to get some shut-eye, but if anything happens, wake me."

"Will do," Sean promised. He watched Faulks disappear down the passageway and then made a turn of the ship, checking on things for himself. Satisfied that the ship was locked down, he made his way to the bridge and checked the sensors, which were unsurprising clear. There wasn't much traffic here other than ore haulers. The *Celia*'s sensor suite was actually in stand-by mode since operating them so close to the town wasn't really safe, but even so she was capable of detecting motion or air traffic.

He settled in on the bridge, thinking about his own future for the first time in a day. His conversation with Faulks kept coming back to him, playing over in his mind. She had sounded sincere, and, as Tony has said, made some solid points that he hadn't really thought her capable of. If he could trust her, and that was still a *big* if, then he was probably better off staying aboard the *Celia* rather than trying to find a new berth somewhere and starting over.

He had to admit that this mystery around Jessica was also pretty intriguing. It was almost worth wanting to stick around just to see how that played out. He wondered what the girl would do now. Staying here, on Gateway, was pretty much out he figured. Sooner or later someone would connect her with the disappeared Jessica from two or more decades ago and then she would be in for a time. She would have to get off this planet and probably stay off of it.

She would need new identification and have to find a way to make a living that didn't depend on her teaching certificate, since that was in the name of a woman who had been missing for twenty-five years, give or take.

His own problems were simple in comparison, at least for the moment. His 'truce' with Faulks seemed solid enough, and he was strangely trusting of Faulks' stated determination to be a better hand for the Captain's sake. Her attraction to Meredith Simmons notwithstanding, being pulled from certain death by the Captain was more than enough to warrant Faulks' undying loyalty.

It was still a risk for him, but he was at risk no matter where he went and that was just a fact. Faulks was right in that at least here he knew the risks and could counter many of them. He was also fairly sure that Faulks meant it when she promised she wouldn't do anything to jeopardize his safety. The rest of the crew could almost certainly be counted on not to give him away except by accident.

Staying here would be a risk, but it was a calculated one. The crew would be careful in what they said about him for fear of giving him away. His face wasn't on any wanted posters anywhere and there was no official notice of his being wanted by the Commonwealth or anyone else. He knew there were people looking for him, some for the same reason Faulks had, some for deeper, more sinister reasons. Either of those reasons was enough for him to kill whoever came looking without pause and he didn't spend more than a few seconds worrying over that.

His main worry was that staying would endanger the others should someone actually discover him and come looking. Risking them being hurt or killed as collateral damage wasn't something he wanted to do, yet they all seemed to want him to stay on despite knowing the risks.

And honestly, were the risks any higher than they had been when the crew *hadn't* known who he was? That thought hit him square on for the first time and he almost laughed at his stupidity. If someone had discovered him before the rest had known who he was, they would have been in just as much danger as they would with him staying on now that they did know. Somewhere in his determination to remain unknown to those around him he had overlooked that simple fact. If he was targeted, it wouldn't matter if the crew knew his real identity or not. In fact, knowing who he was might actually make them more careful.

Faulks could likely handle herself against any reasonable threat. Tony was equally capable of taking care of himself, despite his attempts to hide it. And he was obviously well connected to someone, considering his ability to get information on Hartley Station. Sean still didn't know who Jerome Delgado was, but whoever Tony's father might be, it was obvious he was *Someone*. And Tony was definitely able to take care of himself.

Lincoln and Meredith were not, but that's what they paid the rest of the crew for when it came right down to it. The Captain had never made any bones about the fact that Faulks was here as much to serve as muscle against trouble as she was on the cargo floor.

Jessica was a wild card at the moment, but he had already seen her in action at least once, even if she couldn't remember it. He was fairly sure at this point that the girl really didn't remember it, too. She might just be a really good actress, but the more he thought about it, the more certain he was that she simply didn't know what she'd done. That made her both more dangerous, and yet also a possible asset in protecting the ship and the owners. *Possible* being the operative word.

Digging out who she was and what she was capable of would take time, especially to do so safely, but if she remained on the ship they could probably manage it over time.

And he was pretty sure that the Captain was going to decide to let her stay aboard. Maybe even try and talk her into it. She hadn't come up with the idea to use her maiden name on the fly, or call Jess her younger sister, either. Meredith Simmons wasn't stupid. Stupid people didn't rise to command warships, at least not in wartime. She had obviously been thinking about the problem ever since it had arisen. The name and cover story were obviously part of her plan, whatever the rest might be.

Celia did need a pilot, at least for a while, he mused, leaning back in the seat and staring out at the darkened skies through the screen. Jessica could fly, and do it well. She now needed a place to be and a way to make a living. It seemed to be a good fit all the way around, and if Sean could see that, he assumed that Meredith Simmons could see it, too.

All of these thoughts bounced around inside his head as Sean continued to stand his watch into the daylight hours, allowing the Simmons some much needed rest. As he'd said, this problem was sitting square atop them more than anyone other than Jessica herself.

A good night's rest could only help, if they could get it.

-

Linc woke slowly, his eyes blinking several times to clear away the fog of sleep. He rolled slightly to look at the clock and swore softly, realizing he had slept through most of his watch. Rising, he went to the sink and threw some water on his face, dressed and headed for the bridge, being as careful as possible not to wake Meredith. She had obviously been very quiet when she'd come off her own watch earlier.

He found Sean Galen on the bridge, gazing out at the slowly breaking dawn. The engineer turned to see him and grinned.

"Morning."

"Why didn't you wake me?" Linc demanded. "It was my watch four hours ago almost."

"No need," Sean shrugged. "I couldn't sleep, and Faulks had already stood the Captain's watch, so I figured to do the same for you. You guys needed a good night's sleep for once. You got a lot on you at the moment."

Lincoln blinked at that, then shook his head slowly.

"You guys didn't have to do that," he said finally, moving to the co-pilot's seat and taking it.

"No, but we wanted to, and there was no reason to wake you when I wasn't going to sleep anyway," Sean shrugged again. "I had a lot of thinking to do and this was a good time to do it."

"What are you thinking on this early in the morning?" Linc asked conversationally as he took his seat.

"Just this and that," came the reply. "Some about Jessica for sure, but also about what I'm going to do next."

"And what are you going to do?" Linc asked. "You know you can stay here, Sean. I think we've made that abundantly clear to you. If not, let me do that now. We want you to stay. Need you to stay even. Not just as an engineer, but as someone we can count on."

"I appreciate that," the younger man nodded. "Faulks and I had a long talk about that when we were reorganizing the bay back on Liberty Vale."

"Seriously?" Linc's eyebrows rose at that.

"Yeah. She pointed out that I wasn't going to be any safer anywhere else than I was here. Maybe less so, since I'd have to start over wherever I went. She also promised that she'd never turn me in, and even help me if someone came after me."

"Wow," Lincoln didn't know exactly what to say to that. "Maybe you should have held a knife to her throat before."

"Wasn't that," Sean shook his head, missing the attempt at levity. "I think she meant what she said about the others. That she would have killed them herself, had she known. Faulks may have her faults, but she has her own code she lives by. What happened to my people violated almost every part of it."

"Hadn't thought about that," Linc leaned back in his chair. Of course, he hadn't considered her capable of much more than an average thought process, either, he admitted.

"The real problem is the risk to you all," Sean told Lincoln flatly. "The people who would be after me, happens they knew I was here, wouldn't care at all about collateral damage to the people around me. All of you would be at risk if that happened."

"Would have been anyway, whether we knew who you were or not," Linc said, echoing Sean's own thoughts.

"That wasn't something that ever occurred to me until maybe two hours ago," Sean admitted with a nod. "Now, I'm wondering if all my bouncing around was worth anything."

"Made you felt a bit safer, so it was an effective defense mechanism," Linc pointed out. "And, knowing that we are aware of your past, who you are, might make it easier for you. We don't care what you did in the war, Sean," he said bluntly. "None of us do other than maybe Faulks, and like you said, she's had an epiphany about that."

"Not just that, either," Sean turned to look at him. "I think you'll see a big change in her from now on. May take her a bit to overcome bad habits, but. . .she's determined to make up for any problems she's caused you two. Really determined."

"I'll believe it when I see it."

"Don't blame you," Sean agreed, "but I think you'll see it. If you're like me, you'll refuse to see it at first, not trusting it. But I think she means it. In fact, I'm as sure of it as I can be."

"Sure enough that you think you might stay here with us, now?" Lincoln tried to keep the hope from his voice, but it leaked through anyway.

"Yes," Sean replied simply. "I like it here, and I like most of the people on the ship. I enjoy my job, Lincoln, and I'm pretty good at it. I'd like to keep doing it."

"Then as far as I'm concerned that issue is settled," Lincoln said at once, smiling. "Meredith will say the same thing. She's tried for the last two months to figure out a way to get you to stay."

"Have to be careful," Sean warned. "We'll have to be watchful and aware. If someone starts asking too many questions about me, I need to know it right away. I'll have to leave rather than put all of you at risk."

"I appreciate your willingness to protect us," Linc replied, "but we're either a crew, a family, or we're not. If someone does come after you, then we'll all help you."

"I'd rather you didn't," Sean said bluntly. "Too much risk to you, and to the life you have. If something happens, I'll just slip away and you can say, truthfully, that I deserted you. That would probably protect you from any harm, considering that Meredith holds the Navy Cross and is considered a hero."

"Maybe," Linc mused. "We'll cross that bridge when we get to it. How about that?"

"Works for me."

-

"Jessica, I've been thinking about your situation."

Meredith's voice cut across the table as the crew finished their breakfast. She hadn't been especially happy that Faulks had taken her shift, but she admitted that she felt pretty good after a night's uninterrupted sleep.

"Yes ma'am?" Jessica's voice was smaller, today. She seemed that way too, Tony thought. Like she was drawn in on herself.

"You realize by now that you can't stay here, I imagine," Meredith was blunt, but not unkind.

"What do you mean?"

"I mean that whatever is going on here, you're technically someone who disappeared twenty-five years ago and was never heard from again. You're still the same age as you would have been back then, too. I am amazed that your ID hasn't been tagged by now as a missing person, to be honest. Not to mention that you have no way of making a living here, anymore. Your teaching certificate won't be any good to you if you're using another name, which you would absolutely have to do. It's clear just from what we learned yesterday that your family is still well remembered, as is your disappearance. People aren't going to miss your return."

"This is all wrong," Jessica shook her head, a single tear escaping her left eye to run down her cheek. "If I disappeared, when did I come back, and why is it just five years to me?"

"I don't know," Meredith admitted. "I really don't. All I do know is that you have to make a decision about what you're going to do. We can't stay here like this much longer. Honestly we should already be on our way, but thanks to your flying we've got some time to spare. But only so much."

"I don't have anywhere else to go," Jessica said helplessly. "As far as I know, I don't have any other family, anywhere. Not here, not elsewhere."

"You can stay with us," Meredith said flatly. "I don't know what happened to you, Jess, but I want to find out, and we can't do that here. It didn't happen to you here. You can stay with us, fly the *Celia*, be a part of our crew. We'll figure out a way to get you a new ID, something that will pass muster, and create a new background for you. I don't have any family either, anymore. No one will question you as my sister if you want to keep using that name. We'll work it out, somehow."

"Why are you doing this?" Jessica asked. "I've been nothing but trouble to you since I got here. Why would you be willing to help me like this?"

"Well, for one thing, we need you," Meredith admitted. "Could probably get by without you but there's no doubt that we'd do better with your help. We've always had too few crew on this ship and we've discovered that having two pilots is a good idea. Even once Lincoln is well again, it's obviously a two-person job to fly and land this ship."

"And because something happened to you, somewhere," she continued. "I don't know what it was, but I don't like it. I don't like the idea that somehow your life was turned upside down like this and you were taken from your family and a dream that you had was just cast aside as not important. I know what that's like. I've had a dream taken from me, too."

"I want to find out what happened to you, Jessica," Meredith repeated. "Even if we can't, there's a place for you here. It's not the same as being at home, with your family around you I know. But it's not bad. We're good people for the most part, even if we're sometimes rough around the edges. We can't replace your family, but we can offer you a home, safety, and a new family of sorts. Offer you a chance to have a good life even if it's not the one you wanted. And whenever we get the chance, we'll be looking into what happened to you. We travel a lot, and sooner or later we'll be back to Beria, or maybe somewhere else that might have some information that will help us."

"We've got time," she leaned forward. "We'll figure it out eventually, if it can be figured out. We're a fairly smart bunch, all totaled."

"Yes, you are," Jessica agreed. "Too smart to take on the risk of having someone like me around."

"What about me?" Galen asked suddenly. "You don't think there's risks to having me on board?"

"You're leaving because of them, though," Jessica reminded him.

"No, I'm not," he grinned at her. "I'm staying. There's no point in trading devils I don't know for the one that I do, as Faulks put it. She convinced me to stay."

Faulks sputtered slightly, her face reddening, but she nodded nonetheless. She seemed satisfied that Sean was staying.

"You're not leaving?" Jessica asked with renewed interest.

"I'm not leaving," Sean confirmed. "And I'll do everything I can to help find out what happened to you, and keep teaching you in the meantime. How about that?"

Jessica looked at the assembled crew gathered around the galley table, wondering what stroke of luck had led her to them. Wondering also what had happened to her that she seemed to have jumped forward in time twenty-five years with no memory of anything happening to her at all.

They had all been good to her, even Faulks after a while. She admitted that she felt at home here, even though she'd been aboard only a short time. *Celia* was a comfortable ship and the people aboard her were equally comfortable to be around. She trusted them.

And Meredith Simmons was right. There was no way she could continue her life as Jessica Travers, considering what they had learned yesterday. Even if people accepted that she was who she said she was, there would be an avalanche of questions that she had no way to answer. Questions that she wanted answers to as well, but had no idea where to get them.

So, she couldn't teach anymore. By the look of her small hometown and from the reports of the others, that need had been met already. The quality of life in the Mills was considerably higher than she remembered it being as a girl. They didn't need her anymore.

But the *Celia* did. She could fly, and *Celia* needed a pilot. That was something she could do. A way to earn a living and have a home at the same time. A place of safety while she tried to figure out what had happened to her. People that would help her figure it out.

"So, I'd have a job working for you?" she asked, almost timidly. "I'd be earning my living and not just. . .not. . .charity, I guess," she shrugged.

"No charity," Meredith said sternly. "You'll be paid just like everyone else is and have duties aboard ship just like the rest of us. You'll move into crew quarters and assume the role of pilot. Once Lincoln is squared away you'll still be needed, as we've already seen."

"And you're highly intelligent," Lincoln added. "There will be plenty you can do besides pilot, Jessica. Don't forget that this ship is more than our home. It's a business. We always need smart people," he grinned.

"And it's a great way to see the galaxy, too!" Tony spoke for the first time. "You'll see places you might never have gotten to see otherwise. Meet people you'd never get to meet if you weren't here."

"You're sure I won't be a burden on you all?" Jessica wanted to say yes. She wasn't quite sure why, but the desire to stay on the *Celia* was almost overwhelming all of a sudden.

"Not only will you not be a burden, I expect you to be a valued member of the crew," Meredith said firmly. "We'll teach you the things you don't already know. You'll be a first rate spacer in no time."

"Have to get you a license in your new name as soon as we can," Lincoln added. "Won't be a problem. I'll help you prepare for the test. And there's no reason you can't fly without it for now, especially with me on the bridge with you."

"How will I get a new identity?" she asked.

"Ah, let me deal with that," Tony said carefully. "We'll need to decide who you are, where you're from and all the particulars, and then I'll see to it that you have everything you need."

"How can you do that?"

"I have friends in low places," Tony admitted. "It won't be a problem, and it will be ironclad once it's done. I promise," he added, this to Meredith, who looked at him questioningly but nodded her agreement.

"So you'll become Jessica Trenton, then," Meredith stated firmly. "Pilot, crew member, and part of the *Celia*'s family. Right?"

Jessica looked around the table once more and saw nothing but genuine concern for her on their faces, including Faulks.

"Well, sis," she smiled suddenly. "Looks like you've got yourself a new pilot."

"Outstanding!" Meredith stood. "Now, is there anything you want to do before we go?"

"I...I'd like to see. . .I mean, if you guys would take me to where. . ." she trailed off as she looked at Sean and Tony. Both understood.

"Of course," Tony replied and Sean nodded. "We'd be honored."

"If I could just do that, Captain, then I'll be ready to go," Jessica told Meredith. "It's not like I have anything to pick up. Everything I own in the world is in my bags."

"We'll make sure you have whatever you need, girl," Faulks' voice wasn't quite gruff. "Don't worry over that."

"Faulks is right," Meredith nodded, giving her Chief a smile of approval. "Go and see to your business, Jessica, and then we'll be on our way."

CHAPTER TWENTY-ONE

Jessica stood between Sean and Tony, looking at the granite slab that identified her parent's grave.

"Seeing this. . .it makes it real, doesn't it?" she said softly. "Until I saw it, I didn't have to believe it."

"I'm sorry, Jess," Tony said softly, placing a comforting arm around her slim shoulders. "I wish it wasn't so."

"I hate that they died not knowing I was still alive," she sniffed slightly. "Out of all of this, that's the worst, I think."

Neither man spoke, allowing her to process her feelings. Both knew this was probably the last time she would step foot on her home planet, or see any evidence of her parents and the lives they had lived. Sean had bought her a flower arrangement on the way to the gardens and now Jessica knelt to lay the small wreath carefully on the grave site, taking the time to place the small stake on the flowers into the ground so that it would hold in place. After a moment she stood, taking one of their hands in each of her own. Both men lent what support they could to her as she stood in silence, saying goodbye.

"I see you've returned," a voice broke into her reverie after a minute. The three of them turned to find Willie Poole standing behind them at a respectful distance. "Hello again."

"Mister Poole," Tony nodded slightly. "We just thought we'd pay our respects. This is Jess Trenton, our pilot. And the boss' little sister."

"Miss Trenton," Poole nodded.

"Mister Poole," Jessica returned his polite nod, searching her memory for the man's name, or face. She came up empty, despite knowing that Poole had told her friends he had known her parents.

"That's a pretty arrangement," Poole said, gesturing to the flowers. "Did you know them?"

"Just a way to pay our respects," Tony offered when Jessica was unable to reply immediately. "Since we were late by a long time delivering our message. There's not much else we can do."

"It's a nice gesture," Poole told them. "Not many bother with anything like that anymore. At first," he leaned on the rake he was carrying, "people held remembrances for the Founders once a month. Then it was twice a year, then annually. Now it's just a day for people to have a bar-be-que and be off work," he sighed. "It's a shame, too. Those people were a hardy bunch. Carved this town out of rock and mud, built the mines and the mills that make this place what it is. Worked to make it a home and not just a workplace. They deserve to be remembered. To be honored."

"It's obvious that you take that seriously," Sean noted. "This place is immaculate."

"Thank you, young man," Poole smiled gently. "I do take pride in it. I suppose once I'm gone that someone will still maintain it, but I worry that they won't respect it like I do."

"Likely not," Tony agreed. "It seems that later generations rarely appreciate what those who came before did for them."

"All too true, I'm afraid," Poole sighed. He looked at Jessica again, his eyes narrowing in study. "Miss Trenton, was it? Have we met before, young lady? You're not from here, are you?"

"No sir, I'm not," Jessica managed to strangle out the lie. "My sister and I are from Idlewilde," she added, remembering the story they had concocted earlier.

"Odd," Poole shook his head after a minute. "I'm getting old, I guess. Memory ain't what it once was. I'm sorry, you just look vaguely familiar. Like someone I once knew, perhaps."

"Maybe she just reminds you of someone from back in the day," Sean offered, warning bells sounding in the back of his mind.

"That's probably it," Poole agreed. "Well, it was good to see you young men again, and to meet you, Miss Trenton. I'm afraid I have work to do, so I'll leave you to your visit. Good-bye."

"Good-bye Mister Poole," Sean spoke for all three. "It was good to see you again, sir." The older man waved again over his shoulder as he returned to work. The three of them stood watching him until he was out of earshot.

"That was close," Jessica almost breathed rather than spoke. "I think he knew me when I was a child. I can't remember him, but. . .that doesn't mean anything, really. Not anymore."

"No, it doesn't," Tony agreed.

"I'm ready to go," Jessica announced suddenly. She refused to turn back to the stone with her parent's names on it again. That was behind her, now. Whatever her life was going to be, it lay ahead of her. Gateway was as lost to her as her memory of what had happened to her all those years ago.

Neither man replied, but simply walked with her out of the garden, back toward the ship.

Toward whatever the future held for her now.

-

"We're green across the board, Captain."

Meredith stood behind Jessica and Lincoln as they prepared to lift off. Jessica had returned subdued and quiet. She hadn't said much of anything about her trip to the garden and Meredith hadn't pressed her on it. It was private and if she wanted to share, she would. When she felt like it.

"Very well," Meredith replied. "Mister Galen, are we ready to get underway?"

"*That we are, ma'am*," Sean's voice came across the I/C. "*We can lift anytime*."

"Chief, is the bay secure?"

"*Aye, Cap'n. We're good in all respects. Ship ready for departure*."

"Tony, what's for lunch?" she added suddenly, a slight grin on her face.

"*Assuming the Dynamic Duo can get us off world without exploding, you mean?*" the medic/chef replied without missing a beat. "*I'm making roast beef sandwiches with homemade chips.*"

"Sounds delicious," Meredith stifled a laugh at the looks of mock outrage on both Lincoln and Jessica's faces. "Well you two, see if you can get us to lunch so we can enjoy Mister Giannini's hard work."

"You know," Lincoln said as he completed his checklist, "it's comments like that that make me want to perform sub-par, just to see you and the others sweat a little."

"I was thinking the same thing," Jessica agreed, her hand busy at the controls as she prepared to get them airborne.

"I'll pretend that I didn't hear that," Meredith told them flatly, but was secretly pleased. Both seemed in better spirits. She hoped that would continue. Despite how things had turned out for Jessica, things really were looking up.

"Pretend away," Lincoln shot back. "We'll pretend we can fly. Jessica?"

"Here we go," the young woman nodded. "Next stop, Sidewinder."

Celia shuddered slightly as Jessica applied power to the thrusters and the ship left the ground. She was careful to ease them away from town and gain altitude before increasing their speed.

"Safe distance reached, Jessica," Lincoln told her after a few minutes. "Preparing to light off."

"Go for it," Jess nodded.

"Three. . .two. . .one. . .burn!" Linc counted down and then hit the engines. The ship shuddered again, stronger this time, as the massive power plants kicked in, and *Celia* began to move faster, her nose up, clawing for space.

In what seemed like just a few seconds fire flared across the screen as *Celia* exited atmosphere, entering the vacuum of space. Once through, the ship settled into a smooth flight. Hands flicked across the board as the two pilots set the ship for space travel. Jessica entered their destination into the navigation computer and then locked their course into the auto-pilot.

"And. . .we're on our way," she announced as she turned to look at her 'sister'. "I guess Tony will have to fix lunch after all."

Laughter rang through the ship as the I/C carried her announcement throughout the vessel.

A lot had happened to the *Celia* and her crew over the last three months or so. A gamut of emotions had been crossed, pain had been endured, suffering had been inflicted, loss encountered. Yet the crew remained unbroken, for all that they had bent almost to that point.

Lincoln was still facing the possibility that he would not recover completely from his beating on Hartley Station. Jessica had discovered that her entire life, her past and her dreams of the future, had turned to dust in the face of the mystery surrounding who she was, what had happened to her, and where she had been for twenty-five years that had left her ageless as well as homeless.

Faulks had discovered that her secret wasn't so secret, and been made aware that her desires were not going to bear fruit. She had come face to face with a heretofore 'faceless' enemy that had almost been her undoing, and had learned that the man she had admired and looked up to above all others had been completely unworthy of that respect. That he had deserved what happened to him in spades. And that the man she had thought to be little more than a punching bag was in fact one of the most feared men in the galaxy.

Tony had learned that his friend was not what he appeared to be, and had been forced by circumstances to share the secret of his own background. He trusted Sean Galen not to give him away, but acknowledged that his offer to help with Jessica's new identity had opened him up to questions from the Captain and the others about his own identity and background. While he still wasn't sure that he wanted them to know who he really was, he was starting to believe that it wouldn't be the end of his travels should they do so. If they could keep Sean's secret, and Jessica's, then why not his own?

Meredith had discovered that she could let Tony help her manage her pain without sliding into dependency as she had before. The yoga exercises that Jessica had taught her were also helping, and she found that her pain level was the lowest it had been since her rehab and withdrawal. She had also learned that she had to loosen up a bit. Her attitude had nearly caused her to lose the man that she loved, the man who made her life worth living and her pain bearable when nothing else could. It had also nearly cost her the services of a good engineer.

Her poor decisions had led to their being taken, and to Lincoln's injury. An injury that might yet end his piloting of the *Celia*, something he had worked hard to earn. He had sacrificed much for her and she had put him in harm's way when there was no need for it. Her guilt over that still hung over her, and probably would for a long time. If Linc couldn't recover, then that guilt would be with her the rest of her life. The fact that Lincoln didn't hold her responsible for what had happened didn't ease that guilt, either. All she could do now was move forward as best she could. Just like the rest of the crew.

In the engine room, Sean Galen sat back in his chair, considering the bridges he had crossed in the last few months. There had been a target on his back for a long time. So long that it had become the natural state of things. He didn't regret his actions. Those he had hunted, they had it coming. Those who came after him and died for it, they knew the risks, or should have. They made the decision to try and kill him, and failed. Failure carried a high price in that kind of game.

Now, however, he was faced with a new dynamic. For the first time in a very long while, he was traveling, working, even living with people who knew exactly who and what he was. His secret was out. And yet he was still here.

He had accepted that he could, perhaps, trust at least some Commonwealth people. That he could co-exist with at least those few. He didn't know how things would end up, but for now, he was content to keep going. The *Celia* was a good place, and the crew were good people. Well, mostly. Tony was as good a friend as he had ever had, at least since the attack on his home, and friends weren't something that Sean had a lot of. He didn't want to give that up if he could avoid it.

So, he'd keep riding along for now.

He knew it wouldn't last forever, of course. There was one thing he hadn't shared with the others the night when his background had come to light. He still didn't know who had ordered the attack on his home that had resulted in the death of his family and most of the people he'd ever known. He had searched for that person long and hard, but was no closer to finding them than when he'd started.

But he *would* find out who had ordered the death of his people. And why. When that happened, the person or people responsible would ride the lightning when the Stormcrow would fly once more.

Until then, he would let the *Celia* do the flying, and he would keep her moving.

THE END

THANK YOU FOR READING!

If you enjoyed this book, we would appreciate your customer review on your book seller's website or on Goodreads.

Also, we would like for you to know that you can find more great books like this one at www.CreativeTexts.com

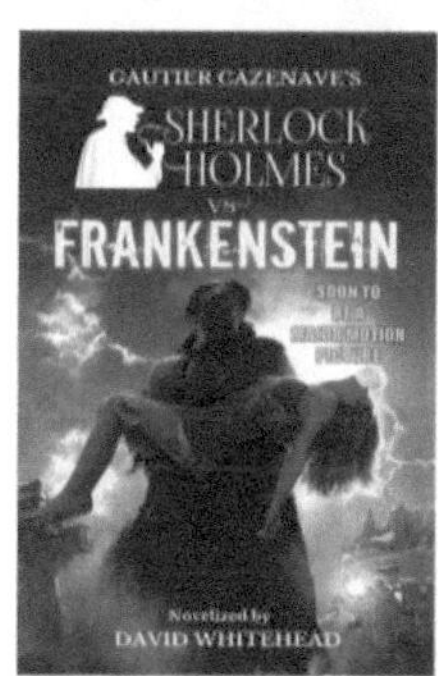

www.ingramcontent.com/pod-product-compliance
Lightning Source LLC
LaVergne TN
LVHW091045080826
845145LV00002B/630